MY SISTER AND OTHER LIARS

ALSO BY RUTH DUGDALL

The James Version

The Woman Before Me

The Sacrificial Man

Humber Boy B

Nowhere Girl

MY SISTER AND OTHER LIARS

RUTH DUGDALL

This is a work of fiction. Names, characters, organizations, places, events, and incidents are either products of the author's imagination or are used fictitiously.

Published by Thomas & Mercer, Seattle

www.apub.com

ISBN-13: 9781503942288
ISBN-10: 1503942287

Cover design by Mark Swan

Printed in the United States of America

For Mum, with love.
Thank you for sharing your stories.

But it is going dark and I must go in.
Memory's fog is rising.

Emily Dickinson, Selected Letters

Memory is the diary we all carry about with us.

Oscar Wilde

CHAPTER 1

30 December

My body is eating itself. My brain too, apparently, is being consumed in its eternal search for sustenance. This is what the staff tell us, one of the topics of our enforced education, *the damage we are doing to ourselves.*

What the staff don't get: that is the goal. Every lecture, dished up daily, is not a scary warning but solace. My body is self-consuming and if it succeeds, taking my brain into the bargain, then great.

I want to disappear, all five of us do. That's the point; it's so obvious that I have to sit on my hands to stop from slapping whichever well-meaning staff member is trying to save us that day. We were ready for the sessions to stop, we needed respite, and the final lecture before they left to celebrate Christmas was on food and celebrations. How turkey and fruit cake shouldn't be feared, but savoured, a teen-mag slice of motivation before the Xmas exodus, relevant to every other girl but not to me.

As Manda talked to us about mince pies and the magic of marzipan, I exchanged glances with Stacey, while Fiona and Joelle whispered behind skeletal hands, but all four of us were thinking the same thing:

Fucking idiot. Mina gazed at the floor; what she was thinking was anyone's guess, but she can't have been looking forward to going home.

Times like that, I have to shut myself up, though my body is already screaming as loudly as it can. And still the staff, that small team of dedication, compassion and superiority, persist in believing they can help us. But there is no help for a group of girls who want to starve.

Autophagy. That's it, the word Manda scribbled on the flipchart last week. It seemed a wonderful word to me, starchy-medical, so comforting to have a label with gravitas. 'Auto' meaning self. Ah, that's the thing, though. The self, *myself*: that's the real problem here on Ana Unit. We are all, each of us self-eating females, our own worst enemy.

Autophagy may sound stern and scholarly, but it feels primal and real. It leaves me drunk with fatigue; my bones push to come out of my flesh, my stomach is an animal in its death throes. And all of this is so absorbing that I can think of nothing else; there is no space for thought or memory, just a wonderful gap.

It's so effective that I can feel my jaw creak; my cheekbones are perfect sharp corners in my face. Self-eating is the gateway to an empty body and mind, a nothingness to which I am dedicated.

I don't want food now; I've risen above it. My body is so empty, so clean, as though my insides have been scrubbed with salt. I ache with hollowness; the air that travels in my intestines is pure, and my mind is clean of memory. I haven't needed to shit or piss in days. I am simple and clean and perfect, and very, very tired. Sleep is no good for me, though; sleep is not oblivion from the news that came today.

I want to disappear. I close my eyes and wait.

The other girls are gone now, off to fight the good fight against the temptations of chocolate roulade and laxatives, turkey curry and compulsive training. They won't be back until after New Year, and the unit has been deathly quiet without them. Poor Manda had the task of telling me the news of my mother's death. It hurt her to bring the news; she was sorry about the timing, as if it made any difference. I am too exhausted to feel; my emotions have been put on hold since I started to starve. I couldn't even think of an appropriate response, of what a normal person would say, so I said nothing and let Manda give me the details.

It was a neighbour who alerted the police, and I imagine Mrs Read with her notebooks, twitching the curtain and realising she hadn't seen my mother leave the house since Christmas Eve. When they broke the door down, they found her in her chair; rigor mortis had set in days before.

'There will have to be an autopsy,' Manda told me. 'Under the circumstances.'

The circumstances: my mother was alone when she died. Her body was undiscovered; no friends, no family even noticed. Just a nosy neighbour peering through the letterbox at the pile of junk mail and unopened Christmas cards. Maybe one was from Dad; I wondered if he knew yet, that she was dead.

'I'm afraid it will delay the funeral. But when we have a date, we can apply for a release pass for you to go.'

'I don't want to go.'

I haven't seen my mother, or anyone else, for eighteen months. I refused to see her or even think about her, preferring to scrub my heart of a need for her, just as I have stopped needing food. I chose emptiness, and a clean heart, and so I won't mourn. But still, when Manda left me, I felt very alone. I couldn't help a rogue thought creeping in of my mother, in that chair. Her body stiff and cold.

I wish Stacey was here to talk to, but she's at home with her family, celebrating Christmas and the New Year. She stuffs her head with trashy stories and problem pages from bitchy fashion mags, so she knows things. She'd be useful right now: she'd make me laugh with her anecdotes, she'd fill my head with her talk-show wisdom of coping with grief, and make me forget.

Even though she pisses me off a lot of the time, Stacey has talents: lip gloss and too-tight tops and talking. The other girls, Joelle and Fiona, don't like her much. I don't think Mina likes anyone, least of all herself. But Stacey is the best friend I've ever had.

Finally, I sleep.

The brain is not like the body: it does not let go so easily and is harder to control, and as I drift to sleep it takes me elsewhere, to the place of all my nightmares. Grief plays tricks like this.

In my dream, I am back home, in Ipswich. It is 25 April of last year, the day of my sixteenth birthday.

I'm in the kitchen. There is the table, taking up most of the room, set for a birthday tea with a cake shaped like a heart. It's a memory, a vision, and I flutter around the room hopelessly, and touch the pile of unopened presents, feeling again a whiff of longing, that heady sensation of being loved that I have managed to rid myself of so effectively when conscious.

One present is already unwrapped. A camera, a special vintage one, gifted to me by my dad. It was his when he was a boy, his most special possession, and then it was Jena's. On my sixteenth birthday he gave it to me.

I hear my sister's words, so clearly, her hurt and anger: *You can't give Sam that camera! It's not right, Dad. You promised you wouldn't. How can you do that to me?*

I feel again the intoxicating cocktail of guilty victory because it had been *her* camera, *her* special prize. Hours she'd spent, in the dark room, developing her prints or helping him edit the home movies he loved to make. But she'd stopped doing that. Dad accused her of losing interest, so he was giving the camera to me.

It made Jena furious and sad, and it was why she stormed out that afternoon.

The kitchen door hangs open, a pool of water oozes into the room and rain slaps hard on the windows. Outside, the world grumbles, and inside is a yellow flash; the fluorescent light blinks once then dies, creepy shadows are cast on the wall. I call into the silence, 'Mum?'

In my dreams I call for her often, but she never replies. She never will again.

The dream is a fever; it sickens me. So real, I can feel the rain on my head as I step out into the weather, to search for Jena, who left in such a rage, and also for my parents who followed her. My T-shirt is soaked in seconds, water squelches in my shoes, and my cheeks are pricked by needles of rain. I make my way along the path at the back of the houses, trampling through long grass and nettles. The path eventually comes out beside the petrol station on Orwell Parade.

I have that sense all dreamers have of danger. I should wake myself, to control these feelings that threaten to crack me open, but I'm too exhausted. Instead, I abandon myself to the pull of the memory and head down the scrabbly path, a narrow alley of overgrown elders. I feel it all, every sensation: shivery and wet, brambles scratching my arms, branches tugging the hem of my dress and pulling strands from my hair, but I carry on like a sleepwalker. Rain in my eyes, in my ears even, feet sinking in the mud, shoes slipping, but I don't stop, can't stop, because twenty feet ahead the path opens up and there will be light.

There is never any light. Someone blocks the exit, up near the petrol station. My dream is playing tricks, and I see an impossibly large person in a dark raincoat, a hood covering their head. I wipe rain from my eyes, and see the hooded person raise a red crab of a hand towards a young woman, who is small and crouched. The hooded figure lunges, and the woman falls backwards, circling her hands, grasping for the raincoat and pulling it down with her.

There is an almighty crack as the woman's head hits concrete. A sickening sound that repeats again and again in my memory.

The monster who attacked the young woman looks up, and seems to move towards me; with the hood now removed as the coat is torn away, I see a pale face and dark hollow eyes. A face with no features, a terrifying blank.

I wheel my feet in an effort to backtrack through the mud, but slip and land smack on the ground. Just twenty feet ahead the young woman is sprawled on the pavement. Her face is turned towards me, her neck twisted, her head split open like a ripe fruit. The storm is directly above, and an arrow-flash of lightning reveals to me her face, and the fact I should have always known: the woman on the ground is my sister.

Jena.

CHAPTER 2

New Year's Eve

'Sam!'

A voice, tugging me back from the past. Bringing me back here, to my bedroom on Ana Unit, to the fact of my mother's death. Voices throb in and out of my hearing, staff talking urgently above my head.

'Sam. You need to wake up. Come on, Sam, stay with us.'

I will not wake. I want to disappear.

'Okay, Sam, I've got you. Stop struggling.'

Of course I struggle. Sian pins me like a butterfly, while Manda coaxes me and readies the tube. They've done this before; they play the bad cop/good cop routine often. I twist and pull back, but they are strong. Eventually, I surrender.

'Good girl. I'm going to pull your head right back, so don't slump. That's it. I'm just going to lubricate the tip, and then we'll get started.'

Sian has me held fast on the couch as Manda inserts the naso-gastric tube. Because I refuse to eat, they will feed me through this tube; it's a sign of how close I am to winning. I'm panicking, because what I'm doing is giving up control; I'm fighting, but it's a battle I've already lost.

'Now, Sam,' Manda coos, 'you need to relax or this will hurt. I'm just going to slide it . . . That's it . . . You're doing great.'

I can feel it there, at the back of my throat, coming down through my nasal passage. I gag, a reflex of rejection, but Manda doesn't stop.

'Just relax and it'll be quicker. Keep still.'

I retch; my throat is dry and painful. I manage to say, 'Fuck you,' but the words burn and Sian grips me tighter. It doesn't stop what's happening.

Before she fed it into me, Manda measured the tube, placing it around my ear and then seeing the length needed to reach my sternum, but now that it's inside it feels endless, too long.

'Nearly there. That's it. Now, no purging while this is in, Sam. You puke, the tube comes up too. And that wouldn't be pleasant, now would it?'

Patronising bitch.

'Once this tube is in place, we can give you all the nutrition you need. It was our last resort, Sam. We can't have you refusing to eat. Or eating and then purging, hiding food under your napkin.'

'I never hide food.'

Sian looks at me in a bitter way that says, *You are lying and we both know it.*

I like Manda as a rule, though right now I want to hit her. But it's Sian that has me held down, her fingers digging in harder than they need to; she's the mean one.

I try to feel nothing as I sip the water to help the tube find its place, as Manda tapes the feeding end to the side of my cheek.

Finally, Sian releases me and says, matter-of-factly, 'You nearly died today, Sam. You were slipping into a coma.'

Oblivion. I felt it, the closeness. To be where Mum is, that place beyond all feeling.

'You've given us no choice; we have to take drastic measures.'

'Violating me.'

There is a slight twitch to her lip that makes me think she is enjoying my anger.

'As well as the tube, we've got something extra, just for you. You could call it intensive therapy. Controversial, even. But it's our last shot. Afterwards, if you still succeed in killing yourself, we won't be to blame.'

You have to admire Sian's candour.

Intensive and *controversial* arrives an hour and a half later, after I've been x-rayed to check the tube isn't in my lungs, and while I'm lying on my bed studying the ceiling for new stains. It doesn't knock, it just opens the door and walks in. My room is small, cell-like, and the man fills it with the smell of worn leather and pipe-tobacco. It's Clive, the director of the unit and a bit of an oddball.

'Hello, Sam. I see the medical team have finished with you. How are you feeling?'

Clive was the first person I met when I arrived at the Bartlet Hospital, that terrible day. I'd met a tag-team of professionals before I was transferred here, men and women with letters after their name, who wore glasses before they needed them just to enhance the image; people paid to assess me and give me a label. *Mad* or *Bad*? I quickly got skilled at reading therapists: I could spot a cognitive behavioural from a transcendental on the shade of lipstick; I could tell a psychologist from a psychiatrist on the colour of tie. But I could not easily categorise Clive and that made me nervous, so I've stayed in the shadows when he's doing a ward visit, and up to now his visits haven't been for me.

Today, he wears a tweedy jacket with old-school blue jeans, and his beard is pure vagrant. His face is crumpled, wind-beaten, but he probably treats his skin like he treats his clothes, and the smoking can't help. He may be younger than he looks.

Clive pulls out the old wicker chair from under the desk, and sits on it, his bottom filling the seat, meaty hands in his lap. He is holding a paper bag, the kind that American moms use for their kids' packed lunches.

'What's inside?' I ask, but he smiles as if telling me to be patient, places the bag on my desk, then returns his hands to his lap.

'We haven't really spoken recently, have we? But I've been monitoring you, keeping up to date with your progress. Or lack thereof.' He pauses, as if to emphasise that I have disappointed him. 'Do you recall our first meeting, Sam? You were in a terrible state that day.'

Of all the five patients on Ana Unit I've been here longest. Some girls stay a few weeks, usually a few months, but I've been locked away for almost eighteen months, most of it here.

'I have a great deal to do managing the Bartlet, administrative decisions and so forth. Fundraising and lobbying in the main, trying to keep our little cottage hospital viable, despite the council's wish to sell it to the highest-paying property developer.' He sighs, and I can hear his criticism of their greed.

'I only get directly involved in a case if the staff have failed with every other route.'

I hate him and his fat bottom. I hate his scratchy-looking beard and his tiny glasses. Most of all, I hate that the brown paper bag is on my desk and I don't know what's inside.

'Sam, on 1 February there is a board meeting, to discuss your progress. You could be released, if it's agreed you're well enough.'

I curl into myself near the wooden headboard. I just want him to go away, and to disappear into the shadows again. I don't want his special attention.

'I understand that you have just had some very sad news yesterday about your mother's passing. I'm so sorry. Things must feel overwhelming right now.'

I am not overwhelmed. I feel nothing. If I begin to feel then I simply starve some more and that fixes me. Empty body, empty thoughts.

'But you have been here a long time, and as you are not dead yet, I can only assume that you wish to live.'

Quite an assumption, considering the size of me. Considering the tube running from my nose.

Having established himself as my personal saviour, Clive reaches behind him for the bag and takes out a clear plastic bowl, the type they use in the dining room for our salads or fruit. Inside is a small pile of sliced carrot.

'Twenty calories,' he says, and in my head I correct him: *Eleven.*

He then takes out a can of Enliven; this is what they force down the tube, thick as condensed milk and disgustingly rich. Just seeing the can makes me want to puke.

'Or two hundred and twenty calories.'

I watch as he places both back on the desk, side by side.

'I have a proposal for you. I'd like to see what progress we can make before 1 February. I'll be writing the report on you, with a recommendation about release.' He smiles, as if he is about to suggest a choice of two fun outings, and I have to blink away bad thoughts. 'I want us to make a start, right now. If you talk to me, and let me be your therapist, at the end of the session you will eat the carrots. But if you refuse, or I am unhappy with how the session has gone, then you will be tube-fed the Enliven.'

I sit up, so fast my head spins. 'A whole can?'

'That's right.'

'You can't do that! I'm on a controlled plan.'

'And I'm now part of that control.' He smiles again, and his eyes twinkle; he would resemble a kindly Father Christmas if he wasn't offering such a horrific choice.

'I'm not a lab rat,' I say. 'You can't just force-feed me arbitrarily.' The can would go straight under my skin, a layer of ugly fat.

'But I can, Sam. You see, one of the conditions of your hospitalisation is that you co-operate with treatment.'

I look at his pompous face, his scratchy, hairy, fat face, and hate him. I breathe in, every bit of air I can, and say with force, 'Piss off.'

He pauses, nods, then takes a radio from his jacket pocket. His fat thumb hovers over the talk button. 'You're sure, Sam?'

'Fuck you,' I say, though with less conviction this time.

'Very well.' He presses the button on his radio. 'Sian, could you join me in Samantha Hoolihan's room, please? She has chosen to be fed by tube.'

I won't tell you how I screamed and fought, how the tube came out and had to be re-inserted. I won't tell you about the slow inevitable journey of fat from can to tube to stomach, and how heavy and ugly I felt, how sad and lonely.

I will only tell you this: Clive is wrong. I do want to die.

CHAPTER 3

New Year's Day

Fireworks crack and hiss across the sky, heralding midnight and lighting my tiny room in pink, purple and blue flashes. I'm huddled against the radiator, wrapped tight in my lumpy duvet. Tensing with each screaming whizz and braced for the gunshots of dynamite, the shocks of light. I long for dark again, but the curtains are too thin to block out the celebrations.

Beyond the hospital's security wall, on the beach across the road, families and couples are huddled, mittens clasped, gazing into the night. I imagine them clinking champagne flutes, kissing each other as a new year begins. Making resolutions, knowing it won't matter that they'll break them before January is through. No point in resolutions for me, I won't even make it to 1 February. If I'm lucky.

Though Clive has a different idea. Five hours ago, my door opened, unannounced, and there he was, blocking the doorway with his bulk and filling the room with the liquorice tang of his pipe-smoke. He was wrapped in a long winter coat that had seen better days; under it was a dark suit that looked like it wouldn't fasten over his belly, and a shirt that may once have been white. His bow tie was perfect, though.

'Bit overdressed for a therapy session, aren't you?' I said.

He laughed happily, because of course he wasn't here for a therapy session but on his way to a restaurant or a party. I was just a task for him to complete before the fun started.

'I wanted to give you a present, Sam.'

He placed it on my desk, and I felt glad it wasn't a can of Enliven until I saw what it actually was; so much worse. It wasn't a present, of course.

'For you.'

He tapped the brown wrapping so it crinkled under his red hand. Skin was peeling on the knuckles, and I thought his wife should have bought him warm gloves for Christmas, that the cold weather doesn't suit him.

'We can make a start tomorrow. No better day for it.'

'If you don't have a hangover,' I said, drily, and he chuckled good-naturedly.

I peeled back the brown paper, and saw it was my old chocolate box, black with a raised red rose and the words 'Black Magic' on the lid. Once the box was empty of chocolates, it had been too pretty to throw away, and Jena had used it for her jewellery and hair grips, bits and pieces like that. And when she started doing photography she used it to store her pictures.

I'd found it in the attic, after she was attacked, when I was searching for something to help her remember. I began putting my own photos in it too, photos I thought of then as evidence.

I pushed the brown paper back in place, desperate to hide the box.

'How did you get this?' I demanded. He had the temerity to look sorrowful.

'It was sent in by your sister. She found it when she was clearing out your mum's home.'

A final poke of rage, directed at my heart. Jena knows how important this box is, what it means to me. If only I could turn back time, back to when the box wasn't a place I kept photos, but was just a chocolate box. The chocolates were eaten years ago, in a snug front room, passed around by a woman wedged into a high-backed armchair. A happy family, enjoying a treat together.

Tentatively, just to check on the contents, I lifted the lid, and in the light cast by a shrieking crimson comet the top photo gleamed with glossy perfection. It was a photo of Jena, the terrible one taken when she was still in a coma. I closed the lid, sat on my bed and turned my face to the wall.

Clive spoke gently; he moved closer, and I sensed him resisting the urge to comfort me. *Don't touch girls who are destroying their bodies; they don't like it.*

'The post-mortem will take place this week, Sam. Do you have anything you want to ask me, about the process?'

The wall was all I saw. I was thinking of nothing, my best talent. He can't break me; no one has yet.

'Okay, well, I'll come back tomorrow morning. All you have to do is talk for fifteen minutes, each day for the next month, about one of the photos in your box. That's all I ask, and when each session is over, you get to eat the lower-calorie option. It will be a step towards recovery, Sam. If you co-operate, they can decide to release you.'

'Fuck you, Clive.'

No matter how much the therapists over the eighteen months have told me that talking will help, I don't believe them. Control and secrets are things I understand well.

'I'll see you tomorrow then, Sam,' he said, hesitating as he jingled his car keys. Then he turned to leave. 'Happy New Year. Let's make it a good one, shall we?'

I heard him whistling as he walked away, and the room went colder.

True to his word, Clive arrives just after breakfast on New Year's Day.

It's quiet on the unit, too still, like a pause between strangers, but the other girls return tomorrow. Manda is on duty, and she's in the office reading a book she got for Christmas, some historical bonkbuster, and eating toast. I'm back in bed, trying again to find undiscovered cracks on the ceiling so I don't think about Mum. I can feel my tube-fed breakfast heavy in my stomach, seeping under my skin like a layer of blubber. I haven't looked at the Black Magic box since I woke, which is an achievement, a sign that I can win this battle with memory if I only focus on my body. Empty body, blank mind.

And then Clive walks in, smelling sour and with a bleary look to his eyes, which are small behind his glasses. There are crumbs of food or dandruff in his beard. The suit of last night is gone, the tweed jacket and flannel shirt have returned. He must shop at either Gentleman's Outfitters or Oxfam. He is carrying two items: an apple and a can of Enliven.

I roll towards the wall and close my eyes.

'Fuck you, Clive. I'm not talking.'

'Not even for fifteen minutes?'

'Not even for fifteen seconds.' And then I shut up, because silence is my friend, as is hunger. Memory and thought are noisy imposters, but I am strong and can beat them. I've been beating them for eighteen months, and my final victory is so close I'm dizzy with longing. Oblivion.

There is a pause, then I hear him speaking into the radio-mic for Manda's assistance. He sounds reluctant, even sad, and I want to scream at him to not give up on me, to please try again, but I keep the words locked inside and close my eyes, waiting. I tense, my body ready for the hands, the struggle, then the creamy fat they will force into me, though my stomach is still full from the first can. But I will not give in.

I start to cry, I can't help it, and I hold myself in a hug that feels pathetically limp, thin arms around scraggy body. I know how skeletal I am; I do not suffer from body dysmorphia. I hug myself, even though I am my own enemy; I cannot protect myself from me, from the thoughts that keep intruding. My dad is gone and my mother is dead, and I miss them both. Fuck you, Sam. Fuck you.

CHAPTER 4

2 January

I'm glad when the other girls return; their noise and drama distract me.

Fiona's bed is sunken in the middle from the weight of designer-shop bags, ones featuring half-naked teenagers and ducks wearing top hats. She's showing us the Christmas presents her parents bought her. Joelle is sifting through the bags with the tips of her fingers, looking superior because her family know better than to buy her clothes; she's drowning in her uniform of black sweater and black leggings.

Fiona is a pony-club anorexic; her symptoms are so recent that her blonde hair is still thick and glossy, she doesn't yet have any down on her face, and there are no dark circles under her blue eyes. She didn't even get NHS funding to be here; her darling parents are paying for her to be counselled and cured.

Fiona just loves having a label – *AN with BM tendencies* – meaning she starves herself until she gives in to chocolate. She's not even that small, not even in children's sizes yet, but Clive must have felt unable to say no to the extra money. Treatment here costs the earth, and we have three empty rooms. How can they keep the place going with only five of us to treat?

Stacey is pretending to be disinterested in the bags, but really she's as shocked as me by how much stuff Fiona has. She's always on the look-out for what the other girls get, especially clothes or make-up. She'd like to be one of their gang, but they don't want her, so she's stuck with me. I put up with her as she pops sugar-free pink bubbles and reads about Paris Hilton's new haircut or Brangelina's messy divorce. Shame really; she's not as dumb as she makes out. Her brain works well enough, but she stuffs her head with what nail polish doesn't chip, what spray tan will make her legs look slimmest.

What's best about Stacey is that she doesn't ask about my family. I told her once, in a weak moment when the feelings wouldn't disappear, how Jena had been attacked, how I've been refusing her visits for eighteen months, not replying to her many letters. Seeing her, seeing anyone, would break me. Jena needs a fresh start after all she's been through.

Stacey listened and didn't judge. That's what she's like: Angel perfume and shaved legs and hugs and not too many questions. It's why we get on. We let each other be. After my disclosure, I punished myself with hunger, and the feelings disappeared again, leaving me to focus only on my body.

Also in the room is Mina, but you could forget she's here. She's sitting in the corner, and she's made herself small. She never speaks, just sits there nibbling her fingertips to the quick. I daren't ask how her Christmas was, but she should never have been allowed to go home. She didn't want to leave, she told us in therapy group, but her father insisted and she can't say no to him. So she says no to food.

Unable to stop herself, Stacey reaches forward and lifts a lace red vest from one of Fiona's bags; her fingers run over the silk and she admires it until she sees it's a size 2 – she herself is a 0 – and drops it like it's on fire. She glances at me, and in that second I know we are both thinking the same thing: Fiona is a fraud. She doesn't belong here with us.

'Did you eat much?' I ask Fiona, my treacherous thoughts sneaking back to Manda's Christmas lecture, starring turkey and chipolatas and cake with marzipan and jellied fruits. And chocolates in black boxes. Fiona looks sheepish. I know the answer anyway; her face has filled out. She'll be home for good before long.

Joelle won't be, though. She looks skinny as always. I tell her so.

'BMI of fourteen,' she boasts, running a hand over her hip bone. 'Not my all-time record, but acceptable. Looks like you win the prize, though, Sam. You must have really done well to get this.'

She reaches to tentatively touch my tube. I let her; it's something we do here, touch each other, though we're prickly about outside people doing it. This is a tight club. We are all fascinated with starving bodies, not just our own, and because we are beyond anything sexual we study each other with the detached interest of clinicians. She feels the tube with wonder.

'Lucky,' she says. 'Now you don't even have to eat.'

Joelle is a blue-blood anorexic, a pedigree. She's third generation; Mummy and Grandmummy taught her all they know. They're proud of her, though they wouldn't say so directly, of course. They visit every fortnight, three wasted women in designer clothes, sculpted from the same source, with dark hair cut pixie-short to show their cheekbones. Her mother was an actress, and Joelle used to model for catalogues before she got too skinny. Unlike Fiona, Joelle doesn't have a chance of recovery, not in that family. Their Christmas present to her was a silver-plated handheld mirror, which is a fucked-up gift because anorexics simply love gazing at their own reflection, checking for changes, worrying over a spot or downy hair on the cheeks. They understand that, though, and that's what makes the gift special. It's like Joelle's family are with her.

My own family are only with me when I can't control it, like in dreams, or the photos in the Black Magic box.

I can't fight the need anymore; I open the lid and look again at the first picture in the pile, the first one I ever took with the camera, secretively taken when Mum and Dad were out of the room, talking to the surgeon, just after Jena came out of the operating theatre. In the picture, she is in a coma. Her face is red and puffy, her right eye half-closed and purple; she looks like she's been in a fight. There are metal grips, studded across her head to keep it from breaking apart, and her eyes are taped shut. I took the picture on impulse, not knowing where it would lead, but unsure what else to do with the camera round my neck in the awful silence of the hospital room.

How I loved my broken, bruised sister.

When my sister's head hit the concrete she was knocked unconscious. I cradled her and cried, calling to her all the time, oblivious to the blood on my hands. I couldn't tell you how long I was there. I was only vaguely aware that Mum and Dad had joined us, that someone, we never did discover who, had called an ambulance to take her to hospital.

Still unconscious after surgery, Jena had her own room in Intensive Care. Only the inhuman beeping machines and the changing of drips marked the passage of time; her hands swelled as the liquid became harder for her body to process. For four days this part of the nightmare continued, with Jena unreachable. The hospital gave us a pager so that if we weren't by Jena's side – if we'd gone home for a sleep or were in the hospital café eating a sandwich – the nurses could contact us. Dad disappeared into himself, weeping silently, letting Mum do all the talking, but even she didn't want to carry the pager; she said it made her panicky, and she'd hold it like it was a bomb. It had a belt-clip, but the waistband of her skirt was already tight, so it dug in and hurt her. Dad didn't offer, and I could see Mum hated that pager, so I wore it instead, tucked into the belt of my jeans. I remember going to the loo and thinking, *What if it rings now?* I was afraid it would go off when we were at home, trying to get some sleep, and I wouldn't hear it. I knew that the hospital calling could mean Jena had woken up, or it could mean that she'd gone into an even-deeper sleep.

Those first few days, I felt so tired. Depressed, I suppose, though I didn't know it then. I wanted to go back to school, think about my upcoming GCSE exams. But Mum was so stressed that if I said anything about that she'd get angry and shout at me for being selfish. Dad cried silently and hugged me so tightly I felt my bones crack. Mum and Dad were almost always in each other's arms, that's what I remember. The two of them, totally united.

We would sit in a line by Jena's bed like the three wise monkeys, gazing abstractly out on the Ipswich skyline, listening to the beep of the machine. We watched nurses press buttons, shine a torch into Jena's eyes and clip her finger with a gadget to measure her pulse. Minutes ticked by with no change. Meanwhile, my presents waited unopened on the kitchen worktop, all except one: the camera hanging around my neck. I couldn't bear to take it off.

Dad never talked about it, how the gift of the camera had caused the argument and sent Jena spinning from our home and into the path of her attacker, but I could feel his guilt like a heavy coat that shrouded him. He was remote from me, insulated by his agony, and only Mum could soothe him. Mum and the dark room, where his old pictures of Jena could show him the girl he longed to have back. Maybe for a while he could forget that she was gone.

We'd get beeped if Jena moved violently; we'd get one when she was too quiet and too still and the nurses wanted us to come in so that we could shout at her to bring her back from whatever dark place she was in. Whenever we heard the beep, we moved fast.

It was 29 April, four days since the attack. We were on the bus, on the way home, having been at the hospital all afternoon. *Beep beep.* Mum leaned across the pregnant woman in the seat by the window and pressed the black strip that sets off the bell, over and over until the bus driver shouted, 'All right, love! I get the message!'

We jumped off the bus as soon as it stopped, Mum half-walking, half-running ahead of me, Dad holding me by the hand as I stumbled to keep up. When we got to the hospital, Mum stopped in her tracks, so that we almost knocked into her.

'She's dead. I can feel it.'

Dad crouched on the ground and moaned; he was worn out by the whole experience, too tired to cry. Mum knelt down beside him and cradled him like he was a baby.

'It'll be okay, I promise. We've still got each other. We've still got Sam.'

The three of us began to walk again, not rushing this time, making our way back to the hospital slowly, thinking we were too late. But when we got there, Jena wasn't dead. She was awake.

The doctors tried to explain it to us, the unpredictable nature of brain injury. They told us that some degree of personality change was to be expected, and that Jena might appear to regress; that her childhood memories would be stronger than more recent ones, that she might lose skills she'd had or gain unexpected ones. One nurse told us about a man in the next ward who woke up speaking French, a language he hadn't used since he was at school. And all the time Jena lay on the bed, blinking like a doll at the ceiling, as the staff spoke about her to us, like she wasn't even there. And I felt that she was listening to every word.

Her progress was miraculous, they said. She could speak, with only a little slurring, and though she had no memory of what had happened to her, she knew exactly who she was. Sometimes she seemed just like her old self; at other times, a poor impression. Three days later, they said she was stable enough to be moved to a community hospital in Westerfield, and placed on Eastern Ward, a specialist unit for dementia, a place she didn't belong. By the middle of May, to the relief of us all, she was moved to Minsmere, the long-term rehabilitation ward. She had her own room, and a timetable of therapy; she was walking around and talking, and sometimes making jokes. Though still not remembering who attacked her.

When Clive opens my door after lunch, I'm waiting for him. I'm seated on the wicker chair, refusing to be vulnerable in my own room, facing the doorway. He pauses, the handle still in his grip, surprised, and I steal my advantage.

'What are you, Clive? Really, I mean? This unorthodox torture you're putting me through. Are you even qualified?'

He bends his head down, as if I have asked something interesting, and points to the bed, as if I have the power to stop him sitting down. When he is settled on the thin mattress, each hand clasping a food item, he says, 'So long as someone is trying to help you, does it really matter?'

'Of course it fucking does.'

'Okay.'

He reaches forward and places my two options on the desk behind me, next to the Black Magic box. This time, the alternative to the Enliven is a celery stick, chopped into inch-long pieces and zip-locked in a plastic sandwich bag. Only ten calories, and chewing celery expends more than that. Clever man: he is offering me negative calories versus 220, if only I will do as he says.

He must be getting desperate.

'You know who I am, Sam. Director of the Bartlet.'

'I mean, what sort of therapist. Are you even a doctor?'

He laughs, enjoying a joke I wasn't aware I made. 'I'm a consultant psychiatrist, though I may be better suited to management.' He laughs again, as if amused by the joke inside a Christmas cracker. It makes anger run right up me like a shooting pain; it shoots from my mouth.

'So what are you even doing here with me? Am I just some lab rat for you to poke about with?'

Strong words, but I feel powerless, frustrated that he has all the control and he hasn't even had the courtesy to label the work he's doing. He's working outside any box, not using the worksheets and words I've become familiar with, and that scares me. I could get caught out. I could lose control.

'I hate you,' I say, and mean it.

'Good,' he replies, evenly. 'That will avoid any complications when we are working together more co-operatively.'

'I'll never work with you.'

I watch as he slides the radio from his jacket pocket and begins to ask for assistance. On the desk is the celery. It's only celery, for fuck's sake; it's almost water.

'Okay!' I snap, exhausted and broken. I can't face another can of Enliven. 'What is it I have to do?'

There is silence. He is watching me.

'Well, Sam, you've already established I do not use conventional methods, so I don't know. But I'm happy for us to improvise. Let's try this. You take a photo from that box and talk about it for fifteen minutes.'

I glare at him, but he continues to gaze at me as if it is the simplest request in the world. I turn, and take the Black Magic box in my hands. Inside, the photos shift as if woken.

'And if I can't?'

'You know the answer to that, Sam. You know that the board won't release you on 1 February if they can't see any progress. Don't you want to be free?'

Free. The possibility is as tempting as any food or drink, as necessary in that moment as breathing. I quickly open the lid and take out the second photo from the top. It's of Ipswich Police Station. I know exactly when I took it, on the first Monday in June, six weeks to the day since Jena was attacked. On 6 June everything started to go wrong. It was also the start of a heatwave.

Oh God, I can almost feel the camera pressed against my cheek, closing my left eye for a moment so everything was pinky-bright. I can almost hear the satisfying click of a moment captured.

And, despite myself, Mum comes back to me, full-focus in my memory. Hair tight in a bun, trowelled-on make-up. Her foundation was melting in the heat, streaking orange down her neck. She was wearing her best heels, the white leather stilettos she'd bought for her pearl anniversary party, so she had to walk slowly and carefully up the steps, clinging to the railing.

Oh Mum.

'I can't do it,' I say, closing the lid so I can no longer see the picture. I can't talk about my mother. It's too raw, too sad.

'Come on, Sam. Fifteen minutes. I know you can do it.'

I look at the can of Enliven. I can't have more calories, either. Nutrition brings back thoughts, brings back feelings, brings back pain.

'Just try, Sam. Try to talk.'

I take a breath. 'Just promise me, Clive.'

'Promise what?'

'That you're not lying to me. That she really is dead.'

He looks confused by this, and his voice is full of concern. 'I promise, Sam. I would never lie about something as sad as a death. I'm sorry for your loss.'

I feel something loosen inside, a letting go. I wonder if I can actually do this.

By 6 June, my family were regulars at the police station.

Six weeks since my sister Jena was attacked, and a man was helping police with their enquiries. He'd been remanded into custody, though we didn't have any other details yet. But Detective Sergeant Penny Rickman, who was responsible for Jena's case, had asked us to come in, so we were hoping for more news. We wanted to know when we'd get our day in court.

People passed us, on their way to the Job Centre or DSS, flagging in the heat. Across the road, Ipswich Crown Court slumped low under red tiles. Girls in skimpy vest tops, skin turning pink in the blazing sun, gathered in groups to gossip. Boys in white trainers and school shirts talked to pale, blinking men in pinstripe suits who were about to persuade the magistrates that the boys were sorry or pissed or innocent.

No one cared about victims, that's what I'd learned.

The police station was a dump. A line of orange plastic chairs edged the back wall under a shabby green-baize notice board, layered with old posters and half-thumbed community leaflets. Hanging around were people I knew at a glance to stay clear of; they were the bad sort that Mum was endlessly warning me about.

A white, skinny bloke, grade 1 haircut, shoes for running, leaned against the notice board and grunted some instructions to his mate, who was slouched in the seat next to him. His mate had slightly more hair and flesh, but was still lab-rat pale. Next to them sat a middle-aged woman with purple hair wearing silver flip-flops. An elaborate tattoo on her ankle said LIAM. I imagined the tattooist dabbing away the dots of blood as he sent the needle again and again into her skin.

Mum took the seat as far from them as possible, the plastic squeaking under her, and took off her right shoe, rubbing her foot with her hand. Her heel was pink and sore with a blister-bubble of fluid raised over the bone. She winced as she prodded it.

'These shoes have never fitted right.'

Mum got tetchy when she was in pain.

'I can't,' I say to Clive, gasping as if I've been held underwater.

I have to freeze my thinking, though my real wish is to freeze the past, stop everything right there, with Jena's case unsolved, and me and my parents getting on with our lives as best we could. I'd just turned sixteen, was taking my GCSEs that month. In September, I planned to start college. I still had a future.

'Come on,' says Clive gently, tapping the can of Enliven. 'You're doing so well. Just another four minutes.'

I take a deep breath and tell myself that she can't reach me now. I don't want more calories; I need oblivion. If I'm to disappear I have to talk, and four minutes isn't long.

At the entrance to the waiting area a flame of colour caught my eye. I recognised Monica immediately; she was in the year above me, the first year of sixth form, and a drama student. An attention-seeking lot, the sixth-formers had loud arguments in the common room and made up seconds later, hugging each other with lover-like intensity.

Monica walked like a catwalk model, yanking on a red lead, on the end of which stood a bulky British bull terrier with one black eye. For all its tough appearance, the dog seemed nervous.

'Oi!' Gloria called from her reception booth, banging her knuckle on the glass. 'Get that dog out of here. Now!'

Monica pulled the reluctant terrier back outside and tied it to a railing, where it gratefully curled up and put its head on its paws. Turning in their seats, the men eyed Monica through the window the way you might an unusual fruit that looks interesting but difficult to eat. She had hennaed hair, golden eyeshadow and skin like cream – an exotic bird caged within notice boards and grey walls.

The men made me nervous, a feeling that was constant since the attack, and to shield myself from their eyes I lifted the camera. It comforted me, covering half my face and giving me the distance I craved. Through the lens, the scene around me suddenly seemed manageable, because I was distant from it. The camera gave me the objectivity I longed to feel.

Through the viewfinder, I caught Monica in profile and pressed the shutter, just as she was pushing the dog's bottom out of the way with her foot. I would ask Dad to help me develop it, work some effects into the picture. I'd only had the camera a few weeks, so I still had a lot to learn.

She came inside and saw me. 'Hey, Sam. Why you take a picture of me?' Her Eastern European accent made her sound like she was singing. She wrinkled her nose. 'With that smelly old dog.'

'Okay, just you.'

She slipped her T-shirt off her shoulder, and the men began to jeer, enjoying the show. She winked at them and smiled flirtatiously. I was hidden behind the camera, but still felt I'd been pulled into something sleazy.

Mum waved her hands in our direction. 'Oi, young lady! Don't distract my daughter. She's taking photos for her art studies, not for some tacky magazine.'

'Who you say is tacky?' Monica gave Mum the full benefit of a pout, but Mum couldn't see that Monica was joking and pulled herself up to her feet.

Ah Mum. Back to her, always.

Her scent was a mix of cheap bubble bath, Oil of Olay and nicotine. When we hugged, she felt like a bag of marshmallows dressed up in scratchy nylon; her kisses were dry and powdery, her cheeks thin, like paper. Mum was chipped nails, gossip mags and bingo. She was bleached blonde (though under the dye she was as dark as Jena and me), and her eyes sparkled when she'd had a Bacardi or two. Just forty-six, she had married my dad when she was seventeen and already pregnant, something neither of her parents forgave her for. And she was protective as a guard dog, ready to attack, if she thought anyone – anyone at all – was trying to hurt her precious family.

She was the fixer in the Hoolihan clan. Dad had retreated into his pain, too bruised to accompany us to the police station, preferring his dark room and photos of the past, but Mum was still ready to take on the world.

'Dressing like that. You ought to be ashamed.'

'Like what, you think I dress?' Monica stalked forward. I tried to steer Mum back to her seat, but she shrugged me off.

'Flaunting yourself!'

'Ha!' Monica went up to Mum, her petite nose level with Mum's flat, red one. 'Who you thinking you are, my mother?'

I felt a lurch in my intestines, a familiar sick feeling rising from my gut.

'Don't mind her,' I said to Monica. 'It's just we hate this place. You must have heard of what happened to my sister. Well, the police have—'

'Shut up, Sam!' Mum clawed at me, catching my forearm with her nail, and I staggered backwards. Along the inside of my arm was a raised blood-red scratch, thin as a piece of thread.

I stop talking, and turn the photo of the police station over so it is facing down on my thigh, the paper sticky on my leg. I look at my arm, but there is no mark. All my wounds are inside.

For the first time, I remember Clive; I was so lost in the past he seemed to disappear. There he is, still seated on the bed, one leg over the other, his hands neatly clasped in his lap. But his face is ruddy, and his eyes twinkle behind the glasses. His voice, when it comes, is rushed with emotion.

'I was right, then,' he says, breathing deeply. 'You do want to go home.'

And then I feel cheated; he's tricked me into talking with threats of extra calories, and now he's taunting me with my own weakness. He hands me the celery, watching as I chew and swallow every sinewy piece.

'Would you like to go to the funeral, Sam? When we have a date, I can make arrangements for you to have a release pass. I could escort you myself.'

'Can you please piss off now?' My words are a string of despair. 'I need to sleep.'

CHAPTER 5

3 January

I need to sleep, but I can't.

It's ten past three, darkest velvet outside, but my brain won't rest. It's Jena's fault for sending in the box, my fault for opening it. I should have kept my mouth shut; now my memories are unravelling like a thread being pulled, everything coming apart since they told me of Mum's death. I wonder about Dad, who has now lost all of his family, and then prefer not to wonder. I erase him from my thoughts, and think only of my shifting bowels, the extra calories sluggishly making their way down my lower intestines. But the toilet is at the end of the echoey corridor; it will be cold in there, and I'll have to pass the nurses' office, where whoever is on duty will see me and mark it on the log to be passed over, commented upon, when the day staff arrive at seven.

I leave my room, bare feet pattering on the ancient red tiles, the huge arched windows all along the corridor like eyes, the moon casting a white eerie glow along my path, though the edges darken into shadow. The nurses' room, halfway along, is a beacon of light. I see a canary-blonde mop of hair covering a face, a head propped up by a hand and arm. It's Birute, who's Lithuanian and my favourite of all the night staff, mainly because, even though she's been in Suffolk for fourteen years, her English is terrible, so she can't ask many questions. She compensates in physical ways, hugs and pats, and I can just about tolerate that. It's words that break me.

She hears me and lifts her head. She looks tired, and also sad, but then Birute doesn't understand why we girls just can't eat. Her grandmother was a prisoner of Stalin and had to beg for food; why would anyone choose to starve themselves? Her logic, of course, is impeccable.

I like that Birute still has pity for us, even when she can see our starving is self-imposed. Other staff members aren't so generous, like Sian, who thinks we're just idiots who need to snap out of it.

Birute makes a sound of concern. 'No sleep, Sam? What matter, hey?'

I shuffle up to her and rub my distended tummy. She places her warm hand over mine. 'You have pain here?'

I nod. 'I need the loo.'

'Okay, sweet.' And she gets the key.

Together we walk to the end of the corridor, where the toilets and showers are. We pass Fiona's door with its poster of One Direction, and she's prettified her nameplate with stickers of the band. Joelle's door has a pin-up of Audrey Hepburn, and alongside her nameplate is a glamorous photo of her with Mummy and Grandmummy. Stacey's door is a mess of magazine clippings, reality stars and actresses; I can hear her snoring softly as we move past. Mina has nothing on her door, and the nameplate is blank. No sound comes from within.

I know these girls' measurements like my own, their stories told in snatches at night; even Mina tells her story in forced instalments at therapy class. I am the only one who refuses to talk. Most anorexics literally die for attention, but I told you I was odd.

Our feet smack on the tiles, our breathing bounces off the high ceiling, and Birute shivers.

'Is haunted, this place.'

'Probably,' I agree. Many souls must have died here; after all, the Bartlet is an old convalescent hospital, built when people perished of TB and consumption if they weren't sent to the seaside to rest. The windows all along one side face the North Sea; its crashing waves are the soundtrack to our days. The building is red brick, a curved grand structure, gifted to the town of Felixstowe by Dr Bartlet, hence the name. But convalescence is a thing of the past; why go to the seaside to recuperate when *Real Housewives* is on TV and there is pizza delivery in every town? Most of the building is abandoned, used to store broken equipment and old chairs. One block is still used for occupational therapy, offering seated exercise classes for the aging population of the town. The middle building is where Clive has his office, surrounded by empty wards. And then there's us. A unit on the end of the curve, eight bedrooms for girls who starve themselves, only five of them occupied.

Us girls, we call our home Ana Unit. It's not really Ana Unit, of course; it's Cobbold Ward, but anorexia is our friend and foe so it's right that she's our home too.

Birute waits while I take a shit, as she's required to do. I hear her yawning, then try not to hear. Privacy is something we don't have; we would abuse it. When I re-appear, she is leaning on the far wall, looking out of an arched window to the sea. It's too dark to see it properly, though the moon and stars shed some light, but the waves can be heard clapping against the shingle. I stand next to her, and she puts her hand on my shoulder, tutting as she squeezes my bony arm. We both watch the dark scene, knowing the beauty that will be revealed at daybreak.

'You want drink with me?' Birute asks, and of course I don't, but the idea of sitting with her rather than returning to my monastic room is appealing.

'Yes, please.'

She smiles, happy to have company, and we walk to the office. I take the comfy chair, and she puts her coat around me while she boils the kettle. Why does everyone have such faith in tea?

Her coat is thin, not heavy enough for January in Suffolk. Ana Unit is an expensive place for the local health authority to keep running, and the Bartlet is a drain on resources, but Birute isn't the reason it costs so much. She's an auxiliary; she'd likely earn more doing the night shift stacking shelves at Sainsbury's, but instead she chooses to sit in the nurses' office and wait for one of us to need her.

I cradle the tea, which is as orange as the brick wall of the hospital, not intending to drink a sip, as she gazes at me. At my tube.

'Oh Sam,' she says. 'Poor girl.'

And though she hasn't the words, I can hear in the way she speaks my name that she is sad for my loss, and confused about my illness. I think Birute thinks we're mad, her poor girls.

But in many ways we are as sane as salt; it's the rest of the world that's crazy.

After she's finished her tea, Birute takes me back to my room, tucks me in like I'm a child, and sits on the wicker chair as I try to sleep. Having her here is so different from when Clive sat there, making me talk. But he's unlocked something, or the box has. Or the fact of my mother's death.

Birute strokes my hair, which used to be so long and is now short and severe.

As sleep comes, slowly and stubbornly, I can't fight anymore. I'm back there, at the police station. I'm with Mum again.

Detective Sergeant Penny Rickman led us to a tiny interview room with no window. On the desk was a grey file titled JENA HOOLIHAN, with a photo clipped to the cover. I felt the familiar tightening in my chest and I breathed deeply, like the asthma nurse had taught me.

Mum shuffled in the chair, which creaked under her. She touched her lips with her thumb, smudging her coral lipstick in the process, and I knew she was gasping for a fag.

'What's the latest on the man you arrested?'

Mum's fingers closed together like she was praying as she waited for Penny to answer. Penny started to tap her biro against her front teeth. *Click*, *click*. It made me tense and I wanted her to stop.

'Penny?'

She dropped the pen, and it rolled across the table on to the floor, then she placed her hand on the file. There was silence, and I felt an intimation like a breath of cold air at the back of my neck that this time was different.

'Has he admitted anything? Have you got a court date?' I asked.

Penny hesitated.

'Well, the problem with a case like this is small communities come together and keep secrets. Someone on Orwell Estate knows what happened to Jena and why; they must do. We've interviewed everyone who was on the estate on 25 April, customers in the fish and chip shop, staff in the petrol station, teenagers hanging around the park. Our other hope is that Jena will be able to tell us something.'

I could feel the pain behind my eyes. For six weeks we'd been waiting for Jena to get her memory back and give us some information, maybe just a tiny detail, something that would give the police the description they needed to nail her attacker.

Mum shook her head firmly. 'Jena remembers nothing.'

'Mum, that's not true.'

She placed her large hand over mine. 'Shush, Sam.' I looked at my arm, the scratch from when she had told me to shut up in the waiting room. I kept my mouth closed.

Penny gathered some loose papers and neatened them in the file.

'I'm afraid that we haven't produced anything but circumstantial evidence against our main suspect. We can place him at the scene of the crime on that day, but that wouldn't be enough for a jury.'

Mum spluttered, started to murmur something, but then fell silent.

'I'm really sorry, but unless something else comes up, I can't see the Crown Prosecution Service proceeding with a court case. We won't know for sure until the bail hearing in two weeks, but he could be released.'

'What?' Mum reached inside herself and found a strangled voice. 'But he was there, when Jena was attacked!'

Penny nodded. 'Several witnesses saw him in the area, and he admits being in the vicinity. But he denies ever meeting with Jena, and no one saw them together. Or no one is telling us they did. Unless something more concrete comes up, he'll be released.'

'And what will happen then?' I asked, in a small voice.

Penny looked at Mum when she answered. 'If he's released, I'd like to act straight away, that same week, and hold a press conference to appeal for more information. I think we should hold it at the hospital, with Jena. Pull at people's heartstrings.'

Mum put her fist in her mouth and started to shake. 'No. I've told you, we won't do that.'

Penny looked annoyed. 'I'd like to go ahead and plan it anyway, for as soon as possible after the bail hearing. I'll liaise with Dr Gregg and have everything lined up, and we'll just have to hope it doesn't come to that. The next two weeks leading up to the bail hearing on 20 June are crucial, Kath. And we're running out of time. If there's something you'd like to tell me, maybe something you've forgotten? You were at the scene just minutes after Sam found Jena. Or maybe your husband remembers something? Sometimes just one detail can help solve a case.'

Penny had said this many times over the past six weeks. She didn't want to give up, and neither did I.

'Is there anything, Mum? Before you found me and Jena, did you see anyone?'

She was curled into herself now, crying hard.

'Okay, Kath,' Penny said, 'I'll keep you informed of any new developments, and I'll speak to Dr Gregg about the press conference. Of course, if Jena starts to remember, that would help immensely.'

Mum murmured unhappily, and squeezed my hand too tightly, like she used to when we were crossing a busy road. 'My girl, oh my precious little girl,' she said to herself, softly and sadly. And I didn't know if she meant Jena or me.

She looked done in, her head hanging down, hair falling from her bun, so much older than her forty-six years. Her breathing got shallower, her chest heaving with effort, and tears splashed on to the plastic table top. I pressed a tissue into her hand, but it didn't do any good. She was gasping in short, huffy breaths, trying to shore herself up like a leaky dam.

'Actually, Kath, there is something I'd like to ask you. Perhaps without Sam?'

Penny looked at me apologetically and I felt like screaming, *I'm sixteen now, not a little kid. The worst has already happened; you don't need to keep anything from me.*

'Okay, but I need a fag first,' Mum said, then added, 'Is there a loo?' and finally, 'Oh God, I think I'm going to be sick.'

She retched loudly, a hand over her mouth, and Penny jumped up, taking Mum by the elbow and launching her towards the door.

Mum stumbled, crippled by her anniversary shoes, a line of blood around the white leather heel as she limped out into the corridor, retching again.

The door slammed shut and I was alone.

I could hear Penny in the corridor, talking to Mum, and then another door slammed. The case file was inches from my grasp. I saw my chance and grabbed it, flicking quickly through Dr Gregg's reports until I came to the photos of the bloodied pavement by the petrol station where I'd found Jena. There was another photo, of Jena in a coma, her face swollen like a purple balloon, her head white and shaved. I turned the page quickly. Mum's statement came next, detailing how she'd found Jena, with me bent over her, just as the ambulance arrived, after someone made an anonymous call.

Next was Dad's statement. Just seeing his name made my hands tremble as I leaned over the words, mouthing them as I tried to work out the handwriting in places. He said we'd been preparing for my birthday tea, that Jena left the house just as it started to rain. He said she'd gone to get food, which wasn't true. He didn't say anything about their argument over the camera.

Finally, a statement, a long one. This must be Penny's main suspect, the man who was currently remanded, who had been placed at the scene of the crime.

I read his name, scribing it on my memory: *Douglas Campbell.*

I heard Penny's voice again, then Mum's, louder as they got closer. I read the statement as quickly as I could:

> On 25 April I'd arranged to meet Jena. I didn't want to, with all that's happened. I don't trust her as far as I can throw her. But I was curious when she started messaging me on Facebook and I agreed to come back to Suffolk. I haven't been back in sixteen years.
>
> I was hanging around behind the chippy, which is where Jena said I should wait. I was late because it had been raining, and I'd waited for the storm to pass, so I thought I'd missed her. I decided to walk down the alleyway that leads to her house, thinking I'd catch her up. That's how I found it, the raincoat. I picked it up. I could see it was a decent coat, even though it was wet. Then I saw it wasn't wet from the rain. There was blood on it, so I dropped it. I gave up on finding Jena, decided it was just another one of her cruel games and I should get out of town as soon as I could.

Later, when I was at the station about to catch the train back to Scotland, I saw the bulletin-board headline. A 29-year-old woman had been attacked on Orwell Estate. I guessed straight away that the woman was Jena, and the bloody raincoat must be connected. I missed my train, and went back for it.

But the coat was gone.

I heard Mum calling weakly in the corridor, 'Sam? I need my Sam . . .' Then Penny's voice said, 'I'll get her for you, Kath.'

The door opened just as I closed the file. But now I had a name, I had a place to start. Douglas Campbell.

CHAPTER 6

3 January

Room search. Six thirty in the morning I'm woken by the banging, and then the door opens to reveal sour-faced Sian in her plastic gloves.

'Happy New Year to you too,' I say, sitting up in bed and rubbing my eyes. Just like in prison, room searches on Ana Unit are random. We can never predict what day they will happen, what hour, but this early on a cold January day is sadistic even for Sian.

'You know the drill, Sam. Up you get.'

She opens a clear plastic bag, keen to start fingering my possessions, looking for anything sharp or sweet or salty; anything that I could use to harm myself or binge on; anything emetic. The bag already has my name written on it. So much for trust, but what do I expect?

I stand in the doorway, as Sian peers inside the toilet roll, pinches the pillow, checks inside photo frames. She looks inside my shoes, smiling up at me as she finds my dirty secret. Into her plastic bag goes the mustard sachet I sneaked from the seafront café, last trip out.

'Tut tut, Sam. Not a great start to the year, is it?'

I won't give her the satisfaction of a reaction. 'Can I get that?' I ask, pointing to the Black Magic box.

'I need to check inside first.'

She lifts the lid, rifles through the photos like they are a pack of cards. But there is nothing she considers sharp or dangerous or too sweet, so she hands the box over. Sian is wrong, though. My memories are all of those things.

I wander along the corridor, where the curtains to one of the huge windows have been opened, so I can see the beach is empty, desolate. I slump against the wall, a heap of bones on the cool red tiles. Along the corridor, the other girls are doing the same; daylight sneaks through the open window and casts a yellow light on their faces. Stacey is curled around her huge teddy trying to go back to sleep. Fiona is leaning against Joelle, whispering and yawning, but Joelle is studying herself in her silver mirror, lost in another world. I can't see Mina at first, but then I spot a shape within the folds of the curtain. As usual, she has made herself disappear.

The far door opens, the one that leads from the main part of the hospital on to our unit, and in walks Clive, blinking like a surfacing mole. He looks in need of caffeine; his clothes look like they spent the night on the floor. He greets the other girls, stepping over their bandy legs, but keeps walking until he is next to me.

'Morning, Sam.'

It's a struggle for him to sit down, and the cold floor tiles can't be good for his saggy old bum. His pocket is bulging, and I can see the silver lid, one I recognise as belonging to a can of Enliven.

'Really?' I'm incredulous. 'We're doing this now?'

Clive yawns into his meaty hand, then looks back down the corridor. The other four girls are lost in their own worlds, sleeping or chatting or hiding. No one is listening to us.

'I have an emergency admission to see to, but I didn't want to miss our meeting, so thought I'd come early.' He yawns again, then smiles at me. 'I'm not really a morning person.'

'Admission for here?' The idea of someone new arriving isn't pleasant. None of us like change.

'We'll see. My priority right now is for us to have our little chat. I want you to know I'm reliable, Sam. That whatever crops up, I'll still come and see you, like I said I would.'

I scowl at him, hating that he wants me to trust him. I'd prefer to simply be a chore for him, something to get done. It weakens me, him being nice. And I'm exhausted, unable to fight this early in the morning. Fifteen minutes. Surely I can manage that? Give him just enough to stave off another can of Enliven. Try and stick to the bare facts.

I take the third photo from the Black Magic box. A front view of a single-storey concrete block with a front entrance reached by a slope, and a line of windows glinting like eyes. Minsmere Unit, the rehabilitation ward where Jena had been moved in mid-May, once she was deemed stable enough. She'd had a room behind one of those windows.

I close my eyes and wish I could return to sleep, but know that I have to carry on telling my story or I'll be force-fed.

And then it occurs to me: there is no one to stop me speaking the truth anymore.

Mum was in a state of shock that in just two weeks the police's main suspect could be a free man. I helped her down the steps from the police station, and her tears made her make-up look clownish. She gripped my arm, limping badly, and winced with each step.

'Mum, you need to rest. Let's get a drink or something.'

'I'm not resting till I've seen Jena.'

We made our way to Ipswich train station, as we had for six weeks now. Mum stumbled every time she used her right foot, and leaned on me. A vapour of heat rose from the baking streets and I felt damp beneath my arms. Her face was mottled and beaded with sweat. She tugged off a shoe, and I saw the blister had popped, revealing pink, raw flesh underneath.

'Come on, Mum. Let's just go home and tell Dad the news. Jena won't even notice if we don't visit today.'

'And what kind of mother would that make me?'

She clicked open her bag and rummaged through tissues and pieces of paper, first finding her small pill pot and taking a white tablet to stop the panic, her atenolol, then finding the mirror. Peering into it, she licked the corner of a crumpled tissue into a tip and tried to tidy herself up.

'I'm a bloody mess.'

Mum caught the train to the hospital, and I walked home. As I followed the well-trod route, I thought about what I'd just read.

The police's main suspect was a man named Douglas Campbell, who said that on the day of Jena's attack he had arranged to meet her, and that he'd found a raincoat covered in blood, but it was gone when he returned. How convenient. And why would Jena want to meet him? Why message him on Facebook?

I longed for a trial and justice, for an end to the nightmare that started on my sixteenth birthday. For an end to my own guilt; I'd seen it, you see. Seen the attacker bend over Jena, coat puffed by the wind. If the rain had been less fierce, if I'd been taller, if I'd had the camera my dad had just given me, if I could only find that raincoat . . . But it wasn't, I wasn't, I hadn't. My testimony was fucking useless and the only other person who'd seen everything was Jena. Vital information was locked away inside her broken brain.

Images of the past are useful in encouraging the brain to remember; Dr Gregg had told us that, when Jena had moved to Minsmere and he asked us to bring photos for her room. Mum collected some from around the house, to try and stir her memory. But now I felt we needed to push faster, to go further.

And if the past was the key to unlocking Jena's brain, then I knew just what to show her: Dad's home movies.

'Dad?' I called, as I opened our front door.

There was silence.

He was likely in his shed, developing pictures, editing films on his computer, losing himself in old images of Jena to forget about 'now'. Film-making and photography were always his hobbies, but they had now become his therapy. He'd been in the shed almost constantly in the six weeks since the attack.

I moved quickly up the stairs to the landing, where I pulled down the ladder using the blue rope, and then climbed the rickety steps to reach the attic. The attic was crammed with boxes, a bin bag of old clothes, broken bits of furniture. Laid on the rafters was the spindly Christmas tree (still with baubles attached) that came out each year, and propped against a joist was the freaky Easter Bunny costume Jena wore on fun days at Pleasurepark, the local theme park, where she worked as part of the entertainment team. Dad worked there too. He was the chief engineer, though he'd been on compassionate leave since the attack; it was him that got Jena the job. Also in the attic was a TV with a built-in DVD player, put up here when we upgraded, but still useful for watching the home movies on: long-forgotten films of birthday parties and Christmases past.

In the corner I found the Asda cardboard box where he kept the films, along with older camcorders he'd discarded. The box had torn sides and the base was strengthened with duct tape, but inside DVDs were neatly lined up in chronological order accompanied by envelopes of photos. My childhood was in that Asda box, recorded by Dad, and I hadn't watched the movies in years. Films showing a normal life, when the worst thing that could happen to me was falling off my bike or scabbing my knee.

Also in the attic was stuff belonging to Jena, things she'd stored here, as she'd packed up boxes ready for her move to the new flat. It was a big deal for Jena to leave home. I looked inside the nearest box and saw a collection of the romance books she loved, a sewing kit that had never been opened, and an old chocolate box. I recognised it: it was the Black Magic box.

The old Black Magic chocolate box she used to put hair grips in, but it had more recently become her memory box. I opened it, and saw some of the photos she'd taken and developed, back when she was really into photography.

An emotional need to visit the past tugged at me, and I found the plug socket in the attic wall, hidden behind a bag of old toys, juggling clubs and diablo sets, and brought the dusty television to life. I pressed 'Play' and watched as Jena's face filled the screen.

The camera wobbles as it zooms in, then suddenly Jena's too close, obscured by pink sunglasses and a toothy grin. I'm next to her, a smiley, pig-tailed girl with missing front teeth, wearing a yellow Minnie Mouse T-shirt and red shorts. We are at Pleasurepark, a place we went all the time when I was little, on account of Dad working there. We got in free; we even got free milkshakes and treats from the staff who knew us. It was our favourite place in the whole world.

Dad films the iron waves of rollercoaster track, people surfing the tide of fear and excitement, hands grabbing air as they fall, then he focuses back on his daughters. I run up to a wooden model of a child, chipped paint in primary colours, a height marker sticking out of its forehead: YOU CAN ONLY GO ON THIS RIDE IF YOU ARE TALLER THAN ME!

I jump up by the wooden boy, placing myself under the marker. 'See! I can go on.'

There's a gap between my hair and the wood, wide enough for Jena to slide her hand in.

'No, Sam, you're too little. It's dangerous.'

'Please,' I beg, puppy eyes liable to weep any second.

Off-camera, my dad's voice says, 'Let her do it.'

In the seat of the rollercoaster I look small next to Jena. There's a stomach-churning stagger forward as the coaster begins its climb, and Jena clutches my hand. She's ashen with fear.

An odd angle, the screen shows sky, then the side of Jena's face. Her skin is pulled, her body is slumped heavily against the car. Dad is filming her, even though she's upset.

The camera jolts then and my head disappears; I'm slipping from view, as I slide down in my seat.

Jena panics. 'Sam!'

Her glasses fall on to the bridge of her nose as she tries to pull me up. She screams my name again, terrified, as the car tips forward, plunging us towards the ground.

Jena, my big sister. Always so protective of me, so loving. But now, my final memory before the attack was of her anger as she ran out into the rain. Her vicious anger at Dad for gifting me her precious camera, and at me for accepting it. On my sixteenth birthday we'd all hurt her, and it was too late to be sorry.

I wanted to show her the film; I wanted to show her anything that would help jolt her back to being as she was, but the Black Magic box was easier to carry than an Asda box of home movies. I slid it into my rucksack and headed back to the hospital.

I looked for her in the dining room first, opening the door in a waft of stewed cabbage and fresh bleach. Another patient, Olaf, was by the window, tugging at the curtains to hide a tower of cups that he'd balanced on the window ledge.

'Hey, Olaf, have you seen Jena?'

His eyes skittered over to where I stood; he shook his head and snarled, warning me away from his wobbling tower of china cups. I backed away, slowly. This was a madhouse. Jena shouldn't be here; she was nothing like the other patients.

Along the corridor lolloped Lance, who everyone in town knew because he'd sold the *Big Issue* on the Cornhill for years. He'd always try and talk with Jena, whenever we were passing, and she was kind to him but not interested.

Things had changed now, though. Suddenly, in the few weeks she'd been at Minsmere, he'd become her best friend.

His hair was poker straight and blue-black dark, except where he was scarred down the middle of his head and it had grown back white. Since Jena moved to Minsmere, they'd bonded over a shared interest in game shows; programmes she had thought lame before the attack, she now loved. Last week, they'd watched *Big Brother* in a three-day binge, but it gave Jena a horrific nightmare, and she had spent the following day searching in cupboards for cameras.

'Hey, Lance. Do you know where Jena is?'

He ran a hand over his hair, making the white tuft stand up; his lips turned down at the edges and he said, 'Poor Jena.'

'Why? What's wrong?' That sinking feeling came again.

'She had a fit.'

Dr Gregg said that if she had any more seizures they'd move her back to Eastern Ward, the dementia ward, where she'd spent that first hideous week after she came round from the coma. The thought of her returning there made me shudder.

'Happened just now.' Lance looked at his wrist, as if there might be a watch there. 'I didn't want to leave her, but I'm late for work.' Then he put his hand to his head, showing me a space on his pale, smooth brow.

'She's hurt bad.'

I stop speaking, not because I'm ready to, but because Clive places his hand on my arm and brings me back to myself. The sun is fully risen and around us staff are moving; Stacey is walking sleepily towards the shower room and the other girls are making their way to their rooms. It will soon be breakfast-time.

'You've done well, Sam. You spoke for twenty minutes. But I think that's enough for today.'

He looks nervous, as though my story is worrying him. It should. It's an ugly story and we're only getting started.

I'm getting dressed for breakfast when Stacey waltzes in. She's wearing massive pink sunglasses and a matching boob tube. She's dressed for Spain in summer, not Suffolk in January.

'The weatherman predicts snow,' she says, sliding her glasses on to her head and looking up at my tiny window. 'This is my Après Ski look.' She's been listening to Fiona again, her boastful stories of winters in the Alps and summers in Italy. Stacey loves hearing about Fiona's travels as much as she likes reading *Hello!* magazine, because they show her a better world, one different from her own.

She pulls at my black T-shirt and it sticks to my skin. 'Yuk, is this what you slept in? You need to shower, Sam. You stink.'

'Yeah, well I haven't got any dates lined up. Where d'ya get that pink top anyway? London Road?' That's the prostitute area in Ipswich.

She clicks her tongue, and is about to say something when we hear noises in the corridor. It's a girl's voice, distressed, then Birute's soothing broken English. The door to the next room, the one that's been empty for months, is unlocked and then we hear the sound of weeping, hopeless and heartfelt.

Someone new has arrived.

CHAPTER 7

4 January

I know from the activity in the bathroom that it's a weighing day. The staff do it randomly, so we can't put batteries in our knickers or sneak coins into our hair (anything small and heavy and concealable: we'll cheat in any way we can), but it's impossible to weigh five anorexics without at least three having prior knowledge. Stacey is bent over the sink, glugging water from the tap.

'Not worth it,' I tell her, but she doesn't stop.

A young girl, not yet a teenager, leans against the cold tiles, watching. She must have been Clive's emergency admission interview yesterday, the source of the weeping I heard coming from the next room. Her eyes are puffy, her nose is red, and I imagine the staff had to force her to finally leave her room. She has bushy brown hair that is covered on the top by a flat tartan hat with a red bobble, the sort a Scot might wear.

'I'm Sam, your neighbour,' I say. 'Who're you?'

'Pearl.' Her girlish voice is lost against the harsh ceramic walls. She reminds me of a woodland elf, so slight she could fly away.

'What isn't worth it?' she asks, nervously whispering, dark eyes bloodshot in her sunken face. Her question tells me that she hasn't been an in-patient before.

'Stacey's waterloading. To weigh more on the scales.'

Stacey comes up from the tap like a drowning man, gasping for air, water dripping from her chin on to her Wonder Woman nightdress.

'S'right,' she tells Pearl. 'Don't let the bastards beat you.'

The elf-girl moves forward to the tap, and bends to take some water, holding her hat with one hand so it doesn't slip, and in that moment I see a kid, just a little kid in a funny hat, who needs help. I put my hand over her arm, which is so thin I can touch my thumb to my finger. Her BMI can't be above twelve.

'Don't, Pearl. Please.'

She pulls back from me, nervously running her fingers over her hat and reaching for a strand of hair. She wraps her finger around it and tugs so the curly strands fall away from her scalp, on to the tiled floor.

'But she's doing it.'

'Okay, Pearl. Let me give you some advice. If you start waterloading, you'll have to do it every week or you'll show a big loss. And if you show a loss, they'll tube you.'

Pearl's mouth drops open and I can see where the enamel has been eroded from her teeth, all that stomach acid playing havoc. I touch my tube to show her, and she stares with avid interest.

'Once you have one of these things, you have no control over your food. You don't want that. You've only just arrived; give yourself a chance to get better.'

Stacey makes a sound like *humph*, wipes her mouth with the back of her hand and neatens her sodden nightdress.

'Yeah, well, I'm gonna go for it,' she says proudly, waddling out of the bathroom to the weighing area. 'I must've drunk four litres. My tummy hurts, it's so big. But at least I'll weigh more.'

I look at Pearl and wink. 'That's if her bladder doesn't explode first.' It feels good when she offers a tiny smile in return.

After she's served the other girls their lunch, Manda pops her head into my room. She's holding a finger of shortbread, which is the food I hate and love most. She knows I can't resist the sugary, buttery taste.

'Here, Sam.' She hands me the stick of fat, and crumbs fall on my fingers. 'You know it'll do you good. And I'll write it on your log for the other staff to see.'

She watches me nibble the edge of the biscuit, and smiles. Then she shivers, rubs her arms.

'It feels cold enough to snow in here.'

I don't tell her that I've turned the radiator off. Being cold makes the body work harder, burns more calories. Sian would have realised what I've done, but Manda likes to think the best of me.

'And so bare. Why don't you put some posters up or something?'

She picks up my duvet, feeling the thread between her soft padded fingers. 'There must be someone who could bring some nice things in for you? What about the person who sends you letters? Or the boy who wants to visit?'

I mumble vaguely, suggesting I will think about it, and put down the biscuit. But I'll never make this room comfortable, and I won't have anyone visit me; I won't even reply to Jena's letters. I don't deserve any comforts. This isn't my home; it's a cell.

In the end, Manda leaves, only one tiny corner of shortbread gone. I hear her sigh as she closes my door.

My room is a blank, a nothing, the outside representation of my brain.

I have a plain blue duvet, and a simple desk with nothing on it but a comb; an unbreakable mirror is nailed to the wall over it. Hanging in the open wardrobe are five pairs of identical black leggings, six oversized plain T-shirts and one jumper. And at the back, hidden away from the staff's prying eyes, a black jumper with a pink swallow on the front: my sixteenth birthday present from Jena. I can't bring myself to throw it away, but could never wear it. Some days, because of its link to her, I can't even look at it.

One of my ongoing therapy targets is to go shopping for something pretty and feminine. It's a theory I've heard often: that I'm not comfortable transitioning from teenager to grown woman, so I'm trying to reverse my sexual development. So I need to go and buy a strappy dress to prove otherwise, when I'm well enough to go shopping.

Jena's room at Minsmere Unit was the exact opposite of this. After arriving there on 13 May she turned the room into a toy zoo, filling it with stuffed rabbits and bears, gifts sent in from neighbours and friends. Her favourite was Sid the Sloth, which she'd bought me years before, after we'd watched *Ice Age* together. I took it to her, back when she was still in a coma, and since regaining consciousness she'd slept with Sid every night, hugging him when she was upset. Jena was possessive over how her room was arranged, in a way she never was over her bedroom at home, and she ordered any photos we took her into a neat line on the windowsill. She'd push all the recent photos to the back and move photos from years ago into the best spots, the nicest frames. Her favourite was in the middle, a picture of me as a baby, and she'd stare at these photos, in a sort of trance.

Dr Gregg said it was normal for there to be some degree of personality change – obsessive behaviour was frequently observed after brain trauma – but that we shouldn't worry.

I've been stalling; I know that, of course. For eighteen months, I've refused to talk about Jena, or even think about her; I've never allowed

Dad's face to appear in my mind's eye, as if I can shut away all that happened.

Since I was told she'd died, though, I can't shut away Mum. She's with me, in my deep-set eyes, my sallow skin. The echoes of her are in the pathetic beat of my heart, the faint pain as my internal organs struggle to keep me alive when my soul is dead.

When Clive comes for me, I'm ready for him.

I'm ready to talk for fifteen minutes, and it's time to talk about Jena.

Reaching Jena's room, I placed my hands on the door frame, snatching deep breaths as I peered through the glass panel. Jena was hunched on the bed, leaning against Mum, who was holding her tight. I could feel my fear ebb a little, but my shoulders had risen up to my ears and there was a band round my ribs, an early warning sign that I needed to calm down or I was heading for an asthma attack. I rummaged in my rucksack for my Ventolin and took a couple of puffs before I entered her room.

'Hi, Jena.'

She was holding a framed photo in her hands, one that I'd brought in to the hospital just after the attack, when Dr Gregg told us that photos could help her memory return. Snuggled in her lap was my Sid the Sloth, his pointy nose flattened from being rubbed against her cheek.

I knelt at Jena's feet, my hands over her bare knees, a scab beneath my right palm. I ran my fingers over the ridge, thinking how easily it would lift, how quickly the blood would flow.

'How are you feeling today, Jen-Jen?'

She reached for me, hugged me so tightly I couldn't breathe, my mouth on her tangled hair. After a few seconds, Mum tried to ease her away, but Jena wasn't letting go. She smelt of cheap body spray and piss; she'd probably wet herself when she had the fit.

Mum cleared her throat painfully, a flush rising on her neck.

'I found her on the floor, in full seizure, banging her head on the wardrobe. No staff around, so God knows how long it'd been going on.'

Jena squeezed my cheek. 'Sammy! Don't look so serious. I'm going to tell you a joke to make you laugh.' She grinned at me, and for a moment she was unchanged, my big sister. Dr Gregg said this would happen, these moments when the brain was coherent and the patient seemed their old self; this seemed the cruellest part of brain damage. Jena had always liked to make me laugh – when I fell and cut my knees it was how she'd stop my tears – and it killed me that she was still trying to make me smile, when she was the one with the problem.

'What's the one about bee's milk? I can't remember,' she said, frowning.

Mum sighed.

'What bees make milk?' Jena said with increasing urgency, sitting very straight as she spoke, her hands clasped in her lap. I saw that the strain was showing, and the pleasant sensation that she was the same old Jena slipped away. I was losing her again.

Then she clapped her hands in frustration and her face relaxed with relief. 'I remember! It's boobies.'

Mum stood up, wincing as she put weight on her right foot, then controlled her face so she showed no pain.

'I need to go and talk to Dr Gregg.'

'But, Mum,' I said, panicked. 'She's fine now. Don't tell him about the fit.'

She kissed my forehead, then did the same to Jena. She had that determined look on her face, the one that said she would fix everything.

'I'm just looking after my family. That's my job.'

After Mum left, Jena got twitchy. She jumped from the bed and hopped from foot to foot like a child, then she fell back on the bed, her skirt riding up. Her shins were red from sunburn she'd got last weekend. Mum had got so mad with the staff for failing to put sun cream on her; even though Jena's hair was dark, her skin was lily-white and she burned easily. She was studying me like I'd done something different with my face, perhaps my lips, but she couldn't figure out what.

'Where's Dad?' she asked.

'At home,' I said. 'He'll visit you tonight.' Since she'd moved to the hospital, my parents and I had taken turns to visit Jena, so she never spent too long on her own.

She picked up Sid the Sloth and rubbed his nose to her sad face.

'How's your head, Jena? Mum said you banged it on the wardrobe.'

'That's a lie.'

'You had a fit, Jena. You're still confused.' Dr Gregg told us that whenever Jena said something that was incorrect we shouldn't get frustrated, we should just calmly explain her error. He told us her brain was like a computer, trying to reboot, and some of the stored data may come back corrupted.

'I'm not confused.'

Her eyes became hooded, her brows heavy, and she shook her head, watching as I unzipped my rucksack and removed the Black Magic box of photos.

'Do you remember this, Jena? It's your special box. I found it in the attic, with your stuff.'

Her eyes skidded from the box back to my face. 'You're wearing lipstick!'

I ran my lips together. 'Only chapstick.' My desert-island make-up was black kohl liner and cherry chapstick. I never bothered with much else.

'Don't wear it. You're too young to look sexy.'

I opened the box and started placing the photos in a line on the carpet, but she grabbed my chin, pinching my skin between her fingers.

'Sam, I'm serious. Please listen.'

'I'm sixteen now.' I felt irritated that she was still trying to baby me, given how everything had changed, and wanted her to focus on the task I'd planned. 'Can't you get that, at least, into your head?' I felt rotten as soon as the words left my mouth. Jena was treating me the same way she always had; it was me who had changed.

I finished laying out the photos from the Black Magic box – ones Jena had either collected or taken, images from her life before the attack. She knelt beside me, and reached for a picture of me as a baby.

'Ah look! I remember you when you were this big.' She held her hands about a foot apart, then rocked Sid the Sloth as if a baby were lying there.

'You were so sweet.' Jena smiled happily, turning inwards to look at the crook of her elbow, where she noticed a bobble of wool on her sleeve. She started to pull it, watching the thread unravel.

'Jena, do you know a man called Douglas Campbell?'

She looked up, shocked, and her fingers began to peel the skin on her leg.

'Why?'

I took her hand away from her leg. 'He was on Orwell Estate the evening you were attacked. He says you'd planned to meet him, via Facebook, but you never showed.'

She frowned and looked away. 'I can't say. I don't remember.'

'Okay, what about this?' I showed a ripped-out photo from an estate agent's brochure, a 'To Let' advert for the flat above Our Plaice, the chippy on Orwell Estate. Jena took it from me, the flaky skin on her shin forgotten, and held it close to her eyes, staring at the lace curtain hanging in the front window.

'That's your flat. You signed a twelve-month lease, and you'd just finished painting the walls; it was ready for you to move in on 26 April. Do you remember?'

Her usual nervous energy had gone and she looked almost normal.

'But I hate lace.' She began to swing her legs, her face closing back up. 'Lace curtains make me think of dirty movies.'

'You were going to change them. You just hadn't found any curtains you really liked.'

'I had something else in that window. A dog. White with a black patch over one eye. So lovely.'

My heart lurched with hope.

'Yes, it was a gift. Can you remember who gave it to you?'

I held my breath and waited for her to remember Andy, Dad's best friend. Jena and he were in a relationship, a secret one on account of the age gap and him being her boss. But they had planned to marry.

'I bought it myself, Sam.' She scratched the side of her head above her ear until there was blood under her fingernail.

'No, you didn't. Come on, Jena. Think!'

She squeezed all the muscles in her face to show me she was trying, though it was just a game to her.

Jena had wanted everything to be perfect in her flat.

At twenty-nine she was old to be leaving home. But she had only been thirteen when I came along, and I suppose she got into the habit of helping Mum with me, and we were very close, so that stopped her leaving.

She left school at eighteen, and had applied to art college in Birmingham, but I stopped her going. I was only five, and any talk of my big sister abandoning me sent me into a tantrum. In the end, she promised to stay. Dad got her a job with the entertainment team at Pleasurepark, working for Andy. He was a charmer, and I always thought he was a bit smarmy, with his year-round tan and his gold watch that sat before his wrist bone so everyone noticed it, but she was always whispering to me about him and all the promises he made her – fancy holidays and fast cars that never materialised.

This flat was going to be her first taste of independence. At night, when she was telling me stories like she'd always done, she'd describe to me the big wedding she'd have, with a pink colour scheme. But when she kissed me goodnight, she'd remind me it was a secret. Mum or Dad couldn't know; their relationship was a secret, on account of him being almost thirty years older than her.

Our mum was just seventeen when she married Dad, and her parents were so angry they stopped talking to her. They had never been part of our lives, all because they didn't approve of Dad being fifteen years older. Jena was afraid of causing the same family rift, and with good reason. Both our parents were fiercely protective of us, and Jena wasn't encouraged to have boyfriends.

Andy was Dad's mate; they'd worked together at Pleasurepark for decades, and Jena told me she met him secretly at his flat. The wedding was already planned; she'd even had the dress made by someone she worked with. And he'd given her money for the flat.

Her bright future was about to start. She'd have liked a dog, but the landlord said no pets, as there was no garden, just a backyard that was shared with the chippy and petrol station, and was full of Biffa bins.

The weekend before the attack, Jena took me swimming, and afterwards she showed me the flat. It was almost ready, and with her artistic talent she'd made it lovely, painting the walls a delicate pink and accessorising with cushions she'd embroidered herself. She planned to move in on the day after my sixteenth birthday. There was a room for me too; she wanted me to think of it as a second home.

'You've got to close your eyes.'

I put my hands to my face so all I could see was pink light around my fingers.

Jena put her hands on my shoulders and guided me forward. I stepped cautiously, but she said, 'Trust me, Sammy.'

Then I heard a noise, like a whimpering puppy, and my eyes flicked open. The whimpering had come from Jena, who had dissolved into happy giggles.

In the centre of the empty room was a wicker basket, cosy with a red fleece blanket, and in the middle of the blanket with one paw slightly up, as if it wanted to shake hands, was the sweetest Staffie puppy.

I shrieked, because I thought it was real, but when I reached the basket and picked it up, I saw it was just a really good imitation.

Jena opened her arms to me, and I stepped into the hug, feeling her warmth, the pottery nose of the dog nestled into my neck.

'It was a moving-in gift,' she said. 'From Andy.'

I didn't wonder why he wasn't there, why I'd never seen them together, as I knew the relationship was secret. But now I did wonder: why hadn't he visited her? When she was in the coma, and on Eastern Ward, only immediate family could visit, but he could have come to our house to ask after her.

I'd seen him once, at the corner shop near my school, just after Jena came out of her coma. I was leaving, when I saw him by the magazines, flicking through one on photography, and I said hello. He didn't recognise me at first, and I said I was Jena's sister. 'How's she doing?' he asked. And it was such a normal, small question that I couldn't even bring myself to answer. How could I sum up the pain of thinking she would die, the elation of her regaining consciousness, the hell of her living on a dementia ward? So I said, 'Fine.'

And he just smiled and said, 'Glad to hear that.'

If this was love, it didn't amount to much.

Now she said: 'I'd like my dog back, Sam. I want to go home.' She lifted the photo of the flat to her heart. 'What bees make milk? I can't remember. I'm scared, Sam.'

'It's okay.' I tried to calm her. 'No one's going to hurt you, Jena.'

I took the photo from her, and put it back in the Black Magic box, which I returned to my rucksack. As I did, my camera fell out and Jena stared at it.

'Why have you got my camera?' she demanded. She'd forgotten that Dad gave it to me on that terrible day, that it caused the argument.

'It's mine now, Jena,' I gently reminded her. 'It was my birthday present. But I promise I'll look after it.'

'No! Give it here!' she said, angrily. Even now, her jealousy was close to the surface. I tried to zip my rucksack up, to hide the camera from her sight, but she grabbed for my bag and tugged hard; I had to yank it away, and she fell back, her head knocking against the wall.

Her eyes slid out of focus, watering, and she twitched. *Oh please, don't let her fit.*

'Tell me! Is it boobies? No! It was Andy wasn't it? No! Oh Mum . . .' She was confused; nothing she said made proper sense. A blue vein throbbed in her temple and her face went ashen.

'Okay, Jena. It's okay.' I made my voice low and soothing, but inside was a renewed sense of rage. 'The police have arrested someone. They just need more evidence to make it stick. If only I could find the raincoat, or you could remember, Douglas Campbell will go to prison for a very long time.'

'I'm scared, Sam.'

She was shivering, and I held her, as she used to hold me when I had a bad dream. 'He can't hurt you now. I promise.'

Her eyes fixed on mine, fully understanding for thirty seconds before she twitched again and her eyes rolled back in their sockets. The twitch became a convulsion, and she fell forward, into my arms. But she was bulky; I couldn't hold her, and she slid to my side, pulling me along with her. We fell off the bed, like two sailors tied together and thrown overboard. Jena was half on her stomach, one arm under her as the other jerked in time with her thrashing legs, saliva dribbling from her lips, a gurgle in her throat.

Trying to hold her with one hand, I reached for the chair and yanked it out of her way, pushing the bedside cabinet nearer the window with my feet. I tugged the pillows on to the floor and kicked them against the skirting board, buoys to buffer Jena's head.

Her whole body was seizing and thrashing. I was scared, wretched with regret. The snot ran from her nose, and I could smell the sickly, malty scent of piss.

'It's okay. I'm here, Jen-Jen.'

I tried to touch her, but my hand was thrust away. I held her head, hugging it in my lap. Blood started to seep from her tight mouth; she'd bitten her tongue. *Oh God, please don't let her choke.* I turned her head down, and a froth of scarlet blood spread on the carpet, spiking me with fear as I rooted around blindly for the emergency cord that hung from the ceiling, an orange string that would bring help, then stilled my hand. Afraid though I was, I didn't want the staff to know about this fit. I didn't want Jena sent back to Eastern Ward, with the crazy dementia patients.

Holding Jena as the convulsion ebbed, trying to control my panic, I gently eased her head back on to my lap and stroked her face, which was webbed in saliva and tears, my finger pulling down her lip to check her tongue was intact. Her eyes were closed and she was pale and sleepy. I tried to rouse her, stroking her cheek.

'Jena? Can you open your eyes?'

She tried, but all I could see were the whites before her eyelids closed again. I sat up, awkwardly pulling her with me to try and put her into bed, but she was too heavy. I looked again at the emergency cord, but steeled myself. I didn't need help; I could do it alone. I pulled the duvet on to the floor and gently covered her.

'It's okay, Jen-Jen.'

Her mouth twitched in what could have been a smile.

'Everything is going to be okay. I'm going to get the evidence Penny needs. I promise.'

Clive waits for more, but I have nothing left to give. He pats my shoulder, the only physical comfort I can allow, but he knows better than to ask me if I kept my promise.

'Well done, Sam,' he murmurs. 'I think the board will be pleased.'

A reminder that my time here is running out. That on 1 February a panel of three, including Clive, will decide my fate. Clive hands me the plastic container, the six grapes that I have won, and leaves me to eat them alone. This, I know, is his way of telling me he trusts me and believes I'm making progress.

But Clive is wrong. When he's gone, I hide the grapes in my shoe. And then I weep for what I've given up, my silence, and the pain that is being released with every word I speak.

I'm not the only one who's angry that I'm suddenly talking.

Later, when the girls are gathered in my room, it seems light-hearted enough. Joelle takes Stacey's pink Jackie O sunglasses and puts them on, walking around like a supermodel. Fiona starts to sing, a song playing on the radio in the staff room: *This girl is on fire*. They grab each other, singing louder, and start bouncing on the bed. Stacey grabs my pillow and starts whacking them on the legs, belting out the chorus along with Alicia Keyes; even Mina joins in, not singing, but clapping her hands lightly to the song. *She's just a girl, and she's on fire.*

Giggling, clasping each other, they land in a heap. I'm laughing too; this is a good moment.

Next to me, Stacey's patent handbag bulges open with a magazine and a can of Diet Coke. Under it, I spy a Snickers bar and wonder if she has laxatives in there too.

Mina remains in the corner, slightly more relaxed than usual, until Fiona and Joelle turn their attention to her, and begin to ask her questions about her father. They want to hear her story again. It's like a horror film for them; they forget it's real.

'Leave her alone,' I tell them, and they look defensive but they stop. Mina gives me the smallest smile.

Stacey plops down next to me on the bed, opens her can of Diet Coke and offers me a swig. I shake my head. I watch her knock back the can, then re-apply her candy-pink lip gloss.

'What was that meeting you had yesterday, in the corridor, with Clive?'

'Nothing.'

'He's such a dork. Why has he taken an interest in you suddenly? What's going on?'

'I just said: nothing.'

'But you've got your board hearing coming up. Getting scared, are ya?' Stacey smirks and it makes her ugly. 'Joelle said you'd have to talk one day, but not to us.'

Joelle looks like she wants the ground to swallow her up. Her face is crimson. 'I only meant you'd rather talk to a professional than us.'

'But that's *not* what you said, Joelle,' crows Stacey loudly. 'You said Sam will only talk to someone who's very highly qualified because she thinks she's special. Because she thinks that her story is more tragic than ours, or at least more important because she's famous.'

'Infamous,' I correct. Quietly. The press coverage had been fierce, especially in the beginning.

'And a special group of people are meeting to talk about her, on 1 February. Isn't that right, Sam?'

I should never have confided in Stacey about the board meeting. I know she's just lashing out because she's upset I won't open up to her, but it's a low punch.

I gaze up at the ceiling, and try not to think.

CHAPTER 8

5 January

Manda wakes me with a gentle shake and a warm smile.

It's been decided: no tube feed this morning, I am to eat breakfast with the other girls, since I've been doing so well. She doesn't go into details about this, and I don't ask. Did she lie about how much of the shortbread I ate? Or has Clive waxed lyrical about how well our therapy is going? Does he want me to take this step to prove to the board I'm getting better? Manda is delighted enough for both of us, but I don't feel ready for this. 'Only,' she adds sagely, as she leaves, 'we won't be removing the tube just yet. So look upon this as a trial period.'

Which means that whatever progress I'm making, they still don't fully trust me.

I shuffle down the line for breakfast, my feet heavy as lead and my bones like rusted steel, despite the fact that I weigh less now than I did when I was ten. Sian's at the serving hatch this morning, so no hope of getting a little less to eat. Bet when her parents gave her that classy name they weren't thinking she'd be working here. She carefully spoons a measure of porridge (made with full cream) into my 5 oz. plastic bowl, like she's auditioning for a role in *Oliver!*

'Thanks, Sian. That looks yummy,' I lie.

She gives me a tight pinch of a smile as I trudge my red tray down its silver road to the cutlery station. 'Just one napkin, Sam. You should know the rules by now. And if you don't eat all the porridge, we'll use the tube.'

I return the second napkin, which would have come in handy for covering the cereal I won't eat, and I'm turning away when she says, 'It must be going well with Clive for him to say you're ready to self-nourish.'

I can hear in her voice that she thinks he's wrong, that it's too soon after the tube was inserted for this. I bet it was her that suggested the tube should remain in place.

I stop, and wipe the rim of my bowl with my solitary napkin.

'I'm doing very well with controversial and intensive, thank you for asking. We use photos.'

I wait to see if she makes a quip about it being a waste of taxpayers' money, but instead she says, 'I used to study photography. Did an A level in it.'

Her eyes look dreamy, clouded into another place. She blinks and looks down at her shabby housecoat, the aluminium ladle like a crude extension of her own hand. She plunges it back into the porridge as Stacey holds out her bowl. 'Fat lot of use that was.'

Sadness seeps into my heart, a physical ache for what we have all lost.

I turn my back, carry my tray to the brown table and sit nearest to the window, alongside Mina and Pearl.

Manda sits overseeing the brown table. We eat in a line, chewing as slowly as cows in a field, while kindly Manda murmurs encouragement from the wings. Over on the blue table, the girls aren't officially supervised, but they watch each other with professional scrutiny; Stacey and Joelle are competing over smaller and smaller spoonfuls of porridge as we slow-race until twenty-five minutes, the time allowed for breakfast, are up. Fiona seems to have forgotten she's anorexic; she's eating without even watching the food, chatting about the pony she has at home, whose name is Topic. Typical anorexic: even her horse is named after a chocolate bar.

I can't digest the porridge; the grains weren't properly soaked, and I can feel the grit on my teeth, clogging the back of my throat. But I have to leave an empty bowl. If I do, I'll get a star on my chart, and I only need two more to be allowed to watch a film. That's my reward; we all have different rewards on our personal charts. Fiona gets to go ride on Topic, Stacey gets a manicure and Joelle gets to use the internet, though she has to be watched or she'll visit the pro-Ana sites, full of 'thinspiration' pictures of wasted girls, and blogs on how to starve. Those sites are porn for anorexics, and lethal. She used to run one; I've seen the archives.

Mina likes trips to bowling or playgrounds, kiddie treats that were ruined for her when she actually was a kid.

Top of my list, though, is vintage horror, even if it does mean swallowing gruel. If there was a chance to purge I would, but there's no loo, not even a sink, in my room, and a trip to the shared bathroom, with Sian on duty, would be impossible.

When the time is up Stacey sidles towards me, her face flushed with guilt. 'What you doing after breakfast?' she asks. So this is how we'll play it: no acknowledgement of what a bitch she was yesterday, but she'll try to make it up to me. I decide to let her.

'Catching a flight to Paris,' I say. 'Thought I'd start with the Louvre, but I'm skipping the Eiffel Tower. Too touristy.'

She grins, glad I'm playing along and that I'm not going to punish her. She raises one over-plucked eyebrow, a look she must have practised in the mirror. 'What about going back to my room and I'll give you a makeover? I've nicked some scissors from the kitchen, so I could trim your hair for you, give you a total new look. Vampire goth is *so* last decade.'

'You're not touching my hair, Stacey.' She's managed to hide scissors in her room, somewhere clever enough to survive the search. But then we're all experts in deception.

She sighs at me, shaking her head. 'You could be a model if you just made an effort. Why d'you always cover yourself up? It's like you don't want anyone to notice how beautiful you are.'

I don't tell Stacey, but I have a previous engagement. I lie on my bed and wait for Clive, thinking about my fifteen-minute confessional. I have no doubts that he'll turn up, which must mean that I trust him. A novelty for me.

When he arrives I'm ready.

It was Thursday 9 June, three days since our visit to the police station, and I woke abruptly, chest tight with panic, replaying Jena's fit. I'd not told Mum, who was down in our backyard, pacing the concrete in her fluorescent lollipop-lady uniform. After Jena came out of her coma, Mum returned to work. We needed the money, especially with Dad on unpaid compassionate leave. Someone had to put food on the table.

She was having a final smoke before leaving for the morning school run, trampling the grass that had started to stick through the cracks because no one could be bothered to try to make it nice. Jena was the gardener of the family, her artistic flair revealed in nurturing shrubs and flowers, so now everything was running wild.

I opened the window to let some air into my stuffy room, and Mum looked up at the movement. She called, 'Breakfast is on the table, love.'

She didn't need to ready my breakfast. I had all the time in the world to eat. School was closed for classes; I just had to go in for my GCSE exams.

Chloe, our pensioner neighbour, harmless but a bit of a gas-bag, was putting washing out on the line, a peg in her mouth as she worked.

'All right, Kath. Gorgeous day, isn't it?'

'A bit hot for me, Clo.'

Mum tried to make a swift exit into the house, but Chloe stalled her with questions, because she knew we'd been to the police station on Monday. Since the attack, there was only one thing our neighbours asked: *Any news?*

No news on Jena, who hadn't improved much since arriving at Minsmere; no news on the case: nobody had been officially charged yet, and the main suspect might be released soon due to lack of evidence. Chloe mourned the lack of bobbies on the beat, how things had been better when she was a girl, how much less crime there had been. Then they stopped talking because Mrs Read, who lived next to Chloe, was hovering under the apple tree in her garden, listening.

Mum and Mrs Read hated each other; they always had, even though they'd been neighbours-but-one for thirty years. Mrs Read was crazy, and Mum said she was dangerous too, always peeking over the fence to see what was going on, or spying through her dirty windows. I'd been warned to stay away from her. Mrs Read gave me the creeps, and local kids would dare each other to knock on her door and run away before she could catch them. She was our local bogeywoman. But, credit where it's due, she had come round with a gift after she'd heard about the attack: some wildflowers from her overgrown garden for Jena and a book of some kind; not that she had a chance to explain what it was.

Mum slammed the door in her face.

In my bedroom, I booted up the computer, a cranky thing I'd bought in Cash Converters. It weighed a ton, but Dad didn't like the idea of me getting a laptop, even though he had one in his shed; he said if I had one I'd drop it when I was on my bike and break it. I knew that wasn't the real reason. He didn't like the idea of me searching the internet without him knowing, worried I'd stumble across some inappropriate site, or get talking to some pervert. If I was using a computer under his roof he felt it was safe, which was stupid. I might be in my bedroom, but I could be up to anything.

I was a good student. I'd done really well in my GCSE coursework and things had looked rosy before the attack, when I'd missed two exams because I was in the hospital, waiting for Jena to come out of her coma. The school had indicated that if my final grades were too low for me to be accepted on the A-level courses, they would appeal, but they said I should try and revise extra hard for the remaining exams to make up lost ground.

I'd always been quick at finding facts and researching data, good at losing myself in books and essays. My new plan was to find out more about the police's prime suspect.

I started in the most obvious place: Facebook. I went to Jena's page and looked through her 'friends', but there was no Douglas Campbell there. He said she'd sent him a message, but I could only access them with her password. I tried logging in as Jena, trying 'Andy' as a password, then 'Pleasurepark', but both were incorrect. My only hope was to request a change of password, and have it sent to her mobile. Where was her phone? I hadn't seen it since the attack.

My second idea was to use my friend Google.

Douglas Campbell.

Not much to go on; just a name. I googled it and 5,150,000 results came up. I did it again, but added 'Ipswich'. 103,000 – still too many. *Okay, think*. He'd been remanded to prison, so he must have been sent there by a judge. What about adding 'court' to the list? There were still lots of pages, but I skimmed down. I clicked some open – one Douglas Campbell was an interior decorator; he'd painted Blue Hall Court. Free quotes. Close the window, scroll down again. Another Douglas Campbell was standing for the Liberal Democrats, discussing a new court bill. Nope, keep going.

Then I found something – an archived newspaper article from sixteen years before:

> ORWELL RAPE LATEST: LOCAL MAN RECEIVES PRISON SENTENCE
>
> A Suffolk man has been jailed, after being found guilty of rape at Ipswich Crown Court today. Douglas Campbell was sentenced to eight years' custody, and the judge condemned him for putting the victim through an emotional trial. Judge Turner said, 'You believed this would not come to court,

> because you had groomed your vulnerable victim over a period of months, and you were certain she would not speak against you. Today you have been proved wrong.'
>
> Campbell runs a fish and chip shop on Orwell Estate alongside his girlfriend, with whom he also has a child. He befriended the victim, just thirteen at the time, when she became a regular customer, and took her to his house on The Terrace, where the offence took place. The rape was reported after the victim confided in a teacher at her school, who had become concerned for her welfare.
>
> Suffolk Police praised the victim's courage in coming forward, and spoke of its plan to reduce sexual crime in the town by focusing on work within schools to educate pupils about paedophile activity and the dangers of being groomed.

So Douglas Campbell was a rapist. The scene clarified: down the alleyway in the storm he had been trying to rape her, she had fought back, and in the struggle . . . *Her head hitting the concrete. Oh God, her split skull.*

I blinked the image away, looking back at the article as if it might hold answers. The photo showed him arriving at court with a coat over his head, but his girlfriend's face was visible. I recognised her, a face from the estate. Searching my memory for the name: Sonia, that was it.

Sonia was a local woman, and I'd seen her, hanging around at Pleasurepark, back when I was much younger and we went there often, and Jena and she would always exchange filthy looks. And she was at Pleasurepark because her brother worked there. Her brother, Andy, was Jena's boss and secret fiancé. But Sonia and Jena had never got on.

Another time, I must have been eleven or twelve maybe, and it was Halloween. I was too nervous to answer the door to the trick-or-treaters so Jena was doing it for me, passing out sweets, and this teenager arrived, a boy I recognised from school. His hair was as orange as the pumpkin Jena had carved, his face as white as the candle she put inside. Jena had filled a bucket with water and we took turns trying to pick out an apple with our teeth. The boy had been shy at first, standing apart from the other kids who'd gathered at our door, until Jena encouraged him to try. I have an image of his head bent over the bucket, his face rising from it wet and jubilant with an apple in his mouth.

Then I remember Sonia arriving, marching down our front path and shouting at Jena, grabbing the boy by the wrist and dragging him away.

Sonia, taking her son home because she didn't want him playing at our house. I remember it upset Jena, so much that she stopped the apple bobbing. Our little Halloween party was over.

The article said that Douglas and his girlfriend ran the chip shop together, and also that they had a child. This child must be the boy from the impromptu Halloween party, with red hair.

We'd attended the same school, though he was a few years older than me. I'd see him sometimes in the playground, or pass him in the corridors, but we never spoke. I bet I could find him on Facebook dead easy, if I could just remember his first name. But at least, thanks to the newspaper article, I knew where they had lived, sixteen years ago. I could only hope they still did live there; if so, it would take me one step closer to getting something on Douglas Campbell, something concrete. I pressed 'Print' and the machine began to spit out the article, line by noisy line.

'Why aren't you dressed, Sam?'

Mum. Stood in the doorway of my bedroom, glowing in her yellow coat with white flashings, her fluorescent baseball hat already on her head. Downstairs, her lollipop would be waiting, propped by the front door, round end to the floor like she always positioned it when it was at rest. You'd be surprised how much one of those things weighs.

She'd got a cig in one hand, even though she wasn't supposed to smoke around me on account of my asthma; she wafted the air with the other, as if that made it okay. The printer stopped churning, and I made a grab for the printed pages, moving back to the bed, the papers behind my back. Mum was distracted, tutting at the books on the floor and the unmade bed, and started folding the clothes I'd strewn on the carpet.

'Oh Sam! How can I vacuum in here with all this stuff in the way?'

I didn't answer her, and when she looked up she noticed the computer screen, went closer and read a few lines.

'Is this revision for your exams?' Her eyes squinted at the words on the screen, fixing on the photo of Sonia. Then her chest heaved a single time.

'What's going on, Samantha?'

I was trapped on the bed. Mum loomed over me, her face losing all its blood.

'It's about *him*, Mum.'

She bent down, her smoky breath in my mouth. 'Who?'

'Who do you think? The man the police believe attacked Jena.'

She swooped back to the screen and read the article again, the fag getting squashed in her fingers, eyes narrowing like she'd just lost a pile at bingo. When she spoke, her voice was reedy-thin and careful.

'He's been to prison in the past,' I said. 'For eight years.'

'Who's in prison?'

'He's not anymore. He must have been out for a while. But in his statement, he said he was meeting Jena, on 25 April. That's why he was hanging about outside her flat.'

She looked like I'd slapped her, mouth gaping. 'You looked in Jena's case file?'

I felt my skin burn with shame, but jutted my chin defiantly. 'While you were out of the room.'

Distressed, Mum gripped on to the edge of the desk. I was worried I'd bring on one of her panic attacks, but couldn't stop the words tumbling out of my mouth like loose change dropped on the ground.

'His name is Douglas Campbell. Do you know him?' I gabbled.

She turned slightly towards the window, and seemed to be looking at something outside. 'Why would I?'

'Because he's local and he raped a thirteen-year-old girl. It was in the papers; you must know about it?'

She turned to face me, with her back to the window, the peak of her cap casting a shadow over her eyes. Mum panted. She went to the window, swung it wide and tossed the fag out.

'Douglas Campbell told the police that the night Jena was attacked he found a coat, down the passageway, trampled on the ground. And it was covered in blood. Whoever owned that coat attacked Jena.'

'So why isn't it over?' she said, her voice wavering. 'If they've found the coat, they know . . .'

'They haven't found it! When Douglas went back, once he realised the significance, it was gone. Or so he says. I think he must have taken it, realising he'd left it behind. Covering his tracks.'

'God, it's so hot. I can't bear it.' She fanned herself with her hand, but the air in the room was still and heavy. She was leaning out of the open window and gasping. Her panic attacks came quickly, especially these last six weeks. They made it hard for her to breathe, and then she'd vomit. I huddled into my duvet: red poppies in a green field, all faded.

'Stop this, Sam. Let the police do their job.'

'But Penny said they only had circumstantial evidence; Douglas Campbell could be released. We have to do something!'

Mum might have believed that there was nothing we could do, but I couldn't accept that, not anymore. I pulled the printed article from behind me, and held it up so she could see. 'See the woman in the photo? That's Douglas's girlfriend, Sonia. Do you recognise her?'

Mum took the page and stared at Sonia's ravaged face. Then she folded it, running her fingers down the crease till it was sharp as a blade.

'She came here once, to collect her son. One Halloween. Remember?'

Mum closed her eyes for a beat. Her mouth was nipped tight. Her shoulders started to heave. She was leaning so far out of the window it scared me. Her anxiety tablets were down-stairs in the kitchen drawer.

'Get dressed . . .' she gasped, then carried on, 'I keep telling you this – concentrate on your exams.'

'Mum! If we can help the police, if we could find that coat. Or if you know something . . .'

'I know nothing!' She breathed deeply, steadying herself.

'I think Jena is starting to remember,' I said, quietly. 'I've thought of a way to help her. If I can take photos, and gather evidence—'

In a burst of energy she was away from the window and pushing me back on the bed, thrusting me down so fast my head knocked on the wall behind.

'You have to stop!' She leaned over me, her face so close to mine I could see the blood vessels in her eyes.

'I can't . . . I can't . . .' My head started throbbing. My lungs felt tight as the airways became straws; an asthma attack loomed.

'You're breathing funny, Sam,' she said, her own breathing still laboured.

She grabbed my Ventolin from the desk, and shoved it in my mouth. I tried to get up, but she held the back of my head, pressing the spray so the drug fumes whooshed into my mouth.

'Again.'

I struggled to free myself, but she forced another burst into me, making me gasp.

'It's my job to protect my family. It's my duty.'

The drug made my head spin, and it hurt where I'd hit the wall. Mum held me, her sturdy arms around me, using all that strength she'd built up from carrying her lollipop around the estate. I could feel her shaking, and there was sweat on her upper lip.

'Isn't it enough, that Jena was hurt?' She started to cry. 'I can't lose you as well. Look at me, Sam. I want you to swear that this ends right now.'

I looked into her eyes and lied.

I wait for Clive's response. He seems lost for words, and then says, 'So you decided to be a sort of private investigator? To help the police solve the case. You were a regular Nancy Drew.'

But this innocent interpretation is way off. I wanted to be a vigilante, to take control of the chaos that surrounded me. My poor sister, the nightmare of the weeks since the attack, felt like a problem I could fix. By making it my mission to solve the case, by using my camera, I gave myself the distance I needed to not be destroyed by it all.

I believed I was trying to save Jena, but I was trying to save myself too.

CHAPTER 9

6 January

Today, when Clive comes for me, he suggests that we take a walk to his office, which is in the main part of the hospital, beyond the locked ward of Ana Unit. I think he wants me to step outside, even if only to another part of the institution, or maybe he wants a change of scene from my dismal bedroom.

When we reach his office, I see why he brought me here. It's grand, with a large arched window all to itself, and a balcony. What's nice is that his desk is to one side, and in front of the window are comfy armchairs. On the low table is a box of tissues, ready for the next teary arrival, maybe. Did I cry when I arrived here, eighteen months ago? I can't remember that I did, but then I can't really remember feeling anything that day.

I must sit still, must say the right thing, must keep my wits about me, though the chair is soft, and I feel myself sinking into it.

He asked me to bring the Black Magic box with me. I slide it down the side of the chair, against my thigh, because I'm not sure I can bear for him to hear the rest of my story.

'I was sorry about your room search, Sam.'

'Not as sorry as I was!' I turn my mouth up at one side. 'Six thirty, Sian woke me up. And then I had to sit on that cold floor talking to you. I'm thinking of lodging a complaint with the NHS.'

Clive raises his eyebrows. 'You could. But the staff are only doing their jobs. And what's more to the point, we're trying to help you, Sam. I was very sad to hear that Sian found a sachet of mustard, when you seem to be doing so much better. When did you last purge?'

'Weeks ago.'

'I hope so.' He leans forward, placing his hand on my bony wrist. 'You could make this your time for recovery. The board will be deciding where you go next, and it's better if you are well.'

I know this, but I still hate being reminded that my future depends on two strangers and Clive.

'Will I be at the meeting?' I ask.

He's looking out of the window to the sea beyond, and the frown on his face tells me. 'Yes, you will. And it's my hope that together we'll convince the panel that your stay here has worked. But I can't lie to them, Sam. And they will be told about the mustard, about all the setbacks.'

'I'm going to stay here forever, aren't I?' My lungs tighten, and my breath shortens. An asthmatic most of my life, I know how quickly breathing can be a problem, and I try to slow down my heart. I thought I'd wanted to stay, but since Mum's death that has changed.

Clive's face in profile twitches, and I imagine that he's longing for a comforting puff on his pipe. The view from here is so peaceful: the blue sky, the flat North Sea.

Turning back towards the room, Clive's eyes are wet behind his glasses. When he speaks his voice is sad.

'The board can only send you home if you are better, Sam.'

Home. A sudden need to recover feels so intense it winds me, this unreachable fantasy that I have never believed possible. The only release that ever felt real before was oblivion, but now there is the slim chance of freedom.

'But I hope, I really hope, that our sessions will help. That if I can tell them how well you are doing, we can persuade them to look favourably on your case.'

I notice that he says 'hope' as if he's not totally sure this photo therapy will work. Regardless, he places his watch on the desk and makes a note of the time. My fifteen minutes begins.

Jena's phone. I hadn't seen it since the day of the attack, hadn't seen it around the house or at the hospital. It may have been lost during the attack, but there was one other option I needed to rule out: it could be at the flat. If I could find it, I could get her Facebook account re-set, then I could hack into it. The police had searched her flat and we'd been told not to go there, but no one had mentioned the phone, and this was a loose end I needed to explore.

I would have to break in.

It wasn't difficult. The latch was old, and I'd brought a screwdriver from home. The only problem would be locking it when I left.

Opening the back door made my heart pulse with anxiety. Inside was luminous with new paint; a bedroom and a lounge, a small kitchen and an even smaller bathroom.

After she'd painted, Jena had started moving things in. I opened her bedroom door; a sunray glanced off the glass deer on the dressing table, its improbably long tail glittering with a greenish-purple mood ring, its china base full of hair elastics in gold and silver, silky ribbons and elaborate clips. Pretty things Jena liked to decorate her long dark hair with; she was clever with fancy braids.

Suddenly woozy, I sat heavily on the double bed she'd bought on eBay; the pillows were new, plump and soft as I rested against them. Gingerly, I massaged my temples, wincing as I touched the swelling at the back of my head. The pretty bedding was unslept in; the new clock told the correct time.

Everything was ready; she should have moved in the day after my birthday, on 26 April. Instead she had been on a life-support machine.

I searched everywhere for that phone, all the obvious places like the bedside table and kitchen cupboards, then I started rooting through everywhere else. Hanging in the wardrobe were Jena's clothes, and I patted down the pockets trying to find her mobile. All of her comfortable clothes had been taken to the hospital, and what remained was a leather skirt with zips, a selection of cut-away tops and a red bandage dress. Clothes I couldn't remember her wearing, and I wondered if Andy had bought them for her.

Then I saw it: her wedding dress, carefully hidden from Mum and Dad.

I touched the silk, the perfect bodice and full skirt, made by one of Jena's mates from work who was handy with a needle. A lot of the entertainment staff were good at making things, and Jena was always being fitted for a princess costume or, if it was Christmas, an elf outfit. She'd had this dress for a few months, and I'd only seen it fleetingly. At home, she'd kept it folded in a bag at the back of her wardrobe, and whispered about it when the house was quiet and she wanted to tell me her secrets, but here in her flat there was no need to hide it. I picked it from the rail and held it against me, the white heavy satin swishing as I moved, for a moment enjoying the sensation.

Then I saw the label, a tag that told me the dress was from Age Concern for £15.99. How could that be, when Jena had told me her work colleague had made it?

Confused, I placed it back where I found it and shut the wardrobe door.

There was a noise in the street, and I was worried it was the police, that someone had seen me break into the flat, but it was just teenagers hanging around, waiting for the chip shop to open.

I felt deflated. The phone wasn't here; I'd looked everywhere. I imagined it lying on the ground, down the alleyway, covered in blood until somebody found it and took it. Maybe an opportunist, maybe the attacker. Either way, it was a piece of evidence that was lost to me. I would need something else if I was going to nail Douglas Campbell.

I looked desperately around for inspiration, and saw the trunk that Jena had put in the small lounge to use as a window seat. She'd taken it from home, and I'd always known it as somewhere that boring things were stored. Old Christmas cards and baby blankets, that kind of thing. I lifted the lid, and was stunned by the amount of stuff inside. I touched the neat piles, all belonging to the life Jena was planning: a box of wedding invites, yet to be filled in; an Ikea catalogue she'd scribbled ideas in for her new home. Her address book.

I picked it up, and found Andy's name. I saw his address was a penthouse flat, on the docks. Why he'd move in here with Jena, rather than her moving there, was another mystery. I ripped the page from the book and placed it, folded neatly, into the Black Magic box.

Also in the trunk were things from when I was a kid that Mum must have stored in there. My baby record book, the Mother's Day card I made at primary school and a brooch I painted with nail varnish. A clay flower.

And there, sat in a corner like it was being punished, was the Staffie dog. I lifted it out, and ran my hand over the china to check for chips. It was perfect, but was it too soon to show her something she had only just remembered having? I was pushing her, I knew, into an unknown world of hidden memories, and I didn't know what the outcome might be.

But even that didn't stop me.

I stop talking, heart racing, my breath on a loose tether within asthmatic lungs that I need medication to control.

Clive notices, collects his watch, straps it back on to his wrist. 'Well done, Sam. But now I think we should find Manda and get your Ventolin.' He hands me a tangerine. 'Your reward,' he says.

A tangerine that will take me an hour to eat, and I need medication in a hurry. He knows this; he helps me stand, and we begin to walk back to the unit. But Clive is still thinking of my tale; I can see it in his eyes, which are unfocused, as if seeing the pictures I painted in his mind.

'I don't quite understand, Sam; why was Jena's relationship with Andy still a secret, when she'd gone as far as buying a wedding dress?' he asks.

'I need my Ventolin. Now.'

He clicks into now, and sees I'm right. We need to go to the unit, and in just a few puffs of medicine I'll recover. If only my psychological recovery could be so easy. I concentrate on breathing, on keeping my chest large enough to hold the oxygen it needs. Sucking in air, each breath painful to me. But not as painful as the memories, now so close to the surface.

CHAPTER 10

7 January

Today is a group trip to the dentist. My asthmatic episode is under control now, an attack avoided in the night by a nebulised dose of salbutamol, gently administered by Birute, who held the mask in place, careful to mind my feeding tube, as I breathed in the cure. I still feel wobbly from the after-effects. That, and the fact that I managed to purge my breakfast without being caught. A small victory, which has left me raw with hunger.

I'm not the only one struggling today. Pearl is helped on to the minibus by Manda, and eased into the seat nearest the front. She's panting from the effort of walking down the hill; as she catches her breath, circles of mist form on the window. She straightens the red beret on her head; so she's French today, and I wonder how many hats she has, how many people she likes to be. She gives me a weak wave, and though my head tells me to look away because friendship isn't worth the pain, I wave back.

Stacey gets on the bus and plops down beside me. She's dressed in a tight black dress with a wide yellow plastic belt, matching patent heels and yellow bangles. Perfect for a trip to a retro nightclub, but over the top for a hospital group outing. She is equally unimpressed with my attire.

'Why aren't you dressed up, Sam?'

For Stacey, even this trip is an occasion. But I prefer not to engage with the world anymore. It's pissed me off, and I'd rather be somewhere else.

'I am.' I gesture to my sweater, black with the pink swallow. Never worn till now, but it's warm and the day is cold. I tell myself that's the only reason I finally feel able to wear my birthday gift, when before I couldn't even look at anything so associated with my sister. Whatever Clive is doing to me, whatever feelings Mum's death released, big changes are happening.

'Pretty. But you've got no make-up on. Or jewellery. Good job I've got some in my bag.' She opens it up and starts to rouge my cheeks and, surprising myself, I let her.

We get settled in the minibus. Fiona is animated, leaning on the driver's seat, flirting with him, chatting about how it's so cold her skin is goosey, how weird it is that the Christmas lights are still hanging along the prom. Pony-club brat, she hasn't even been ill long enough to have reason to fear the dentist. Finally, much to the driver's relief, Manda tells her to take a seat beside Mina. Fiona then starts bombarding her with questions that Mina won't answer. Joelle sits by herself, pensive. This outing is important for her; it's not good for a model to have bad teeth.

After making us wait for what she deems long enough, Sian joins us on the bus and any chatter soon dries up. While she briefs the driver, poor bastard, I look back at the Bartlet Hospital, proud on the brow of the hill, and wonder how long it will continue to be my refuge from the world. If she were a person, the Bartlet would be anorexic; she's so rigid, so angular and symmetrical. An obsessive building, everything in its place, standing facing the sea, very alone.

In her middle are four bay windows, and I imagine Clive seated in one of the armchairs, reading the files relating to my case, worrying his way through the report he must write for the board meeting on 1 February, to try and persuade them that I'm getting better. That I am no longer a risk to myself, or anyone else, and can be free. That's the nub of it: the risk I represent. Because if there's a danger, still, of me causing harm, to myself or others, I'll be kept here.

And there, on the far left, is Ana Unit, the square rectangles of glass that I look out of during lectures, endless talks on how our anorexia is a form of female rebellion. The next window along is the dining room, place of my prolonged hunger strike: the weapon I have used to express my anger. Sure, I feel like Boudicca right now.

No, wait. I was wrong; the Bartlet wouldn't be anorexic. Not with those curves and arches, deep-red bricks and pebble-dash. She would be a beautiful, curvaceous woman, fully in charge of her sexuality, loved by men. She wouldn't be like me at all, with my orange palms and green-tinged face, and the tube taped to my cheek. She would be a woman I could never dream of being, a woman Jena was never allowed to become.

Both of us had our future selves stolen from us that day in April. Jena's potential was ruined by someone else, a person who pounced on her in the rain. She was a victim.

But the person to blame for my pitiful condition is starting to look like myself.

Finally, when Sian judges we are all present and correct and the driver is properly briefed, the minibus takes us the few miles to the dentist's surgery in Walton, in a white building with a wide sweeping staircase and high ceilings. What would once have been a beautiful home for gentry has been taken over by the sound of tooth-drilling and the stench of mouthwash.

The waiting room is cold, as if its walls have been whitewashed with menthol, and we take up most of the seats. There is only one other person waiting, an elderly woman clutching a tissue. I see a gap in her teeth, and guess she is holding a lost crown, but we are entertaining enough to distract her from this, and her eyes slide over each of us in turn. She must know what we are, where we are from. Six sick girls.

Sian takes a magazine from the pile, *Family & Home*, and I see Joelle straining to see if she will turn to the recipe section. For us, cookbooks are pornography; we are all alert to the possibilities of food. Sian lingers over a travel piece on New England, lifting the page to see a crumble recipe, waiting until we have all noticed the apricots and biscuit topping, then dropping it back. Teasing us with our obsession.

'Samantha Hoolihan? Follow me, please.'

Into her small room, where the dentist has framed photos of fish taken on her diving trips, making me feel like I'm underwater, which does nothing to soothe my anxiety.

I sit on the plastic couch, which she lowers so my head is down near her crotch, her face half-hidden behind a mask that puffs in and out as she breathes. She looks at my tube, the mask billows, then she asks me to open my mouth.

After eighteen months at the Bartlet, I know all the varying theories, about what the mouth represents and why I refuse food, Freudian bullshit, but right now I can't even open it. My cracked lips refuse to budge; her silver spike comes closer.

'Okay,' she says, putting the implement down. 'I won't put anything inside, but just let me see.'

I open, tentatively.

'Like volcanoes,' she says, though I know this. My teeth are thin at the front, smooth and strangely shaped at the back. Last time, she painted a fluoride treatment on them; there is little else that can be done.

'Okay, Sam. You can send the next girl in.'

The next girl is Pearl, and she refuses to leave her seat. Sian sighs, puts *Family & Home* on the table, and proceeds to lift her by the arms. Pearl sinks her slight weight down, but Sian has her easily, and together they disappear into the dentist's room.

I can hear muffled protests, then I choose not to hear.

Later, back at the Bartlet, there is still more to endure. I have my fifteen minutes with Clive, the painful viewing of my Black Magic box of memories. It's like having a dentist drill my teeth, looking at those photos. Painful and unavoidable. Back to the familiar pain of that terrible month of June, when I went hunting for Jena's attacker.

'Why are we even doing this?' I ask, arms folded and mouth nipped. 'You can't fix me.'

'I agree,' he says.

'So what's the fucking point?'

Clive holds up a chunky finger in correction, an earnest frown on his face so deep his eyes disappear for a moment.

'I can't fix you, Sam. But I really believe you can fix yourself. You're doing so well, and the board meeting is soon. Don't give up on yourself. Please.'

He places a saucer of cherry tomatoes on his desk, next to the Enliven.

'But it has to be your choice. It always has been.'

'Some choice,' I say, looking at the can of fat and sugar.

'I know this isn't comfortable, or easy, but if you can peel back those layers of understanding it will be worth it. It will mean your freedom.'

It sounds like a cliché even as he says it. But talking, finally talking after eighteen months, is becoming necessary, like an unblocked river finding its way to the sea. There's a trickle of hope, somewhere unseen, the narrow possibility of a better place, a normal life away from here. Home. My only option is to follow the trickle of hope, so I select the next photo in the pile, of a terraced house on the estate, and talk.

I used a brick to wedge the door shut and left Jena's flat, the dog in my rucksack, and headed for The Terraces.

Under the gaze of the June sun I peddled hard, past closed-up shops, overflowing bins, concrete yards, signs showing snarling Alsatians with speech bubbles warning I LIVE HERE!

I dodged dog shit, drying out in the sun, and zipped around cars parked on bricks. Orwell Estate was built in the seventies, a limp ambition of flat roofs and plate glass, where thin terraces from the last century got boxed in by maisonettes, blocks crammed together in a dip in the world. It was just a few streets from my home, near enough for us to use the same local shops, near enough to hear the ambulance sirens outside Our Plaice.

Orwell Estate is the sinkhole of Ipswich; the path down to The Terraces is steep. I'd spent many hours here when I was younger, roller-skating down with my hands stretched out in summer, balanced on a tray and risking my neck in snow. It was a trudge walking downwards in the heat and my bike felt heavy, pulling me forward so I tripped on the uneven concrete. This was the older part of the estate, somehow forgotten when other parts had a breezeblock makeover, and there was a fair bit of greenery on both sides of the path, trees thriving through neglect.

I stopped just fifty or so yards from the row of terraced houses, the bottom of the sinkhole. I looked around at the long grass, at the spindly crab-apple tree, but there was not enough nature to hide my bike or me. Luckily, there was a recycling bin next to the tree, a huge black box on wheels with YES PLEASE! printed next to pictures of bottles and cans. Some keen councillor's attempt to clean up the estate, but all around were discarded beer cans and family-sized White Lightning bottles. This was where I hid, crouched behind the bin with my bike flat in the grass, holding my camera like a sniper. Jena didn't want me to have the camera, but I was going to use it to take pictures, and keep them in the Black Magic box, until I had enough evidence to bring her attacker to justice. I didn't know how exactly this was going to fall into place, but I had to do something.

Even in the shade of the recycling bin, the heat was intense; my skin itched with sweat. I was starving, but I wouldn't give up my vigil. I adjusted my camera lens to line up a shot. The first terrace had a pink door, a fancy net at the window and a fat orange cat meowing in the garden. An old, hunched-over woman came out, reaching a shaky hand to the marmalade moggy as it wound itself around her varicosed leg.

I moved the camera to the next house. I had a feeling this was Sonia's home, just from the mess. From the itch in the pit of my gut. There was no movement, not even the twitch of a curtain, so after a while I took the printed newspaper story from my rucksack, as if it was going to tell me something different, something I didn't already know. Then I took the dog out, and held it. This was a long shot. I had no idea if Sonia and Douglas were still together, or even in contact. He'd said in his statement that he hadn't been back here in sixteen years, and the article that described her as his girlfriend was as old. But I had to start somewhere. Maybe she'd be able to tell me where he was now.

I was asleep in the grass, the dog in my arms, when a harsh voice roused me. A buggy appeared, then the woman who was using all her strength to push it. A lad a few years older than me was walking beside her, laden down with bulging supermarket bags that looked about to tear. I strained my ears to hear what the woman was saying in breathy sentences, only catching snippets: *. . . put me down to work tonight . . . not even my . . . said to him . . . what am I supposed to do with . . . only a puppy . . . if you don't like it you can . . .*

They came closer, just twenty yards from where I was hiding, my body pressed against the hot plastic bin as I craned my head to hear and see. Finally reaching her own path, the woman stopped pushing the buggy. She wiped her brow and put her hand flat on her bony chest. I attached the zoom lens and focused in, and I could see it was Sonia, looking much older than in the newspaper picture. Her face was hollow-cheeked and her hair was ratty; she'd got the same dragged-down shoulders, even though it was the teenage boy next to her who was carrying the bags.

It was him: the boy I'd ducked apples with at Halloween, though his ginger hair was now more burnt orange, and his boyish face had narrowed; the boy whom I suspected was

Douglas's son. I zoomed too close and the image blurred, so I twisted the lens back until I could see him clearly.

Sonia pushed the buggy, one of those plastic tripper ones, up to the front door. The sound of yapping came from inside. She leaned into the pram: . . . *now . . . get you inside . . . wee-wee*.

The boy had his head down and was fumbling in his pocket, taking out a key, but before he had time to use it, the door opened.

I flattened myself into the grass, my face perilously close to a rusted tin of mouldy peas, camera to my eye, and zoomed in closer.

A man stood in the doorway, partly concealed, and all I could make out was that he was tall with greying hair. He reached up to the top of the doorway and stretched his whole body.

'Bought the whole shop, did you?'

There was a tussle with bags and the pram.

'I told you, Sonia, that dog is meant to be for your protection. It's not a fucking baby.'

As he reached to lift the puppy from the pram, I saw his whole face. It was Andy, Sonia's brother and Jena's secret fiancé.

The surprise at seeing him sent a cold thought shivering through me: he, Sonia and Douglas were linked by blood and marriage, and these relationships somehow all connected to Jena. If I could untangle this, I might find the motive for the attack.

I'm in the grip of my story; I hadn't felt the asthma overtaking me again, the panic at not being able to grasp air. The tube is making it worse, and I'm struggling to get enough air into my lungs.

Clive makes me breathe in through my nose, out through my mouth, five times. His palms cup my shoulder and eventually he says, 'Do you want me to call Manda?'

'No. She'll only pump me full of prednisolone.'

'I should get your Ventolin, though?'

'Please.'

He returns with it, and the drug is like a miracle. He looks relieved, even though his meaty hands are still clasped in anxiety.

'The other board members will ask to see all the unit files, so if I can see you through this without needing to write it up, that might be best. We don't want to add any more doubts about your health.' I breathe, grateful that Clive is not just with me, but totally on my side. It's been a while since I felt anyone was.

'It isn't easy, Sam, digging up the past. I'm glad you're facing it head-on. Just breathe, that's it.'

Clive takes a deep breath in sympathy, and I find myself matching him, breath for breath, and feeling calmer. I don't know whether the Ventolin or Clive is the better drug, but I feel better. There is a silence, just the sound of our matched breathing, and the seagulls cawing outside, drifting on the sea breeze.

'What I'm not understanding, Sam, is why you needed to do all this. You were acting like you had to solve the crime, but why? You could have just let the police do their job.'

I'd let the police do their job for six weeks and they'd fucked up. Finally, I'd felt like I could do something to help my sister.

'I needed to be in control,' I say, grasping for a word that sums up everything that happened then, everything that came after.

CHAPTER 11

9 January

Most of the girls here smoke, but I don't because of my asthma. Still, I join them in the frigid bathroom when the unit is quiet, under the extractor fan so the smoke rises and doesn't trigger the alarm. The bathroom is the one place there are no rules. We can talk calories and weight and triggers, at least until a staff member discovers us. There's laughter too. Today it's about Manda, and how fat she's looking since Christmas.

'She should spend some time with us,' Joelle says. 'Wouldn't take us long to get her back into shape.'

Pearl stands awkwardly on one tennis shoe, pulling at a coil of hair that has released itself from her green serge trilby. Stacey offers her the end of the cigarette, and I blanch but say nothing. Pearl has to make her own decisions; I know that, but she's young and vulnerable, and I want to take her by the hand and lead her away. Her fingers hover in the air, just above the lit stub.

'Take it, kid. It's calorie-free,' Stacey advises in a fake American, have-a-nice-day voice.

Pearl puts it to her lips and sucks, then she starts to cough. Each cough feels like it's coming from my own chest. She passes the fag to Fiona, who pulls a face, so it's returned to Stacey. No one offers cigarettes to Mina, who is also in the room; it's as if she's invisible.

'Yup,' continues Stacey, inhaling deeply and warming to the theme, 'we could teach that fatty some weight-loss tips. Looks like she had too many mince pies.'

It's funny, the thought of fat Manda cutting up her food into the smallest bites, then trying to hide it under her napkin so she isn't made to eat it.

'I've got the best tip ever,' I say, tapping the tube on my face. 'If it ain't liquid, don't do it.'

Stacey laughs, which is what I wanted, but Pearl gives me an admiring look from under the brim of her hat, and I immediately regret drawing attention to my tube.

After taking a final drag, coughing into her bony hand, Stacey concludes, 'We look like the models in the magazines, but we're the sick ones. And the staff look like whales, but they're supposed to be healthy.'

The logic of the fatally ill is a perfect thing.

When I arrive at his office, Clive is seated in his high-backed, faux-leather armchair facing the window, flicking through my case file that is balanced on his knee, a fountain pen in his bear-paw grip. I take a moment to enjoy the view. There is condensation on the windowpane, and outside the sky is white, full of snow yet to fall, over a slate of sea.

'Making notes on me?'

'It's my first draft of your progress report.'

'For the board?' I ask.

I try and make the question light, but really I'm nervous. Clive must see how tense I feel; he disarms me by pushing the case notes over to me.

'I'm not going to write anything I won't discuss with you, Sam. Here . . .'

I walk over to him and read the thick, slanted handwriting, the ink still wet:

Sam wishes to be in control of her body, as a direct consequence of her sister being attacked and the subsequent trauma, which she was unable to influence.

A snort of irony sends a bubble of air up my tube, as I land on the chair opposite him.

'Not rocket science, is it?'

'Maybe not. Shall we pick up where we left off, Sam?'

He leans forward, eager to hear the next part of this story. His pen drips ink over the blank page, hoping to fill it with the story of my life.

'There is no *we*, Clive. It's me telling this story. You're just taking notes for your report.'

'I'm sorry, Sam. If it bothers you, I'll stop.'

He places the pen down, sits back. Then he looks out of the window, as if only interested in the view. The cold North Sea, which will outlast all of us.

'I'll just listen.'

I returned each day, positioning myself outside number 5, The Terraces, like a sniper, hiding behind the bin and watching, waiting for something to happen. On the third day of my watch, late afternoon on Saturday 11 June, Sonia's son left the house.

I didn't have a plan, not really, but this boy was in all probability Douglas's son, and I needed to find out all I could about the man who had most likely attacked Jena. So, I followed him.

He was ambling along, in a familiar direction, and with crawling dread it dawned on me that he was heading for Orwell Parade, the place where Jena was attacked, with its row of shops: the petrol station with its yellow-and-green frontage; the tanning parlour, where you paid by the minute to turn orange, if cancer didn't get you first; then the fish and chip shop, with its glass front and plastic blue fish painted with OUR PLAI – the final C and E having peeled away – once managed by Douglas and Sonia, if the news report was correct. Above was the flat where Jena should have been living.

At Orwell Parade, a group of lads were hanging around on bikes and skateboards, leaning on the wall and eating chips. One called out to the boy, 'Hey, Rob, what's up?'

So that was his name. I must have known it when we bobbed apples together, and this time I wouldn't forget.

I placed my bike against the wall, and rummaged in my pocket for money, walking slowly past the gang of boys to join the queue coming out of the chip shop. I couldn't help but think about the hard pavement under my feet and my sister lying there in a pool of blood.

Our Plaice was doing good trade and smelt delicious – hot vinegar and salt; the man behind the counter was red-faced, sweat dripping off him into the bubbling fat. I waited in line, watching the chips being shovelled on to paper; my stomach growled, reminding me that I hadn't eaten all day. My mouth watered at the sight of the battered fish inside the steamy warmer. Finally, it was my turn, but I couldn't contemplate filling my hunger. How could I carry on, sustaining my body, when Jena's was so wrecked?

'A Diet Coke, please.' Then, made weak by the delicious smells, 'And small chips.'

I clicked my coins on the counter. Beyond the foggy window, I saw Rob take a pew on the arm of a bench, the green band of his boxers showing over his low-slung jeans. His chin was red with spots, and bits of copper hair hung in his eyes.

I took my chips, sprinkled salt, and knocked back the Coke greedily. The fizz made me gag, but that didn't stop me downing it in big gulps, all the time thinking, *What should I do now?* I left the shop and walked over to Rob, feeling the heat in my palm from the greasy chip wrapper. I took a chip and sucked, my mouth a hollow as I pulled in air to cool it. It was a betrayal of my sister, this selfish need for food, when I should be thinking about her and finding her attacker. Finally, feeling stronger, I tossed it away.

'You want these? I'm not hungry anymore.'

Impulsively, light-headed with hunger and daring, I offered Rob the greasy packet and he took it.

He pushed his fringe from his forehead. He should have cut it, since his eyes were a lovely blue-grey, like a June sky before a storm. I was both excited and terrified by his closeness, by the possibility that his father was Jena's attacker, his uncle was her fiancé, and he would know plenty about both men.

'I'm Sam,' I said.

He looked directly at me. 'I know who you are,' he said.

The sky was overcast; the sun had overreached itself, and a summer storm was on the way. My phone vibrated in my pocket; it was Mum. She'd be wondering where I was, when I was coming home for tea.

I ignored the call.

It started to rain, warm drops on my face. We stayed sitting on the back of the bench, the wood digging into my bum, getting wetter.

Rob's red hair dripped into his eyes, and when he pushed it away from his forehead I saw a raised white scar, an inch above his brow.

'How did you get that?'

I could see from its ragged edges that the cut hadn't received the stitches it needed.

'I . . . er . . . fell.' He tugged his hair back to cover it, and looked away. 'The rain's getting heavy. We should take cover.'

As we ran for the bus shelter there was another call, this time from Dad. Again, I didn't pick up.

'I'm sorry about what happened. I saw it on the news.'

He thought I was a pity case, the girl with the damaged sister. He didn't know yet that I was a vigilante too.

'So, you live around here?' I asked Rob, as if I didn't know.

'Yeah. With my mum.'

I quickly said, 'Not your dad?'

'Nah.' He looked down, then recovered. 'But my Uncle Andy is round a lot. Too much, if you ask me.'

'Oh. Sucks.'

Rob rubbed his chin then looked at me in a shy, proud way. 'Yeah, but I'm moving out as soon as a room comes free at The Fold.'

'The what?'

'It's that block of flats by the docks. You get a room and a shared kitchen and everything.'

My phone beeped angrily. Mum had sent a text:

JENA HAD ANOTHER FIT. DR GREGG HAD TO BE CALLED IN TO ASSESS HER AND HE'S MOVED HER BACK TO EASTERN WARD. WHERE ARE YOU???

I stepped out of the shelter, immediately heading for my bike. If I peddled hard enough I'd make the next train. I got on my bike, then turned for a moment.

'What you up to tomorrow?'

Rob looked surprised; pleased too. 'Nothing much. I'm not going to church, let's put it that way.'

I smiled even as the rain soaked me to the bone.

CHAPTER 12

10 January

I'm an expert on hospitals; the NHS should employ me as an inspector. As well as my experiences of Westerfield Hospital when Jena was there, I've lived in the Bartlet for eighteen months, plus I have outpatient appointments at the general hospital in Ipswich.

This isn't done en masse, so today it's just me and Sian in the waiting room of Ipswich Hospital. The room is stuffed with women, all of whom are stuffed with babies. Their bellies, in various degrees of gestation, are smug boasts of their success, their normalcy. The women eye me with unhidden curiosity. Have I had a miscarriage? Why am I here, so skeletal, when they are so fecund? They shiver, rub their stomachs, and make an exaggerated show of looking away whilst keeping me in their peripheral vision.

'Samantha Hoolihan? If you'd like to follow me.'

The sonographer, at least, seems pleased to see me. I must be a change from floating alien-shapes, a bit more of a challenge. Sian doesn't even look up from *Your Pregnancy* magazine, and remains in her seat. She doesn't care if I can have babies or not.

The jelly is cold, then pressed in by the steel probe of the ultrasound machine. Both of us look at the screen, listening to the strange cave-calls of my stomach.

'No period yet?'

Stupid question. I wouldn't be here if there had been. 'No.'

'Hmmm.' She frowns, moves the prod around, left, right. Back to the left, all the time pressing hard on my full bladder.

Finally, she takes the pressure away, wipes my stomach with a yard of tissue, and starts to make notes. Next is the bit I hate most.

Sian is called in to join us, and takes a sturdy seat beside the couch, on which I am still prone, managing to look vaguely interested whilst fiddling with her watch.

The sonographer starts well, talking to me, then turns to Sian and doesn't look at me again. Sian becomes increasingly grumpy as she notes down the sonographer's feedback, shoulders hunched. Basically, my pelvic reproduction organs are fucked. Or rather, if I was fucked, nothing would come of it. My uterus is less than one centimetre, the thickness of my endometrium is just a couple of millimetres and my ovaries are small. All of this means I am drastically underweight. Which, of course, is not news.

As we leave the maternity unit, Sian says, 'Doesn't look like you'll be getting rid of that tube anytime soon, does it?'

No wonder I hate hospitals. No wonder I hate the smug staff who work in them; talk about control – why else would Sian or Clive or even Birute want to work on Ana Unit? It's them who want control, not us.

I'm at the mercy of the staff, just like Jena was, and on 1 February my future will be decided for me. Clive tells me that our sessions are progress, but they hurt, more than starving, more than the tube, more than purging. That kind of hurting can be good, it can be addictive; as a starving girl, I know that more than most.

But this pain, this emotional kind of hurt, is harder to bear. I can hardly stand that Clive looks at me. He *sees* me, he *listens*. And all of that is a tiny scratch across my heart, a shedding of a protective scab, which leaves me vulnerable and raw in a way I haven't been in eighteen months.

His sessions do this, because of his warm smile and crinkled brown eyes, beady behind his glasses. Because he seems to care, and that cuts me most of all.

Once I am in his office, he waits for me to be ready to continue my sad story.

Arriving at the hospital hopelessly late that Saturday afternoon because of my encounter with Rob, I wasn't even sure Dr Gregg would still be around, but I went straight to his office and banged loudly on the door.

'Enter.'

I could see he was getting ready to leave; he was clearing his desk of papers and his briefcase was stood on it, upright and sealed, his job done for the day. When he saw me, he frowned, no doubt thinking about his already-burned tea, and I felt him scrutinising my long unkempt hair, my eyes rimmed with black kohl, ruined by the rain.

'Ah! Hello Sam. What can I do for you?'

He pointed to a chair. The seat was so low I was forced to look up his nose.

'I got a text from Mum. You've moved Jena.'

I sat on my hands, sweaty palms sticking to the plastic chair.

'Yes, I was called in because the staff were concerned about her, on account of the fits. I've moved her back to Eastern Ward, for the time being.'

He said it in a distracted way; in his head he was already home with his wife, eating his tea and relaxing.

'Jena hates it there.'

'Mmm. I want her under closer care. Your sister has had two seizures in the last week.'

Three, I corrected in my head.

He smiled like he was doing me a favour, his thick skin creasing into a grimace.

'There's a higher ratio of nursing attention on Eastern Ward. It's for her own good.'

His gaze went back to his desk and the files he was tidying away, to indicate the conversation was finished.

'But Dr Gregg, she's getting better. Yesterday, she remembered a dog she was given, just before the attack.'

I was babbling, desperate for the old man's attention. I was on the brink of telling him that I'd shown Jena some photos, but his eyes flicked to the clock and I could see I'd caught him at a bad moment. He wanted to leave and I was stopping him.

'Dr Gregg, please listen! Jena put this dog in the window of the flat she was about to move to.'

I lifted the rucksack, and thrust the dog in front of him.

'I'm going to show her and then she'll remember.'

He sighed, and pushed the dog away without looking at it.

'Don't you believe she will?' My chest started to tighten, and my feet did a jig on the floor.

He cleared his throat. 'Mmm. It's very much an art rather than a science when it comes to assessing the prognosis with brain injury. But I've been through all this with your parents. Maybe you should ask them to explain it to you? I'm not sure you fully understand . . .'

'I'm sixteen, not a child!' I returned the dog to the rucksack.

The rucksack slipped from my grasp, and there was the sickening sound of china cracking against the floor.

'Just answer me one thing. Did Mum tell you to send Jena back to Eastern?'

She liked to have Jena there, with the heightened security. Dr Gregg leaned back, his nostrils flaring so I could see the hairs.

'Naturally, Kath gave her opinion, and we are trying to do what's best.' His voice gained speed as he began to lecture me. 'As I explained when Jena was first admitted, one's memory is like a series of computer files. A brain collision is effectively a computer crash. Afterwards, it is sometimes possible for data to be retrieved from a deleted section, backed up on the hard-drive, if you like, but often it's lost for good. Jena's brain was badly damaged by the fall. She may never retrieve what she has lost.'

Eastern Ward. After Jena came out of her coma and was discharged from Ipswich Hospital, they transferred her here. A hospital ward for people who were no good anymore, half-broken zombies who might as well be dead. A prison; the door was always locked, the windows didn't open. I pressed the buzzer and spoke into the intercom.

'Hello? I'm—'

Before I could say my name, the door was released. So much for enhanced security.

The hot air hit me like a wall; it was stiff with warring odours of shit and lavender, the stench of the old. Next was the cotton-wool silence, reminding me of Dad's shed. To my right was the staff office: empty. The day room to my left was full. The ward may have a locked door, but no staff had come to check on me. I hesitated on the strip of plastic between office and day room, feeling lost. I needed to find my mum.

The day room was stifling; the only sound came from the television, where a bubbly presenter was talking about re-decorating or re-locating or some other life improvement that none of these patients would ever make. There were familiar faces from when Jena was here six weeks ago. Ernie sat by the window snoring, and several residents were slouched in chairs facing each other or the wall, not saying a word, wearing clothes that were old and hot: men in long-sleeved shirts, Ivy in her layers of woollen cardigans.

In the staff room, I could see a table with magazines and a plastic tub of sandwiches, a chair with a denim jacket thrown over it, a desk with a jar of pens and a phone. The telephone receiver lay on the desk, upturned. I'd disturbed a phone call, and whoever buzzed me in had gone to fetch someone, or find something, for whoever was waiting on the other end of the phone.

Then I saw the medicine cabinet, steel-fronted with silver locks, three of them. An impulse overtook me.

I walked to the desk, opening the drawers, searching for keys, then I rifled through the pockets of the jacket. Rizla papers . . . chewing gum . . . a used tissue . . . a set of keys! Impulsively, I took them to the medicine cabinet and tried each one, increasingly frustrated, until the smallest one worked. Excited and nervous, I went to check the door, but no one was coming. I opened the medicine cabinet. Inside were boxes and bottles. Brown and white and blue. I read the labels: *Gaviscon*, *lactulose* . . . I didn't know what I was doing, what I was searching for, just something . . .

'Can I help you?'

I spun round. A flustered-looking male nurse was watching me; his badge told me he was MARK and a CARE WORKER. His green trousers and top had fresh yellow stains, and he was holding a cardboard bucket with a sheet of kitchen paper over the top. He noticed the telephone receiver on the desk, and I stepped smartly away from the cabinet, which still hung open, his keys in the door.

'Oh shit, I forgot about that . . .'

I felt my face darken; I'd been caught red-handed, but he was too distracted to notice. He put the bucket down and picked up the receiver, said 'Hello?' then, after a pause, replaced it, giving me time to push the cabinet door shut and slide the key free just before he turned his attention to me.

'You must be Sam?'

'Yes.'

'You look just like Jena.'

I awkwardly tugged at my hair, pulling it to cover my cheeks, which still felt hot. I looked nothing like Jena; she was beautiful.

'Can I see her?'

'Of course.'

He led the way from the office, and I dropped the keys back on the desk, thinking how close I'd come to doing something I shouldn't, how I'd got away with it.

I followed him to the bedrooms, heart sinking at how horribly familiar the narrow corridors were. I wondered if she'd be in the same room as before.

She wasn't. It was a new room, but the bed, cabinet and sink were identical. A woman-shaped huddle shook under the duvet and Mum sat stroking it, speaking softly.

'Sam's here, my darling,' she said.

The duvet flapped open, revealing a puffy-faced Jena, her bloodshot eyes peering at me from swollen sockets, cuddling Sid the Sloth like her life depended upon it.

'Sam!'

She pulled me to her so we were nose to nose, which wasn't pleasant as hers was runny. She'd been crying hard.

'Oh Christ, Mum, look at the state of her!'

Jena was making noises like a fox caught in a snare, and she was shaking.

'You could have been here sooner. She's been crying for you. If you'd answered your mobile . . .'

'I was taking pictures, for Jena. I lost track of the time.'

Mum grunted. 'She doesn't need your pictures, she needs you! Watch her, will you, while I go and call Dad? He needs to know what's happening.'

'No, please . . .' Jena was still clinging to her, but Mum peeled herself free.

'She'll settle down.'

Jena didn't settle. She didn't understand why she'd been moved; she kept saying, 'I'm sorry,' thinking she was to blame for her predicament.

'I'll open the window,' I said, but it only budged an inch. 'Fat lot of good that is. Come on. Let's get you out of these pyjamas and into something cooler.'

Her belongings had been put away with no care. The cuddly animals were tossed in a random pile, the pink photo frame faced the wall and her clothes were squashed in the drawers. After a bit of rummaging, I found a clean T-shirt and some bobbled leggings.

'Come on, Jena. Arms up!'

A sour odour escaped from her. She needed a wash, but the shower room was kept locked, and going to find Mark to ask for the key would mean leaving her alone. I improvised, wiping a towel under her arms and neck and spraying some Impulse over her. Once in her fresh clothes, she climbed back under the duvet, grabbed my baby photo from the cabinet and hugged it, shivering.

'Head hurts.' Her voice was weak, like she could barely finish a full sentence.

'I have a special present for you, Jena.'

Unzipping my rucksack, I lifted out the Staffie dog, guiltily noticing its chipped paw. I placed the dog on the bed, and Jena stroked the paw where the smooth china became rough and flat, then cuddled the dog to her body, her eyes weepy but blank.

'Do you remember it, Jen-Jen?'

A long whine came from between her lips, like air escaping from a balloon. I was hoping for more, some sign that she recognised it.

I took the dog from her, worried that if Mum saw it she'd know I'd been in Jena's flat, despite the police warning us not to go there.

'I'll take it home with me, but I'll bring it back next time I come. Promise.'

As I placed the dog back in my bag, the Black Magic box fell against my fingers. I lifted it free, and showed her; her eyes widened as she recognised the place she kept her keepsakes, her photos. The box where I now kept my evidence.

CHAPTER 13

11 January

Despite the disastrous visit to Ipswich Hospital, where my current infertility was confirmed, I still got an extra star on my chart because I haven't tried to yank out my feeding tube. Good girl, Sam.

Then, when I gained at the weigh-in this morning (I don't know how much by, we're never told), I got another. Two more stars meant a reward: I could watch a film.

Now I'm re-united with the Black Magic box, I know exactly which one to ask for: *Dracula*. The old version, in black and white, with Bela Lugosi. I wanted to test if the film still affected me, like it had when I saw it last. It gave me nightmares for weeks, and turned every potential threat, every bogeyman, into a faceless monster in a cloak.

Manda lets me take over the day room for the viewing, which gets grumbles from Stacey. 'Can't we all watch it? Come on, Sam. I love a good flick.' She winks at me. 'I'll bring toffee-covered popcorn.'

'Sam, I can't . . .'

We looked at each other, and a clear moment of u
standing passed between us, that what I was asking was
painful and dangerous. There was a point when it could h
gone either way. I could have returned the box to my ba
could have chosen to be a good girl.

'We have to, Jena. I'm gathering pictures, to help yo
remember. I've met Rob, Douglas's son. Andy is his uncle; he
was there too. I'm trying to work out how it's all connected, and
I need your help. But don't tell Mum about this, or about the
dog. Remember to forget.'

'Yes,' she said, and her voice was so clear it seemed like
a moment of lucidity. 'I always do.'

But Manda is firm. 'This is Sam's reward. If you want to request a film, you're at liberty to do so, though you'll need to get some gold stars first.'

Stacey's waterloading got rumbled when she couldn't even stand straight, her bladder was so full. And Sian was cruel. She made Stacey wait, took her time with her notes, until finally Stacey couldn't bear it anymore and had to dash to the loo, clutching her sides.

'Yeah, well,' Stacey scowls, 'it's easy to get gold stars when you're fed by a fucking tube.'

Manda closes the thin curtains on the cold sky outside, then leaves me alone, closing the door behind her. I sit on the edge of the long, lumpy sofa as the film starts, my mind drifting back to the first time I saw this film.

Mum was out at bingo with Chloe, and I was supposed to be asleep. Jena was downstairs with Dad, watching an old black-and-white movie. Andy had popped round, and he ended up staying when he saw what they were watching. He said it was a classic. Regardless, I was sent to bed. I suppose I was about twelve years old.

I pretended to be asleep when Dad came up to check on me, like he always did when Mum was out, tucking the duvet around me and kissing my cheek. When he'd gone, I made myself stay awake, fighting off sleep, then sneaked quietly down the landing, where I hid at the top of the stairs in the darkest corner, watching the television. Jena and Andy were sat close together on the sofa, but Dad didn't seem to notice.

The screen was hazy, but I could see a man walking up the steps of a castle in a swirl of fog; spider webs dangled from the walls and his footsteps echoed. He had spooky dark eyes and hair as glossy as a blackbird's wing. Then he disappeared, just like that, and there was a bat bouncing up and down by the open window.

Andy laughed. 'No need to be frightened. Just relax and enjoy it.'

Jena wasn't laughing, though. She said, 'Can we stop now?' But no one did.

In the darkened room, the men were still laughing, teasing Jena. I could tell from her whimpering that she was scared.

I wrapped my fleece dressing gown closer around me, shivering. I wanted to go back to my room, and hide under the covers, but something stopped me. On the television screen, the man was in a bedroom, bent over a sleeping girl. He opened his cape, and then he turned to me. His whole face, so pale, the eyes so dark, and it was me he was going to kill. He opened his mouth wide and, shockingly, he had two prominent shiny teeth, sharp as needles.

Jena screamed. And then, because I couldn't stand to watch any more, so did I.

I have to stop. I switch it off, as scared as I was back then, when I was just twelve.

My heart is quaking with anxiety. This film started my nightmares, the ones I still get, about a man with a hood over his head. With dark eyes and a red mouth.

I witnessed Jena's attack, but I couldn't help the police because I couldn't remember her attacker's face. Because of the rain, because of the hood. So my brain filled in the gap.

The film and the attack merged. My current nightmares aren't really about Dracula. They're about something far more terrifying.

Later, I join Clive in his office. I tell him about being unable to watch the film, and about the first time I saw it. Watching Jena, with Andy and my dad.

'It's all opening up inside you, isn't it?'

'But it hurts,' I say. 'I want to stop.'

'I don't think you can stop, Sam. This is your last chance.'

He may mean because of the approaching board meeting. He may mean because my body is wrecked.

The sky outside is getting dark, though it's not yet evening, and the room is made of simple outlines and shapes.

'I think we need to talk about your mother, Sam. I had a call earlier to say the post-mortem has been completed. It was a heart attack.'

Of course it was. A heart like hers, fighting so hard to keep us together. What else could it do but fail in the end?

'They've set a date for the funeral,' he adds. 'I'm afraid it's going to take place on the afternoon of 1 February, which is also the date of the board hearing.'

Two bad things in one day. How would it be easier if they were days apart? And I can't go to the funeral, not if Jena is there; it wouldn't be fair to her. And if Dad is there, it would be unbearable.

'The board will want to speak with you, though they will make their decision based mainly on the reports. But I wouldn't want this to interfere with you attending your mum's funeral. I can ask for the date to be changed, and apply for a day release.'

I shake my head. 'Don't do that. I don't want to go to the funeral, and I don't want you to get the date changed. It makes no difference.'

'If you don't go to the funeral, you may regret it. You should think about it carefully, Sam.'

When anger comes over me it's a relief, a welcome change from the sadness that I can't stand. 'Why do you think I'd regret not going to see her buried? Because all anorexics have issues with their mother, is that it? You'll start asking me if I was a good feeder when I was a baby next. How early I was potty-trained.'

Clive smiles at this, the absurdity of our interviews, then says, 'I think it's true that anorexics often do have issues with their mothers. The typical dynamic is a controlling mother and absent father, sometimes physically, but in your case emotionally. And it's a fact that, until she died, you refused all attempts at therapy.'

Dad was always in the shed, with his photos and laptop, editing his films. Mum was the verbal one; she did the talking for both of them. He was more distant, it's true. From me, at least. He was always closer to Jena.

Our parents were very protective. It's one reason why it took Jena until she was twenty-nine to decide to leave home. Mum and Dad liked us to be where they could see us; they liked to keep the family close.

Case in point: that September they wanted me to stay on at Orwell Academy for sixth form, so I'd be nearer to home and Mum could watch me walk to school each morning and afternoon, keeping guard in her fluorescent jacket, her lollipop held high to stop the traffic. Dad said I could learn all I needed to at the local school.

I didn't blame them for this, but I needed some control over my life and college was the gateway.

They only gave in after my art teacher called at our house, just a month or so before my sixteenth birthday, and told Dad I had a real talent, and that college was the best place for me.

'Sam has a great eye, and the college will really develop that gift.'

That was the word that swung it for Dad, him being into photography like he was; the temptation of 'developing my gift' was too great to resist. That might have been when he decided to take the camera from Jena, and give it to me that fateful day I turned sixteen.

For me, the plan to go to college that September had represented freedom. But after the attack, everything felt different. I couldn't imagine my future anymore; the only thing I thought about was finding Jena's attacker, or some evidence against him, like the missing raincoat. Clicking with my camera, to try and catch a criminal, viewed through a distancing lens. The camera was more, much more now, than a way to capture images. It was my shield, guarding me from the things I was forcing myself to see, the people I was investigating, the questions I had.

It was Sunday morning, the day after Jena's move back to Eastern Ward. I hadn't seen Dad all weekend, but I knew where he'd be. Where he always was, especially since the attack: in his dark room, the one he'd created by painting the shed windows with black paint and securing an inside lock, so no one would disturb him at a crucial time and wreck his pictures. It was somewhere he would go with Jena, but now the Leica camera was mine, so I could go there too.

I had work to do.

I opened the shed door slowly, not quite sure if I should enter.

'Sorry, Dad. I was wondering if you could help me develop my prints?'

Dad. A short man with a big belly; he was sixty-one and losing his hair on top, but still wore it long at the sides. His straggly goatee was always matted with paint, as he was always starting odd jobs but never finishing them.

He'd worked at Pleasurepark for thirty years, as their chief engineer, but he'd been home on compassionate leave since the attack. I don't know why he'd done that, it wasn't like he was always at the hospital. He never seemed comfortable just relaxing; he had to have a project, and this extended leave just meant he had more time to fill with his hobby.

'Come on in, Sam. My photos are nearly developed. I just thought I may as well do something while I wait for your mum to get back from the hospital and put the roast in the oven.'

That was where she always was. Dad found it harder, though, to see his daughter so damaged, and it distressed Jena too. He came back so upset that Mum had started saying maybe he should stop visiting so much and return to work. He hadn't done that, though.

He was waiting for his daughter to come home, in the hush of the dark room.

Dad showed me what to do, the things he had also shown my sister when she was younger. This photography equipment, the Leica camera, was precious, and that was why Jena was so upset, so angry, when he'd given it to me on my sixteenth birthday. Jealousy, but not just because of him giving me the camera. Before then, the dark room had been their special place, but that gift had been a sign that now I was going to be included. What he gave me, on my sixteenth birthday, was the promise of future attention.

Dad guided me, and we worked silently together in the red glow, my hands fluorescent under the chemical water as he showed me how to dip my photos. Above us, on the washing lines, pictures of life hung out to dry in the cool motionless air, dripping on to the floor. Dad's pictures, taken at the theme park. Teenage girls screaming on rides, toddlers sucking ice creams. Lots of pictures of the entertainment team, which Andy managed, and one of Jena dressed up as a fairy-tale princess. The picture must have been taken at Easter, because there she was wearing a peasant's low-cut dress and carrying a basket of Creme Eggs.

I understood why Dad came here. He could study the pictures and imagine his daughter whole again. The room was a refuge, away from the reality of Jena and her damaged brain.

Together, we watched as my pictures revealed themselves, and he picked out the one of Monica. It was the photo I had taken at the police station that day Penny told us the prime suspect may be released soon.

'Pretty girl,' Dad said. 'Goes to your school, doesn't she?'

'She's in the sixth form.' I decided I'd give her the photo when I saw her next.

He touched Monica's picture, delicately lifting the edge so the print rippled under the single bulb.

'You're a very good girl, Sam.'

His voice was low, and I could hear the emotion in it. All the pain that he'd been feeling for six weeks. I wanted to tell him that the real reason I was taking these photos was to help jog Jena's memory and to find evidence against her attacker. The words were almost out, but he looked so sad, and I was worried that I'd just upset him.

'Are you okay, Dad?'

He moved towards me, giving me a tight hug, and kissed the top of my head, breathing me in. 'I'll be fine soon,' he said. He looked again at my pictures, as if the answer to when he would be fine could be found there.

Silence in the dark room as we both looked at the picture of Sonia's house.

'Isn't that Andy? Stood in that doorway.'

'Yeah. That's his sister Sonia's house. Have you met her?'

He looked again at the photo. 'A few times. She sometimes came to Pleasurepark with Andy, but I can't say I've seen her in years. What were you doing there?'

'Her son, Rob; I know him a bit. I was waiting for him.'

I had so many questions about Andy and his relationship with Jena. She'd always told me that their affair had to be secret on account of him being her boss and the age gap, that Mum and Dad mustn't know about the wedding or that he would soon be moving in with her, that it would be a repeat of the family rift that Mum experienced when she married Dad.

'Dad, why hasn't Andy visited Jena?'

He looked surprised. 'He isn't immediate family. And it's hard, to see her like that. I can hardly bear it myself, so you couldn't expect anyone else to put themselves through it.'

He started to well up again, and I didn't want that; I wanted answers. Was it really true that Andy hadn't visited because it was just too hard? Could it be that he loved her too much to see that?

Whatever the reason, I needed to know.

I stop, no more left to come. I've purged myself, vomited up my past in my monologue, and I'm empty. Exhausted and exposed.

'Good girl,' says Clive.

Suddenly a rage overtakes me and I clench my fist, then run at him as if to punch him in the gut, but he shields himself just in time.

'Sam, whoa! It's okay . . .'

But it's not okay, it never will be again, and I'm not a good girl. I pull free, hot and chaotic, and run from the room. Back to the other side of the building, to Ana Unit, where I feel safe. To my bedroom, where no one can reach me; to my bed, narrow as a child's.

I throw myself down on it, no longer angry but desperately sad. How can this be helping? How can it be fucking helping? I reach for my tube and yank, pull it from my nose, my throat, my stomach. I cry and pull and don't stop until Clive finds me, and fetches Manda, and then the two of them are with me, soothing me, rocking me. Telling me it will be okay.

CHAPTER 14

12 January

I gashed my throat, brought up blood and skin with the plastic, but that didn't stop Sian from re-inserting the tube when she came back on duty. Six cans of Enliven a day, plus a meal in the dining room. It will kill me, if starvation doesn't get me first.

The next morning, I don't go to Clive's office at the appointed hour; I wait for him to find me in my room.

'Fuck off,' I say. As calmly as I can, though my hand clenches and I want to run at him again.

He sits on the white wicker chair, strokes his grey-white beard and breathes deeply, trying to dredge up words of comfort I don't want to hear. His presence suffocates me.

'I'm not doing this anymore, Clive. I mean it. If you want to give me an extra can, you'll have to fight me.'

To my surprise, he doesn't argue. He looks too tired. 'Okay, Sam.'

I notice the local newspaper is folded neatly under his arm.

He stands, but leaves it on my desk. I wait for him to be gone, for his footsteps to be out of hearing, and lift the paper. Then I understand why he didn't threaten me with the tube, why he didn't need to say anything. I understand that I have no choice.

The headline reads:

ORWELL ESTATE SHOOTER: SAMANTHA HOOLIHAN JUDGEMENT LOOMS

After lunch, I find Clive in his office. I'd expected him to look frantic, to be poring over paperwork as I've seen him do before, but instead he is stood by the window, hands buried in his corduroys, looking out at the grey North Sea. He turns and smiles, but his eyes are red. It's the look of a man who has lost and knows it.

'Hello, Sam. I didn't expect to see you again today.'

'Oh yes you did.' I throw the paper on his desk. 'What will happen to me?'

Clive breathes deeply, so his whole chest lifts, a barrel of emotion.

'That, Sam, has always been up to you. I write the report, but you are the one who dictates the content. Believe me, I want nothing more than to tell the board that this hospital order is no longer necessary and you should go home.'

My crime, committed not because I was bad but because I was mad, or so they think. I received a hospital order, on account of severe depression and anorexia, treatable mental conditions, that saved me from prison, but I need to be fixed before I can be free. I need to be not just sane, but safe.

Clive removes his watch, places it on the desk and waits. He knows I can't afford to refuse now.

'I continued to hang around Rob, forging a quick intimacy, desperate to get closer,' I say, thinking back. 'He was my only link to Douglas Campbell, and I needed to do something so he wasn't released, like

Penny said he might be. Evidence was needed, stronger evidence than the police already had.

'I went to Greasy Monkeys, the car project, where Rob had told me he worked. It was just a scrabble of a field, and a rickety outhouse holding knackered cars.'

It was Monday 13 June, seven weeks since the attack, and I was determined to get something on Douglas.

In the yard, there were two old bangers, battered and rusted, both with their bonnets up. Each car had a trio of boys gathered around, and all of the boys wore jeans or blue overalls. No one seemed to be in charge, and there was lots of chatter; a radio on top of the car roof pumped out an old song, RiRi's 'Umbrella'. A few boys had their T-shirts off, and were rosy from the sun and splattered with oil, singing along to the song: *ella-ella-ella*.

As soon as I was spotted, the whistles began. I hid behind my hair as much as I could, eyes to the ground, and walked to the first car.

I found Rob working under the bonnet of a turquoise Datsun. His copper hair was sticky with sweat, and his naked back was puckered with acne. He quickly pulled on a raggy T-shirt.

'How do you feel about bunking off early?' I asked.

He hesitated. 'Mac's just got me a room at The Fold. I don't want to piss him off before I even move in.'

'Who's Mac?'

'Social worker. He's really pushed to get me this room; said to the manager how well I've worked here. He's on my side, Sam, and I don't want to fuck that up.'

'Better make sure he doesn't notice, then.'

I took his oil-stained hand in mine, and urged him to follow me down the dusty track.

The air was heavy with heat, and we bumped along like drowsy bees towards Orwell Park, the straggly piece of grass behind the shops with swings and a graffitied climbing wall. But we'd timed it badly. The park was crawling with children just out of school.

Half a mile away, Mum would be holding forth at the crossing, fiercely lollipopping the cars to a screeching standstill. After the attack, she'd taken a month off work, but the council wouldn't keep her job for her indefinitely, so she'd had to start back.

I sent her a text:

I'm at school in the library, doing some revision. Ok?

Her reply came immediately:

Ok. C u at home 4 tea. X

In the park, the kids skipped and yelled, letting off steam. Their mothers sat on nearby benches, yakking and smoking. No way were we going to get the swings with those mothers on guard.

'Can we go to yours?'

I looked at Rob expectantly, willing him to agree, so that I could see inside Sonia's home. Maybe even meet the woman who'd stood by a rapist, whose brother was secretly in love with my sister. Sonia seemed to be the linchpin.

'It's a bit of a state,' Rob said. 'All my things are packed up, ready for when I move out.'

'Will your mum be around?' I held my breath, silently begging him to say yes.

'Nah, she's taken the new puppy to dog training. Trying to train it not to shit on the floor.'

'So, what are we waiting for?' I reached for his hand.

Rob shifted his feet awkwardly. 'But she'll be home soon.'

'Good,' I said. 'I've always liked dogs.'

My brain jabbered non-stop all the way to Sonia's house, demanding, *What are you doing? Who the fuck do you think you are?* I was about to get inside Sonia and Rob's home, and that might not be so smart, given their relationship to the main suspect. And what if Andy was there? Did he know about Douglas Campbell's arrest? It came to me then that this could be another reason why he hadn't visited Jena: not that it was too painful for him, but that his loyalty to his family was stronger than his feelings for his fiancée.

I told myself to keep calm and focus on the things I knew for certain, like the firmness of the pavement, the hot sun in the sky.

And then we were in front of Sonia's house, standing right where Andy had been when I took that picture of him.

The house had the stillness of no-one-home. As Rob opened the door, the sun lit a runway of rising dust along the narrow hallway, which was cluttered with squeaky dog-toys. A large cage was rammed up in the corner, with stained blankets and chewed toys in it. The house reeked of puppy piss.

The kitchen was cramped, smaller than Dad's dark room. Rob opened the fridge for beer, and the stench of sour milk wafted out. The counter was crowded with used mugs and plates and empty crisp packets.

'So, you looking forward to moving out?' I asked.

'Yup. Can't wait.' Rob poured the beer into beakers, and tipped the remainder of a half-eaten bag of Monster Munch into a bowl, taking one and eating it, saying, 'Pickled onion, mmm.' Just as he was turning to enter the front room, I put my hand on his arm and moved closer.

I touched his cheek with my lips, tasting the tang of motor oil and sweat, and he gasped then kissed me back. Awkward mouths, too wide, then his tongue probed my teeth and I tasted vinegar from the crisps. I tried to hold him back, to make him kiss me slower, but his teeth knocked mine, and it was hard to carry on, telling myself that this was what I had to do if I was going to get any information from him. It felt too soon for this, just two days since we met, but he didn't notice my hesitation, and I needed to act fast. No time to be playing coy.

'Shall we go upstairs?' I said.

He was gulping me down like I was water, pushing me back so the kitchen worktop dug into my spine, the hardness of his penis pressed to my stomach.

He led me up, kicking aside wet newspaper and a bald teddy bear. In the first room, the bed was covered with boxes, a sports bag, a pile of folded clothes, so he pulled me towards his mother's room.

It was a mess. The curtains weren't fully drawn and the bed wasn't made; clothes lay scattered on the floor, a hairbrush was on the bed and there were enough randomly placed tea lights to give a fireman a heart attack. Rob sat on the bed, and tugged me down beside him. I wanted to pull away, but I told myself that I needed him, to help me gather evidence. I wanted something to show Jena, to jog her memory.

'Does your mum have any photos of you as a baby?'

'Hmmm?' His eyes were closed; he was miles away. 'Why?'

It was a good question, and I stumbled to answer. 'It's what girls do when they like a guy: ask to see photos of him when he was little.'

A slow smile rose, making his eyes lighten as clouds drifted away. 'You like me, then?'

I flicked his face with my nail, leaving a half-moon of white on his red cheek. 'Think I'd be here if I didn't?'

He pulled me back on to him, kissing me again. It became less awkward as we discovered how each other moved and our bodies found a fit, legs wrapped around each other and torsos touching. I was fighting my inner voice, telling me to run. I shushed myself with promises of information, of helping Jena to remember, of evidence against her attacker.

'So, does she have any photos, or what?'

A smile twitched the corners of his mouth, and his lips curled back from his front teeth as he tried not to grin. I could feel how badly he wanted me, the way he pushed against me, the way he looked at me like I might have the answer to some important question. He rolled on to his stomach and dug around under the bed, coming back up with a large carrier bag.

'This is where Mum keeps photos and that. Most of this stuff is years old.'

Rob upended the bag, and a wodge of papers fell out along with some Airfix planes. He picked one up and stared at it with wonder.

'This is all Dad's stuff, back from when I was a kid. He spent hours making these. I'd forgotten they were here.'

On the bed was a fan of photos: school portraits in card-board frames, small square ones yellow with age – Rob eating a sticky lolly; Rob kicking a punctured football; Rob as a baby in the arms of a girl who looked too young and vulnerable to have a baby.

'How old was your mum there?'

'Eighteen.'

She looked younger, with mousey-brown hair and small eyes, wearing a too-tight dress, pushing a swing in the playground at Orwell Park. This Sonia was a world away from the battle-weary woman I'd seen two days before.

Careful not to show my eagerness, I continued to sift through the photos. If I could just see his photo it might trigger a memory; Jena's attacker might have a face.

One photo, creased down the middle like it had been folded for a long time, was of a young man holding a newborn baby, gazing down at the child in his arms so his hair was in his face.

I felt a hot probe run through my core. 'Is that your dad?'

Rob rested his chin on my shoulder. 'Yeah, that was his favourite photo. He used to keep it in his wallet . . .' He stopped, and rubbed his nose, looking embarrassed. I waited. Then he said, 'I might as well tell you, if you haven't heard already, that my dad has a bit of a reputation on the estate. He was in prison for a long time. I was just a kid.'

I scrutinised the photo. Was this the person I saw hunched over Jena's body seven weeks ago? The photo was over-exposed, and whoever took it had wanted to show the baby, not the father, so Douglas Campbell's face was only a side view, ruined by the orange-and-pink swirls of a badly taken picture. But if Jena could see it, it might be enough.

I placed my foot on top of Rob's leg, stroked his calf with it, and gave him a wicked grin, as if this was a game.

'What did he go to prison for?'

Even though I knew, I wondered if he would tell me.

'Some scam he got involved in. Fraud.' He pulled his leg away from mine, and a flash of anger showed in his eyes. I realised he was lying. He was lying because he was ashamed that his father was a rapist, and I didn't blame him for that. 'Uncle Andy said it was a good thing; he'd never liked my dad, and he said we were better off without him, but it messed everything up, him being sent down. Mum lost the business – they ran Our Plaice – but all the rumours, things people said; it got too difficult. Then she went really downhill, got mixed up in drugs. It was a bad time, for Mum and also for me. Later, I got mixed up in some bad things too.'

'You took drugs?'

He shook his head vehemently. 'Never. But I got a gun – an old one, de-commissioned; it couldn't have hurt anyone. I used it to threaten the local dealers, to stay away from my mum. Maybe it was the Campbell reputation, or maybe they just saw how angry I was, but it worked.' He smiled, grimly. 'She's clean now. Unfortunately, I got arrested after I got rid of the gun by throwing it from the Orwell Bridge. Like an idiot, I forgot about the CCTV camera that saw my every move. I'm on a Community Order; Greasy Monkeys is my Community Payback. I have to be squeaky clean for two years, or I'll end up inside.'

'But you saved your mum, so it was worth it. It was a brave thing you did.' I closed the gap between us, moving my body closer and touching his cheek. 'So you don't see your dad? He's not with your mum anymore?'

Rob shook his head. 'A long stretch in prison would kill any relationship. I was just ten when he got out, but he vowed never to return to Suffolk, so that was that. He went back to live in Scotland, and the only person who could have driven me was Andy, but there was no way he would do that. He hates my dad, and so we don't have anything to do with him.'

My blood was pulsing so loudly in my ears I felt sure Rob must hear it, because I knew something he didn't. Douglas had returned to Suffolk, to meet my sister. And he was currently remanded, charged with her attack, but he still might get away with it. I wondered if Sonia knew, and was keeping it from Rob.

I smoothed his hair, exposing the ragged scar on his forehead, and peered into his sky-grey eyes. Into giant pools of black within the grey, like the calm centre of a storm. He wrenched the photo from my hand and shoved it back into the carrier bag, then kicked the bag under the bed.

'Let's get out of here before my mum gets home.'

I was still thinking about that photo. We were heading out of the front door when I froze, a shard of clear thought shining brightly in my brain.

'I'll just go upstairs a sec, Rob. I need the loo.'

I didn't go to the loo. I went to Sonia's bedroom, where I carefully pulled the carrier bag from under the bed and stole the photo of Douglas Campbell.

CHAPTER 15

13 January

Birute arrives for her shift wrapped in her thin coat and a home-knitted scarf, carrying a battered Monopoly box. She starts to set it up at the table nearest the window in the recreation room, still wrapped against the elements, and ignoring Joelle, who puts a choking finger in her mouth, and Fiona, who pulls a grimace; both too cool for games. Stacey is engrossed in painting her nails, and she won't play either. But Pearl hovers nearby, her face lit with pleasure. Today, she wears a red woollen hat, shaped like a poppy, making her impossibly fairy-like.

'Come, Sam,' Birute says. 'Is not possible to play with only two. And you, Mina.'

Mina is in the corner of the room, hidden in the folds of the curtains. She shakes her head, and retreats farther from view.

Not able to disappoint Pearl, I join them at the table, and Birute chuckles as she places the car and the dog on the board. With the moon outside, and the cosy glow of the lights along the prom, we could be a family enjoying a game together. Something I used to enjoy with Jena, in the run-up to Christmas, playing Cluedo and drinking hot chocolate. Innocent times.

I pull my knees to my chest, and start to dish out the money.

'I had dog,' Birute says, looking at the silver charm of a terrier in her hand. 'In Lithuania. He look a bit like this.'

Pearl takes the dog from Birute. 'What colour was he?'

'Brown,' says Birute. 'But he had dark bit here.' She makes gestures around her eyes, like goggles, and we both laugh. 'But he was poorly dog, he had . . . what is it you say in English . . . mangy?'

'Mange?' I say. 'From fox ticks, isn't it?'

'Ya, something like this. So poorly, and all his hair, it come out when his skin hurt.' Birute looks at Pearl, at her poppy hat. They exchange a gaze that excludes me totally, and I feel a stab of jealousy. Birute has a new favourite.

'What happened to him?' asks Pearl.

Birute settles in her chair, legs curled under her, scarf to her chin, which means she is getting ready to tell us a long story.

'He was so sick, this dog. First we try shampoo, then we try medicine. My neighbours, they bring olive oil and coal tar. We try it all, and our dog, he such a good boy he let us. Finally, a farmer, he come to see my mother. He say he have special thing he use on his sheep. We dip him like a sheep, every week! It smell so bad,' she says, laughing, holding her nose and shaking her head, as if the smell is in her nose right now.

We play the game and, thanks to a silent conspiracy between Birute and myself, Pearl wins. It takes so long, I slip several red hotels on to her properties when she isn't looking, just to speed things up. When Pearl finally wipes us both out, Birute takes the silver dog and gives it to her.

'Your prize,' she says.

Pearl looks at the tiny silver dog in her hand, so touched she might cry. And then she does something I have not expected: she pulls the poppy hat from her head and lowers her face so Birute and I can both see her scalp.

There is a disc of skin in the middle, like a monk's. A smooth bald patch with no hair at all.

Birute touches Pearl's hand, the one with the dog in it.

'My dog, he got better. After we looked after him, he was beautiful and healthy.'

In the morning, I can't find words easily. I'm still thinking about Birute's mangy dog, about Pearl's bald scalp. How could I have missed that she pulled her hair? It was so obvious, all those bloody hats, that I curse my stupidity.

I'm still feeling guilty when the time comes for me to talk to Clive.

Because of the fits, Jena was back on Eastern Ward, and all the hope I'd had for her recovery felt flimsy. It was my mission to capture something with my camera – enough to help Jena remember – or, even better, to find some actual evidence like the missing raincoat, that got me out of bed that Tuesday morning. But I didn't eat; I was enjoying the hunger pangs, the swishiness in my brain. It made life bearable, because when my stomach growled, demanding nutrition, I wasn't thinking about Jena. I wasn't thinking about my exams either; I barely knew when the next one was, and revision seemed pointless.

There was only one thing that occupied me: hunting evidence. I needed, more than I needed food or a future, justice for Jena.

'It's not that bad. Best thing you can do is get up and get dressed.'

Jena whimpered, but Mum was having none of it. She yanked Jena from the bed, and led her to the sink, where she ran a basin of water. About to lift off her pyjama top, she paused, looking pointedly at Mark. Made redundant by Mum's nursing skills, he left.

Mum stripped my sister, washing her body with a flannel like she was an unruly child. She got her into some clean clothes, and combed the tangles from her hair.

I sat and watched, dumb. How was Jena ever going to say who'd attacked her, when she was in such a state? How was it ever going to get any better? But Mum was undefeated. 'Now, Jena, I want you to go into the day room and have a drink. No good moping about in here.'

In the day room, she found Jena the comfiest chair by the window, next to an old man nursing a toy train, who asked her if she had a ticket for that seat. Mum rummaged in her bag for her used train ticket, and handed it to him. His cragged face lit up, as if he was holding a winning lottery ticket. Then he nodded in a professional manner, folding it carefully and sliding it into his dressing-gown pocket. Mum went busily on with her work, grabbing a cushion from another chair, then started looking about for something to keep Jena entertained. It was as if she didn't see the rocking woman facing the wall, or that the man with the ticket now had one hand in his pants. Mum was good at ignoring things, focusing only on what she could fix.

She left the room, and when she came back she had a magazine she'd probably nicked from the staff room. She placed it on Jena's lap.

'Sam, you watch Jena. I'm going to find Dr Gregg to sort this out once and for all.'

CHAPTER 16

14 January

We're on a trip today. It's supposed to help rehabilitate us, and the fact that I've been invited is a sign the staff think I'm getting better, or at least that Clive has told them that. They've reduced the amount of calories I get through the tube, so I'm back on two normal meals each day, and I know this is all for the parole board and for my benefit, but it feels like I'm being rushed into recovery. I chew everything slowly, carefully, swallowing each tiny mouthful with sips of water. This, they say, is progress.

Leaving the unit is never quick, what with girls being told to put on scarves and hats, and there is an excitement in the air that could turn to hysteria because we don't know what's coming, whether it's good or bad. Last time was before Christmas; we went into Felixstowe to see the lights being turned on, but the trip went sour. Christmas has too many memories, and even Fiona and Joelle, who come from relatively happy homes, felt melancholy. Mina was saddest, though. She watched all the kids with their parents, and then she disappeared. We found her in the back of a toyshop, clutching a brown bear, weeping.

But this trip is to a small café on the sea road, named 'Simpsons' after Wallis, the American socialite responsible for Edward VIII's abdication. A good role model, wasn't she, the woman who pronounced 'a woman can never be too rich or too thin'.

Sian must have spoken with the manager because the sign is switched to CLOSED, but we walk right in, bringing a gust of cold air and the threat of snow.

'Okay, ladies,' she chirps, battling against our stony silence, the various expressions of anger and terror and mild panic. 'Look through the menu and order what you want. Let's say everyone must order within the next five minutes, okay?' She checks her watch.

Next to me, Pearl studies the menu, biting the cuffs of her baggy jumper, eyes wide with anxiety, her rainbow-striped bobble hat pulled firmly on her head. I touch her arm so she looks at me, and smile.

'It's all right,' I whisper, though I'm also tense. But I want Pearl's recovery more than I want my own. She, after all, is an innocent. I scan the list, and try to work out what has the least fat, the least calories. Nothing with bread. A jacket potato may be okay, but not with cheese. Stodgy winter food, not a salad on offer.

Sian looks at her watch.

'Three minutes left.'

If she didn't time us, we'd stare at the menu all day. The soup is homemade, and it doesn't say 'cream of'. It's my best option.

'Tomato soup for me, please,' I say, and Pearl looks relieved and nods in agreement, but Sian gives me a withering look.

'No you don't, Sam. If you don't choose something sensible, I'll pick for you. That goes for you too, Pearl.'

'Be my guest.' I lean back and put the menu on the table. Since when has soup not been sensible?

'Okay. Same as me, then. Ciabatta with bacon and mozzarella.' She's punishing me for not deciding quickly enough. Bitch.

I look away, out of the window, just as a woman is walking past. She pauses to re-adjust her shopping bags, all announcing various sales. She's pregnant, heavily so, and even on this brittle day her coat hangs open and she looks roasting. She catches a breath, looks up and sees me. I assume she's staring because of my bony narrow face, the tube strapped to my cheek, or maybe she knows who I am from the press coverage. But then she smiles. And it's a warm smile, understanding and wise.

She's about Jena's age, about thirty, and in that smile I can see her life. The nursery she's just decorated, the trips to the hospital for check-ups, a visit to see the maternity ward. Her husband, coming home with a takeaway because it's what she fancies, the baby moving inside her.

I smile back, and I don't feel envy. Once again, I feel the sensation of hope.

The feeling has faded by the time I take my usual chair across from Clive, later that day, in his office. My stomach is bloated from the ciabatta, and I know that if I let it, the guilt of eating will force me to purge. So I think about the pregnant woman who smiled, and block out Ana's voice, which tells me I'm pathetic and weak, a fat pig. That I don't deserve to survive.

'You look tense, Sam.'

'I'm trying to be calm,' I say, clutching hard to the feeling of hope. 'I want to be normal, or I did earlier. I had this feeling, like a wave lifted my thoughts up.'

I try not to think about the board, who will decide my fate, about Mum, and her funeral, fast approaching. Of her cold body, waiting in the morgue. A funeral and a judgement, both on the first day in February. How can I bear it?

'Close your eyes,' he says, and I do, even though my eyes move around the sockets and I can feel my eyelids twitching. 'Tell me when you felt that wave of hope before. Maybe as a child, or a younger teen? Go back, and locate a moment of peace or optimism in this painful story.'

Dad's shed comes to mind straight away. It was a place of darkness and quiet, somewhere I felt able to slow down.

'Tell me about it, Sam. Talk to me, about how it felt.'

When I arrived back home from the hospital I needed silence and peace badly, and went outside, meaning to go straight to the shed, but the sun made me pause. I lifted my face to the sun, breathing deeply, letting its rays warm me and take the edge from the coldness I'd started to feel in my fingertips. Then I noticed Mrs Read, in her jungle-like backyard, leaning over the fence.

'Good afternoon, Samantha,' she called, primly. 'Can I ask how Jena is faring?'

Mum would hate me talking to her, even though it seemed like she was just being kind. Both of my parents regarded Mrs Read as crazy, someone best avoided.

'She's doing better.' It was all I could think to say, though it wasn't true, not given she was back on Eastern Ward and having fits.

Mrs Read moved so she was pressed against the fence posts, but separated by Chloe's garden. Despite the twenty-foot distance, I could feel the intensity of her gaze.

'I'm glad. The ambulance was quick, I'll say that. And how are you? You're looking very thin. I hope you're eating?'

And then I saw that in her hand was a pencil. She was noting something down, in a small book she was holding. Mum and Dad were right, she was crazy. She was enjoying our pain; we were just entertainment to her.

'It's none of your business how I am, you old witch!'

I made a hasty exit towards the shed, losing myself inside its darkness to forget her prying eyes following me.

Dad was still there, in his shed. His computer was booted up, and he was peering at the screen. On the floor was overflowing rubbish from the waste bin, what looked like over-exposed pictures, images ruined by too much light.

'How is she?' was what he wanted to know, and I wondered again why he hadn't come with us. Why he only went on his own, in the evenings.

'A mess. They don't know what to do with her, so they're running tests. And she hates being on Eastern Ward.' I let the air fill with silence, as we both had nothing to add to this. 'Mrs Read's in her garden again. It looks like she's making notes on us.'

Dad narrowed his eyes, and frowned gravely. 'Don't even speak to that woman. She's a lunatic.'

I saw then what he was doing on his computer screen. He had scanned in my picture of Monica and was photoshopping it with light and shade, making her look even more glamorous.

'Why are you doing that?'

He stopped moving the mouse, looking surprised at my tone. When he spoke next, he sounded defensive. 'I just thought I could help her, seeing as she's a friend of yours. Send it through to Andy, see if he has any work for her with the entertainment team.'

I didn't understand why he was finding Monica work, when he should have come with us to the hospital. I dug my hands into my jeans and watched as he made the image an attachment; moments later, the computer told him it had been sent.

'Why hasn't Andy visited Jena?'

Dad stilled, his mouth working before the words came. 'We've been through this, Sam.'

'But what you said doesn't make sense. That he might not be able to cope with it. I mean, he's her boss; he's known Jena for years.' It was there, on the tip of my tongue: *Because Jena loves him.*

'Well, he's a busy man.' Dad looked at me, full in the face. 'And men aren't as strong as women. We can't cope with emotional things like you can.'

'That's a pathetic reason.'

'Yes,' he said. And I saw then that he might cry. 'It is.'

I was angry, with Andy, with Dad. He was right: men are pathetic. The only way Douglas Campbell would be brought to justice was if I did it myself. I needed more images for my Black Magic box, enough to push Jena into remembering, enough so she could make a positive identification. Even better, if I could find something tangible, like the raincoat. I needed him to be convicted.

I ignored Dad, didn't care what he thought, as I busied myself with my latest snaps, pegging the wet pictures on the clothes line, next to the other photos I'd taken that week: Andy outside of Sonia's house; Rob on the bench, eating a bag of chips; a queue outside Our Plaice. Pictures that should mean something to Jena, enough to kick-start her stalled memory.

Dad just stood there, watching, his watery eyes filled with emotion. 'Excellent work, Sam. You're such a good girl.'

He really had no idea what I was up to, trying to track down Jena's attacker. I thought he was weak and – as he admitted – pathetic, the way he was avoiding what was happening with Jena.

'I don't want you messing with any of my photos again.' I wondered how it had happened, that since the attack I'd stopped respecting Dad. I'd never have spoken to him this way before; he was always distant from me and preoccupied with Jena. I'd thought that what I wanted was what she had – that close father–daughter bond – but now that it was possible, I was rejecting it.

'Of course,' he replied, brokenly.

Dad sat heavily on the only seat in the room: a low, small stool, under the red glow. He looked like a gnome on a toad-stool, with his white beard and his funny bushy brows.

'Where are your own pictures, Dad?'

He looked down at the floor, where balls of papers had gathered, and I realised he was destroying his images.

'I got rid of them. I'm not as good a photographer as you, Sam.' He looked up and grimaced. 'I've decided to stop all of it, to stay away from the dark room. I'm no good.'

Of my parents, he was the quiet one, the harder to read. It was best just to leave him be, to destroy his pictures and abandon his hobby. Dad simply couldn't handle any more pain.

'It'll be okay, Dad.' My voice was too loud in the space, hollow as the words. I knew I couldn't comfort him, not the way Mum could.

'I hope so, Sam. We're all trying our best.' He cleared his throat, and then he opened his arms. 'I could use a hug.'

I went to him, and felt how tightly he gripped me, as if afraid to lose me. His lips muffled against my hair, touching my ear.

'How about a kiss for your old man?'

I kissed his cheek, then laid my head on his shoulder, relaxing into the hug. I looked at my pictures, hanging above us: my secret mission.

When I finally pulled away, his eyes looked so sad, so clouded with conflict, that I was worried he'd cry again. Before the attack, he never showed much of any emotion. He was always self-contained in a way Mum never was. The depth of his feelings was something I could only sense, as it was all unspoken, though he'd always doted on Jena. It was as if they were in a secret club, the way they'd disappear into this dark room. On my sixteenth birthday, his gift, the camera, had been an invite to join. But fate had robbed me of any pleasure I might have felt in this.

'My beautiful girl,' he moaned, tears very near the surface. 'Oh Jena.'

'Dad . . .' I went to comfort him, but didn't know how. I tried to hug him again, but this time he pushed me away, his palms slamming painfully against my chest, as if suddenly realising that I wasn't Jena.

It hurt that he didn't love me like he loved her.

CHAPTER 17

14 January

Pearl comes to my room after dinner, this time wearing an orange baseball cap. She perches on the end of my bed, writing on her forearms with a black biro, and talks about the voice in her head that belongs to her best friend, Ana.

I have that friend too. I know how she talks, the secrets she whispers: *Don't eat that . . . you're doing really well . . . ignore the doctors . . . they know nothing.*

Pearl is so translucent her skeleton is on show. Her skin is like webbing, strands of her hair fall from her head every time she runs a finger through it, and her breath seems impossibly light. She leaves her hat off now, when we are alone together, and the tender skin on her crown glows like a halo. Sometimes she pulls just one hair and runs it through her teeth, before I gently remind her not to. She told me she pulls hair from her legs and arms, which explains why she looks pre-pubescent – that it feels like a release, the plop of the hair coming out. To me, it sounds like pain she is inflicting on herself, just a variation of the pain of starvation that each one of us is punishing ourselves with.

She looks admiringly at my wrists, narrow enough for her to see the clear outline of bone.

'You're so strong, Sam. You've resisted food.'

'It's not strength. It's sickness.'

Pearl considers her own forearms, which are covered by silvery threads of old scars. She starts to draw over them with curly writing. 'Me, being younger. Newer. I see you as . . . thinspiration. Like, a role model. I mean, you have a tube. You only ate half that ciabatta. I saw you hiding the rest, behind the curtain at the window. Sian didn't notice, but I did.'

Pearl's hero-worshipping horrifies me. Inspirational, to be tubed?

'Don't tell me that, Pearl. I can't bear the responsibility.'

She gazes at me with her large, blank eyes. On her arm she has stencilled I HATE ME.

CHAPTER 18

15 January

Clive is looking smarter when we meet next, though only a tad. He's had a haircut, though it looks like it was done in the kitchen by his wife, and his beard is neater. He sees me noticing.

'Getting spruced up, for when the officials come up for the meeting. I've written up most of our sessions, but I'll leave the conclusion until as late as possible. They've started hassling me; they want to distribute reports so everyone has time to consider before 1 February. But I told them they can't have it yet.'

A pop inside, like a balloon meeting a pin. A shrivelled-up sensation of hope being lost. 'What will happen to me, Clive?'

Despite the minor makeover, he is looking tired. I see that my story distracts him, and he's trying to be positive, but really he's worried about the outcome. He has a deadline, a report to finish, and I'm not doing as well as he'd like.

'There will be three of us: myself and two members sent by the Mental Health Tribunal, who will all have read previous reports on you. They will all know what you've done. To be released, Sam, it has to be unanimous. It has to be deemed that your mental illness, your eating disorder, has been managed, and that you pose no further risk to anyone. We need to agree that you won't commit another crime.'

He shifts in his seat. Here is the nub of it; he hasn't asked me about this yet. We haven't reached that point in the story.

'Before the judgement, you will be invited to speak.'

Invited to speak. What a euphemism; as if there is a choice. As if I would be speaking now, if I could stay silent. I remind myself that Clive is on my side, so I will talk and help him conclude his report.

I have to at least try to help myself.

That night, sleep was elusive; my body's gnawing demands for food kept me focused on my plan. I didn't want to be comfortable, well nourished, because that was when the real terror would come. Clinging to pieces of information in my hazy state, having to concentrate, stopped me grieving for the big sister who was lost to me. At around four, the sun curled its fingers around the curtains and I knew there was no point in trying to sleep anymore. Sleep didn't help either, but plunged me into bad dreams. The only answer was action. It was Wednesday 15 June and I had an exam that morning, but I knew where I needed to be more.

My talk with Dad in the shed had made some things clearer for me.

Firstly, none of the adults around me seemed to want to find Jena's attacker, and so it was down to me. Secondly, Andy's failure to visit didn't make sense, and I needed to face him. I also needed to keep Rob, and Sonia, in my sights, given their link to Douglas. It had only been four days, but things were moving fast with Rob, and I needed to keep it that way. Time was running out, with Douglas's bail hearing approaching.

I should have been taking my seat in the school hall, pencil sharpened, bottle of water on the desk, but instead I rapped on the door of 5 The Terraces, and waited.

'Hi, babe.' Rob opened the door, fiery hair flopping over his eyes, which lit up at the sight of me. He really liked me, I could see that, and any questions he might have had about my sudden interest were being pushed aside. Lucky me. 'Come in.'

His face was pink with excitement as he hopped aside to let me enter, pushing the Leica gently into my chest.

'Why d'you always wear this?'

I had the brief worry that he was on to me, but there was only curiosity on his face. 'It was a gift on my sixteenth birthday. From my dad.'

'Ah yeah. I remember now; you were always into art. I saw some of your pictures on the corridor at school.'

He'd been noticing me, even when I was oblivious to it. That day at the shops, he'd said, *I know who you are*, and I realised that whilst I'd been studying and drawing and wandering blindly around my world, Rob had watched from the sidelines. Now I was noticing him right back.

There was a pile of stuff blocking the hallway: a sports bag with a bulging zip; plastic bags; a guitar.

'I didn't know you played the guitar.'

'Badly.' He looked down at the pile. 'That's my life. Doesn't look much, does it?'

Upstairs, a woman was singing, a pop song, too high and out of tune. Then she yelled, 'Keri! Bad dog! Stop pissing on the floor.'

She staggered down the stairs, holding a stocky white puppy at arm's length, shouting, 'Open the door, open the door!' Rob made for the front door, squeezing past me, kicking his guitar in the process, but Sonia yelled, 'The back door! For fuck's sake . . .'

I heard the door open, and then slam closed. 'Stay out there till you're house-trained, you little bitch!'

Then she was right there, so close I could smell the booze.

The years since her photo appeared in the newspaper had not been kind to Sonia. She had a gappy mouth and dead eyes, like her face batteries had only half-charged. A homely blonde with brown roots, her face sunken. The tattoo on her neck was an unlikely tiger, resting on the ridge of her collarbone, its mouth open as if to swallow her Adam's apple. Her cheeks were red with broken veins, sure signs that this morning's tipple was a regular habit.

'You for the off then, love?'

Her lower lip quivered and she leaned into Rob, hugging him until the *bark, bark, bark* from outside demanded her attention.

'Christ's sake. It's worse than having a baby.' Stepping back on to Rob's guitar, she steadied herself against me.

'Sorry, sweetheart.'

'S'all right,' I muttered.

Finally turning, she focused on me. I could see her brain was ravaged with drink and maybe drugs; even her eyelashes looked stunted. Her skin was a shade of yellow, and the only lively thing was the twitching nerve under her right eye. She was studying me, hard, trying to place me.

'Who are you then? New girlfriend?'

'Mum!' Rob's ears turned red. She gave him an affectionate poke in the ribs.

As she turned to me again, her mouth froze so her broken-toothed smile looked like a grimace.

'I know you.'

My heart jumped; my cover was blown. She leaned towards me, and under the booze I smelt the fake herbal tang of tea lights, the stench of joss sticks.

'You're the Hoolihan kid.'

'Sam,' I said, trying not to show how scared she made me feel. Like she knew exactly why I was there, that I was using her son to gather evidence against his dad. But then her clarity evaporated, her eyes watered and she blinked furiously, reaching for her son.

'Please don't leave me, Rob.'

'It's not like I'm moving miles away.'

She wiped a finger under her eye where the purple eyeliner was running, a stain like a bruise on her skin. Rob shrugged on his jacket and endured it whilst she cupped his face with her hand.

'I've never been on my own before. Even when your dad left, Andy would come round. And I always had you.'

'You've got the puppy.' For a moment, mother and son shared a grin, and I could see warm affection pass between them, until she belched and put her hand over her mouth in mock horror. Rob's face darkened and he picked up his bags. I understood why he needed to leave: he couldn't rescue Sonia anymore; he had to get on with his own life.

Sonia folded her arms, plumping up her small breasts, her frown lines deepening. The tiger tattooed on her neck seemed to be eating her throat.

'Come and give your old mum a hug. Stay here with me.'

Rob was sour with his mum now, and the hug was stiff. I pretended to be interested in my camera, but could feel Sonia assessing me over her son's shoulders, trying to work out why I was in her house, but too tipsy to understand.

'I heard about Jena on the news. The bitch had it coming.'

I felt like she'd thrown icy water over me, and my skin shrank on my bones at the shock of it.

'Don't call my sister that.'

'Oh yeah, who's gonna stop me?' Booze or drugs were working through her system, and Sonia had flipped quickly into her anger. She ground her teeth together. 'Always thought she was a cut above, did Jena. Walking around this estate like her shit didn't stink.'

'You know she was left for dead?' I asked, with quiet venom. 'She was in a coma for four days, and even though she came round seven weeks ago she's still having seizures. She might be brain-damaged forever.'

Sonia looked down at herself, swaying slightly as she picked a bit of something from her cleavage, then said with steely irony, 'Maybe she pissed off the wrong person this time.'

Anger came out as a demand. 'What's that supposed to mean?'

Sonia was so close I could smell the sweet, sickly stench of liquor on her breath, and see her pink nostrils flaring. 'It means she's a lying little bitch and she had it coming to her.'

Rob grabbed my hand. 'Let's go, Sam. My mum's not worth talking to when she's pissed.'

Sonia grabbed his hand between hers. 'You shouldn't trust this girl, Rob. Her family are no good.'

'Fuck's sake, Mum, what's with you today?' He pulled his hand free. 'Is it just booze, or have you been using again?'

'No, son. I'm straight, I swear.' But her now-free hand covered her mouth and nose as if to hide any traces of powder that might remain there.

'Like hell. You promised me, Mum!' In that moment, he seemed to grow a size. His voice had a new sureness to it. 'It's good I'm moving out. We both need some space. You need to call your sponsor.'

'Rob, no, don't say that. I'm just looking out for my boy.'

'But I'm not your little boy anymore, am I? I haven't been that for a long time. Come on, Sam.'

We quickly collected Rob's bags, and made our way out the door and down the path. All the time I could feel Sonia watching, her eyes like bullets boring into me.

CHAPTER 19

16 January

'I don't want to be a role model to any of the girls here. I'm not a good example for anyone.'

Clive listens without response. The clock ticks on the wall and the wind gathers pace outside, the sea crashing into the shingle, ripples of petty chaos. Low-hanging white clouds warn of snow.

I'm thinking about Pearl, though I don't tell him this. She's so young, just a kid, and I want her to get better. But to talk about her, in this session, would be a betrayal. We are all liars here; we all keep secrets.

'It's normal, on an eating-disorder unit, that other girls will see those who are most underweight as being more successful. You know that, Sam. Adoration of this type is part of the mental imbalance. You aren't responsible.'

I feel responsible, though, for Pearl at least. My heart aches for her, so young and so frail, so skilled at starving, and yet fooling the staff into thinking she's doing well. Anorexics lie; everyone knows that. It isn't up to me to tell him this; he knows it already. I can help her more if I gain her trust, I understand her better than the staff ever could. I decide to stay silent about my concerns, for now.

'What about your own recovery, Sam? Do you want to get better?' He touches the lid of the Black Magic box, and I feel as uneasy as if he were touching me. 'Now you're revisiting the past, it could help with how things ended.'

How things ended. I think about Mum then. 'Where is she now? Before she's buried, I mean. Where does she . . . wait?'

'She'll be kept cool, and they'll have fixed her hair, her make-up. Would you like me to arrange a half-day release for you to see the body?'

I shake my head vigorously. 'No way.'

'Would you like me to arrange for you to go to the funeral?'

Jena will be there. Dad too, possibly. Again, I shake my head. 'I can't. The board meeting is the same day.'

'I've said I can arrange to have the time moved. I wouldn't stop you seeing your mother buried, Sam; that would be a breach of your human rights.'

'What about her human rights? What makes you think she'd want me at her funeral? I gave up on deserving rights eighteen months ago.'

His gaze drops to the floor. It interests me that even Clive can't talk about what happened, what I'm guilty of. Instead he says, 'Is this why you refuse any visits? Because you don't think you deserve them?'

Words are bubbling up, and I can't stop them or control my thinking. I don't even know what I really do think until the words escape me.

'I don't want to see anyone; I don't deserve to get better. To eat normally, live normally. Have all the things normal people have. And if I do this, Clive – if I talk aloud about what I did – it could destroy me.'

I look down at my thin body; my hands are bunched in my lap like scrawny birds.

'It's destroying you already, Sam. Anorexia is eating you away, and that's because of your need to control everything, even in the way you blame yourself. You need to let go, go back to that time when things were beyond your control. And not your fault.'

'But I'm scared.'

Clive considers me frankly. 'If you don't continue with this story, you'll never be truly free. Even if the board grant you your liberty, you'll still be a prisoner.'

So I prepare to talk, to purge myself. I pick up where we left off, hoping I'll feel clean after.

Rob was shaken by the scene with his mum; he was walking fast, breathing heavy. It wasn't the time to talk about it, not right then, but I knew I wouldn't get away with it so easily once he'd calmed down. He'd want to know everything.

Rob's new home was a red-brick tower at the grotty end of Ipswich docks. Most of the windows were wide open; several had people leaning out smoking, and carrier bags full of lager cans hanging from the snib. On the wall beside the entrance a gold plaque announced that local superstar Ruthie Henshall opened it. The plaque was just two months old but already marked with graffiti, and no doubt Ruthie had long since forgotten this dump. Still, Rob's mood had switched, and he was grinning like he'd rocked up at The Ritz.

The entrance was a large hallway with posters along the walls and a staircase directly ahead. To the right was the glass window of an open-plan office, where a skinhead in his thirties sat at a desk in front of a pile of paperwork.

'There's Mac.'

Rob banged on the glass and Mac looked up; he put down his pen, and a moment later he joined us in the hallway, extending a tattooed hand, a key dangling from his long, bony fingers.

'This is it, mate. The key to your very own pad.' Mac had a tattooed tear, faded blue like old china, next to his left eye. It narrowed to a comma when he smiled. 'Hello, love. Here, let me take those.'

He relieved me of the carrier bags, but Rob wasn't hanging about. He bounded up the stairs.

'Come up, Sam, see my room.'

'Whoa, Rob!' Mac called after him. 'You need to sign the contract first.'

Rob stopped on the landing. 'Sorry.'

'The previous resident only left this afternoon, but Lance gave it a good clean for you.'

'Sweet.' He came back down, slowly at first, but then regaining his spaniel energy. Because he was free, he now had his own space, and I envied him.

'Don't go taking advantage,' Mac warned Rob. 'Lance isn't here to skivvy after you. Now, give me a few minutes to get the paperwork ready and I'll be right with you.'

Lance was busy getting the hoover into a cupboard that was clearly too small, vacant eyes roaming, his too-loud laugh reverberating. He noticed me and waved, as if my being there was the most natural thing in the world. He must have been so used to seeing people he knew, being such a character in Ipswich and selling the *Big Issue* on the Cornhill all those years, but it surprised me.

'I didn't know he worked here,' I said.

'Yes, it's a community placement. He lives in a flat, at Westerfield Hospital,' Mac said, not knowing about my own link to the place. But Rob watched me, for my reaction. Just like his mum, he knew exactly where my sister was and what had happened to her.

Rob's room was nothing to write home about. A single bed (no headboard), a pine chest of drawers (ring marks on top), a stained mattress naked to the world, and a sink in the corner. The floor was clean, though, thanks to Lance.

'No towels, I'm afraid,' said Mac, helping Rob in with the final bag. 'Did you bring any?'

'No. We left in a bit of a hurry, so I forgot my duvet as well.'

'Should we go back to your mum's to get it?' I asked, though my stomach churned just thinking about seeing Sonia again. Luckily, Rob felt likewise.

'She needs time to come down from whatever shit she's on. I'm sorry, Sam. She's not always like that. That junk she takes makes her aggressive. She should never have said that thing, about your sister. Not when she's so sick . . .'

I wondered how often he'd seen it on the news, about the unsolved attack on our estate. But the police hadn't released the name of the man they were questioning. Only I knew that information.

Mac disappeared, and we unloaded Rob's possessions: his iPod, two pairs of jeans, a couple of sweaters and T-shirts, an alarm clock in the shape of a football, a Swiss army knife that looked junked, a canvas roll of car tools and a plastic model of a car with *007* printed on the door. And a red-and-yellow Airfix plane, the one that had been in Sonia's plastic bag with the photos.

All his worldly goods.

Rob put his clothes away in the chest of drawers, his iPod on top. The car and plane were placed on the windowsill. Ten minutes and he was done. The room still looked bare.

'Here you go, son.' Mac was back, a bundle in his arms. On to the bed he spilt a duvet, still in its plastic wrapping, a cover and a clean towel. 'From the staff cupboard. I don't think anyone'll miss them.'

'Thanks, Mac,' Rob said quietly.

'I reckon a few posters on the wall and you'll make this place look like home.' He patted Rob's shoulder, then noticed the models on the window. 'Aston Martin, of course. Nice. What's with the plane?'

'It's Japanese.'

Mac turned it in his hands. 'Lots of work went into this. You do it?'

'My dad.'

I stilled, willing him to continue. Whatever he had to say about Douglas Campbell, I was desperate to hear.

'They always say the Japs are a cruel race,' said Mac, still looking at the plane. 'But I reckon that's just prejudice. Say something often enough, people think it's true. But what happens if it's a lie and people just go on believing it?'

CHAPTER 20

17 January

Most people's problems stem from their family, but no one wants to know about that. It's in bad taste, isn't it, blaming our parents? So we stay silent, mostly, but stay away. Visit at Christmas and leave it at that. But us starving girls, friends of Ana, we don't stay silent. Not completely. We shout with our bodies.

I've seen Joelle go home plumped, come back emaciated.

I've seen Mina starve herself after any talk of a home visit, or any phone call from her father.

I've heard Manda say to Sian that it makes no sense sending us back to the source of the illness, that it causes relapse. She runs fortnightly family therapy sessions, here on the unit, but no one likes it, least of all the families. The mums and dads and siblings think the problem is the anorexic but, as Stacey once said, 'I might starve myself, but my whole family are fucking sick.'

My family: they couldn't come in for family therapy. Not possible. So it's just me and my illness. My Black Magic box of photos. The only family interaction I have is in my head, the only voice is mine talking to Clive, as the sky becomes black and the room darkens and the past becomes my present.

I can remember it now, though for the past eighteen months I preferred to forget, how good it was being with Rob, despite how determined I was to feel nothing for him. We instinctively knew we were alike in some way. I needed things to move quickly, and we were soon lovers, but it ran deeper than that; Rob understood me, and I felt the same about him. We were both doing the best we could in a world that hadn't dealt us the best hand.

Clive says he's proud of me, opening up like this. Down to the flesh and bone. But this isn't just about me, and I'm not the only one with a sad story.

I was trying to get Rob to talk some more about Douglas. Looking at the plane on the window ledge, and noticing one of its wings was broken, I said, 'Why don't you fix this?'

'It's a reminder,' he said.

He was going to stay silent, but I couldn't let him, not when I knew he was going to tell me about Douglas. I pushed him, until he told me.

'I wasn't very old; I'd only just started nursery, so you'd think I wouldn't remember. But I do.

'I know that it was just before Dad went away, before he was sent to prison, and there was lots of shouting in the house. I've heard since, from Uncle Andy mainly, that Our Plaice wasn't doing so well; business had been affected, and they'd had to close so they could both attend the trial. Dad had this aeroplane collection, parked along the window ledge in his bedroom, all placed just so. When he was building one, I'd sit next to him on the lounge floor, watching. It's one of the few strong memories I have of him.

'He'd have the kit on a tray in front of him, pots of paint and glue lined up. I mean, Mum said he never so much as put an empty beer can in the bin, wouldn't pick up a dirty sock from the floor, but he would arrange his aeroplane stuff like a surgeon preparing for an operation.'

He laughed at the memory, and I tried to make this piece of information fit with what I already knew about Douglas. A rapist with a dorky hobby.

'That was his special plane,' Rob said, warming to his subject, and reaching to take the broken plane from me. 'He'd bend over with a tiny paintbrush between his fingers, making the wings yellow and later adding red circles. Whole days he'd waste, when he wasn't working, hunched over that blasted plane. It was weird, y'know, how those hands that usually just tossed fish into batter or unhooked beer cans could build a plane so slowly and carefully.'

Rob handed the plane back to me, and I studied the carefully painted markings.

'It's from the war,' said Rob. 'One of the Jap planes. Dad told me once, years later in one of his rare letters from prison, that they have the right idea when it comes to fighting. Just dive straight for the target.' He took the plane from me and curved it through the air, diving it down as if to crash it on the table. 'Kamikaze. Means "divine wind". Can't stop someone with nothing to lose, that's what he said. I wasn't allowed to touch the planes. I tried once and had me arm twisted into a Chinese burn.'

Rob fell silent, lost in a painful memory. I realised that he was about to tell me something important. His voice was low and broken when he spoke again.

'I was just a little kid, what did I know? I thought maybe Mum had touched the planes, he was so livid.'

I put the plane down and moved next to him, taking his hand in mine, willing him to trust me. He hesitated, then in a low voice continued.

'I was upstairs in bed, lying in the dark. Downstairs, there was yelling. I always got this heavy feeling in my tummy when they rowed, but that night was much worse. I crept out to sit at the top of the stairs, where it was light, and heard Dad shouting. It was hard to make out the words, but I got that Mum was going over something she'd heard said about him.

'I saw my father push Mum into the hallway, forcing her against the wall. She fought back, screamed something about there being no smoke without fire, smashed her fist into his face.

'She looked up, saw me standing at the top of the stairs. She wanted me to go back into my bedroom, and I could see she was strung out on booze. I ran to the big bedroom, got a stool, and reached for the windowsill. The neat runway of Airfix planes. The red-and-yellow plane was still drying in its special place under the window.

'I stood at the top of the stairs and threw myself down like a kamikaze pilot, along with the plane, letting it fly through the air and crash against the head of my parents. But one of them caught it, mid-air, and turned the plane back to me, crashing it into my head. I still don't know which of them it was. They both have mean tempers and they like their drink.'

I pushed Rob's hair back, touching the scar on his forehead where the plastic wing must have cut into his skin. Then I kissed the place where the cut had been, as if to stop the pain that still remained.

'Yeah,' he said. 'And the only other thing I can tell you about my dad was that just after that he got sentenced to eight years in prison and left our lives for good.'

I felt I could hear our heartbeats, the same rhythm.

'I know why your dad went to prison, Rob. I know he raped a girl.'

He breathed out, a quick pant, his gaze holding me tight. 'Mum says he was set up. But Uncle Andy says he's guilty, and my dad was always bad news.'

I understood the confusion he felt over his father. A man he barely knew.

'Rob, there's something I want to tell you, about your dad,' I whispered, as if that would soften the blow. I placed my hand on his, to show him I was on his side. 'He's in prison, right now, on remand. They think it was him who attacked my sister on 25 April.'

Rob pushed me away, as if he could push away the truth. He tried to get up, but I pulled him back. He sat down on the bed, the weight of being his father's son heavy on his back. 'That cunt.'

It was a relief to me, to know he wouldn't defend his dad. I couldn't have handled that.

Finally, he asked, 'How do you know?'

'The police file. I'm sorry, Rob. It doesn't change how I feel about you.'

It was true. He was a victim in this, as much as me. Neither of us were responsible for the people around us.

He let me hold him, and though he was still tense, I tried to soothe him. 'It's okay, Rob. Whatever your dad has done, it has nothing to do with you. Or how I feel.'

We kissed, so close his eyelashes caught my cheeks, and then we moved together, on the bed. Clothes were a barrier; they had to go. We needed to be one, because we alone understood. The sex was quick but intense, leaving us in a tight tangle of sweaty limbs.

'I think I love you, Sam. I know it's soon to say it.'

'I love you too.' I kissed him again, my taste in his mouth, and felt the truth of it. We were alike, he and I. We understood each other because we were both damaged goods.

'I'm so sorry, Sam. If he was the one who hurt your sister, then he deserves everything he gets.'

'Then will you help me? If you love me, like you say. Please help me.'

CHAPTER 21

18 January

I miss my mother. Two weeks today is her funeral, and then she'll be gone for good, but I still can't bring myself to let her go. I try not to think about her because it hurts too much, but I can't stop the small things seeping through, like how she was always there for me, making the house warm with the smell of fried food, wafting the smoke from her cigarette out of her face.

I close my eyes and she's there, in our kitchen with her back to me, bum wiggling as she cuts fat chips over a muddy sink full of spuds, ciggie hanging from her mouth, humming between smokes. Hearing me and turning, taking a final drag and grinding the butt out on a saucer.

Smiling, warm and loving.

This is what you want, isn't it, Clive? For me to just talk, let the words flow. Memories pushing against each other as they rise up to the surface.

I barged through the back door to find Mum at the sink, peeling potatoes with manic zeal.

'There you are, Samantha! Mobile switched off again. I've been trying to reach you.'

'Why?' Warily, fearing Jena had had another fit. I carefully eased my rucksack down under the kitchen table.

'That fool Gregg has decided to return your sister to her room on Minsmere Unit.' She curled her hands around the rim of the sink and stared at the window, then went back to her paring knife.

'But that's great, Mum.' Relief filled me like a flurry of blown bubbles in my chest.

'I went to see him today, refused to leave his office until he saw sense. But he was adamant; he says she's stabilised enough and that they need the bed for other patients, so he's moving her back first thing tomorrow.' Mum stopped peeling the spuds and started to cut the round white flesh into chunky fingers. 'Cat got your tongue?'

'Jena will be happy to be out of Eastern Ward,' I said lamely.

'At least in that madhouse the patients are safely locked in. I don't like how slack they are with security at Minsmere, all those patio doors that open on to the courtyard. Anyone could just walk in!' Mum winced like a pain had bothered her, and turned back to her potatoes, no longer humming as she cut them into wedges.

I set the table, poured three glasses of juice and buttered the bread. Dad came in from the shed, where he'd been all day, and put his hands on my shoulders.

'When's your next exam, love?'

I had to think hard, it seemed so irrelevant. 'Tomorrow afternoon. English Literature.' I'd already missed the Language paper. The time when I worried about such things was a lifetime ago.

Mum dropped the cut chips into a pan of oil. The smell made my stomach growl in anticipation. It still didn't understand that I was in charge.

'The first smart one in the family,' he said, and surprised me by kissing my cheek.

I felt, in that moment, that it could be like this, with Jena gone. I could be his new favourite. All the years I'd envied Jena, her close bond with him, and now it could have been mine for the taking, only I was set on a different course. One that would drive us farther apart than ever.

'You need to eat more, Sam,' Mum said, frowning. She liked to see me eat, but I wasn't going to give in just to please her. I nibbled the edges of a chip and it felt like a weakness. The chips were fluffy in the middle. Perfect. But the hot potato in my mouth, going down to my stomach, made me feel weak, like I'd lost something precious, given away some of my power. I was frightened I'd give in totally and wolf the lot.

Mum and Dad both chewed in a business-like way as I pushed the food around my plate, fighting my body's demands. Then Mum swallowed hard, and said, 'Penny called. She's thinking it's more likely their suspect is going to be released, so she's lining up that press conference for exactly a week later, on Monday 27 June. She says it can always be cancelled if it's not needed.'

Dad dropped his fork; it clattered on his plate. 'It's exploitation. They want people to see Jena, how sick she is.'

He put his head in his hands, and Mum reached to touch him, offering him support. Although I also found the thought of Jena talking to a room full of journalists horrible, everyone seeing how damaged she was, I agreed with Penny. Whatever it took, to get more information, for justice.

'Tell her we won't do it,' he said. 'All those journalists, prying into our private business. And what if there are questions?'

They looked at each other; my dad had a desperate look on his face, and I wanted to scream at how pathetic he was, but Mum's face was alive with sympathy and fierce protectiveness. In her concern for Dad, she'd forgotten about Jena.

She took his hand tightly in hers and looked at him for a long moment. He was the quiet one; Mum spoke for him a lot of the time, but when push came to shove we all knew where the real power lay. She touched her lip like she always did when she needed a fag.

'Shouldn't we do what the police tell us?' she asked.

Finally, he said, 'You're right, Kath. We have no choice.'

I dipped a cold chip into a smear of yellow yolk with no intention of eating it, just to do something in the awful silence that followed.

'Penny wouldn't put us through it without good reason,' I said. 'And she needs more evidence, if Douglas Campbell gets released.'

The energy in the room became electric. 'Don't say that name in this house!' Mum snapped.

Dad's head jerked up. 'That bastard.'

'Why? What do you know about him, Dad?'

Dad looked down at the table. His shoulders heaved.

'That's enough, both of you!' Mum started to clear the plates away. 'The important thing is that we still have each other. That we keep strong as a family.'

She battered the table with a dishcloth, scattering crumbs.

'You know something about him, Dad. What is it?'

He rubbed his thumb over his teeth. 'Don't go digging into things that will hurt you, Sam.'

'What can hurt me any more than what's already happened?'

Mum was washing the cutlery vigorously. 'Enough! We need to get on with our lives. What's done is done.'

A tear escaped from the corner of her eye, and she lifted a hand from the steaming water to wipe it away with her wrist, still holding the knife she was washing, the blade dangerously close to her face.

'Mum, be careful!'

I understood why she didn't want me to talk to anyone about the attack: it was just too painful. Her panic attacks were frequent, and I knew the image of Jena's unconscious body must always be there, hanging over her, just as Jena's faceless attacker was never far from my thoughts.

'I want to tell you both something. I'm hanging out with this boy, called Rob. He was here once, a long time ago, on Halloween. And his mother said some things about Jena.'

'What things?' Dad said.

I took a breath of courage. 'She said Jena's a little liar. She called her a bitch.'

Mum whipped round to face me fast, still holding a soapy mug.

Dad said, quietly, 'How dare you repeat that in this house!'

I felt angry then, because I could see they were holding something back; they'd lived on this estate for thirty years.

'Rob's father is Douglas Campbell. The rapist.'

The mug smashed on the linoleum tiles, breaking into three pieces.

Mum crouched down next to the broken china, collecting it in her shaking hands.

'Let me do that, Kath,' said Dad, moving towards her.

But she pushed him away, and as she did so a shard cut her hand, causing a streak of blood to appear between the heart and lifeline on her palm. 'Look what you've done now! Why do you always have to ruin everything?'

As I watched my parents, hunched on the floor over the broken mug, their pain and hurt spilling out as anger, the feeling of guilt that I'd caused this was overwhelming. It made me feel sick, and I knew I'd soon vomit what little food I had eaten.

But they were keeping something from me; I knew it. Bright blood was dropping on to the plastic flooring, splashing into patterns like butterfly wings.

'I think you should put that cut under the tap, before it gets worse,' Dad said to Mum.

Sweat beaded on her lip. Her eyes were losing focus, and I could see a panic attack looming.

'Mum, you need to take your atenolol.'

'You know nothing about what I need, girl. You're just a child.'

She wiped her hands on a tea towel and threw it viciously at Dad, then picked up her fags and lighter, and went outside, banging the door behind her. Within a few seconds, I could see gusts of smoke rising past the window.

Her anti-anxiety tablets were in the cupboard with the tea and sugar. I took two from the packet and poured a glass of water. Outside in the overbearing heat, Mum was leaning against the wall, lighting a fresh fag, but struggling to stay upright. Her free hand was against her stomach, a sign that she felt sick.

'Here, take these.'

Her hand shook as she picked up the tablets with her fingers, slipping them into her mouth.

'What is it, Mum?'

She swallowed the tablets with a gulp of water, handing me back the glass.

'So, Rob Nicholls is your friend?'

I hesitated, because it seemed such a small word, *friend*, inadequate for what I felt for him. 'Yes. Do you remember him coming here, one Halloween? How his mum came and dragged him away like he'd done something wrong by being here.'

Mum swayed towards me, unsteady, the tablets not yet taking the edge off her panic, the hot end of her fag in my face, backing me to the wall.

'Don't make me out to be an idiot, Sam. This is because of that newspaper article you found on the internet, isn't it?'

I had to explain, to make her understand. 'Douglas Campbell was seen hanging around near Jena's flat the evening she was attacked. I need to know why he would want to hurt her.'

Mum's eyes watered from the heat of her cigarette, the wall hard against her spine. 'Oh God . . .'

I held her upright. The drug would kick in soon, hopefully before the panic won. Her face was twisted.

'Don't you get it, Sam? His rape conviction: it was back when Jena was thirteen.'

'So?'

She looked at me, straight in the eye, as if suddenly making a decision.

'So, how old did the article say his victim was?'

She waited while I understood. I caught my breath, more shocked than I deserved to be. When she saw I did understand, she said, 'Jena was very brave, to speak out.'

Douglas Campbell raped my sister. 'Does Penny know?'

'Of course. It's why he was remanded, why he was questioned in the first place. We wanted to protect you from that, Sam; it's why we spoke outside the room last Monday. And now Penny's saying they haven't got enough evidence, that he'll be freed, and we have to do this awful press conference . . .'

She started to weep.

'Mum, you're hyperventilating.'

She leaned against me, her weight in my arms, dry retching again, forgetting about the tip of her fag close to my cheek. In a violent retch she vomited potatoes and ketchup on to the overgrown flowerbed, her hand thrusting forward and her cigarette catching my face.

'Mum! You're burning me!'

I pushed her away, but the solid brick behind me blocked my escape. Falling back, she saw what she'd done and tossed her fag away, cradling my burned cheek, her chin wet with red dribble.

'Oh Sam, look what you made me do.'

She hugged me to her. Then she started to sob and shake, and I felt sad for her again. I breathed her in, addicted to her soft love, the comforting aroma of nicotine overpowering the sickly stench of warm vegetables. I breathed her in, and tried to lock it in my heart.

As I looked up, I saw that, from her own garden, Mrs Read was watching us. I had the disturbing feeling that she'd been there the whole time.

CHAPTER 22

19 January

I arrive for my session at exactly nine o'clock. Clive is waiting for me in his usual chair, in front of the bay window. Outside, the sea is a line of slate under a white sky, rectangular boats sat upon it like tanks in a grey field, container ships heading for the port.

'How've you been sleeping?' he asks, apropos of nothing.

'Fine,' I lie. I can't go a whole night without waking; thoughts that I banish when I'm awake seep into my unconscious brain and startle me. Mum in the kitchen with her knife, Dad in the dark room, Jena lying on the ground with her brain leaking pulp. Freud was right: we can't suppress stuff; it finds us in the end.

'No nightmares?'

'Nope.'

'Please, Sam. I'm trying to help you.' His hands are clasped, a gesture of prayer, and I see that he wants me to be honest. He knows anyway: Birute heard me cry out last night, and came to comfort me; she will have written it up. There are no secrets in here, and everything written will be shown to the board. I abandon my pretence.

'My dreams have been bad,' I admit. 'Since we started this.'

He unclasps his hands, and relaxes a little because he sees I'm not going to resist today. Makes a note in his jotter. 'Well, I think it's a good sign,' he says optimistically, his preferred mood. 'Think of your dreams as your unconscious unblocking.'

I have the image of him pouring Mr Muscle down my feeding tube to clean me out like a drain, and unexpectedly laugh aloud.

'Tell me about the nightmare, Sam.'

I don't like feeling he's experimenting with me, trying different tricks to open me up. I don't like feeling that everything I say will be used against me on 1 February.

'I can't remember it. Besides, you're not Freud. Shouldn't we be focusing on facts?'

He puts the jotter on the table and threads his hands together in his shapeless lap. I can see he's thinking about giving me a pep talk.

'No, I'm not a dream therapist or a psychoanalyst, or any of that fancy stuff. Just a bog-standard consultant psychiatrist.'

He's being ironic. It would have taken years of training to get where he is, and to the other staff he's God.

'But I've also studied counselling, and psychotherapy, so despite the job title, I see myself as more of an odd-job man. For many years, I didn't believe the standard combination of drugs and therapy worked with eating disorders. I got disillusioned, which is why I diverted from the clinical side into management. I came to believe that what worked best was a structure, tube-feeding to give the patient strength, and most of all space away from toxic family dynamics. Time away from everyday pressures, and the patient would grow out of it; that's what I came to think. But that wasn't working for you, so I've gone old-school, back to the talking cure. And you're making such progress, I'm revising my earlier opinion that therapy doesn't work.'

'You sure about that? I'm still underweight. I'm still hiding food.' Spitefully, I add, 'And I purged my Enliven feed last night.'

Clive looks surprised and also sad. He lifts the leaves of his jotter, letting the paper fall, as if measuring the worth of it with his fingertips.

'Don't you want to leave here, Sam? Don't you want to get better?'

His question hits me, in the centre of myself, because sometimes I do want to get better; I want to leave the Bartlet and live out in the world again. But I prefer the idea of oblivion.

'They could decide to keep you here indefinitely. Don't you want to go home?'

Home. Mum is gone now, things are different, and I must push forward with my story. He must see this, because he leans forward, the notes forgotten. 'Speak to me, Sam,' he says. And I hear that he wants it, so much, for my own sake. And so I decide, once again, to trust him.

'My nightmare last night. In it, I was feeding Mum. She can only take food from my hand, but she keeps rejecting everything I offer, and I know she'll die if she won't let me feed her. I need to feed her, because if she dies, Dad will be all alone. Her mouth is open, but each time I come closer with a piece of bread or meat, she closes it tight. And then I see her teeth, sharp as needles, and before I can scream, I feel them puncturing my neck, and she's taking my blood. I'm saving her, but I know I'll bleed out. I know she'll kill me.'

Once again, I'm aware of the clock ticking on the wall. In just over an hour it will be time for lunch, and then classes. Clive will be going home later today, eating the tea his wife has prepared, watching TV. Whatever it is that normal people do with their evenings.

Clive waits, as if thinking about my dream. Then he says, 'Delving into your Black Magic box is bringing back memories.'

'That wasn't a memory.'

He acknowledges this, but then explains. 'Not literally, no. But your brain is re-living those weeks when you were hunting down Jena's attacker.'

'And you think that's good?'

'I do, yes. You must carry on with your story, Sam. The only way to go home is to move through the past.'

Jena's hospital was like the Bartlet in many ways.

For a start, mealtimes were supervised. On Jena's unit, the staff were supposed to eat with the patients, but they couldn't even finish a slice of toast before one of them had to reprimand Olaf for hiding pats of butter in his pockets, or pull Susan out of a cupboard.

On Thursday 16 June, Jena was moved back to Minsmere, and that morning things looked quite peaceful in the dining room when I arrived. But then Jena saw me and began waving her arms, calling.

'Sam! Over here.'

Mum, who must have arrived on the early train, was seated a little away from her. She hadn't seen me since she'd burned my cheek, and didn't look up from her coffee; I didn't know if she was still mad with me, or ashamed.

'Hi, Sam.' Lance, wolfing Weetos, showed me a mouthful of half-crunched mush. The scar on his left eyebrow glowed purple, his badger tuft shower-wet but drying in a spike.

Jena pulled me on to the empty seat between her and Mum. I could see how delighted she was to be back on Minsmere and with her new best friend.

'It's Lance's birthday next week. Tuesday.'

''S'not, Jena.' He tapped her nose with his finger. 'We're just celebrating on Tuesday because you was in the secure ward when it was my real birthday and they wouldn't give you a community pass.'

'How old are you, Lance?' I asked.

'Twenty-five.' He grinned. 'Jena's toy boy.'

They sniggered, heads touching. I remembered, before the attack, how Jena would buy the *Big Issue* from Lance, how kind she always was whenever she saw him about town, chatting with him and sharing a joke. But she'd never have wanted him for a boyfriend; she was far out of his league, and though she accepted his doting, she would never give him any false hope. Things had changed; the attack had cut her down to size.

I wondered if that was Douglas's motivation, returning to destroy her after the rape conviction destroyed him. Rob had told me he'd lost his business, his marriage, his son . . . That was motivation enough.

And he'd succeeded; my sister wasn't going to move into her flat, she wasn't going to marry Andy. I recalled Sonia telling me Jena *always thought she was a cut above*. Not anymore. But then I thought something else too: did Sonia know what Douglas had done? She implied that Jena deserved to be attacked. And if she knew, did Andy?

'Lance has a job,' she boasted, oblivious to my addled thoughts. 'He works at . . . What's it called? I forgot.'

'The Fold.' Lance started on his toast, covering it with a dollop of Nutella. 'Sam knows that. She goes there too.'

'That's a lie,' Jena said. Her usual response when she wasn't able to make sense of something.

Mum wasn't listening; she was gazing at me sadly. She reached a hand to my hair and brushed it from my face, leaning close to me as she touched a finger to my burn, where it had scabbed.

'I'm sorry I hurt you, love. But you shouldn't have provoked me.'

'I know, Mum. I won't do it again.'

I felt wretched, knowing that Jena had been raped when she was just thirteen, the impact of that on all of them. I'd been protected from it all, and that made me feel guilty; the three of them, trying to cope. Thinking the worst had already happened.

Mum squeezed my arm, and her touch was like a balm. With Dad, we three were all the family Jena had. She needed us to be tight.

'Let's draw a line under it now, and concentrate on getting Jena well again.'

Mum put on her coat and grabbed her bag. 'I have to go, or I'll be late for work.'

'Okay. See you later?'

Mum hesitated, looking again at the circular scab on my cheek. She leaned to whisper into my ear, and I thought she was going to apologise again, but instead she said, 'Don't go upsetting Jena.' She tapped my Leica. 'No photos today. Okay, love?'

'Don't worry, Mum.' I meant it; my sister had suffered enough.

And with a wave she was gone.

Flora Matthews, the art therapist, came over just as Jena started on another round of buttery toast. 'Hi, Sam. I saw your mum leaving, and she said I'd find you in here. I wanted to catch you.' She turned to Jena. 'Both of you.'

Flora was like some woodland creature, with nut-brown eyes and long, grey straggly hair, speckled with purple paint. She fidgeted with her hessian bag, and poured some juice. 'Aren't you eating anything?'

'Nah.'

'Maybe you should? You're looking a bit gaunt.'

'I ate earlier.'

My stomach protested at the lie as I watched Flora take a slice of toast and eat it with relish; small squirrel bites, cheeks pouchy with food. She smiled at Jena and Lance. 'Look at you two lovebirds. Excited about your date next week?'

Confused, I said, 'What date is this?'

'We told you, Sam. To celebrate my birthday!' Lance's eyes shone with happiness as he looked at my sister. 'We're going for pizza. To Pizza Hut.' He was as proud as if he was taking her to Venice.

I didn't want to upset Jena, I really didn't, but I was so confused, and the question bubbled up again inside me; no one else was going to answer it. I leaned over, close to my sister, and whispered, 'But you're engaged, Jena. What about Andy?'

And she looked at me, her eyes as clear with understanding as they always had been, and for a desperate moment I thought she was her old self. She hesitated, and I leaned forward, ready to hang on every word that might explain what was really going on with her and Andy, and why he hadn't visited; how she seemed to have erased him from her heart. But she simply said, 'I love pizza. My favourite is with black olives and pineapple.'

'I'm chaperoning,' Flora said. 'But I'll sit one table away and close my ears.' Lance kissed Jena full on the mouth, and Flora added, 'And my eyes.'

Lance laughed at that, his mouth wide open and Jena kissed him back, a full French kiss this time, then seemed to be watching for my reaction. She looked defiant, and I felt queasy. What was going on in her head?

Flora finished her toast, and made to stand. 'I wonder if I could show you something, Sam?' Her nails, bitten short and splodged with fluorescent pink, made a journey to her squirrel teeth.

'Mum will be back later.' It was her that the therapists or medical staff talked to if there was a problem, and I was feeling ill. I wanted to get out of there, and quickly. I needed space to think, and the hospital wasn't the right place.

'Erm, well, actually I was thinking you might be the best one to show. For some reason Jena is shy about showing her artwork to Kath and . . .' She looked at my Leica. 'And you're creative. You see, Jena started a new picture yesterday. She spent hours on it, didn't you, Jena?'

Jena carried on eating her toast, but I sensed she was listening.

'It's very . . .' Flora searched for the right word, her hand like a butterfly in the air.

I was getting impatient. 'Is something wrong with it?'

Flora showed her teeth again, this time in a small smile. 'There's nothing wrong with it. It's quite wonderful.'

'Oh. Well that's good, isn't it?' Daft cow.

'Oh yes, but . . . I wondered if you'd like to come and see it? That would be easier than trying to explain. I could take you now, while Jena is finishing her breakfast.'

I followed Flora down the corridor, watching her bright gypsy skirt move in and out of her legs, to the quick pace of her feet. Occasionally, I caught a flash of a purple satin shoe. The art room stank of clay and turps, and I sneezed.

'Bless you,' Flora said.

I was about to sneeze again, the dust particles floating in the air, when shock stopped me. There, on the giant canvas, was something that stole my breath away.

Flora's hand danced in front of it. 'Even though she's only just begun, you can see what Jena has already achieved. These pink and reds and whites . . . So beautiful. Like swarming petals – or snow – veiling what is going to be a quite exquisite portrait.'

As perfect as a photograph. Alive with sunlight and warmth: an ivory white, a sunshine yellow, baby pink, on a black background. Assuming my default position, I lifted my camera and focused the lens, blinking away the watery film that had come from nowhere. Only then did the picture come together and I saw a young girl's hopeful face.

'Jena was always good at art,' I said. Guiltily remembering that she would have gone to art college, if I hadn't begged her not to.

Flora was warm at my side as I aligned my shot. This picture would go with the others into the Black Magic box, proof that Jena was regaining her skills.

'Yes, she's a wonderful artist. The art-therapy sessions I run aren't about the skill of the patient; they are about helping the memory to return, but working with Jena is such a joy. The girl in the picture is beautifully rendered.'

I clicked the shutter and told her what she should have realised immediately.

'She's not beautiful. It's me.'

The girl I once was, young and innocent.

'You are beautiful, Sam. Jena has captured you perfectly. There's so much emotion in this picture.' Flora moved closer to the canvas. 'Such pretty green eyes. Are they really that colour?' She turned back to check, then her eyes fell on the cigarette burn. 'What's that mark on your face?'

'Just a spot.'

'You want to put some TCP on that. It looks infected.' She frowned.

'Yeah,' I said weakly. I didn't want her to ask more questions. 'So, why did you want to show me the painting?'

She paused, and when she spoke her voice quivered, dreamy. 'It's as if Jena has poured all her love on to the canvas. That's what my sessions with her aim to do, to call on those deep emotions and connect the patient with their inner world, which is often so damaged. Art therapy is a very powerful tool, and with Jena it seems to be working beyond even my hopes. Maybe because of her creative past. She used to be a keen photographer, didn't she? And she's involved in acting?'

'She works for the entertainment team at Pleasurepark.' I caught myself using the present tense, but ploughed on. 'There's a small theatre for shows, and she dresses up as a princess to have her picture taken with little kids.' I added, meanly, 'It's not exactly Shakespeare.'

I lifted my camera again, using a sharper eye, and saw something else. Something that did not belong. Behind my face, in the dark background, was a shadow. Jena had sketched a menacing shape, hunched over and huddled in a dark coat, hood up so it looked like a cloak. Its face was blank. I gasped in recognition.

'That's what I remember too. That figure, in the cloak.'

My heart was beating fast. This was a turning point: despite the recent fits and being placed back on Eastern Ward, there were still signs that Jena was getting better, maybe even recovering her memory.

Was the art therapy shifting something?

Or was it that she remembered far more than she pretended to?

I tapped on the door, then entered Jena's bedroom.

Eight weeks' worth of get-well cards adorned the walls, from us and people she worked with, and also from strangers who'd read about Jena's case in the newspaper. Even Mrs Read had sent one, though Mum tossed it in the bin after reading the scribbled message.

A gust of cold air lifted my hair, and I realised the patio door was open, though it was supposed to be closed at all times for security reasons; if open, anyone could access the hospital without having to go past the main reception. There was supposed to be a catch to stop it opening all the way, but it had broken, and no one had thought to fix it. I could hear laughter, coming from the courtyard.

Jena was lounging on the bench, her head in Lance's lap, sunbathing like a lizard on a rock, her legs splayed apart, arms dropped at her sides, perfectly still, and he was stroking the top of her ponytail. One of her pink flip-flops had dropped to the ground, while the other dangled on the toes.

It was a moment of happiness for Jena, and she'd had few enough recently, but I still didn't understand how she'd forgotten Andy and all her future plans. I was sick of being alone in the dark.

'Jena, I need you to come with me now.'

I watched her untangle herself from Lance; she looked sleepy and content, and I was about to ruin that feeling for her.

I hurried Jena to the television lounge, which was empty. Not that any of the other patients being there would have stopped me; my need to *do something* was overwhelming. If Flora's art therapy was working, then this should too. I rummaged in my rucksack and removed a DVD, one I'd taken from the Asda box in our attic, recorded by Dad and labelled in his heavy, slanted handwriting. When Jena saw it, her eyes widened and her cheeks flushed pink, and I thought about my promise to Mum, the one I was already breaking, about not upsetting her.

'No, Sammy, I can't watch a bad film.'

'It's not a bad film,' I said, wondering if she was still paranoid about Big Brother watching her.

Every film in the box had been watched a dozen times, and none of them showed anything upsetting. But Jena grabbed the DVD, staring hard at the label. It was a relic from when she was normal. Precise, dark letters in faded ink: *Sam's 6th Birthday*.

She frowned. 'It's not a bad one?'

Now it was my turn to be confused. 'It's a nice tape; it's a party. Look!' I pressed play and on the screen my sister's beautiful face came into focus.

Jena's in the kitchen, bent over the counter, her hands moving slowly as she concentrates on her task. Lovely and shimmering, like a cut-price Angelina Jolie at a film premiere, she's dressed for a party: silver dangling earrings, and a top with glittery thread, a halter-neck that shows her pretty neck. Dark hair falls around her face, loose and curled and glossy.

Jena is squashed against the kitchen worktop, but keeps her hands steady while the camera moves to get a good view of the table, where a chocolate sponge has been cut in half, sandwiched together with buttercream and covered with chocolate buttons.

Dad's voice dominates over the sound of the whirring tape. 'What's the cake supposed to be? A football?'

Sat next to me, Jena answered the question. 'It's a hedgehog.'

Dad says to Jena, 'Thought you was supposed to be artistic?'

She gives him a withering look. 'As if you couldn't tell. Look, that's its nose!'

She turns the plate, and the camera zooms in on a glacé cherry balanced on the tip of a mound of buttercream, two Smarties above for eyes, chocolate buttons for hedgehog spikes.

Dad's laughter makes the camera wobble, and his hand comes into the frame, making a grab for a chocolate button. Jena nervously slaps him away with a tea towel.

'Please don't, Dad. You'll ruin it.'

The screen went blank, and then came back to life.

My six-year-old self sits like a princess on a throne at the end of the table decked with pink streamers and brightly coloured food: yellow crisps, red strawberries, green cucumber. I'm wearing those colours too, and a plastic crown. Hair floats around my face in ringlets, eyes glittering greedily at the spread laid out in front of me. On the table is the hedgehog with its cherry nose, and by my side Jena strikes a match and bends forward to light the six candles pushed into its chocolatey back. Mum bustles into the frame, neatly turned out, hair newly permed in tight corkscrews, eyeshadow toothpaste-blue, but her smile forgivingly natural. She looks slim; young too. But the biggest difference is in her shoulders, and her back, which isn't stooped with grief.

Candles flicker. Mum, Dad and Jena all sing 'Happy Birthday', badly out of tune, enjoying the rowdy noise of their own singing as I smile and clap and blow out the candles. Then Jena kisses me; she's so happy there are tears in her eyes.

Jena had become wrapped up in the action on the tape. The dividing wall in her damaged brain had crumbled, the gap between the life she was living in the hospital and her past life captured in the videotape was gone. She turned to me and said, 'Make a wish, Sammy!'

Sadness filled me, and I ached inside. There was so very much to want. I took her hands in mine, feeling the dry skin, thirsty for moisture, and longed as I've never longed for anything else.

'I wish you'd remember who hurt you, Jen-Jen.'

She pulled away, and I saw that she was back with me, in the television room; the party she had just enjoyed was only a film. The life she had returned to was frightening. But I had to continue; I needed her to remember, even if it caused her distress.

'Jena, I know about the rape.' She didn't react, but I kept going.

I scrambled through my rucksack for the picture I'd stolen from Sonia's bedroom, of Douglas Campbell holding the baby. I placed it in Jena's lap.

'Was it true that you sent him a message on Facebook, that you arranged to meet him? Why, Jena? After what he'd done to you . . .'

Beat of silence. Everything on pause. She held the photograph like it was made of snow, looking at the television screen with longing. She wanted to escape, to lose herself again in the past.

I tapped her wrist. 'Do you remember?'

She shook her head, looked back at the TV screen. Frustrated, I held her chin this time. 'What happened, Jena?'

'He said it was my fault. Because I was so pretty.'

I wanted to tell her that was crap; she was just thirteen and he was an adult, but I could see she wanted to say more.

She leaned towards me, so close our noses almost touched, and whispered madly, 'I didn't say no. I didn't say anything; I just let it happen. Because I didn't know what to do, and I thought it would be over soon. He always found me when I was alone, and he said he loved me. He does love me, doesn't he?'

'He raped you, Jena. That's not love.'

Her eyes were wild, and the whispering grew louder. 'And Mrs Read, she started to ask questions. She saw that I was changing; she wanted to know why.'

'Our crazy neighbour, Mrs Read?'

'She was my PE teacher.'

I hadn't known this. 'So what did she do?'

'She called Social Services. And they spoke with me, for such a long time. The same question, again and again. *Who did this to you, Jena? Tell us who.* But I'd promised to forget.'

Her shoulders started heaving. Her eyes were glittery with fear, but I couldn't let that stop me. We'd opened a wound, and I needed to dig inside. I retrieved the photo of Douglas Campbell, stolen from Rob's home, from my rucksack.

'You just have to look at this, Jena. You just have to say that he attacked you.'

She looked down at the photo, then turned her head away at a sharp angle.

'No!' And she tore the photo in half, a violent rip that sent me into a rage.

I grabbed her shoulders and shook her, yelling, 'I'm trying to help you, you stupid cow!' My voice was loud and unsteady, and I knew I'd reached breaking point. 'Fucking snap out of it, Jena.'

I shook her, again and again, her head wobbling as she pleaded with me to stop.

The door swung open and Mum pulled me off Jena. A quick hard slap on my cheek, over the scab.

'Enough!'

Mum panted, caught her breath, her hand pressed hard to her body, as if she was fighting the urge to commit more violence. She picked up the torn photo, placing the two pieces together. She peered at it, and I saw the dawn of recognition as she stared at Douglas Campbell's face. When she finally spoke, her voice was uneven and shot through with fury.

'Samantha Hoolihan, you need to get out of my sight right now, or I will not be responsible for my actions.'

I was propelled by anger and need, my hunger keeping my thinking in straight simple lines. Train back to Ipswich. Bike ride back home. But I didn't go home; I went to another house. Next door but one.

I knocked on Mrs Read's door, but there was no answer, so I scuttled down the side alley, a mirror image of our own, and found her in the overgrown garden, as motionless as a tree. She was looking over the fence, in the direction of my house, and in her hand was a notebook.

She jumped when she saw me, and put her hand to her chest, then said, 'Well, I thought you'd come round at some time. I just expected you to knock.'

'I did.'

Bird-like, she twitched her head, and I saw what had attracted her attention. Dad was walking down the path towards his shed, unlocking the padlock and looking around before disappearing into its dark interior. She took a pencil from behind her ear, made a note in her book, then she turned to me.

'Let's talk inside where they can't hear us.'

Although Mrs Read's house was the same as ours, it was nothing like. There were books everywhere, open and tossed, and I saw from the covers that they were mainly the biographies of criminals: Crippen, Fred and Rose West, Hindley and Brady. The place was a mess of old wrappers and half-drunk cups of tea. Piles of newspapers, large broadsheets, seemed to be in some kind of order, judging from the many faded yellow Post-it notes that stuck out from the pages. A feral-looking cat with pink eyes wound its way around the mess, and my chest tightened as lost strands of white fur floated before me.

Mrs Read smoothed down her trousers, which I saw now were baggy tracksuit bottoms, wearing thin on the legs and none too clean. Her top was a polo shirt, which must have once been white, and I remembered that she had been a PE teacher.

'I need to ask you about what happened to Jena.'

'Naturally.' Mrs Read had a very proper way of speaking. 'I'll get us some tea.'

She left the room, and I looked again at the chaos around me. Mrs Read was a hoarder, and as I read some of the Post-it notes I saw that they related to various articles, all about high-profile cases. Madeleine McCann, Holly and Jessica, Sarah Payne. Her spiky writing on the yellow notes, when I managed to decipher it, said things like: *links to other countries?* And *both blonde. Swedish heritage?* And *neo-Nazi connection?*

Dad was right: she was a lunatic.

'Tea.'

She placed a silver tray on top of a pile of papers. The spout of the pot was stained, and when I peered into the milk jug, I saw skin on the surface. Nevertheless, Mrs Read poured, and I accepted a cup.

'So, you have finally come to see me. Good girl.'

I felt like I was back at school and had done well on some test.

'Jena said it was you she told about the rape?'

Mrs Read drank her sour tea delicately, making my mouth tingle in sympathy.

'Not exactly. Her body told me.'

Loopy old bird. 'Eh?'

Again she smoothed her trousers; I realised it was a habitual gesture, the reason for the thinning fabric over her ropey thighs.

'As a PE teacher, one of the tasks is to monitor shower activity. Some teenagers avoid water like they will melt!' She laughed at her own joke, but I thought that showering under Mrs Read's piercing gaze would be enough to deter anyone. And she smelt none too fresh herself.

'So what did her body tell you?' I was going with it, but already feared the woman was too mad to be of help.

'That she wanted to die. She was starving herself.'

'Jena was? No, I'm sorry. You must be thinking of someone else. Jena's always had a good appetite. She's slim, but not skinny.'

Mrs Read tutted at my ignorance. 'Remember, this is before you were born. She was a different girl back then. What happened when she was thirteen changed her; she grew into a woman with a scarred soul, but she was a survivor. But the danger was always there, in the background. I thought she might just make it out, but I wasn't watching closely enough. They got her first.'

Mrs Read gazed sadly at her newspapers, as if thinking of the other girls she was so obsessed with, who had also been 'got'.

'Okay, so she was starving herself. Then what?' I was irritated. I felt I'd wasted my time coming, and I just wanted to hear what Mrs Read had to say, and leave.

But Mrs Read focused on me now. 'She looked like you. Skinny. Starved.'

I said nothing. I waited.

'There were no bruises; there rarely are in cases like this. But the body shows its pain anyway. I tried to help her; it was my duty.'

'What did she tell you about the rape?'

Mrs Read raised a quizzical eyebrow. 'The *rape*. Dear girl, Jena had been systematically abused for a long time. What happened to her was not a one-off event but a pattern of activity.' She gestured to her stack of articles. 'So many young girls are groomed and violated. I knew I had to help her before it was too late. Did you know that in almost all cases like this there are warning signs that people ignore? At Praia da Luz there had been twelve sexual assaults before Maddie was taken. Twelve missed opportunities, and twelve occasions for the kidnappers to practise before their ultimate coup.'

I'd had enough. The woman was clearly a conspiracy theorist.

'Okay, Mrs Read, well, I really must be going now. Thanks for the tea.'

She stood and smiled. 'You are welcome. I'm glad I could help.'

I headed quickly for the back door, desperate to get out of this crazy house and away from her crazy brain. As I opened the door, she asked, 'But what happened to the baby?'

I whipped around. 'What?'

'Jena's baby. They said she'd lost it, but I think it must have been taken away. Sold into slavery, or given to a childless couple. What do you think?'

I thought she was certifiable. I thought I needed to go.

CHAPTER 23

20 January

In our lesson on Food Facts, the six of us sit in a semi-circle on squishy beanbags in primary colours. They are presumably meant to make the food-tech room 'fun' or 'relaxed', this being such a touchy subject for us, but only serve to make us feel like children as we squish about on thousands of polystyrene beads, trying to find a comfortable position.

Manda scribbles on the whiteboard:

How much fat do we need in our diets?

Inwardly, I groan. This is her pet subject, and always provokes heated debate.

'The food we have here,' says Joelle, leaning back in her red beanbag like it's a throne. 'It's way too fatty. Chicken nuggets on Thursdays.'

'And chips!' adds Fiona, joining in the game. 'That's not healthy food.'

Manda could answer this question in her sleep. We all could. It doesn't make us believe it, though.

'The diet you have here is not low-fat. It is giving you the fat you need, which is a third of your calories.'

'So, why do the government bang on about healthy eating, then?' says Stacey, trying to sit upright but failing as the material bulges and sags under her skinny frame. 'You don't need Jamie Oliver to tell you that chicken nuggets are shit nutrition.'

The three of them have the energy to play, but I've heard it all before, and Pearl looks too sick to enjoy the debate.

Mina is sunk into her blue beanbag like she wants it to swallow her; usually her eyes are cast down, but not now.

'Shut up, please,' she says, quietly, but with enough force that there is silence in the room. 'I'm tired of hearing the same stuff.'

Manda clears her voice as if to reply, but then doesn't. The rest of us just wait; we have waited a long time for Mina to say anything.

'I know,' she says, simply. 'I know about fat and calories, good and bad food. We all do, much more than you ever could,' she says to Manda. 'Why don't you get that?'

She's right. The hours, weeks, months that we have studied our calories – we are all experts. We are united by our shared illness, our shared expertise.

'So then why not eat healthily?' asks Manda, gently. 'Why starve?'

Such a simple question. Such a fucking impossible question.

For once, Mina has an answer.

'You can't be healthy in a sick environment.'

Later, at our scheduled time, I find Clive in his office. I've been thinking about Mina's words, and wondering if the sick environment is this hospital, or the world outside. We may all have anorexia, but for each of us the sickness is different.

I can no longer hide behind the others, like in group sessions. Mina's story is not Fiona's; Stacey's is not Pearl's. And none of them have this story.

In Clive's office, it's only my voice, continuing my sad tale. The only story I know.

Friday 17 June broke with heat and a low sun, and I felt a renewed hunger to fix the case, to bring Douglas to justice, burning inside.

Rob was in the workshop, a wrench in his hand. I didn't want to tell him what Mrs Read had said about Jena having a baby, and anyway he had news of his own. A letter had arrived, at his house.

'From my dad, the bastard. No contact for years, and then this. But it sounds like he's sent a few and Mum hasn't been passing them to me. I was there when the postman arrived, picking up my duvet, so it was only a fluke I got this.'

He was agitated, and when he thrust the envelope into my hand, I sensed it was the very thing I needed: access to Jena's attacker.

Inside, the paper was thin, with HMP BISHOP'S HILL stamped on the top, then a scrawled prison number. Douglas's writing was cramped and spiky. The writing of the man who raped my sister when she was thirteen, who had most likely attacked her nearly eight weeks ago. And here I was, with his son, who was lacing his arms around my waist.

> Hello Rob,
> Still waiting on your reply, son, and I'm hoping you aren't mad at me because I'm in prison again. I tried to explain it to your mum, but she just hangs up on me. She won't believe me, but it's a conspiracy, another bullshit accusation, but they have nothing on me.

They'll have no choice but to release me. My brief says it might not even get before a judge – CPS will likely pull the file first thing Monday before my bail hearing.

I know I said I'd never return to Suffolk, but I've had enough of all this crap. It's taken everything from me – my business, my marriage, my son.

I'm going to put an end to it now, so I'll need somewhere to stay. Tell your mum I need to kip on the sofa. It's the least she can do, giving up on me like she did. Sonia and me need to talk anyway. I have some questions for her.

So, since she won't talk to me, this is the only way I can let her know. You tell her, son. Once I'm free, I'll be on the first train to Ipswich.

Dad

Douglas Campbell was coming home.

If I could see his face, up close, then I might fill in the blank I'd had since the attack. I wouldn't need Jena to remember; I could remember for us both, and then Penny would have evidence that wasn't just circumstantial. She'd have an eye-witness identification.

'That bastard can't just show up at Mum's,' Rob shouted over the sound of the revving cars and yells of the other mechanics. 'She's on a suspended sentence, and the police will be watching, waiting for her to fuck up. Anything happens, any violence or drugs or just anything, she'll be sent to prison. I'm not having that.'

I coughed away some fumes, and sidestepped into a dusty gully to get away from the prying eyes of the other mechanics. I touched Rob on the shoulder.

'That's right, you need to protect your mum. Just like I need to protect Jena. Douglas hurt them both, Rob. We need to work together on this to make sure he doesn't do any more damage to them. And to get him sent back to prison where he belongs.'

Rob was flustered, moving jerkily around the car. His face was patchy with sweat and I had the urge to wipe it away with my fingers.

'The sooner the better, as far as I'm concerned. He's no dad of mine. Uncle Andy always said he was no good – he's been more of a father figure to me.'

I shelved this positive image of Andy, to reflect on later. Right now, I needed to focus.

'So, you won't feel bad? Helping me get something concrete on your dad?'

'Why should I? I don't owe him anything. Do you know what it does to you, knowing your dad is a rapist? The things people on the estate said about my family . . . After he was sent down, Mum lost everything, got into drugs. You saw how vulnerable she is right now. I'm not gonna let him mess up our lives a second time.'

'Then help me get him sent back to prison,' I said, holding him tight, my eyes not leaving his conflicted face, willing him to be on my side.

There was a warning whistle from one of Rob's mates, who pointed to the open doorway of the workshop, where Mac stood, arms folded.

'Hey, Sam. It's not that I mind you being here, love, but this boy has work to do. Come on, Rob. Play the game.'

I waited for him to finish his Community Payback hours for the day, seated on a broken chair in the restroom, the prospect of Douglas's imminent release buzzing in my brain. The workshop was rowdy, with the radio competing with the shouts to *Pass that hammer* and *Give us a hand here, mate*. I felt dirty just being there. Finally, Rob was done. He picked at some jump leads under the Datsun's bonnet, pulling one out with a yank that seemed to satisfy him. I could tell he'd made a decision.

He turned to me, and took my hand. 'The most important thing for me is to protect my mum. He can't come back into her life. And no one should get away with what he did to your sister. I'll help you, Sam.'

And I kissed him, deep and long and with every beat of my weakening heart.

By the time we reached The Fold, hand in hand and heads together, Rob and I had come up with a plan. Lance was hoovering the hallway, a path of clean carpet between the graffiti-marked walls and battered doors. He grinned stupidly at Rob, his friend for life.

'Hey, Lance. 'Sup?' Rob high-fived him, and Lance snorted with delight.

'Just cleaning, man.'

Once we were in Rob's room, he started to move things around, making space on each of the shelves as he went over our plan. 'Okay, so I'm going to write and tell Dad that he can stay here. Then we can keep an eye on him, follow him, see what he does. Keep him away from my mum and your sister.'

'What about Mac? If he finds out your dad is here, will you be in trouble with your probation officer?'

'Yup. He'd do his nut if he found out, and it wouldn't look good for me. It's in the contract: no overnight guests.' I saw a flash of something defiant in his eyes. 'I'll have to get him a blow-up mattress or something.'

He pulled out some Rizla papers and baccy from a drawer, and began to roll a joint.

'We should meet him from the train. Make sure he doesn't wander anywhere else.'

Rob licked his paper, and sniffed. 'Fuck that. I'll pick him up at Bishop's Hill. Take my Datsun.'

It wasn't his Datsun; it belonged to Greasy Monkeys. Mac sometimes let him drive it on the disused airfield, but I doubted he'd be insured on the road. Rob inhaled his spliff, and his shoulders relaxed. After his second tug, he said, 'I'm going to be there when he gets out on Monday.'

He took another drag, hollow cheeks as he sucked, a glow of orange at the tip, and passed it to me, touching my fingers as I took it and breathed deeply.

'Me too.'

I felt a twinge of excitement, and went to Rob, kissing him deeply and unbuckling his jeans. Our pact, our shared goal of monitoring Douglas, drew us closer, close enough to call it love. I let him pull off my clothes and lower me to the bed, and felt his weight, like he was a part of my own body. But my thoughts were racing, thinking how close I was to seeing Douglas Campbell, to knowing if it was him I saw in the alley, standing over my broken sister.

I closed my eyes as Rob touched me, entered me, and I could almost feel the rain, almost see the hunched figure, dark slick head, and the devastating emptiness where a face belonged.

CHAPTER 24

20 January

Elsewhere on the unit, girls will be sleeping, and Birute will be in the office enjoying a magazine with lots of photos, *OK!* or *Heat*, by the light of a study lamp, relishing the peace of an uneventful night shift, flicking glossy pages with her sturdy fingers. My fingers are so pale now, almost blue, and so thin. Touching them, I think of the trick that Hansel played, offering up a chicken bone to feel so the witch would think her too skinny to eat.

I bury my head in my pillow, smothering out the past, the future I rejected, and don't hear Birute arrive with the night-time meds until the door is open. Her hand touching my shoulder startles me; I am so lost in the past that for a second I think it's Rob and I'm being given a second chance at being loved. But I rejected that with what I did, and have kept on rejecting it for eighteen months. He has tried to visit, many times.

Birute peers closely at me with an expression of concern.

'What wrong, sweet? You cry, and this not like you.'

And I'm so rocked by my memories, so undone by her concern, that I tell her. 'I'm scared. It'll soon be February, and I don't know what's going to happen to me.'

'I think it will be okay. You are a good girl, Sam. They will see.' She notices the Black Magic box, the photos clasped in my fist. 'All this you are doing with Clive is upsetting, yes?' She sits next to me, her hand stroking the bumps of my spine.

'Look at this,' she says, shaking the small plastic cup in her hand, showing me an oblong white horse-pill and a small round one, sugar-coated. There's a new pill, diamond-shaped and blue, which has started appearing in the pot.

'These can help you get better. But this' – she pokes with her index finger at my temple – 'this is the most important of all. My mother, when she was sent to Siberia, she was just a little girl. I don't know how my grandmother kept her alive, but she manage. Is possible, always, to live. But what I see, with all you girls, you want so very much to die. And this is something I don't understand.' She shakes her head sadly, blows her fringe from her face so I can see her eyes more clearly. 'My grandmother had no food; she was starved and cold. But Stalin did this to her. You, all you girls, do it to yourself.'

When I first came here, I would hide the pills under my tongue and spit them into my hand once her back was turned, but now I'll swallow them all, even the blue one. I won't even ask what it is for.

'I do want to get better, Birute. I'm just not sure I can.'

'You can.' She sniffs and fixes her clear eyes on me. 'My grandmother, she was not afraid of Stalin when she came home. She kept his picture, to show her that he is just a man. Maybe visiting the past with your special box of photos is medicine you really need, so you are no longer afraid.'

I sleep fitfully, but the next morning I feel something has woken inside, a tentative faith that carries me through the day as I think about what to tell Clive at our next meeting. I decide to be like Birute's grandmother, and face my fear.

At the scheduled hour, Clive sits in his usual chair, hands clasped together, waiting for me to begin.

Okay, Clive, here we go.

I was about to meet Douglas Campbell. It's time for you to meet him too.

Monday 20 June, eight weeks since the attack. To be at the prison for eight in the morning, we had to leave Ipswich by seven fifteen, latest. It was five past already, but I was still in the bath. Cold water, a soap-scum ring round the edge. Wedged the wrong way, my back against one side and my feet on the other, knees to chin. My stomach ached with hunger, and the water wasn't helping. Felt dirty, and the soap wasn't helping either.

My head was scrambled with what I knew and what was missing. I didn't want to think about Jena, but she was there anyway. This was all for her, so I could positively identify her attacker, and give Penny the evidence she needed. If Douglas was convicted, it would mean justice for Jena, and safety for Sonia. Rob and me, both heroes.

Mum rapped on the bathroom door with her knuckle. 'You've been in there ages. Hurry up! I need the loo.'

I stood, a wave of cold air making my flesh pimple, water falling off me like a shed skin. My stomach cramped in on itself, and I sat on the toilet, dripping. Then I turned round and retched into the bowl. Trying to empty myself of what hurt inside, to rid myself of hunger so I could focus on what was important.

'Sam!'

She sounded narked, and I instinctively touched my cheek, the round scab that had started to peel, revealing baby skin underneath, pink and raw.

Then, through the window, I heard the frustrated sound of a car horn.

'Who's that in the car outside, beeping?' Mum asked.

I flushed the toilet, rinsed my mouth at the tap, and grabbed a towel, rubbing my arms and chest so hard the skin reddened.

Mum banged harder on the door.

I opened up, and she stood there, arms crossed, glaring at me.

'Where are you going so early anyway?'

'Just for a drive.'

'Where?'

'Pleasurepark.' We got a free annual pass, a small compensation for the crap pay Dad and Jena received, so it was believable.

I shuffled past to the bedroom, where I pulled on jeans, sticky on my damp legs, baseball boots and the T-shirt I slept in. I felt better covered up, but Mum was still on guard in the hallway.

'You better not be lying to me. Again.'

That subject of the photo of Douglas Campbell, and my showing it to Jena, wasn't closed, and we both knew it. Suddenly, I wanted to kiss her, for her to love me, more than anything in the world; wanted to tell her the truth and stay at home, safe. But it felt too late for that.

Outside was the Datsun, with its rusted doors and botched paintwork, ramped up on the kerb, vibrating to Kiss FM. Rob had both hands on the padded steering wheel.

'Morning, Sam. Got your camera, I see? What about a shot of me driving this beauty?'

'Later. Let's go.'

As the car pulled away, I saw Mrs Read, looking down at us from her bedroom window, make a note in her book.

Forty-five minutes of cars beeping, second-hand smoke and Kiss FM. The sickness hadn't eased, even with the windows down. Fresh air wasn't enough to settle my feeling of dread, but I didn't ask Rob to pull over.

He stroked my hand. 'You all right, babe?'

'Yeah.' I felt panicky, weird, but best to keep it in; just try and keep breathing.

Finally, we had arrived at Bishop's Hill Prison.

I could see two guards opening the oversized steel doorway to release a white van with blacked-out windows.

'That'll be on its way to some courthouse,' smirked Rob. 'Some scally'll be getting the return trip.' He'd been like this the whole journey, mouthy with a fidgety energy. Deep down, he would be as scared as I was.

There was a wall either side of the gate, grey concrete with barbed wire on top. The gate closed and a prison officer, schoolboy-formal in black trousers and white shirt, came out of the door within the gate. He whistled his way across the car park. Other cars were parked up with people waiting, just like us. A woman in a flowery dress held a toddler as he did a wee on the grass; he struggled in a shirt and trousers, stuffy in the June sun. The woman had tried her best.

I flashed back to the newspaper article, when Douglas was about to be sentenced for rape, and recalled the picture of Sonia, walking side by side with Douglas to the courthouse, crying. Not because she was thinking of the thirteen-year-old rape victim, but because she was thinking of herself.

The woman called, 'Morning! Lovely day, isn't it?' to the prison officer, but he didn't even look up. Her special day, this release day, was just another shift for him.

Rob clicked his fingers, hummed, filling the heavy silence before his dad appeared. He held my hand, and our fingers slid together, clammy but still comforting; we were united in our purpose.

The prison gate opened, and a man stepped out. A man with a shorn head, wearing a plain blue T-shirt and badly fitting jeans, carrying a white sack with H M PRISON stamped on it. He scratched his head, and dug into his sloppy jeans' pocket, bringing out a packet of chewing gum.

'That's him,' said Rob, his voice bringing me back to the present.

How could he be so *ordinary*? Just a worn-out version of the young man in the picture.

Douglas Campbell put his sack on the floor while he popped some gum in his mouth, then he gathered the bag at the neck and hoisted it over his shoulder, walking out of the car park with the loping gait that the patients had at Minsmere Unit, the ones who'd been there a long time and had no reason to hurry.

Rob scrambled out, calling to his dad. Douglas turned, surprise then pleasure registering on his face. He reached to hug Rob, who held back, forcing his dad to cup his head and pull him forward so he could kiss his forehead.

When they arrived at the Datsun, Douglas bent down to look at me.

'Don't mind if I take the front seat, do ya love? Only I'm an old man, see. Arthritis is a killer, y'know.'

His Scots accent still had a blur of Ipswich yokel mixed in, like there was a bit of gravel in his throat.

I squeezed myself between the seats, to the back. When Douglas climbed into the car, I saw him properly, for the first time. I held my breath, and waited to see this rapist and violent man, hoping it would adjust my memory of the attack into sharp focus, but nothing happened. He wasn't that old, mid-forties, but his skin hung heavy on his bones. His lips were cracked.

He saw me too, and I wondered if he could see in me a likeness to Jena, his victim twice over. I stared right back at his sad, ordinary face, willing myself to remember him, to know beyond doubt that I had seen him before, but nothing came.

He turned towards the front, chewing the gum with his mouth open. I could see him in profile, the lines around his mouth, his eye narrowing when he chewed. His large knuckles were blue with tattoo stains and a silver cross gleamed at his neck.

'That's Sam,' Rob said, proud like I was a prize he'd won.

Douglas turned to look again, making me feel hot and trapped as I wondered why his face meant nothing to me. Why it didn't fill the gap in my memory. After a moment, he said, 'She's pretty.' He released his gnarly hand from his rollie and pushed it through the gap.

'Pleasure to meet you, Sam.'

Because he didn't know who I was, he had no idea that it was my sister he'd raped and then attacked, that I had a plan to send him right back to the place he'd left, if only I could get something on him, something concrete.

I steeled myself, and touched his hand. The skin was loose and his grip was soggy. I pulled my fingers free.

Rob and I exchanged a look, a secret promise. He wouldn't give me away; he'd chosen water over blood. He turned the key, and the car staggered out of the car park, Douglas giving a final one-finger salute to the gate.

Rob revved so fast the car made a whirring protest on every sharp corner; he slammed the dashboard to the beat of the music until Douglas turned the radio off.

'So, Dad. What's your plan now?' asked Rob.

Douglas glanced at Rob, then addressed the window. 'One thing about being locked up for a few weeks, it gives you space to think.' He touched the silver cross at his neck. 'God told me, when I was released from that bullshit sentence years ago, to go home to Scotland and make a fresh life, that coming back to Suffolk wouldn't be the right thing for me. But eight weeks ago, I was pulled back to this fucking county; the past caught up with me. Now I think God is telling me something different: that I can't run. I have some sorting out to do and it involves your mum.'

Rob said quietly, but with menace, 'You leave her be, Dad. She's been fine without you.' His hands moved too much on the wheel, his foot kept peddling the accelerator.

'You should slow down, boy,' Douglas warned. 'An old banger like this attracts attention. Is it even taxed? You don't want to get stopped by the cops.'

Rob's hands fisted on the steering wheel in response.

Douglas asked him, 'How is she really?'

'Fine. Which is why you need to leave her be.'

'Stop repeating that same bullshit, son. I heard she was into some bad shit?'

'That's in the past. She's been clean for four months.'

There was a silence for a beat, and I knew Rob was remembering the last time we saw her, how she'd stank of booze and her eyes were like dinner plates.

'Your mum was always weak. If she'd been tougher, she could have kept hold of the business when I was sent down. She could have campaigned for me, organised an appeal, got the papers to cover it. Anything, just so long as she got me out.'

Rob's leg started to wiggle up and down. 'Look, Dad, she just needed to get on with her life, you know? I mean, I was only a kid, so she had enough on her plate. Let it go already. And you shouldn't go and see her. You can stay with me.'

Douglas seemed to think about this, as if he had several options to choose from.

'I'd like that, son. I'd like a chance to get to know you, catch up on all the years I've missed. The police, the courts, they set me up, and I've let them get away with it. And as for letting it go, well I tried that. I'm not gonna let them stitch me up a second time, like they did to that American guy on the Netflix show. I'm back in Ipswich, and I need to sort this bullshit out once and for all.'

Douglas wound the window down, breathing in fresh air like a dog, the silver chain around his neck catching the sun. I swallowed a mouthful of bile, sick of hearing his lies. I needed air, needed to leave the car.

As Rob pulled the Datsun into a side road near The Fold and came to halt, I opened the car door and spewed watery puke on to the grass.

At The Fold, we sneaked past the office, mercifully empty. It would have been obvious from Douglas's bag that this wasn't just a quick visit. Rob sent Lance into the staff area, to check the coast was clear, while his dad waited outside.

'Everything okay?'

Lance nodded. 'Yup. The staff are still in their meeting.'

'You didn't see Mac?'

Lance shook his head, his eye weeping with the effort.

'This is our secret, okay? Don't go telling anyone that you saw me, or anyone else.'

'Our secret,' Lance echoed.

Douglas paced the small square of Rob's room, touching this and lifting that, kicking a jumper that lay on the floor.

'This it, then?'

I was tempted to say, *No, we just came here for fun. His flat is the penthouse suite.* Jerk. It couldn't be worse than a prison cell.

'I'm only on an apprenticeship, Dad. I haven't got the money to buy nice stuff.'

'What apprenticeship? Hope you're not getting ripped off, son?'

'They call it Community Payback, so I don't get paid, but I'll get a certificate.' Rob bristled and said, with spite, 'I want to make something of myself, carry on and train as a mechanic. Don't want to waste my life.'

Still feeling sick, I took a seat on the ledge by the open window, fiddling with the kamikaze plane. I sensed Douglas watching me, then turning to speak with Rob.

'So, how long has Sam here been your bird?'

I couldn't stand that sort of thing: 'bird', 'missus', 'other half'. Talking about me like I wasn't there. But at least he had no clue that I was Jena's sister.

Rob caught my eye, and said with a smile, 'Doesn't matter how long; it's how we feel about each other. We have a lot in common.'

'Early days, is it?' Douglas offered me his hand to shake. 'Well, thanks for coming to pick me up, love.'

Blue letters were tattooed on his hands and I could see an E between two knuckles. It probably said HATE, with LOVE on the other hand. Orange stains along his fingers.

He made himself comfy on the bed, while Rob and me watched, exchanging a glance. We were together on this: his dad was a wanker.

'Chuck my jacket this way, son.'

Rob grabbed the scruffy denim from the back of the chair and threw it at him, harder than necessary. From the inside pocket, he took a packet of chewing gum and slowly started to unwrap a stick. 'Takes my mind off fags,' he said, sliding it into his mouth. 'So, how old are you, Sam?'

'I was sixteen eight weeks ago.'

He chewed thoughtfully, and I wondered if he realised what date that was. 'About to leave school are you? Then what'll you do with your life?'

Make sure you're locked up, you bastard. 'I was going to go to college and do A levels. Now I'm not so sure.'

'What's that you're fiddling with?'

'My camera.'

'Show me.'

I wanted to say no, but courage left me, and I lifted the strap from my neck and handed the camera over, tensing as he peered at me through the lens. He pressed the shutter and took a picture, touching the Leica with his clawed hands.

'Where d'ya get this?' he demanded.

'Birthday present.'

He examined it closely before handing it back. I saw the indigo letters tattooed on his fingers.

I was wrong. The word on his flesh wasn't LOVE or HATE.

It was JENA.

CHAPTER 25

22 January

Pearl wakes me up by jumping on my bed, landing painfully on my left foot. 'Ah shit, Pearl. Where's the fire?'

She's like a girl a toddler would draw: mad fuzzy hair with a circle of smooth skin on the crown, sticks for limbs, Hello Kitty nightdress riding high on her bony thighs. Big toothy grin.

'The weatherman says it's going to snow later this week. And Sian says you're getting your tube out today.'

I don't know which of these pieces of information is causing her to be so manic. My fingers reach for my tube, touching where it's taped behind my ear. 'You sure Sian actually said that?'

Pearl nods, smiling wildly.

'I want a tube.' Her eyes are big and shiny, but her face is skin on bone surrounded by a halo of hair. I wonder when she last pulled some out.

'No, you don't, Pearl. Keep eating.'

'I am,' she says, giggling. 'But I'm getting away with it. The staff think I'm doing great.' She grins at me, showing a neat row of enamel-stripped teeth.

The pride in her voice sickens me, but who am I to judge? I share that desperate need for love and attention.

'Can I get a hug, Pearl?'

She places her head on my shoulder, one arm over my body. Her hand drifts to her head, and she wraps a finger around a strand of hair. I loosen her grip, but keep hold of her hand.

'Just think about nice things. Think about snow.'

We hold each other in silence on the narrow bed, two starved waifs, and I wish more than anything that I could help Pearl, but it's impossible. I can barely help myself.

'I'm sad to see you so despondent today, Sam. Why do you think you can't recover?'

Clive always asks questions like this, so glaringly obvious I can't even bring myself to answer. Today, I can hardly lift my head. I don't want to engage with the world, let alone him.

'Sam, please consider; just eighteen months ago, you were fearless. You were investigating a crime that even the police couldn't solve; you resolved to find Jena's attacker.'

'And look how that ended up.'

He shifts in his seat. 'The point I'm making is that a warrior spirit must still be inside you. Where is she?'

'Dead.'

'Nonsense, you just need to give yourself a chance. When you talk about your family, or about your friends here on the unit, I can see the powerful emotions play on your face. You look like you could achieve anything; you glow with life.'

Ah, the beauty benefits of an indoor life, eighteen months away from the damage of both wind and sun! But what he says pleases me and I relax, just a little.

'It wasn't just a warrior spirit that kept me going. It was Jena. She remembered her attacker.'

'She told you so?'

'No,' I say, thinking back to that day when I saw Jena's painting. 'She showed me.'

Douglas got settled on the bed, and began unwrapping another stick of gum, folding the silver paper until it was tiny. Rob said he was going to get some food, and I decided it was a good time for me to make my exit.

I wanted to stay, to find out more about Douglas, but I needed to see Jena too. Conflicting pulls, not sure which way would help most. All I wanted was some information, a way forward. Now that Douglas was free, it was even more urgent.

At the hospital, Jena was in the art room, working at an easel with Flora at her shoulder. I could tell she was really concentrating from the way her mouth was nipped tight, and the fixed focus of her eyes. Mum had that same look on her face when we were in the supermarket and she was working out whether to buy their own brand of cornflakes or splash out on Kellogg's. I lifted my Leica and tried to capture Jena, not as evidence for Penny but for me, proof that Jena was recovering. In the moment before I pressed the shutter, I saw my own face in the lens of the camera.

The sound of the shutter closing was so loud, Flora jumped. It took Jena a few seconds to register who I was, and then the smile burst.

'Sammy! Give me a hug.'

Jena held me so hard it knocked the wind from me. 'Okay, take it easy. I'm feeling a bit fragile.' Sick since I woke, and the journey to the prison hadn't helped. Somehow, it wasn't getting better.

'Come see what I did.'

She gently led me to the easel. I froze; in the picture with me in the foreground, Jena had started to add to the figure behind. She was filling in the blank face of her attacker, though it still wasn't clear that this was the same man I had met from prison earlier.

'Oh, Jena . . .' But words failed me. I kept staring at the empty space where a few pencil marks suggested a nose.

'I'd like to start here.' She pointed with her pencil to the area where eyes should be. 'But I don't have any black paint.'

'I'll get some.' Flora swished her way across the classroom and disappeared into her cave of art supplies.

Dumb and frozen to the spot, not wanting to move in case I should break Jena's concentration at a crucial point, I watched as she fell back into her art, mesmerised by what she was creating. I was spellbound as she drew a pencil line that became a jaw. Another curve became a cruelly dropped eyelid. The face was still mostly blank, and I was waiting for something definite, something that clearly identified this person as Douglas Campbell.

Flora returned, and handed Jena a tube of oil paint that she'd managed to daub on her shirt cuff. She touched my arm.

'Are you okay, Sam? You look peaky.'

'Bit sick. Just too hungry, I think,' I stammered, forgetting that it was a secret, that I'd stopped eating. My secret weapon, which made my thinking run in only straight lines, a thread I had to concentrate to keep hold of, but the only one I could follow. I'd missed several GCSE exams now; an academic future path was closed. Justice was my only ambition.

'Why don't you go get something to eat and come back when she's finished? It's best not to distract her.'

I couldn't leave, and I didn't deserve food. That would come after, when I had got something tangible for Penny. The raincoat would have been perfect, but an artist's sketch of the attacker, drawn by the victim, would surely work too.

Jena's face, as blank as the one on the canvas, was calm, but her arm moved rapidly as she swapped her pencil for a paintbrush and layered the paint, building the light and dark of the burly figure, with dark paint specks around the edge of the picture, which I took to be the storm.

It took me back to 25 April. My feet slipping in the mud beneath me, as I watched through the rain and saw Jena fall to the ground, her head cracking on the concrete.

Jena scrutinised the splatter effect.

'This brush is too thick!'

She was annoyed; she dropped it on the floor and started to drum on the edge of the easel.

Flora found a finer brush in a paint-ridged pot, and Jena grasped it, turning back to her painting, her hands moving quicker as she painted the pinky-red flesh of the face.

She washed her brush clean, and began to fill in the neck with a pale ivory colour, stroking and smoothing in such a way that the hairs on my arm tingled.

Flora put her hand on my arm. 'Gosh, Sam, you look like you've seen a ghost.'

'Not a ghost.'

It had to be Douglas; there was no possible alternative. And when Penny saw it, when she identified his face in the painting, then she'd have to re-arrest him. It was strong evidence; Jena was giving a visual description of her attacker.

But the details still weren't clear enough; the face was undefined. Jena needed help, to join the pieces together. I had to prompt her, but with what? The stolen photo might have worked, but she'd torn it in two, and then Mum had taken it.

Then a better idea came to me: Jena needed to see Douglas Campbell, face to face. That would be powerful enough, surely, to make her memory snap back in place. Then she could complete her picture, Penny would re-arrest Douglas, and the world would be normal again. I could re-do my GCSEs and start to eat.

If only I could get Douglas and Jena in the same place.

CHAPTER 26

22 January

Have you ever had that feeling, when something physical is being done to you, how you rise above the pain and let your mind go elsewhere?

I'm lying in the medical room (we girls call it the 'Weighing Station') on the plastic couch, and Manda is tugging the tube from my nose. Around me, the walls are pristine-white, and there are stainless steel gurneys, shiny medical cabinets and the dreaded calibrated scales.

'Just another pull should do it.'

She leans over me, hair falling loose. It's a tricky process and she breaks into a sweat, concentrating so hard that her eyes become crossed as the tube rises from my stomach, through my nasal passage.

I look down on the discomfort. My thoughts drift.

Jena's name is tattooed on my heart. So is Mum's. And Dad's.

And they are with me now, all three of them, not just in my memories or images in a photo. In my dreams, in my waking thoughts too. I feel unlocked, like my heart is open and warm, and fluttering out are feelings and thoughts that had been frozen.

I'm afraid that without the tube Ana will take over again. I'm suddenly afraid of dying, without resolving everything. 1 February is approaching; I can't escape it: the day when everything will be decided by the board and the day Mum will be buried. Big things, looming, and it's too late to change anything. My body is giving up; my organs are breaking down, even as my heart and mind thaw to life.

They won't release me; I don't deserve it. Once I tell Clive the next part of the story, he'll agree. It's not just that I'm mad, I'm bad too. Sick to the core.

It wasn't hard to persuade Douglas that we should eat at Pizza Hut the next night, the place I knew Lance was taking Jena for his belated birthday celebration. I'd spoken with Rob, and he agreed; placing Douglas and Jena together was a perfect way to see his guilt, to capture it on camera if I could, and to witness whatever it was he would say to her. Rob wanted his dad away from his mum – Scotland or prison, it was all the same to him. We were united in our purpose, and it was intoxicating, having someone so much on my side.

We held hands tightly, trailed by Douglas, who walked into Pizza Hut on 21 June like the world could wait, feet dragging, arms hanging and shoulders hangdog. The bastard had just been released without charge, but still wasn't happy; he'd spent the day since his release grumbling about the conspiracy against him and expecting sympathy. Rob was as sick of it as I was.

The town centre was empty except for a few latchkey kids on micro-scooters. Anyone with money or sense was at Cardinal Park, the leisure complex by the docks with a multi-screen cinema and snazzy restaurants. All the high street offered was boarded-up shops, a Poundland and fast-food joints. And Pizza Hut, a restaurant where it was forever Christmas: red chairs, white walls, green salad bar. Bright lights and glass windows, beyond which waitresses in red caps carried over-large pizzas (red tomatoes, green peppers) to groups of teenagers or weary families.

Plastic benches, booths, laminated menus, and the smell of burning cheese. On the table a flyer advertised the *Summer Sizzler Family Feast* for £20, and that's what we ordered: a gigantic pizza, garlic bread and Cokes.

Douglas drooled over the pictures. 'I had dreams about pizza when I was in my cell.'

So much for rehabilitation; it seemed all he thought about was food.

Then it happened, the very reason we were all there, though only Rob and I knew it. I nudged him, and gave a slight nod so he saw her: Jena had arrived.

She didn't see me. Too busy messing about with Lance. They were giggling, and Jena was lit up like Angelina Jolie on the red carpet at the Oscars. I tried to remember when I'd seen her so happy. Her dark hair had been washed and carefully braided, her face was lightly made up with soft colours, a peach blush and a touch of mascara accentuating her green eyes, and she'd lost that drooping quality. She looked beautiful, and though I guessed that Flora had helped with the make-up, I knew the real reason was Lance. He had his arm protectively round her shoulders and was talking to her, making her smile, and I thought how the few times I'd seen her with Andy, mainly when I'd been to see one of her shows at Pleasurepark, she'd always seemed nervous and desperate for any attention he gave her, whilst he had been charming and a little too smooth, always well-dressed and smiling, but never very warm.

The accident had robbed Jena of so much, of her job and her flat and the secret future she might have had with Andy, but it had given her this: a pure relationship built on simple terms. For a fleeting second, I felt it had been a good exchange.

The waitress led them to the booth in the corner, down-mouthed like she'd just won the last prize on the tombola; no tip tonight. Flora followed in a billow of lilac satin, hair clipped up into a colourful bird's nest of plastic grips, taking the table nearby and looking around as if she'd just landed on the moon.

The glum waitress slid a pepperoni pizza on to the table and a plate of garlic bread, hard as cardboard. Douglas closed his eyes.

'For what we are about to receive, may the Lord make us grateful.'

He crossed himself, then dived in, biting the bread with sharp teeth, spraying crumbs, then wolfing a slice of pizza, cheese stringing from mouth to plate, filthy nails dug deep under the crusty dough.

I took the smallest slice, and started to pick the cheese off. The rest of the pizza was sucked down in record time. Douglas was already eyeing the dessert menu, in a sticky plastic box on the table.

'I wouldn't mind Death by Chocolate.'

I stood up. 'Won't be a minute.'

I didn't look towards Jena and Lance's table, but went straight upstairs to the loo.

The droning fan wafted the smell of piss and pine around the warm room. Sat on the loo, knickers still up, I thought about my next move and felt a tide of sickness rising, even though my stomach was empty. I needed to keep calm and think. Douglas and Jena had to see each other. But what if she freaked and had a fit? What if he attacked her again? I put my head between my knees. If only I was ill, then someone would take me home and put me to bed. So ill I had to be knocked out. Made to forget. I held on to the toilet seat; the floor swum upwards.

Jena looked so alert and happy, and I was about to wreck that. It had been easier when she was safely locked away on Eastern Ward. For a moment, I understood why Mum had wanted to keep her there.

I left the cubicle, splashed cold water on to my face and faced the mirror above the sink. 'Samantha Hoolihan, get a grip. This is the moment you've been planning, so don't fuck it up.' The water was icy; that was why I was shaking.

The door opened, and I heard Flora say, 'Mind that step, Jena.'

Before I had chance to move, Jena was in front of me.

'Sam!' She held me too tight, saying happily, while kissing me on the cheek, 'I'm having pizza!'

'Everyone's having pizza.' I tried to free myself, suddenly hot after shaking with cold.

Flora, in various shades of purple with clashing green, looked like an exotic bird that had got lost.

'Come on now, Jena. You can see Sam another time, because she's with her friends tonight. And you're with Lance. So let her go now.'

'Your cheeks are wet, Sam.' She wiped my face with her fingertip, making me shake even more. She looked at me with such concern that I wanted to hug her hard and tell her to run away. I braced myself until the feeling passed.

'I need a wee,' she said, dashing into the cubicle.

Flora and I both pretended we couldn't hear Jena taking a piss. She was back out in seconds, tugging her jeans up.

'Hands, Jena.'

'Yes, Miss.' Jena grinned at me like I was in on the joke, but it was in moments like this that she seemed most changed, disinhibited by the accident. Or was it simply that she was bouncy with happiness, and I'd forgotten what a happy Jena was like?

'I'll see you later, Jena.'

'Back at the hospital?'

'No. In just a few minutes. I'll be waiting downstairs in the restaurant.'

Back in the booth, the pizza plate had been taken away, and Douglas was halfway through a mound of chocolate sponge swamped with cream. Rob gave me a questioning look, and I made a small motion to tell him, yes, this was the moment.

Douglas sucked up the last of the chocolate sauce.

'We need to pay,' he said, but he didn't make any move for his wallet. Instead, he leaned across the table. 'Get mine, will ya, son? I'll owe you later.'

'This one's on me,' I said, smiling sweetly. 'My treat.'

'Thanks, girl.' His eyes wandered over me. Then he stopped. Mid-sentence. Mid-movement.

He was staring over my shoulder and I knew he'd seen her because his eyes were wide as saucers, and I could hear Jena, talking loudly to Flora, on their way back to their table. 'I want Knickerbocker Glory, but if they don't do that I'll have . . .'

I turned, and sure enough, she'd stopped too. Uncertain which way to turn, her gaze fluttered then landed on Douglas.

I turned and looked into his eyes, to see if there was any clue written there. Though I desperately longed to watch Jena, to see if she remembered him, to confirm that he was guilty, I couldn't look away from Douglas's stricken face. White as a sheet. Pale anyway, at that moment he looked deathly, his eyes dark as seaweed, jaw slack. Was that what guilt looked like?

Jena said, 'Oh no. Douglas . . .'

Her beautiful face split open with a grimace of pain, her hands risen to her neck as if to protect herself. I moved quickly to her side, afraid of the memory I was ripping open like a scab.

'It's all right, Jena.'

She clung to me, her weight against me like my own guilt, turning in so we were in an embrace that felt like drowning. I had planned this, caused this.

A hand braced my shoulder, pulled me away from my sister, and I expected to see Flora's paint-splattered nails. But the hand was larger and the knuckles tattooed.

'Let her go.' Douglas was still touching me, pale as death, looking at Jena. 'I've been wanting to see you. You and me need to talk. Seems that whoever hurt you had the same idea.'

Her deep frown, her quivering down-turned lips, made my mouth ache.

A few yards away, Flora started fluttering, uncertainly hopping from foot to foot.

'Why didn't you meet me that day, Jena? Why get me all the way to Suffolk and not turn up?'

'I wanted to. I was going . . .' She started to weep, words struggling to come through between sobs. People had stopped eating to stare, and the waitress was by the till, talking to a young man in a red cap and waistcoat who must have been the manager. Lance was the one person who didn't keep a distance; he came beside us and put his arm around Jena's waist. Douglas was still waiting for Jena to finish her sentence, looming so close his face distorted. 'Go on, talk!'

'I was going to meet you,' she said, desperately. 'But then there was . . . someone. Stopping me. I hurt my head.'

The manager was walking towards us, pulling his cap more firmly on to his head. Douglas reached out, put a firm hand on her arm to silence her crying.

'So what about now, Jena? You can still tell the truth, sixteen years too late, but better than never. Only you can end this, and you know what you promised me.'

'No.' She shook her head, she backed away, into Lance's embrace. He comforted her as she repeated, 'No, no, no, no.'

'I'm afraid I'm going to have to ask you to leave,' said the pimply manager, sweat beading on his temples, but resolute. 'Or I'm going to call the police.'

It was over. The confrontation I'd planned, over just like that. Moments later, Flora was comforting Jena, coaxing her back to her table to collect their bags and coats. I paid quickly, and the manager sent me, Rob and Douglas outside in his bid to restore order.

In the street, Douglas sucked air and glared at me, his face high above mine and his voice pinning me with each syllable.

'You're Jena's sister? Did you know this, son?'

Rob moved forward, to stand between us.

'I know everything, Dad. So leave Sam alone.'

But Douglas wouldn't move back, and as he crowded me my heart pounded, hands clenched, and I felt rage pump through me.

'I just want justice. For Jena.'

Douglas scowled. 'For that lying bitch? She wasn't no innocent, you know, even at thirteen. She kept coming in the chippy, hanging around like a pretty stray. I felt sorry for her, fool that I was. I didn't know she was about to fuck up my life with her lies.'

My fingers itched to push him to the pavement, to see his head cracked open.

'She was just a child and you raped her! And then you came back, all these years later, to hurt her again.'

He stepped forward and held my arms to still me.

'You better hush your mouth, girl. That's slander.'

'Get your fucking hands off her!' Rob moved forward, against his dad, just like he did when he was a child and got that scar. But Douglas held him off.

'You don't believe this crap, son? You don't really think your old man would do those things?'

Rob moved, so he was closer to me. 'How would I know? I don't even know you.'

Douglas's eyes welled with tears. 'Because they stole me from you, son. Their lies. Jena's. Andy's.'

'What's Uncle Andy got to do with this?'

Douglas's tears disappeared as his eyes narrowed. 'He never wanted me to be with your mum, so when he had the chance to stick the knife in, he did. Went and made a statement supporting Jena's, some crap about me fancying her, so I looked guilty. Turned your mum against me, and sounds like he turned you against me too.'

Rob's face was crumpled with confusion, and I knew just how he felt. But he was my ally, and I needed him.

'Don't listen to him, Rob. He's a criminal and a liar!'

Douglas swivelled, his eyes still fixed on me, so close I could smell the garlic on his breath.

'There's things you don't know, girl, about your sister. After they arrested me for rape the police said there would be some kind of evidence, something physical. They said she was pregnant. But when my legal team asked about doing a DNA test on the foetus, they said she'd had a miscarriage – how convenient. She's a liar. A lying little bitch, and there are people in this town who have very good reasons to want to hurt her.'

Rob still had the look of confusion on his face, and I saw how strong the desire to believe his dad was. I felt I was losing him, and I had to show Douglas for the liar he was.

'Who would want to hurt her?' I demanded. 'Tell me!'

'I'm not telling you anything. I don't owe you, not after that stunt you just pulled. Making my son stand against his own father; it's not natural. You're just like Jena: a scheming little liar . . .'

'You're the liar!' I shrieked. People in the street were stopping to watch the commotion. 'I know things too, Douglas. That you were in Suffolk, outside her flat, eight weeks ago. That you found a coat with blood on it.'

He looked shocked; his jaw fell slack. 'You saw my police statement?'

Rob had got a hold of himself, and was trying to calm me; he tried to put an arm around me, but I shrugged him off. 'It's all right, Sam.'

'It's not fucking all right!' I was screaming, not caring that everyone nearby could hear. The Pizza Hut manager was standing in the doorway with his phone in his hand. 'Jena's in a hospital; her home is a crappy ward called Minsmere, and she can't even take a shower without asking permission.'

Douglas caught the collar of my jacket in his fist, and I heard the manager speak into his phone, asking for the police. Rob heard too, and started to steer us away.

We left before the police arrived, and as we walked Douglas pulled my face close to his, his hand under my jaw, so I could feel every word.

'A terrible thing happened to Jena that day, and it wasn't the first time something bad happened to that girl either. Maybe she asks for trouble. But if you think it was me who hurt her, you're dead wrong.'

CHAPTER 27

23 January

I find Pearl beyond the door marked FIRE EXIT, an outside area that is off-limits to patients (unless there's a fire), and for good reason.

'Fifty-four steps,' Pearl tells me through huffed breaths, her bare feet slap-slap-slapping on each one of the black iron steps, then she presses her palm flat against the red-brick wall, propels herself into a spin and goes right back down again, the knot of her bandana bobbing as she moves up, then down. It's exhausting just to watch.

'How long have you been here, Pearl?'

She doesn't even have to think about it. 'Enough to do this one hundred and eight times. One hundred and nine . . .'

I sit on the top stair, squeezed against the wall so I'm not in her way. Sweat drips from the tips of her elbows, and the hair not covered by the bandana is matted around her face.

'When can you stop?'

'When the staff make me. Until then, every step burns a calorie.'

Starving. Exercising. Purging. Pearl is a perfect anorexic. I'd like her to sit beside me and tell me why she does this to herself, but I'm not sure I could bear to hear the answer. Because I know, even without asking, that love and family and hurt will be at the heart of her problem.

I look out, to the North Sea, and feel the chill in the air. Snow is coming.

This time, when I arrive at his office, I expect Clive to ask how I'm coping without the tube. He doesn't.

'Aren't you even going to ask if I'm eating?'

Clive's jowls sag, and I see a conflict cross his eyes. 'If I do, would you tell me the truth?'

It is a stand-off; he knows I purged my feed yesterday, and he can see from my narrow face and frame that food and keeping it inside are still battles I fight. We could waste many hours talking about it.

'Probably not,' I admit.

Clive rests his head on his hands, elbows on the desk, as if he needs to support himself or he might melt. Today, he looks defeated, and I don't like this. One of us must be strong, and it should be him. If he stops believing in my recovery, then like a parent losing a love of Christmas, he will destroy magical possibilities. I am that child, and I need him to have faith.

'Do you think it's too late for me, Clive?'

He lifts his head and forces a smile. 'We still have some time left, Sam. But we need to use it wisely, and I think my role here is to ask you about the past. It's the road we are travelling, and we shouldn't deviate. Though we are getting to the very part that will cause you the most pain, that can't be avoided. I'm sorry, but it's an exorcism of sorts, and very necessary.'

Anger runs through me, quick and sharp as a blade.

'You in your fucking ivory tower up here, thinking you've got all the answers! But you never really say anything. It's me doing all the talking.'

His face returns to its earlier despondency. 'I don't think I have the answers, Sam; I wish I did. I just don't know what else to do to make the board look favourably on your case. On 1 February, I want to tell them that we have talked about everything that happened, and that you are now mentally stable and also remorseful. I want to be able to say that, whilst there is still healing needed, most of the work is done, and that you should be free.'

Free. Free from here, and free from the past. Is it really possible? How I long to believe, like a child; how I long for a touch of magic in my wretched life.

'Okay. Then let's get on with it.'

I don't even know if I deserve this special attention. I'm a mess, a bag of bones, head full of crap. I think about telling him that Pearl needs him more than me; if I told him about the Fire Exit marathon, he'd realise her need was more urgent than mine and leave immediately, my session forgotten. I'm a selfish bitch; I don't want to share his attention.

Still, Clive waits and I don't tell him about Pearl. Instead, I return to that terrible June, when the sickness surfaced.

After we left Pizza Hut, I went home. Rob didn't want us to part; he was worried about me, but I needed to be alone, and I needed to be away from Douglas. Thoughts were crowding my brain, and my forgotten body was begging me to sustain it, weakening me with the idea of food and calories, when I knew better. A single thought, capturing Douglas, was the line I needed to cling to, to follow to the bitter end.

That night, sleep offered meagre relief, a threadbare covering that lasted fleetingly, deserting me totally long before dawn. Douglas had said that Andy gave a statement against him, back when Jena was raped at thirteen, and I liked that he had tried to protect her, but still wondered why he seemed to have abandoned her now. And Douglas had been so adamant that he was innocent, both of the rape and the attack, that it raised doubts in my head that I didn't want. Only Jena could answer my questions.

In the quiet house, the empty kitchen, I cut an apple into twenty-nine pieces, one for each year of Jena's life, and sucked and chewed and swallowed. Hard cuts of apple, white down my throat and into the liquid of my stomach. The only nutrition I would allow myself until this was over.

I dressed without looking down at how my body was changing, melting into the very bones of me. I gathered up my camera and my Black Magic box, placing them in my rucksack, and biked to the train station.

I waited for the rest of the world to catch up with me and wake, and then boarded the first train across town to the hospital. I was there just as the day staff would be arriving; I saw Flora's lime-green Cactus pulling up in the car park, and quickly darted round the side of the building so as not to be spotted. I cut across the courtyard, bypassing the reception. Jena would still be in her room; I just had to bang on the glass and she'd let me in.

When I saw my sister, she was not alone.

At first, I assumed it was a member of staff helping her dress, that her arms were animated because she was putting on a top of some kind. But then I noticed her hands were open, palms up; she was pleading with someone. And that someone was not a nurse or care worker; it was a tall, lanky man with tattoos on his fists. Although my eyes saw him, my brain couldn't believe it.

Douglas Campbell was with Jena, in her room.

My hands fell limply to my sides, then my heart thrust itself into a frenzy, and I tensed as if to run away. Flight. Or fight? I squared my shoulders, ready to kill him with my bare hands if I had to.

I slid open the patio door. 'What the fuck are you doing here, Douglas?'

Douglas stepped forward and grabbed my arm, his firm, tattooed knuckles wrapped around my wrist, and pulled me into the room.

Jena was on the bed, her fingers in her mouth as she nibbled her nails, dark hair over her face, but I could still see she looked terrified. The world tipped as I realised that I had no chance of escape, no way of fighting him off. I was frozen with fear.

'Quite the stunt you and my boy pulled last night, wasn't it, girl? Trying to catch me out like that. Your little trick told me where to find Jena, so here I am.'

'You stay away from her! The police are on their way. You should leave!'

Douglas narrowed his eyes and I could see he didn't believe me, or if he did, he didn't care. He produced a ball of gum from behind his ear and played with it between his fingers, the silver cross hanging from his neck.

'I've done enough leaving for one lifetime. It's time people listened to what I have to say.' He positioned me on the bed, forcing me to sit next to Jena. 'You know why Jena wanted to meet me that day? She was going to tell me the name of the person who really raped her. Together, we would have finally set everything right. I would have been able to appeal my conviction.'

I leaned into Jena, so our shoulders touched, willing my love to melt through my flesh to her, to strengthen us both.

Douglas stood over us, and I internally begged for someone to arrive, so we would be saved. He placed a hand on Jena's right shoulder, the one nearest me, trapping her, his fingers so close to my face I could see the JENA tattoo. He saw me looking at it.

'See this? I did it in prison, sixteen years ago, serving time for a crime I didn't commit. Inked her name on my skin to remind me not to be so fucking gullible. Not to forget either.'

His fingers drummed her collarbone and Jena shrank into herself. He was so close I could see the creases around his lips, his brown teeth. And that cross, hanging round his skinny neck.

'Now tell Sam the truth, Jena.'

She was hunched beside me, like a child being told off.

'I lied,' she said. 'He didn't rape me.'

Douglas let out an almighty sigh, and released her. His hand free from her neck, he caressed the place where her name was forever tattooed, then focused on me; I could smell the mint on his breath from his last chewing-gum fix. I could see the white skin peeling around his nose, the red blood vessels in his eyes, the relief in them. For a moment, I believed him, that he had been wrongly convicted; he looked so determined to prove his innocence.

'Look, Sam,' he said, speaking quietly but making every word a slap. 'The police can't see the truth, even though it's staring them in the face. I didn't rape Jena sixteen years ago, and I didn't attack her on 25 April.'

Jena had started crying. There was blood on the tips of her fingers, where she couldn't stop biting her nails to the quick.

'What you read in my police statement was true. That afternoon, we'd planned to meet, but Jena never showed. And later, less than an hour after we should have met, I found a raincoat covered in blood, on the ground down the alleyway that leads to your street. I just thought it was someone had got in a fight, or maybe a worker at the chippy had had an accident. It was odd, but I didn't know what to make of it, and it was only later, when I saw the news bulletin, breaking news, that a woman had been set upon on Orwell Estate, that I knew it must have been Jena. And that the raincoat must belong to her attacker. So I went back, to get it. I'm not fucking stupid, Sam; I don't want to speak to the cops any more than I have to, but I wasn't going to keep quiet about something important like that. Only when I went back, it was gone. And next thing I knew I was the prime suspect.'

I leaned back, desperate for more space between us.

'But if you're innocent, then who attacked her?'

'That's the question we should all be asking. And one thing I know in my bones: whoever did it was the same person who raped her sixteen years ago. The two things are linked; I'm sure of that.'

My thoughts were all tied up in knots; I was unable to see where one rope ended and another began, but someone out there knew everything.

I took a gamble. I said, 'Penny is planning to hold a press conference on Monday, here at the hospital. There will be reporters, cameras, everything.'

Douglas leaned in again, and placed a hand on my shoulder this time, a threatening but also intimate gesture. 'What are you thinking, girl?'

I hesitated; I was about to suggest something risky.

'Jena could tell everyone that she lied about you raping her. If she said it when cameras are rolling and reporters are taking notes, then the police would have to act. There'd be a public outcry if they thought you'd been scapegoated and the real attacker was still walking around. He couldn't hide anymore.'

Douglas's expression turned dreamy for a moment. 'I'd have everyone's support, just like that guy in the Netflix series. A public petition. Compensation, maybe.' Douglas gave me what could have been a smile, but up close it looked like a snarl.

There was no smoke without fire; everyone knew that. Didn't he realise that even if Jena said he was innocent, she looked so pitiful and damaged that she was hardly reliable? And simply resurrecting the spectre of the rape case would remind everyone that he'd served time for it. The reporters would see to that. Then the police would have to try harder with their investigation. I wasn't trying to save Douglas, or make a hero out of him. I was moving him directly under the spotlight.

'That'll do nicely,' he said. 'Now I'd better go and tell Rob the plan, 'cos that poor boy has been poisoned against his own father, and he needs this as much as I do. I'll leave the same way I came. After all, I don't want to cause any trouble.'

After he exited by the patio door, I comforted Jena, who was still crying, but in my head I was sifting through what Douglas had said, that the bloodied coat was on the ground of the alleyway. If the attacker was someone other than Douglas, that coat belonged to them.

The coat had been in the alleyway that came out near the back of the fish and chip shop. Above which was the flat, with the lace curtains and the pottery dog, that Jena was about to move into with Andy.

Andy. It seemed that all roads led to him, all the strands I'd been following; his name kept coming up.

He was Jena's secret fiancé, yet hadn't shown his face since the attack. He managed Jena at Pleasurepark and was Dad's friend, but he hadn't been to our house either. Douglas said Andy had always hated him, and was happy to see him convicted of rape. He was Sonia's brother and Rob's uncle, and deep there in the mix.

And his address was written on a piece of paper, torn from Jena's address book, and folded neatly in my Black Magic box. It was time I paid him a visit.

CHAPTER 28

24 January

This afternoon is group counselling, called 'Share and Care', probably by Sian in a moment of ironic humour, and this time Clive is going to be there, to monitor how I cope. He said it would be good for the report, if I perform well in therapy, like a fucking circus clown. He also said it would be like a rehearsal, for when I have to speak in front of the board. The day of judgement is approaching, and I have a lot to prove.

Share and Care happens once a fortnight and is usually a time for patients to air grievances or sort out squabbles, to get things off their chest. The hot seat is a pine chapel chair, the same as everyone else sits on, but it's placed in the centre of the room, and whoever sits there must be honest and answer questions.

Some of the girls volunteer to be in the hot seat; Fiona likes to talk about feeling fat in jodhpurs, and how the girls at her private school bullied her for having wobbly thighs. We're all a bit sick of hearing about her privileged life, but it's easy listening. Joelle doesn't mind talking either, though it always goes sour when Manda gently points out that the lessons darling Mummy and Grandmummy taught her weren't an act of love. 'They said I looked beautiful,' Joelle says. 'The more weight I lost, the more they admired me.' Three sick women in one house. And this is where she'll return, when she's deemed well enough.

Mina won't often talk. Manda tries to persuade her, and sometimes she succeeds, but it's always a long process, and before she's spoken for many minutes she's in tears. We aren't sorry when she stops. Some people's stories are just too painful to hear, and I fear for her, knowing that she'll one day have to return to her father's house.

As for Pearl, though she hasn't been here long, she seems to enjoy chatting. I get the feeling, though, that she's not really revealing much. It all sounds too good to be true, how she now wants to get better, how being at the Bartlet is the best thing that's happened to her. She looks pretty and cool, wearing a beret or a bowler, but I know what's under the hat. Pearl is a good actress.

Today, I'm in the hot seat.

Clive told me that I should bring my Black Magic box to the session, so I have an idea what's coming, but first we all pretend to listen as Manda goes through the warm-up act: a lecture on the importance of knowing ourselves, understanding why we starve, so we can heal. I can't stop shaking.

'Okay, everyone, so today Sam is going to share with us some of the therapeutic work she's been doing, and talk about one of the photos in her memory box. Okay, Sam? You ready?'

I'm not, but I gather my box and prepare to leave the circle and sit in the centre. Clive is next to me, and reaches to pat my shoulder as I pass; an awkward gesture, and it feels bulky, but it's not his size that's wrong, it's mine. I take the seat, feeling like I'm in the dock, back in Crown Court, accused and needing to explain myself. The other girls are the jury today.

'Okay, Sam,' Clive gently prompts. 'We're all listening.'

I take the photo of Andy's penthouse from my box, because this is the photo we've come to in my individual sessions with Clive. It's him I most need to convince. The photo is passed around the circle, and the other girls – fellow sufferers or survivors, or whatever you'd choose to call them – gamely contribute, saying they're impressed by the open-plan design, shiny floorboards and black leather sofas. Pearl says she likes the cushions; they're zebra and cow print and scattered on the floor. Stacey is wowed by the large plasma screen above the fireplace, always impressed by a bit of bling. Everything looks clean and minimal.

When the photo is finally returned to me, I say that what I like best of all is the window: a whole wall of glass, looking out on to blue sky.

'Why have you chosen this photo?' asks Clive, though unlike everyone else in the room he already knows that we have reached this part of the story.

I sense Pearl hanging on my every word, Stacey leans forward to listen, and for the first time I get why some of the others love being in the hot seat so much.

'Because,' I say, almost in a whisper, 'this is where Andy lived. I hadn't been to his flat, but I knew Jena had, many times. I'd known for a long time that they were in love, and that a secret wedding was planned for when she left home and had her independence. But since she was attacked, I'd only seen him briefly, at the local garage buying a magazine, and he hadn't shown much interest in how Jena was. He hadn't visited her once.'

Stacey interrupts. 'How has this got anything to do with your anorexia?'

No one stops her asking this question, no one suggests it's too early in my talk to prod me to be explicit, to make links between then and now. They want me to answer.

'My sister had been attacked, and I didn't know who by. The whole world felt wrong and muddled and confused. Stopping eating was something I could have power over. For the first time, it occurred to me that Andy could have attacked Jena. Maybe, deep down, I'd always thought it, but just couldn't face it. She said he loved her, that they were getting married. I didn't want her to be wrong.'

'We can't always know what motivates people,' Clive said. 'Human beings are complex.'

'Some are,' I say, looking at my own hands and thinking what they'd done. 'But some people are simply evil to the very core.'

It was Douglas who first put the idea in my head that Andy may be Jena's attacker, but I needed Jena to confirm it. After Douglas left the hospital grounds, and still reeling from hearing her say that she'd lied about him raping her, I knew that she had to finish her picture. It was the only way she could prove if Douglas was guilty or innocent, and my mind was so messed up I didn't know anymore. I needed Jena to show me.

The outline of her attacker was on the canvas, but the face remained almost blank.

She frowned at the picture, and I saw that she was still shaken by what had just happened, but sympathy wasn't what was needed, and I tapped the edge of the canvas impatiently with my fingertip. I pointed to the incomplete face.

'So you say you lied about Douglas raping you, and he says there's a conspiracy against him. If it wasn't him, then who is this, Jena?'

She looked stricken. I wanted her to remember the events of 25 April so much, and it was coming slowly, the layers of memory peeling back like the kids' game of Pass the Parcel.

She dabbed with her brush, working again on the black hood when it was the face she needed to complete.

'Who was wearing that black coat in your painting? The coat that got covered in your blood? Who, Jena!' If only I could find that coat. If only I had more to go on than my sick sister's daubs.

She turned to me, wide-eyed, as though a shard of recollection had punctured her daydream. 'I was always special, he said. He gave me things, and said I was beautiful. Then he stopped. He stopped loving me.'

Andy. He had stopped loving her, hadn't he? He showed it plainly by not visiting. I felt like she was stepping on water; a miracle was happening.

'He hurt me, Sam.'

'Do you mean Andy?' I asked, pushing more than I should, but desperate for confirmation.

Her eyes looked weepy. 'Doesn't he love me anymore? He's hardly been to visit. You know what happened, don't you?'

'He's not come at all, Jena. I know fuck-all. And it's killing me.'

I reached for my sister and hugged her like my very life depended upon it. She pulled away from me, and there was such a wise expression on her face that it broke my heart; she was my protective elder sister once again.

'I'm not there to look after you. And it's dangerous. You must remember to forget, Sammy.'

But I couldn't promise that. Not anymore.

I stop talking, and look around at the other girls, who all know what I did, what I'm guilty of. This is the closest I've ever come to describing the build-up to my crime, and I can see their eagerness for more.

Pearl nibbles the ends of her hair nervously, while Stacey gazes at me with frank curiosity. Joelle and Fiona look as though they're watching a soap opera that's just paused for adverts. Only Mina is so shut down that it's hard to know what she makes of my story. But Clive looks proud.

'Well done,' he says. 'That wasn't so hard, was it? We can continue this in our individual session later.' And this alone makes me want to weep.

When we leave the therapy room, everyone sort of breathes out and starts talking, real loud, like they have some sound to catch up on. Stacey's at my shoulder.

'That wasn't so hard,' she mimics, making a crude gesture with her right hand on her crotch. 'Patronising wanker. But why can't we hear what you did next? How come only he gets the big reveal?'

She's wearing a lemon top, a black skirt and red shoes, so she looks like a fruity stick of rock, so sweet any boy would want a lick. So happy with herself, with her *not hard* joke and her bubblegum-pink lips.

'Fuck off, Stacey. It's not *Coronation Street*.'

'Whoa, what did I do to deserve that? God, Sam, I'm getting sick of your attitude. I thought you wanted to talk! What's got into you at the moment?'

I'm so busy calculating how much I've just revealed to the other girls that I don't know what she's on about. 'What?'

'What do you think? Being all secretive. Opening up in the hot seat for once, just because Clive is there, but not with us. Not even getting to the juiciest part!'

She pouts, as if she's thinking more about how she looks than what she's saying.

'We're supposed to be mates, but I haven't got a clue what's going on in your head at the moment. You're so moody.'

'Oh get off my case, Stacey. Go and suck some water.'

'See? I'm only saying what I think, and you speak to me like that. I'm your friend, remember? I reckon you need help.'

'I can look after myself.'

'You reckon, Sam? You're so . . . angry. All the time.'

'Yeah, well, maybe I've got reason to be.'

She thinks about this. 'Maybe you have. I mean, I know your mum's funeral is coming up. And what happened to your sister sucks. I mean, I can't even imagine how it must feel, and I don't blame you for being mad about that. But I'm on your side, Sam. Don't you get that?'

Sweet Stacey. Who says she's not clever? She knows just how to make me feel like a piece of shit.

CHAPTER 29

25 January

We're approaching February, the coldest month, and after days of the weatherman's empty promises, it's finally snowing.

I wake to discover the Bartlet Hospital has been wrapped in a huge white duvet, insulated by the falling flakes that gather on the window ledges and hang heavy on tree branches. The snow on the beach is met by the frothing white sea, a magical land, untouched by humans. I stay inside, where it's so quiet my breath echoes. The other girls are out on the hill, sliding on plastic bags and metal trays down to the sea road below.

Watching them through the window as they catch snowflakes on their tongues and scoop balls of snow to pelt at each other, I realise how old I feel, much older than seventeen, and decades older than them. Pearl is spread-eagled on her back in the snow, moving her arms and legs vigorously, laughing. When she jumps and sees me at the window she waves, pointing to the shape she's left behind.

A snow angel.

With her pale, almost-blue skin, her wide eyes, a pink knitted hat with a white pom-pom covering her head, a few curls escaping, she looks like nothing less. Too good for this world.

When she finally comes inside, her teeth are chattering and her lips are navy. I hold her hands in mine, but rather than giving her my heat I can feel my arms turning icy.

'I think you should see Manda,' I say, when her skin hasn't regained any colour after twenty minutes.

'I'm fine.'

But she isn't. Her body is thin. Her bones are sharp and visible under her skin. She removes her hat, wet with melted ice, revealing her bald patch. It looks bigger, and red at the edges; she has been pulling hair again. I feel helpless, knowing she's sick but that I'm too sick to fix her.

Also, there isn't time. I have just seven more days to sit with Clive, as he tries to fix the bad thing inside and order my thoughts. Attempting to free myself from the crushing guilt of the past, but on 1 February I will be judged anew.

'You need to be assessed as being mentally stable enough for discharge, as well as being morally stable.'

'What the fuck does that mean?'

'It means taking full responsibility for your crime, being remorseful. The board need to be certain you don't represent a risk to society,' says Clive, carefully talking me through the board's possible decision.

He doesn't threaten me with extra calories anymore. He knows that I no longer have a choice.

I have to finish my story before it's too late.

On Thursday 23 June, I came downstairs to find Mum and Dad huddled over the table, untouched mugs of tea in front of them, Mum's anxiety tablets in their green-and-white box in the middle of the table, and a letter propped against the cornflakes box. It was from Penny and had already been opened – in fact, I saw that the postmark was from two days ago, and it was sent first-class, so I guessed it had arrived the day before and that Mum and Dad had been keeping it from me.

I read it quickly:

> I'm sorry to inform you that the person remanded, pending our investigations, was released without charge by the court this morning. There was insufficient evidence to detain him, and unless anything new arises he is not considered a suspect at this time.
>
> Given this, and the lack of other leads, I would like to go ahead with the press conference on Monday. I have spoken with Dr Gregg, and he has agreed that it can take place in Jena's room at the hospital, at 2 p.m., and I'd like you all to arrive around one thirty to prepare. National press have been alerted, and we expect at least two television networks to attend, as well as local journalists.

My parents had watched me read the letter, and were waiting for my reaction. Both of them had faces as blank as babies', and I didn't know what to make of it. Unless they'd both had some atenolol.

'It's all been arranged,' Mum said, her voice taut with suppressed rage. 'She's not even asking for our permission.'

'We don't need to be there, though,' Dad said, quickly. 'She can't make us go, Kath.'

I read the letter again. Mum was right: Penny wasn't asking for our permission, but she did expect us to be there.

'I've called Minsmere,' Mum said to me. I saw that Dad already knew this; he put his hand up to his brow and leaned in. 'Even if that fool Dr Gregg has told Penny that Jena is well enough to speak, I said we didn't think so, and we're her next of kin. I'll see a solicitor if I have to. He's meeting us later today. We need to persuade him to cancel the whole thing.'

'But I don't agree with you, Mum! This is the best way to solve everything.'

Her face paled, then mottled up with a blood rush. She shook her head, grabbed the letter from my hands and screwed it into a ball.

'Sam, I'm trying to protect my family from more pain. You've got your GCSE exams; you just need to just concentrate on them.'

Everyone wanting to protect me. *Remember to forget, Sammy.* And Mum would find out when the results were issued that I hadn't even turned up for the stupid exams.

'I don't need protection; I need justice for Jena. And the press conference is the answer.'

'It's cruel to put her through it. To put us through it.' She took Dad's hand, clasping it tightly over the kitchen table. 'I want you at the meeting today, to support us. He'll be getting all of his staff to say Jena is well enough for the press conference, and we need to persuade him otherwise.'

'But, Mum, this conference could—'

Mum shook her head violently, and snapped, 'Stop, Sam! It won't make any difference; she can't remember a thing.'

'You're wrong, Mum. Jena is painting her attacker. I think it's Andy.' I blurted it out, not even sure I believed it. I still hadn't totally ruled out Douglas.

Mum touched her chest, heaving under the fluorescent layer. I could see she was trying to control her breathing.

'Have you never wondered why he hasn't visited Jena?'

She looked at Dad, as if he would answer, though he always left the speaking to her. 'Stop it, Sam! Only close family have been visiting Jena, you know that! Why would he be allowed in? He's only her boss . . .'

'He was more than that. They were close, closer than you know.'

'Rubbish! I won't hear any talk like that.' She shifted to try and get up, but anxiety had her in its grip. Suddenly she was taking shallow, panting breaths. She rocked herself, head down with nausea, words like tumbling gravel as Dad tried to steady her.

She held out a grasping hand to him for support. 'Pass me my medicine, Sam.'

Standing over her, I felt again the strongest conviction that she was hiding things from me. I reached for the green-and-white packet, next to the letter, and closed it in my fist.

'You don't need this shit, you need answers! The press conference is our best chance, Mum. We get to say something publicly, something powerful. Who do you think attacked Jena?'

'Give it. Please.'

She tried to stand up, but fell back down on to her chair awkwardly. Dad steadied her, and reached for my hand to get the pills, losing his grip on Mum as he did so. She fell on to the floor, hyperventilating, eyes rolling.

'Oh Kath, love . . .'

I chucked the tablets at her where she lay on the carpet, Dad over her trying to help her sit up as her panic attack took hold and she retched.

Hot with guilt and anger, I grabbed my rucksack and headed for the front door, slamming it closed behind me.

As I walked down our front path, I had the sensation I was being watched, and turned to see Mrs Read, standing in her bedroom window, gazing down at me. She pressed her palm to the window, her face twisted with concern, her hand a gesture of *stop*.

Bike. Get on it and ride. Away. Away from Mum and her panic attack, from Mrs Read's conspiracy theories. I rode hard, all the way to the docks, the air singing in my lungs as I struggled to breathe through swollen airways. I hadn't showered or eaten in days; I was a mess, but none of that mattered. I had an address, a place I needed to be.

Andy's penthouse was easy to find. It was eight floors up, a balcony across its width. Even from the ground I could see the view would be impressive.

The entrance lobby had a pond, with a few fish glimmering below the surface. There was an intercom buzzer, a panel of numbers. I pressed lucky number 7.

'Hello?' Andy's voice.

'It's Sam Hoolihan.'

I could hear him breathing into the mouthpiece. I wondered if he was worried about what my arrival could mean. Questions. An accusation, maybe.

'I'll buzz you in. Take the lift.'

I had to wait while the lift swooped down, the doors opening terribly slowly. When it was fully open, there stood Monica, the drama student from college.

She was dressed in every shade of sunset: orange hair, yellow dress and red lips, eyeliner smudging down her face. She looked rough and tired, but still pretty.

'Hey, Sam.' She didn't seem overly surprised to see me; then she noticed my face and became concerned. 'Why you cry, hey?'

She pulled a tissue from her cleavage and blotted my cheeks. 'Cheer up, it may not have happen, yes?'

'It already has.'

'Why you here?' She looked me up and down. 'You're too skinny to be an actress. You come with me instead.' She gripped my arm and started to tug me outside. 'We go to Spoons Café, yes? Is good there, good cake, and I have money now. We have tea and talk.'

But I pulled away from her and stepped into the lift. 'I can't.'

I jabbed number 7, afraid she'd drag me away, but she remained outside, watching me as the door closed. She looked sad, and I felt like I was abandoning a friend.

The lift took me high; a glass panel revealed the world falling away beneath me. There was a ping as it reached the top floor and opened on to a small landing, with potted plants either side of its shiny surface. In front of me was a closed door. I pressed the doorbell, waiting a long minute until the door opened. A British bull terrier with a curved nose and a black patch over one eye bounded up to me, pushing its nose into my crotch. I tried to shove it away, but it was all muscle, sniffing into me.

'Get back, Bullseye.' Andy pulled it off me by its thick collar. I'd seen the dog before, with Monica at the police station. Andy must have been there, in one of the interview rooms. Was he one of the leads they were investigating? Or was he trying to set Douglas up, as Douglas claimed he had sixteen years ago for the rape?

A prickle of sweat on my scalp, under my hair. My heart pounding with nerves.

Bullseye whined, watching me, its pink tongue hanging wetly out; if Andy let go of the collar he would pounce on me. Andy pushed his cow-licked fringe to one side. He was dressed casually in skinny jeans and a Hollister T-shirt, young clothes for a man with a receding hairline and grey sideburns. He smelt of sweat.

'Hi, Sam. This is a surprise. How did you find me?'

'Your details are in Jena's address book.'

Andy stepped back over the threshold, hands in pockets like it was just any encounter, though his face was tight, and I could see a muscle twitching near his eye, where crinkles had set in, probably decades ago. This was why Jena said their relationship was a secret; he was almost sixty, though he didn't look it.

'Come on in, then.'

Andy's flat was picture-perfect. My eyes were greedy to take it all in: the famous monochrome print of a kissing couple by Robert Doisneau on the wall, the fluffy white rug. It was nice, in a predictable, Ikea kind of way. I mean, way better than my home, but not what I'd have chosen if I had cash to flash. I thought about Sonia's house, and wondered why he didn't do more to help his sister out.

'Well.' He rocked, hands still in his pockets, wondering what to do with me. 'Can I get you something? Milkshake?'

When Dad took Jena and me to Pleasurepark, back when I was a kid and she was still a teenager, we'd always drink milkshakes. They had a machine in the staff room to make it really frothy, but that felt a long time ago now.

'Water's fine.'

He walked to the far corner, where a door led into a kitchen. Silver and slick, it had a designer coffee maker, over-sized pepper grinder and a kettle with a spout shaped like a bird's beak on the granite-tiled work surfaces. And a milkshake machine, just like the one at Pleasurepark.

He got my water from a cooler in the door of the huge American fridge. It was so cold my teeth ached.

'Well, you found me.' He leaned on the worktop, both hands returned to his pockets. He was watching me, wary but concerned. He rubbed the stubble on his chin, and his eyes were blurry.

'Have you just got up?'

'I wish! I've been awake all night. Working.'

'What work?' Not Pleasurepark. That place closed at six, even in high season.

'New film. The actors didn't leave till this morning.'

'Is Monica one of the actors?'

His head jerked up. 'Do you know her?'

'She goes to my school. She's in the sixth form.'

'Oh yeah, I remember now. Your dad sent her photo to me, but I'd already talent-spotted her.' He chuckled. 'Ipswich is a small town for beauty.'

And then I remembered when I took that photo. 'I saw her in the police station. With your dog.' As if it knew it was being discussed, Bullseye gave a whimper and moved to Andy's side, rubbing its nose on his leg. 'Why were you there, Andy?'

'The police are interviewing everyone who was close to Jena. And your sister's on my team; I've known her for years, so . . .' His sentence trailed off, hanging in mid-air. He smiled, like that was enough, and I realised he was used to people believing him, doing what he wanted.

I knelt on the floor, hiding my face in my hair, and Bullseye came to me. I reached to stroke him, and he gave a shiver of pleasure.

'What sort of film is Monica acting in?'

He inspected his buffed nails then said, 'Art house. Low-budget but high-quality. I have a studio at Pleasurepark; they let me work on my own stuff as long as it's in my own time.'

Bullseye whined again, then gave a sharp bark.

'All right, boy.' Andy turned to me and said, 'Problem with living in a flat. I just need to take him for a quick walk or he'll piss on the floor. Why don't you wait in the lounge? Switch on the TV if you like. I'll only be a few minutes.'

Once I'd worked out how to use the remote control, the plasma screen blinked into colour and sound. Above the tag-line *Who's the daddy?* Jeremy Kyle was shouting at a weary and worn pregnant teenager, who sat between two scag-heads, presumably the potential fathers. Jeremy opened an envelope and waved the answer before reading it out, saying, 'Well, well, well. The DNA test results show that . . .' He paused dramatically, simpering into the camera. The audience waited and then, right on cue, they heckled and booed: it was neither of the men on stage. The woman hid her face in her hands.

I switched it off, disgusted with myself for no good reason. As if shoddy behaviour was contagious and I'd been touched by it.

I walked to the window. Outside was a balcony with white shiny chairs and a glass table, and a few oriental-looking plants in white square pots; red blossom had dripped on to the white tiles.

The flat gave nothing away. Everything was impersonal and perfect, and none of it satisfied my curiosity. A white, sturdy cabinet was against the wall, the kind that might be used for books or a home office. I wondered what Andy kept in there.

The cabinet opened soundlessly. Inside were bundles of wires and gadgets; so this was where he kept his film-making stuff. There was a tripod and a camcorder: top of the range, thin and ultra-sleek. On the floor was a wooden chest. I lifted the lid to reveal a bounty of tapes. I read labels and realised these were the films he made.

Hello Klitty (Nita), *Breakfast with Fanny* (Tracey), *The Iceman Comes* (Monica). The DVD covers were lurid, creepy rip-offs of better-known films, with pictures of girls in sexy clothes, showing flesh and smiling provocatively. The last DVD in the box was called *Wedding Day*. And the smiling girl in the picture, wearing a wedding dress, was Jena.

Just then, the door to the flat opened and Andy walked in with Bullseye. I was still on the floor in front of the open cabinet. He came towards me, Bullseye straining at his side to sniff my neck.

'What are you doing, Sam?' He closed the cabinet with a slam, and though his face remained genial his voice was threatening. 'Didn't your mum ever tell you not to snoop? You'd regret it if you watched those films.'

I pushed the dog away and stood up, unsteady.

'Why? Are they porn?'

''Course not; they're just a bit of entertainment. But you can't just march in here and start nosing in my cupboards!'

I took a deep breath. 'I know about the wedding, Andy.'

His jaw dropped so I could see his teeth, perfectly neat but sharp incisors. 'Jena told you about the film?'

I shook my head, trying to straighten out my thoughts. 'I know that you were moving in with her. That you were going to get married. I've seen the invites. And the dress.'

He stared at me like I was crazy, then he started to laugh. 'We weren't getting married. Your sister lives in a dream world, she always has; that's what made her such an asset on the entertainment team.'

I couldn't believe he was denying it. 'Why would she lie?'

'It's not lying, is it, to have a little fantasy?' He chuckled to himself, and stroked a preening hand down his T-shirt, where grey hair bloomed at the neck. 'She's a born actress. And I'm sorry about what happened to her, Sam, truly I am.' Then he looked at me as if suddenly seeing me for the first time. His face changed, and his eyes seemed to be inspecting me.

'Perhaps you've inherited the acting gene too? You're very pretty, Sam. Maybe you'd like to be in one of my films? It's just a bit of harmless fun and a good way to make money. Lots of money.'

He stepped towards me, smiling confidently, eyes alight with something like curiosity, and I pushed him away, hard on the chest so he stepped backwards in surprise, his mouth open, teeth glinting.

I had a premonition, a moment, when I saw another figure in a cape, with teeth like needles that wanted to sink into my flesh and kill me.

It was Andy. Oh God, it was him . . .

I stumbled to get away, tripping over my rucksack, frightened. I grabbed it and made for the door, struggling with the lock, as Andy came towards me, looking angry, and every instinct ordered me to get away from him, to get free.

The lift door was open, waiting, but he caught me up and held me by the arm. 'Sam, what's the problem? I'm sorry if I scared you.'

Panicked by his hands on me, thinking of what he did to Jena, I yelled, 'Get off me!'

He dropped his grip, holding his hands up in submission, and I stepped into the lift just as the doors closed. As it began its descent, I could hear his voice, calling me back.

CHAPTER 30

26 January

Pearl is opposite me at the brown dining table, pretending to eat lunch. Sian's our supervisor today, but she doesn't take a seat. Instead, she stands over us at the head of the long pine table, leaning on it, fixing each of us in turn with her assessing eyes as we swallow each mouthful of water, each spoonful of soup. She'd have been better suited to working in a prison. Isn't that ironic, given my own predicament?

Pearl lifts her English muffin to her mouth, but before she takes a bite she squeezes the bread so that butter trickles down her arms, then she crumbles a bit off. She swishes her hair so that her fingers can hide the pieces of muffin in its tangles and under the crazily patterned woollen hat she has pulled low on her head. There is no colour in her face, and her eyes look bloodshot.

Sian doesn't notice Pearl; she's watching Stacey, who is struggling with even one mouthful. 'Muffins are bad,' she tells Sian, who replies that there is no such thing as bad food. Pearl tries her trick again, and gets away with it. Half of the muffin is gone now, and she hasn't eaten any. Delighted, she winks at me, and despite my inner qualms we are conspirators.

As the twenty-five minutes tick past, I nibble around the edges of my own muffin, infuriating Sian.

'Eat it, Sam, don't play with it.'

I sip my water, and notice Pearl hasn't touched hers. Does she want to get tubed?

'Come on, Pearl!' says Sian, who has also noticed. She has little patience generally, but for some reason even less with Pearl. 'You can't believe there are any calories in water?'

'I do,' says Pearl, fixing Sian with her large saucer eyes.

Sian's own eyes narrow. 'Really? Haven't you ever read the back of a bottle? Zero calories.'

'I've read it,' says Pearl, sweetly. 'But I don't believe in labels.'

Later, Pearl joins me in my room. She sits cross-legged on the floor with her Sylvanian toys, a family of rabbits, each no taller than her thumb. The mother rabbit is distinguished by an apron, and Pearl has placed tiny plastic cooking implements into the rabbit's paws. Mrs Rabbit is baking an invisible cake. I lie on the bed, watching.

'Do you really believe there are calories in water?'

Pearl continues playing. 'I used to think I could get fat just by smelling food. And I used to think water had calories because it made me feel heavy. But now I know that's not true.'

'So why not drink it? They'll tube you if you don't.'

Pearl smiles manically. 'I like to feel the pain.'

She means the dehydration, the way it intensifies everything, the dizziness and tingling. Looking at Pearl's young, frail body, she seems so much sicker than I ever was. That can't be true, though; it's a distortion. I was very sick, only no one realised it. Not until afterwards, when it was too late.

When I arrive at his office, Clive is slumped in the chair. For the first time, he isn't wearing his jacket; instead, it is strewn across the desk. His shirt has sweat stains under the arms, and his beard is straggly, in need of another trim. He looks like he slept at his desk, and I feel concern for him, a strange shifting of roles.

'Clive?' He rallies himself, and sits up, trying to put his professional mask on, but I still see he's troubled. 'Are you okay?'

'I'm fine. I'm just getting worried about the board meeting; I want this report to be right.'

I see then that the papers he is worrying over are my own case file notes. His jotter is full of scribbles, and on an A4 pad is a neater text.

'Is that my report?'

'Without the conclusion,' he acknowledges. 'I have to be honest with you, Sam. I want the best for you, and I want you to be free of this place, but I think we'll have an uphill struggle. The judge who sentenced you said you showed no remorse, though at the time that was put down to your poor mental health. We need to demonstrate this has altered. If it has?'

I look out of the window, at the snowy beach beyond. 'I don't know if I'm sorry for what I did.'

He puts his face into his cupped hands. 'That's what I was afraid of. The condition of your release is sanity, and that would include remorse.'

'Do you think I'm sane?'

Clive looks blankly out of the window, at the snow starting to fall.

'I think you're getting close. And I'll have to submit my assessment by the end of tomorrow, so the other two board members have time to read it before the meeting. If you're ready, you could go home.'

Home. I don't respond to this. There aren't words enough.

'We don't have long left. You need to finish your story.'

And, for the last time, he prepares to listen to me. The sky breaks open and snow taps the windows, closing us in.

Although I am not hopeful that it will make any difference, I talk anyway.

I arrived back home from Andy's flat confused and upset.

Mum was in the kitchen, on her knees in front of the oven, her arm lost in its greasy depths, working the Brillo pad so hard her whole body was jiggling to the frantic rhythm of her scrubbing. The sound of it made me shudder.

'I don't feel so good, Mum.'

She came out of the oven then, her face dripping with sweat, concern in her eyes.

'You've not been right for days.'

A stab of guilt shot into my heart; I'd been so angry with her recently, when none of this was her fault.

Arms hanging, head down, I burst into tears. She came to me, pressing her hand first to my forehead, then to my cheek.

'Well, you're not hot. Cold, if anything.' She gave me a hug and I was enveloped in the scent of Mr Sheen oven cleaner and Yardley and her. 'I'll tell Dr Gregg the stress is making us all ill, and that's why he needs to cancel the press conference.'

'Oh Mum . . .' I wanted to be protected, but my obsession had gone too far for that. It was time for the truth. 'I think Andy attacked Jena.'

She sucked her teeth. 'Why would you say that?'

'Because he was leading her on, saying he loved her. Telling her they were getting married. But it was all a lie.'

Mum frowned. 'He was just her boss, Sam. They were never getting married, that's crazy.'

It didn't make sense to me either. Why would this fantasy lead to my sister being broken on the ground?

'But he's sleazy. And he makes dodgy films.'

'Stop!' She gasped, confused and angry, with me, with all that had happened. I could hear the tension simmering beneath the words. 'Andy has been a friend to this family for years, employing Jena, looking out for your dad. Your father would trust Andy with his life.'

Suddenly my head was against her chest, her heart pulsing in my ear. Then she placed a hand on each of my shoulders and pushed me back so she could see me. She looked close to tears too.

'We need to focus on the future, on keeping this family together. That's what matters. You're so pale, Sam, so thin. You're wasting away. Dad and me, we worry about you. It's time we focused on you for a change. But first we need to make sure the press conference doesn't happen.'

Defiance rose in me. Anger broke free into a moment of clarity.

'I'm the only one who wants to find out who attacked Jena, aren't I? You don't even fucking care.'

Slap. Hard and fast, on my left cheek.

'Shut up!'

There was stillness in her, in both of us. We were both stunned. She smoothed her dress, and breathed out.

'Now, that's an end to it. We are getting the next train to the hospital for the meeting with Dr Gregg, and we are going to stop the press conference taking place. Understand?'

Dr Gregg was behind his fortress of a desk; Mum, Dad and me on the low chairs in front. Dad hadn't said much on the journey to the hospital; he'd just stared out of the window as the train sped down the track. I hadn't forgiven Mum for slapping me, but I sat close to her side as she pretended to read a magazine.

Jena didn't join us for the meeting. Whatever was about to be decided, she would not have a say.

Dr Gregg knew what was coming; he was prepared. He'd asked all staff to submit a mini-report stating if they believed Jena could cope with the stress of a press conference, and everyone was agreed she could.

He handed us the pile of papers to read, just like a bloody school report. Even the cook had written a comment: *Jena's not eating as much fruit as she should.* What would she know about whether Jena could speak to a roomful of journalists?

'It seems we have no choice, Kath,' said Dad, after reading every slip painfully slowly, a finger under each word, taking it all in. 'Everyone is against us.'

I flicked through until I found Flora's slip and placed it in his hand. 'This is more important than how many apples she eats.'

Dr Gregg pointed with a pencil to his copy. 'Ah yes, Flora is really pleased with the progress Jena is making in art-therapy sessions and she thinks she's closer than ever to being able to speak about the attack. She tells me that Jena has a natural gift.'

Dad breathed deeply. 'She's always been creative. You should have seen her performing at Pleasurepark; she'd sometimes get nervous, but she stole the show every time. She came alive on stage or in front of the camera.'

I felt irritated by this sentimental bullshit, though Mum was dabbing her eyes and Dr Gregg was smiling indulgently.

'It's what she's painting that's important. Her memory of the attack is returning. Which is why the press conference needs to happen,' I said.

Mum frowned at me, a warning that I should shut up, then she gave Dr Gregg a meaningful glance. 'Sam hasn't been well recently. It's the stress. I don't think she could cope with Monday.'

He cleared his throat and peered over his glasses at me.

'I'll agree, Kath, that Sam's obsession with retrieving Jena's memory is upsetting, for both of them. But I think we have a solution for that.'

A cold thump of rage. 'What?'

Mum took my hand firmly in hers, not for comfort but as a warning. With my free hand I lifted my hair to my mouth and chewed on the ends, staying silent as Dr Gregg lifted a cardboard box from under his desk. The Asda box, from the attic at home!

'Sam, you've been seen going to the storage room with Jena. It was clear from the layout of the room, the TV being switched on standby and what-have-you, you've been watching films with her, family films. Emotional jolts like that could set Jena back and should only be conducted under strict supervision.'

I turned to face Dad. No one else used that attic but him.

'Why would you give him our family films? This meeting isn't supposed to be about this!'

Dad looked at his hands. Mum cupped her hand over his, a sign of her support, their unity. I felt like a trapped animal, brought here to be neutered. My mission aborted.

Dr Gregg cleared his throat and tried to explain. 'Samantha, your parents and I have talked about it and we've agreed. The box will be stored here, until such a time as Jena is well enough to view the films in a controlled therapeutic environment. It would be unethical to influence Jena's memory just now. What she says on Monday must come from her own recollection; showing her films may influence her adversely.'

'Bullshit!' I reached for the battered lid and pulled the box towards me. 'These can help her to remember. She should watch them this weekend.'

'Sam, you need to stop. This is making you ill.' Mum was getting weepy. As if I was the one in need of help.

'I thought this was about Monday,' I said. 'Why has this become about what I'm doing with Jena?'

Dr Gregg exchanged a knowing look with Mum, then Dad, and I realised they thought I was a problem.

'Jena is a special case, and her brain may be more suggestible than you realise. In patients with ante-retrograde amnesia we would expect to see evidence of hippocampal sclerosis, especially when Jena has experienced left-lobe seizures. But we found no evidence: hence, she is MRI negative.'

'So, her brain is better?'

I thought of all the times I'd shown her a film or photos and saw genuine understanding on Jena's face; all the times I'd felt that she was just pretending to be brain-damaged.

'No, ah, no,' Dr Gregg said, stifling a smile at my stupidity. 'It's simply an anomaly. Just one diagnostic tool that, in Jena's case, is of no use, I'm afraid. I'm just trying to explain that her brain is still processing memory, and she is very vulnerable to current events.'

'Her brain isn't damaged!' In a flash of inspiration, fully realising the truth finally, I was about to list everything that proved she wasn't: the lace curtains; the dog; all the other things she had remembered.

Mum silenced me. 'Shut up, Sam.'

It was always more frightening when she spoke quietly, seething underneath, her patience worn thin. I felt my cheek burn, as if re-experiencing the slap.

'Listen to what Dr Gregg is saying. He's confiscating the films for Jena's – and your – own good.'

'The press conference will go ahead, Kath,' he empathised. 'But we can agree on certain conditions. If you can sign here, to say so?'

Dad stood, bent over the desk with a pen in his grip and signed, then handed the pen to Mum. I was one of the conditions: I wasn't allowed to do anything to influence Jena's recollection before Monday.

I felt Dad was signing Jena's death warrant, condemning her forever.

CHAPTER 31

27 January

I arrive late for breakfast, hung over from my dream, and take my seat wearily before noticing that Pearl's place is empty. I rub my eyes and stretch, thinking that she doesn't usually lie in, but then I see her. She's at the blue table, sat as proud as punch, and she gives me a delicate wave with the tips of her fingers, grinning broadly.

The blue table is where unsupervised patients eat.

How has Pearl managed to get herself upgraded, when her weight is so low? When just a few days ago she was doing the Fire Exit marathon, and yesterday she was hiding food in her hair?

As we settle in for group therapy, Manda sighs. She checks the clock, which isn't easy, as the shimmering numbers are glued to the wall in a giant collage. Funky and fun, but totally fucking useless.

Manda looks around her group, trying to think of something constructive to say. It must be hard, keeping positive, with a group of girls who want to disappear. Relief flowers on her face as she looks at Pearl, who is seated next to me on a green beanbag, looking as ethereal as a fairy on a leaf.

Unlike Sian, who prefers us to feel wretched, Manda likes her sessions to have a positive vibe.

'I think this would be a good moment to focus on achievement, on the fact that each of you have a life to look forward to when you do leave here. Would you like to share your news with the group, Pearl?'

Pearl blushes, two pink apples on her cheekbones. She looks down at her bitten nails.

'I got my period today.'

There is a hush in the room, then a ripple of whispers. A period is an elusive thing. Most of us, we haven't menstruated for months, years. The return of blood is a sign of recovery.

Manda claps, and we all join in, the applause gathering pace as we share in Pearl's happiness. Then she catches my eye, and my hands clasp together, refusing to clap anymore, because I don't see triumph, I see fear.

I hurry to Clive's office, and find him lost in a sea of paperwork. He smiles in greeting until he registers the panic on my face.

'I want to tell you something.'

He puts his pen down, and asks me to sit. I see my case file is open on the desk, recognisable from the battered cover; I interrupted him when he was halfway through a sentence.

'Okay. What's wrong?'

I hesitate. I don't believe Pearl got her period; she's pretending. But to tell Clive so would be a betrayal of her, and the code we all live by here on Ana Unit.

'If I tell you something, can we keep it secret?'

'Sam, you know confidentiality is always limited. If you tell me something that means you or anyone else is at risk, I will have to act.'

'Even if I tell you it's a secret?'

His face crinkles with concern for me, and I see that he thinks I'm talking about my story, about something I'm about to reveal. I want to scream at him that Pearl needs him right now, more than I do.

'There can be no secrets between us, Sam. I'm writing an assessment on you that must be defensible, and there's a lot at stake. But that doesn't mean you shouldn't tell me.'

If I tell, he'll leave me. He'll go to Pearl and help her, and this session won't happen. And I need it; I need him to listen. To finish what I started.

'I'm nervous. About talking.'

'Which is understandable. You're uncovering so many layers of memory, and we've got to such a crucial point. Fear is very natural, given the board meeting in just a few days' time. And, of course, the trauma of your mother's death. It's to be expected that you feel highly anxious.'

Fucking psycho-babble. 'Clive, please. Will you listen?'

'I am, Sam. I have every day for almost a month now. And we still have to finish.'

Maybe my worries over Pearl are displaced anxiety because I'm delving into the past, and I can't remember to forget anymore. I don't say her name, and I don't tell him my concerns about her. I decide to keep him to myself.

Clive moves away from his desk, and sits beside me in the other armchair, looking out to sea, no longer as a therapist, but now simply an audience, as I continue my story.

'So Dr Gregg and your parents had effectively stopped you using any films to help Jena remember, but you only had a few days until the press conference. What did you do next?'

I went back, to the person who I now believed was Jena's attacker.

Just three days until the press conference, and the family films had been confiscated, and my own photos weren't helping. But I had a better idea: a film that might help shift Jena's memory once and for all.

'I'm sorry about yesterday, Andy. Can we start again?'

He was surprised to see me, but stood aside so I could enter his flat, smoothing his hair as he did. He smelt clean, even from a distance, but there was a red spot on his chin from a shaving nick, and it made me relax slightly, to think that he was vulnerable.

In the lounge, I tried to avoid looking at the cabinet, in case I gave away why I was there. Andy had said that if I watched those films I'd wish I hadn't, but I didn't believe that. Nothing was worse than ignorance.

He scratched his chin. 'So, you came back. Why?'

It was a good question, one I had to give a believable answer to. Then I remembered Monica.

'I was thinking about what you said, about me being in one of your films. My mate, Monica, told me about it. She says it's cool and, y'know, fun.' Even to my own ears it sounded phoney, but Andy was too sure of himself to notice.

'Monica's a good girl. And it's decent pocket money for you girls too.' He chuckled and made a gesture around the flat. 'Think of all the nice things you could buy.'

He was so unfazed that I felt the futility of my task. Even if he was guilty of attacking Jena, he would never admit it. I'd have to force him into a corner, break him so he willingly confessed. Or get evidence of some kind, which would mean continuing to humour him.

'What is it I'd have to do?'

'Monica didn't explain?'

I shrugged. I didn't want to give myself away by saying the wrong thing.

'First, we need to see if you're photogenic.' He looked at me hungrily; I could sense an eagerness being restrained. 'We need to go to my studio for that. That's where all my equipment is.'

'Now? To Pleasurepark?'

He looked at his watch and smiled confidently; he was a man used to getting his own way.

'Why not?'

Thirty minutes later we passed a huge plastic rabbit holding a sign: WELCOME TO PLEASUREPARK. Above, the big wheel drew a circle of screams in the air. I longed to feel like a child again, wanted so desperately to go back in time and be that happy kid who was brought here by her dad and big sister.

Andy led me through the turnstiles to the pay booth, where a woman with pink hair was chatting to a friend on her mobile. When she saw Andy, she put her phone down and touched the tips of her hair, face radiant with a smile as she passed two wristbands under the grille. Andy rewarded her with a cheeky wink. 'Looking good today, Yvette. Catch ya later, babe.'

He turned to me, pulled his Ray-Bans down and gave me a grin. Despite being almost sixty, he was still handsome, and I hated that I noticed this.

'Do you want to go on the rollercoaster first, Sammy? Get some adrenalin in your system.'

Andy put his hand on my shoulder, and I tried not to flinch or to enjoy it, but his hand warmed my skin.

'No.'

'Too babyish for you? I keep forgetting you're a young woman now.' His hand skimmed my bottom, squeezed it, sending a pulse through me against my will. I moved away from him and, longing for the perspective of my camera lens, lifted my Leica to my face.

Everywhere, there were children. Sucking lollies, screaming. *Snap*: a group of teenage girls in cut-off shorts and cropped vests passed us and he winked at them, making them giggle. Litter covered the ground like fallen leaves. *Snap*: the paintwork on the food stalls was chipped, the chrome on the rides was smeared. Even the smiles on the painted children on the signs looked strained.

Everything was damaged.

Putting my camera down, we walked around, watching the rides. Everyone who worked here knew Andy; he was greeted warmly, especially by girls, and sometimes with a certain wariness, like by the worker on the gun range who handed us rifles and quickly busied himself elsewhere. We both tried shooting rings from the edges of jars containing iPods and money, but no matter how vulnerable they looked, the rings stayed put. And I was a rubbish shot.

'Do you remember,' I asked, trying to sound sweet and nostalgic, hiding the bitterness I really felt, 'when Dad brought me and Jena here?'

''Course.' He looked at me sideways. 'Your dad kept you amused on the baby rides, and I took Jena off for an hour or so, to do more grown-up things. We all had fun.'

He put his arm around me, and this time I didn't move away.

After about an hour, he'd had enough of playing happy families.

'Come on, Sam, I haven't got all day. Let's go shoot some film.'

'Can we get a drink first?' I asked. 'I'm parched.'

'I have milkshakes in the studio,' he said.

We walked into the staff area, through the restroom where a few people sat around eating lunch, reading magazines and watching the TV. Andy waved at them, and they seemed to sit to attention as we walked by, then down an unlit corridor and through a door with the sign: ENTERTAINMENT MANAGER, ANDY NICHOLLS. It opened into a small office, and he then went to another door, behind his desk. He took a key from his fob and opened it.

'This is where all the magic happens,' he said. 'My studio.'

It was a larger, darker space. I'd been here before, years ago, but it seemed different. I didn't remember that the walls were covered in pictures of women in swimwear and skimpy dresses, Marilyn Monroe laughing alongside Kim Kardashian, or that the floor was dirty plastic that sucked at my feet.

'Here's my pride and joy.'

He tapped the plastic lid of the milkshake maker, which I'd loved so much. It was old and there were stains on the plastic. It was just a blender; how could I have ever thought it was special? A couple of half-empty bottles of syrup stood beside it, the glass sticky with dead fruit flies.

'Chocolate or strawberry?'

'Either.' I knew either would make me sick, especially when he opened the small fridge for the milk and I saw the cans of Red Bull, beer, and – at the back – a half-used tube of KY Jelly.

Andy pointed me to an empty plastic chair next to a wonky table, splattered with spilt soda. As he prepared my shake, I saw him as a stranger might: good-looking, well groomed, smart in jeans and shirt.

He didn't look violent. But the room had a bed, and there was a sheet on it, not too clean. The camera was set up on a tripod, directed at it.

'Here you go.'

He put the frothy brown drink on the table, and got a beer from the fridge for himself, swigging from it greedily, then he reached an arm around my shoulder. He moved closer.

'You're really pretty, Sam. I bet you'll look great on camera. We'll have some fun and make a lot of money at the same time.'

I moved away, my eyes catching the grubby bed. Had my sister been here?

'When you were at the police station did they tell you about their prime suspect?'

He swallowed hard. 'A bit. Just that someone was remanded. They've let him go now; it was in the papers. No name, though.'

'I know his name. I read the police file.'

I watched him digest this information. He took a long drink, and put the can on the plastic table.

'So, spill the beans. Who is it?'

'Douglas Campbell.'

Andy's eyes widened. 'But he doesn't even live in Suffolk.'

'He came back, to meet Jena. The night of the attack he was waiting for her, around the back of Our Plaice. He said he found a coat.'

I paused again. Andy was strangling his can, and his face was drained of colour.

'The raincoat had blood on it.'

Andy gazed at the blacked-out window, open enough so we could hear screaming coming from the rollercoaster.

'So why have the police let him go?'

'Not enough evidence to proceed with a trial,' I said.

'Bloody typical. The police round here are so crap, they couldn't even win at Cluedo unless someone told them who was in the envelope.'

I tried to control my voice. 'They've organised a press conference for Monday, and Jena will be speaking publicly about the attack. She's going to say what she remembers.'

'Fuck. Well, that's going to be some show, then.' He ran a hand through his thinning hair, then moved it to his mouth, as if he was about to cover it, to stop the words falling out. 'Having someone banged up for years won't change anything, Sam. I used to think it would, but that was stupid. People still do what they want, make the same mistakes. Do you have any idea what I'm talking about?'

He sounded genuine, and I felt myself losing ground. He was playing me, with this sympathetic act, but I did have an idea what he meant. In my darkest thoughts, I sometimes hated Jena. Not that the attack was her fault, but I had to put the anger somewhere.

'Jena's my sister,' I said, as if this concluded all my muddled thoughts.

'Well, I have a sister too. Sonia and me, we're closer now. It was awkward, y'know, when she was with Douglas. They were fighting all the time; it was chaos. But since she's been on her own she's doing okay, and I do what I can for her boy. I'd like it to stay that way, so there's no love lost between me and Douglas. I'd pay a lot of money to see him banged away again.'

He finished his drink. I still hadn't touched mine.

'Poor Sonia,' he said.

'What's Sonia got to do with this?' I snapped, and he frowned at me.

'Oh shit, you don't get it, do you?' He almost laughed, but then stopped himself. 'If Douglas is back in town, then he'll soon be showing up at her door, and he's bad news. When he was locked up, it was a blessing for everyone, and a good job he went to Scotland after he was released. But if he's back, he'll be stirring things up again.'

'Like what?'

'Jesus, Sam, think about it. He's told the police he'd found a coat covered in blood near the chip shop he used to manage with Sonia. He's trying to set her up!'

'Set Sonia up?'

There was a long silence, and in seconds his skin paled and his eyes looked heavy; he looked his age for the first time.

'Think how this will look to the police: when Douglas went to prison for rape, Sonia lost everything. Her man, her shop. Even her boy, if Social Services had had their way. She hates Jena, and she's got good reason. She'd be a perfect scapegoat.'

My brain clicked over the words, replaying them. Yes, I knew that Sonia hated my sister, and I'd seen her temper first-hand.

'She couldn't be scapegoated, though. I saw the person who attacked Jena. I didn't get a good look at the face, but it wasn't Sonia.'

Andy looked at me with pity. 'Of course not, Sam. Sonia wouldn't do something like that. But that doesn't mean the police won't start sniffing around her. And she's on a suspended sentence.'

I closed my eyes and saw it, Sonia pushing Jena to the ground, standing over her as blood pooled around my sister's head like a halo. I didn't know if it was a memory, or just my imagination, as I tried to think how much bigger than Jena the attacker was. Sonia wasn't very tall, no more than average height, and in my imagination the attacker had mythic proportions. Had I imagined Douglas as the attacker for so many weeks that I'd forgotten the height and build of the figure in the raincoat? Could it have been a woman?

I didn't know what I was doing, or who I could trust. I looked at my hands and they were shaking. I looked at the floor and it spun up to meet me.

'I don't feel good. I've had enough of Pleasurepark, Andy. I'm not going to make a film, now or ever. Take me back to your place and I'll walk home from there.'

'Yeah,' he said. 'You've kind of brought the mood down anyway. Maybe another time, yeah?'

Back at the flat, I didn't hesitate. I took the first chance I got, when Andy went for a piss, and opened the drawer in the cabinet where I'd seen the *Wedding Day* DVD.

It was still there; he hadn't even thought to move it. And it was my last hope.

CHAPTER 32

28 January

'How did you fool them, Pearl?'

Today, Mrs Rabbit has brought her rabbit baby, in its tiny plastic pram. Pearl bends over her animals so that her hair covers her face, but her scalp is clearly visible: a perfect disc of white skin. I kneel next to her on the floor, though my knees hurt from the pressure on the scratchy carpet. She continues to push the tiny pram with her forefinger, back and forwards, cooing to the baby bunny as Mrs Rabbit looks on.

'Come on, spill the beans. Did you borrow someone else's sanitary pad?'

I've known girls do that before. In a place where so many things are not allowed, a black market always exists. Perhaps Pearl has bartered with one of her precious tiny animals.

'No. It's my blood.'

I gently take her chin in my hand, and lift her face so it's level with mine. Her anime eyes are wide and innocent, but desolate.

'Tell me, Pearl.'

She moves away from me, and lifts up her skirt. On her inner thigh, close to the knicker line, is a long cut, red at the edges and puckered where a scab is trying to form.

'Shit, Pearl! You can't fool them like that. You'll have to show them a bloody pad every few hours for at least three days. You'll have to open that wound again and again. It could get infected. You could bleed to death!'

'Please don't tell on me, Sam,' she begs, her eyes erupting with tears. 'I borrowed Stacey's scissors. I just wanted the staff to stop watching me; I couldn't bear it. Promise you won't tell.'

She pushes her face into my shoulder and cries, the cradle with the bunny baby held tight in her fist.

'Of course I won't tell, Pearl. I promise.'

Clive looks up blearily when I barge into his office the following morning, determined to break my promise and tell him about Pearl's deceit. It will get her in trouble, and she'll hate me for it, but at least she'll be safe.

A watery sun is attempting to rise on the horizon, the slushy sand a sick yellow in its light. He pushes the newspaper across the desk towards me.

'Have you seen this?'

I lean on his desk. 'Clive, I'm worried about one of the girls. I think she's seriously ill.'

'Everyone is seriously ill here, Sam. But if you tell me who, I'll make sure I look in on her after our session. Please don't panic; the staff here are all highly qualified to address whatever it is you're worried about. But right now we really need to focus on you. And this.'

He taps the newspaper, the *East Anglian Daily Times*, and my eyes drift to the headline on the front page.

ORWELL ESTATE SHOOTER: LATEST NEWS

The Ipswich teenager, who was just sixteen at the time of the shooting, may soon be released, officials have said. Samantha Hoolihan has been in a secure hospital since the shooting. See page 3 for the full story.

I don't turn to page three, though I know Clive wants me to.

He leans back, and reaches for a typed report. 'This report has to be written, Sam. Your future is in the balance, and my responsibility is to you. And to the people of Ipswich who want the correct outcome, and need to know that you aren't a danger to them.'

Clive looks at me directly for the first time, and I see how bad he looks. Uncared for, unwashed. I've got under his skin; the weight of responsibility for this report hangs heavy on him. Another person affected by my crime, another casualty.

He fiddles again with the newspaper, unable to resist glancing back at whatever the journalist has written. It unnerves him, the attention in the paper; since the shooting, I've been a freak show to the press; they can't get enough of my ugly story. Whatever he concludes, his report will be judged by the media. Especially if he recommends release.

'Write whatever you like,' I say, getting up to leave. 'I don't give a fuck.'

'Sam! Sam, guess what?'

Stacey's yelling like something amazing just happened. She runs down the corridor, grinning madly. 'I'm getting released this weekend. They say I'm well enough.'

'You were always going to be, Stacey. The NHS can't afford to keep you here forever.'

She looks stung. 'You're such a bitch sometimes, Sam. You just can't bear for it not to be about you, can you?'

'What's that supposed to mean?'

But she turns and walks away from me without saying another word. I've pushed her away, which is what I've always done to anyone who cares for me.

Back home, after stealing the *Wedding Day* film, I found the house empty. Mum would be at the hospital with Jena, and when I looked out of the window to our garden, I could see Dad was in the shed, so I was safe.

I pulled the ladder down by its blue rope, and climbed up into the attic.

Jena's Easter Bunny costume was still propped against the joist, one ear flopped at a painful angle. The fairy on the Christmas tree still dangled from a single gold thread, her arms above her head as she gazed at the ground. The black bin bag meant for charity had been moved, so I knew someone else had been up here. I reached inside, curious, but when I saw it was just more discarded clothes I didn't delve further. Instead, I took the *Wedding Day* DVD from my rucksack and slid it into the player, pulling my knees to my chin as the screen flickered into life.

Jena is sat on a bed wearing a white wedding dress; I recognise it as the one hung in the wardrobe of her flat. She has her hair pinned up in a chignon, like a bride, and she looks nervous as one too. This film is old; she looks younger, maybe only seventeen or eighteen. But her eyes are the same, old beyond her years and full of fear.

As the camera pans back I see she's in Andy's studio at Pleasurepark. They've put a bottle of Buck's Fizz on the table, and flowers, trying to make it look like a hotel room, but I can see the plastic table is still stained, the sheets on the bed aren't hotel fresh and the flowers are dying.

Jena looks up at the screen, and says hesitantly, 'I was waiting for this night. I'm a virgin.'

'That's okay, I'll be gentle.'

It's Andy's voice. Playful, coming from somewhere off-camera. Whoever is filming doesn't care about him, and zooms in to focus only on Jena. In the reflection of the window I can see two, no, three other men are in the room. One is hidden behind the camera, the other two are just leaning against the wall, watching. The picture is filled with Andy's naked back, the muscles pronounced, as he squats on the edge of the bed and reaches behind Jena to unzip the dress.

She looks directly at the camera, a tight smile. 'I'm so happy right now. Can't wait for everything that's coming, the honeymoon, moving to our flat.'

Andy has released her breasts. He's not responding to anything she says; it's as if only Jena has a script. A script of her own fantasy.

'Let's take this dress off.'

She sits straighter, staring intently in the direction of the camera. 'What do you want me to do now?'

She's asking the cameraman; it's clearly him who is in control.

Jena shields her eyes with her hand, as if the lights in the room are too much, and when she removes her hand, I see how sad her eyes are, how her mouth has turned down at the corners. Her face looks sad but determined, as if she won't allow herself to cry, even though there are tears in her eyes.

The man reflected in the window, the cameraman, looks bulky and familiar. But his face is hidden.

The attic was silent, except for my heavy breathing. I stared at the empty screen, feeling just how alone I was, blood whooshing in my ears.

Andy had used Jena. This was why he had befriended us, why he'd taken us on trips. Not out of friendship to Dad, or us, but because he wanted Jena to star in his porn film.

I wondered how many times it had happened, and if it was still happening. Jena had worked at Pleasurepark since she left school: was this why? All of these years, had she been involved in this seedy film-making? Was that how she had finally afforded the flat? It looked like she was a willing participant, lost in some imaginary world where Andy was her boyfriend, not just someone she was paid to have sex with.

Shaking, hardly able to gather up my things, I staggered down the ladder, trying to make sense of the world.

I hadn't heard Dad come inside the house, and was shocked to see him stood there, waiting, at the bottom.

'What are you doing, Sam? You have no reason to be up there!'

I swallowed, hard. I couldn't tell him.

'Just looking at old photos. Thinking about Jena.'

As I stepped from the final rung of the ladder, he reached to help me, and I fell into his arms. I cried and cried and let him hold me and didn't say a word, not to him. The only person who could tell me what I needed to know was my sister.

I caught the next train in a hot sweat, and at the hospital I found Jena in the art-therapy room, working on her painting. She looked up, wide-eyed as a girl. 'Sam! Where have you been? Come give me a hug.'

Her embrace took my breath away.

She danced in front of me, making me giddy. Words didn't come, wouldn't come.

The film you were in. The lies you told about your relationship with Andy. The rape. I need to know!

My hands felt clammy as I grabbed hers, pulling her off-balance. I looked at the painting. It was finally finished; the whole picture was splattered with paint to show it had been raining. Despite this, the face was completed, whole.

And unmistakably female.

Jena smiled at me, wise and sane. I was at the end of my reserves. There was only one thing I could ask.

'Who hurt you, Jena? You need to tell me. Because I'm close to crazy, and it's going to kill me if you don't.'

Jena leaned towards me. She whispered, one finger on her lips, as if warning me to keep it a secret.

'It was *her*.'

It felt like the moment I'd been working towards for weeks had arrived, and still I wasn't prepared. In just a few days I'd learned so many truths, but the one that resonated to my core was what Andy had said: *Your sister lives in a dream world, she always has.*

I'd thought Douglas Campbell was to blame, then I'd thought it was Andy. But now Jena was telling me it was a woman.

'Who's *her*?'

Jena pulled her mouth inwards, as if to stop herself from saying any more. One woman's name came to me, a woman with a good reason to hate my sister. A woman that Douglas and Andy had both mentioned.

'Was it Sonia?'

Jena looked alarmed and grabbed me by my arms. She squeezed me so hard they hurt, her face contorted with worry.

'Sam! We must remember to forget.'

My thoughts clicked together like magnets; pieces that had made no sense suddenly belonged. Sonia had said that Jena was too pretty, that she'd thought herself a cut above the others on the estate. And she was with Douglas when he was accused of rape; Jena was the reason he went to prison, then left Suffolk, leaving Sonia and Rob to fend for themselves.

'Why now, Jena? Why attack you sixteen years later?'

And Jena's lovely green eyes were wide and fearful. But she nodded. 'Jealous. Of me. Because I was about to be free.'

'Free? You mean because you were moving into the flat?'

'Yes!'

Of course Sonia would be jealous of that, given her own chaotic existence. Unstable, because of drugs. Jealous. Angry, because Jena's accusation had ruined her life. But how the fuck would I make her confess when everyone around her was willing to lie? Rob, poor Rob, had been so willing to help me when I thought the attacker was his dad. But he wouldn't help me with this.

'Too pretty, she always said so,' Jena whispered, oblivious to the chattering madness in my head, repeating again, 'I was about to be free.'

I felt capsized; the ground shifted beneath me, but Jena caught me, held me tightly, and started to sing. A lullaby, and I wanted to scream or weep and fall into her embrace like a child.

CHAPTER 33

29 January

I can still feel that madness surge through me, its firm hand on my back, pushing me forward, the urgent need to right the huge wrong that had been done to us. To my family.

What I wouldn't give for one scrap of that conviction now, one burst of that energy, so I could fix Pearl. But I'm pathetic; here on Ana Unit I have no power.

I wait until evening, when Birute brings me my meds. Finally, I'm going to alert someone, and stop thinking only of myself.

'Pearl isn't doing as well as you think she is.'

I long for a dramatic reaction, but she looks sad, and her mood is slightly flattened as always. 'All you girls are so poorly. It hurts me here.' She touches her ribcage with her palm. 'Is something I never understand.'

I've heard this before. It comforted me once; now it makes me want to scream.

'But Pearl is worse than the rest of us, Birute. And she's good at hiding it.'

'You care about your friend. I see this when we play Monopoly. And soon you will be apart, if you are set free, so this is upsetting for you.'

She turns to go, and I have to stop her.

'But she's . . . It's just . . .'

Birute's busy; I can see that. She has other medications to distribute; she's tired.

I understand what it's like, to be consumed by a thought, unable to think of anything else. My Black Magic memories have taken me back to that blistering June, eighteen months ago, when my sickness began.

'Sam?'

Pearl is in the doorway of my room. Hands resting on her skinny hips and an angelic smile on her narrow, finely boned face.

'Come on in, Pearl. I've been worried about you. How are you feeling?'

She sits close to me on the bed, and puts her hand in mine. It's small and cold, and her breathing seems rapid. 'I'm fine,' she says. 'I just missed you today. When you go and see Clive, I have no one to talk to.'

'Well, I'm here now.'

She presses against me. 'But you'll be leaving soon. On 1 February, they're going to let you go home.'

'Maybe,' I say, slowly.

'Do you want to leave?' She looks up; her deep brown eyes, liquid-rimmed, are so full of affection that it breaks my heart. I can smell the candyfloss of her lip gloss, and remember again just how young she is, how vulnerable.

'I didn't. But that's changed now.'

And I'm tired, or maybe scared, because everything is getting real close, real soon, and I'd like someone to talk to, just one person. I just want one person who knows me to know what I'm going to do. I'm sick of feeling alone.

Pearl is listening, and she smells like spun sugar. She smiles at me like I'm a decent person and I want to tell her the truth. Real bad, like it's burning in my throat, the words.

I take a deep breath, till it feels like I'm drowning in air, just to stop myself from cracking up.

'The thing is, Pearl, I've got a lot to prove. I'm here on a hospital order, as an alternative to custody. I shot someone.'

Whatever she's heard about me from the other girls, the gossip in the bathroom, she didn't know this, and she shifts slightly away, her mouth dropping a little. I'm losing another person who cared about me, and still I can't stop myself from making it worse, from self-destruction.

'I'm not just here because I'm sick, Pearl. I'm here because I'm bad.'

My thoughts were circular and obsessive:

Sonia had been Douglas's girlfriend. She was Rob's mum and Andy's sister. She was also a fucked-up drug addict, full of anxiety and rage, and she'd hurt her own son – hadn't Rob shown me the scar? And she hated Jena.

She was the glue between Douglas, Andy and Jena. Penny and the police had been looking for a madman and they had missed the truth, we all had. That a woman can be evil too.

So, then, the pressing need for justice. I was a sixteen-year-old kid, weak with hunger and lacking in strength. How to get a grown woman, a spaced-out drunk, to confess?

I needed something to make me brave, and make her weak. A weapon. But what?

The thought of a knife made me wince; I could picture Sonia seizing it from me, plunging it into my own flesh. Anything that required strength could be used against me.

A gun didn't require strength. A gun in Ipswich, elusive as snow in the desert, but not unheard of. And didn't I know someone with a firearms history?

At Greasy Monkeys garage, the trainee mechanics barely looked up from their oil-stained, messy jobs. In just a couple of weeks I'd become part of the furniture. Rob was sitting on an old tyre, basking in the sun, blue denim and oily fingers. He watched me approach with a look of warmth in his eyes, and I felt bad, bad that I was about to betray him. He didn't deserve that.

'Hi babe,' he said, coming up and kissing me. And I kissed him back because I wanted to; it felt good, even though my plan had changed and we were no longer allies.

I nursed something pure in my heart for this messed-up boy who saw the world the same way I did. Who was also one of life's victims, but doing his best to survive. We had been united against Douglas, but now Sonia was my target. I knew he wouldn't take my side against his mum.

Oblivious to all this, Rob moved me around so I was backed against a rusting car. Desire hung from him like musk.

'I've missed you these past two days. Don't leave for so long again.' He was warning me, that I could hurt him. I knew I should step away, let him be, because no good would come of it, but instead I kissed him. The kiss was deep, desire was there, but what good could come of that now?

'I'm sorry with how it went at Pizza Hut. But Dad told me he went to see Jena the next day, and that she said it wasn't him who raped her. Is he lying to me again, Sam?'

His face was so full of hope, and I envied him. I'd lost the capacity.

'He's not lying. Jena says it wasn't him.'

Hope went to a flicker of despair and confusion. 'So everything he lost, all those years in jail, and he was innocent?'

'So she says. And she's going to say it publicly on Monday, at the press conference. Douglas needs to be there. You should come too.'

'I wouldn't miss it! Christ, all these years, being known as the son of a rapist . . . He deserves compensation! We all do.'

'So where's Douglas now?'

'At The Fold. Eating my food, drinking my beer. He's been happy since he spoke to your sister; keeps talking about how everything's going to change. He thinks he's going to be rich. I don't know how much longer I can keep him away from my mum; he's desperate to tell her the good news. But I've said he should wait.'

'Until it's public,' I agreed. 'On Monday.'

Rob was hopeful, thinking about his dad's name being cleared, but it left me with a huge question. He held me, kissed me, and I knew that if he let me go I would fall to the ground; I feared I'd never get up again.

Rob pulled away, and when he saw my face he asked, 'You okay, babe?'

'Not really.' I was shaking. 'I mean, if it wasn't Douglas who attacked Jena, then who did? And how do I find them?'

'It's not your job. You should let the police work that one out.'

He came close, his breath on my forehead. His eyes caressed the outline of my body, and I felt myself shiver. I was nervous, but I knew what I needed.

'Can you get me a gun, Rob?'

'What is it you want?' he said loudly, as if he'd suddenly gone deaf.

I looked around for listeners, then whispered, 'If I had a gun, I'd feel better. I need to carry on, and find Jena's attacker.'

He had an eyebrow raised, an amused smile on his face. He wasn't taking me seriously.

'But you have no idea who it might be or what you'll do next? I'm serious, Sam, leave it to the police.'

'Please, Rob. It's just a prop. To make me feel more secure.'

He whistled between his front teeth, staring at me like I was a weird but interesting zoo animal, but not one that might bite.

'A prop?'

He gave an ironic chuckle, wheezy from rollies and exhaust fumes, which gave way to a hurt silence. His shoulders hunched over; there was tension in his muscles. I felt sure that if I pushed just a bit more he'd help me. He was the only person who could.

'Look, you shouldn't even joke about that stuff. Leave guns to the grown-ups.'

'Do I look like I'm joking?' My body was humming, energy running from my core to the tips of my fingers. 'How much would it cost for you to get me one?'

'Fuck, girl. You have no idea what you're even asking. It's mandatory prison for shit like that.'

'I know you've got a criminal record; you know drug dealers, so you'd know how to get me one.' I felt fury rising up in me, hot and powerful. 'You saying you can't?'

He studied me. 'Not can't. Won't. I like my freedom.'

A pulse throbbed in my forehead. 'Come on, Rob! You know people with guns. I don't.'

'No one's gonna sell a gun to you.'

'Why not?'

He sighed, then counted the reasons on his fingers. 'One, because you're a girl. Two, because no one knows anything about you, and frankly, Sam, you're acting like a nutter right now.'

'But they'd sell to you.'

'Only I don't want one. And I don't understand why you do.'

I was losing him, I could feel it. The kiss, our embrace, was forgotten now. He was suspicious of me.

'I know you could help me if you wanted, Rob. You're known round here; you've got the Campbell reputation to keep up.' I raked my fingers through my hair and they got caught in the tangles.

'Sam, I've already got a strike for firearms. I got it from Spoons Café; that's where all the dodgy deals happen in this town. It was deactivated so couldn't hurt a fly, and back when Mum was into some heavy shit and I was needing to protect her. I was lucky to get away with Community Payback and Mac breathing down my neck.'

Rob reached to ease my hand away from my tangled hair, smoothing it down, in a gesture that was so tender it made me want to weep.

'That would be perfect. A deactivated gun would be just dandy.'

He sighed, and released a curl of my hair so it grazed my cheek.

'The bottom line is, I probably could get you a piece, but it would cost. And if I got caught, I'd be banged up. It's just not worth it.'

'Could I make it worth it?' I bit my lip and moved towards him, my hands hovering near his belt.

He touched my face, near the scab. 'What happened here?'

I could feel the grease from his fingertips in my pores as his finger lingered on the place where Mum burned me.

'Please help me, Rob. Is it cash you want?'

'How much ya got?'

I thought about the birthday and Christmas money I had saved. 'Three hundred pounds.'

He laughed. 'Not even close.'

'It's all I have.'

'Forget it, Sam. You're the smart girl with the camera, not the low-life with the gun. You're better than that.'

'Let me show you how much better I can be.'

I pushed myself towards him, so I could feel his penis through my jeans. I wiggled against him, and let him nuzzle into my neck. He pressed me back against the car; we were so close I could feel his eyelashes on my cheek. I felt desperate, grasping for the final grains of sand before the hourglass emptied.

I thought about Andy's offer: quick money to appear in a film. If that was what it took, it would be worth it. 'I can get more money.'

'I don't want your money. I want you. I love you, Sam. Even though I think you're crazy.'

He pressed into me. I could smell the coffee on his breath, see the sweat on his collarbone. His lips touched mine, and on instinct I opened for him. We kissed, deep and wet this time, before I pulled away. We were drawn together; we both felt it.

'I love you too, Rob. Please help me?'

'I'm sorry, babe. Not with this.'

But he'd already helped me, more than he knew. *Spoons Café . . . that's where all the dodgy deals happen in this town*, he'd said.

Spoons. The café on the waterfront. Monica's hangout.

CHAPTER 34

30 January

Pearl died in the night.

Sian woke me with a gentle shake, her face so puffy I could tell she'd been crying, though her voice was as sharp and serious as ever.

'Heart failure,' she said, sitting heavily on the edge of my bed. 'The staff on duty the other day should never have let her go out in the snow.' And then she stared at the window, at the water dripping from the melting icicles along the gutter, her hands clasped in her lap.

The news seeps into my soul like poison. Snow angel, little Pearl, has starved herself to death. I let her down. I knew she lied about getting her period, I knew she was hiding food, and I said nothing. I let her kill herself.

But so did everyone else.

Sick with who I am and everything I'm responsible for, I curl up under my duvet.

I think about Jena, and how I have abandoned her too. Not allowing her to visit, refusing any contact. Reading all of her letters, treasuring them, but never once replying.

Clive comes to find me when I don't turn up for our meeting. I'm curled on my bed, cried out. Wretched with memory and regret.

He tries to comfort me. He tries to tell me Pearl's death was not my fault. That I'm not to blame.

'Just let me finish, before you tell me I'm not to blame,' I say to him. 'Please.'

And so he sits on the wicker chair, pulling it close enough to hear my weak voice, and to be of some comfort as I let myself leave this place and return to Ipswich docks, to the ancient houses, beamed and timbered with lopsided roofs and doll-sized windows, back to Spoons.

Saturday 25 June.

Spoons was a small and crooked place, just a stone's throw from the house that was once Thomas Wolsey's butcher's shop before he became a cardinal. A butcher's boy could soar like Icarus with the right ambition, the right brain. At least, he could in Tudor times.

The tiny oblong windows were steamed up with the heat from inside and covered with scraps of paper advertising: *Paczek z dzemem and cuppa just £1*. Another one said *Free mince pie with any drink*, and someone had drawn a holly leaf in the corner, with berries in blue biro. The poster was either six months too early or too late.

I pushed the door; it dragged over the thick doormat. The room was small and still held the sooty memory of when it had been a front parlour with a cosy fire in a yawning brick mouth under one wall. But there was nothing comforting about the room anymore; it had a brick floor and a handful of mismatched tables. A balloon-bodied woman in a violent-green headscarf and wrap-around pinny eyed me from behind a ramshackle counter, upon which a plastic tray was stacked with brightly wrapped chocolate bars and biscuits. Her fat hands busied themselves in arranging a broken wicker basket stuffed with every flavour of crisps. On the wall behind her was a fluorescent star advertising *Cola or Panda Pops 60p*. The dry smoke smell of continually boiled water filled the air.

There were only two other customers. In the far corner by the fireplace, a man in his twenties was reclining against the wall, his long legs stretched out on the chair in front, arms limp and head low. He poked the brim of his baseball cap higher so he could see me. His face was narrow, feline, and his bony scalp was shaved and tattooed, though I couldn't make out the pattern. The other customer had her back to me, neat and straight, and her hair was as red as a blood orange. She was reading a book propped against the sauce bottle in front of her.

'Can I help you?'

The woman behind the counter crossed her arms over her firm bosom, unsmiling. The man was watching from under the brim of his cap.

'Er . . . yes, please.'

On hearing my voice, the redhead turned, her face lighting up when she saw me. I was equally glad to see her, familiar as she was when everything else had become strange and frightening.

'Hi, Monica.'

'Hey, Sam! So, you come for cake after all? Come, sit.'

She called to the woman in a quick, lyrical voice, in what I assumed was Polish, pausing to check with me. 'Tea, you like? Or Panda coke?'

'Water. Please.'

'Vater, okay.' She resumed her instructions to the woman, who stepped back into the second room, which was a make-shift kitchen. On the shelf was a drum of teabags, a steaming cob of bread, and green sausages, hung from a string, cold and cured. Also, stacks of plastic tubs, the kind used for ice cream, which were filled with a lumpy brown soup. The woman busied herself, and despite her bulk she moved nimbly, reaching mugs and opening the tap on the silver urn.

My plastic chair had a snapped back, so I sat at an awkward angle, rocking on the uneven brick floor. The whirring air conditioning droned on like the world's battery was out of control. A drip of condensation dropped from the ceiling, blooming on the table like a rose.

'Nice to see you, Sam,' said Monica, pushing aside the book she had been reading, titled *An Actor Prepares*. 'This make my head hurt.'

The headscarfed woman bustled back with tea for Monica, four chocolate squares on a saucer and a glass of water for me. As she bent over, I caught the scent of soap powder, and thought of Mum.

I sipped, but the water was warm and made me feel slightly sick. The chocolate was filled with marshmallow so sweet my mouth felt sore. Monica glugged from her mug of brown liquid, topping up from a bottle labelled *Poema di caffe*, leaving a smear of pink lipstick behind. She looked longingly at the squares of chocolate.

'You no like the *Ptasie Mleczko*, Sammy?'

'It's too sweet.'

Without needing further invitation, she grabbed one and sucked it into her mouth, her eyes narrowing with pleasure as she chewed, taking her time. I waited until she dotted a fleck of chocolate from her lips.

'So. We talk, yes? You tell me why you go to that place. I help you.'

'Which place?'

Monica stroked the bottle; her nails were square and strong. Practical. But veneered with a glowing orange paint, newly done.

'Andre's flat. Is no good for you there, not when you are going to be famous photographer.'

'Well, Andy's a photographer too.'

'Ha!' She scowled. 'He think so. He makes promises of money that never comes, false promises to girls who need to make a new life.'

'Did Andy bring you from Poland?'

She laughed, a dismissive snort that told me what an idiot I was. 'I'm not Polish. I'm from Czech Republic.'

'Oh,' I said, thinking about a map of the world in my head, but unable to think where this was exactly. 'Czechoslovakia.'

'No!' she snapped. 'Is not that for many year. Is now Czech Republic.'

I'd offended her in some way that I couldn't fathom, and our conversation was clearly getting me no further in my quest for a gun. I reached into my rucksack and brought out the picture I'd taken of her when we met at the police station. A peace offering.

'Here,' I said. 'I promised you a copy.'

The photo had come out well; Dad's improvements had made her look fun and glossy and very pretty. Monica squealed with delight. 'Ah! Just like a model, yes? I like this for my portfolio.'

I wanted that for her too, proper modelling on a catwalk somewhere, far from here. She smiled at me happily, her head angled with surprise at my kindness.

'Thank you, Sam.'

'So, what about Andy?' I asked, sad that the question would wipe the smile from her lips, but seizing the chance anyway to find out more.

'He is someone who says he can help me, but afterwards I always think he is the one who has been helped most. A cat who always lands on his feet, you know?' She leaned forward and twitched her nose, her fingers making paws as she placed them on the table, making me smile. 'What is he to you?'

I thought of the porn film I'd watched, the way he'd unzipped Jena's dress.

'He's nothing to me.'

Monica considered me frankly.

'I envy you, strange girl. You have choices. Me, I am still learning how to be in this town, and the best thing is that I can go to school. You do not have to struggle like me, a foreigner in this place, never getting even Saturday job because people don't like that I am different, but I need money to help my family stay here.' She flicked her hair over her shoulder defiantly. 'You are from here. Clever, with your camera, click click.' She tapped the picture of her, smiling at her image. 'So, you will be okay.'

'So will you, Monica. You're clever too, studying A levels at college, like I'm going to. We both have choices.'

She ate another sweet, thoughtfully dabbing chocolate flakes from her lip with her finger. 'Maybe the same as you, and I am clever in another way too. I think you need a clever friend like me, yes?'

'Is it that obvious?' I looked down so my hair covered my face and said quietly, 'That I need your help?'

'I know this when I first saw you, at the police station. With your mother, yes? I see it then.' Monica looked concerned. She sipped her drink again, leaving foamy milk on her upper lip that did nothing to detract from her Slavic beauty. She was right, she could be an actress. Her eyes were a film reel of emotion.

'So, we are both clever. And you are sad girl, so I am kind. See?' She snapped her fingers together as if it was explanation enough.

The man in the hat looked up again, his eyes fixed directly on me. He scratched under his cap, revealing more of the tattoo, which I could now see was the markings of a leopard. He replaced his hat, and appeared to settle back to his slumber, his eyes half-open, but I sensed he was listening to every word.

Monica tapped her hand against her empty mug, her jaw working on possible words. I felt the table with the tips of my fingers, where the wood veneer had been peeled back, revealing smooth plastic.

'I do need your help, Monica. You may be the only person who can get me what I need.'

It was time, it seemed, to tell the truth.

'My sister was hurt. Badly. On 25 April.'

'Yes, I know from the papers, and the news.' Monica's eyes were wet. 'I am sorry for this, Sam.'

'The thing is, Monica,' I said, haltingly, re-directing my sorry tale, 'the police still haven't found her attacker.'

At the word 'police' the tattooed man fully opened an eye, and Monica made a guttural sound in her throat like she needed to spit.

I leaned forward, mindful of the woman in the headscarf drying up a plate, watching us.

'But I think I know who did it, and I think I could get a confession. If I had a gun.'

'No.' Monica moved back, away from me and my request.

I reached for her hand, trapping it in my grip. 'It's just for show. I won't even load it.'

'Ha! You think?'

'I mean it, Monica. I can't make an adult confess to something like that without help. That's all it'll be for. You're an actress; you use props all the time.'

'Sure, props I use! I get you a plastic one from the drama room.'

I lowered my voice further.

'The gun has to be real. I have money.'

She released her hand, still leaning away. 'I not help with this. Is no good.'

She wanted me gone, then, and so did the woman. But the man, alert in his slumber, had been listening with ears pricked.

Outside, in the midday heat, I leaned on the crumbling wall for its support. I put my forehead to the red brickwork, rocking my head, tempted to pull back and bang my head hard, damage my brain, so I could be the one with no memory. I pressed my nose into a dusty crack and was thinking of how useless I was, when I felt a hand press my shoulder. I jerked round, and saw it was the man from the café, his baseball cap low over his eyes, which glinted in the sun.

He moved towards me.

'You have money, you say?'

'Three hundred pounds.' I pressed my back to the wall, afraid. Was he going to mug me? My hands instinctively gripped my camera.

He leaned so close I could see where the inked leopard spots were bloody from the needle. He must have had the tattoo done recently.

'I get you a gun,' he said.

CHAPTER 35

31 January

Pearl's family came to collect her things, her mother and father and a younger brother who was so like her I caught my breath when I saw him. They packed her clothes, her Sylvanian animals, her collection of hats into a box.

I longed to ask for one of the hats, as a keepsake, but I couldn't bring myself to speak to them. Ashamed, I stayed in my room with the door shut, occasionally wandering into the corridor, pretending to need the loo when really I wanted to see how they were coping with her death.

It's wrecked me.

Wrecked all of us. Stacey and Joelle were quiet at breakfast. Fiona spoke about wanting to go home. Mina was even more invisible than usual. Pearl has shown us our own possibility; death feels closer. It lingers over us, waiting.

My bones are still sharp, my skin is furry with lanugo. Pearl is gone, but oblivion is here.

The past is here too, pressing against me.

Because Pearl's death is making me think of Jena, and how I've let her down. Eighteen months, and I haven't so much as sent a card or replied to any of her letters. She's been turned away at reception, and I've refused calls, thinking that seeing me would only remind her of the bad things that happened, or what I represent. Rob too. I've refused to see anyone who loved me, feeling unworthy of their love, and unable to think about home.

Jena and Rob were innocent victims. And it's them I've continued to hurt.

Clive is busy now. He has to explain to the authorities, to journalists, to the family, how a girl in his care has ended up on a mortuary slab. There will be an inquiry; the press will have a new story to report. I could have saved her, but I chose to keep quiet, and now it is too late.

Now there is no one to listen to the end of my tale, yet still it must finish, I have to reach the bitter end.

The Spiral car park was sunk into the ground, an underground helter-skelter in grey concrete, parking for 360 cars deep down beneath the world. The cheapest parking in town because the walkway down to the cars was a narrow corridor of graffiti.

A woman had been raped there on Valentine's Day; it had made the local news, but only for a few days, and the main message was that single females in Ipswich should be more careful about where they went. No escape in a place like that.

No escape for me either. This story, pulling me down deeper. No choice but to sink before I can rise, but I can't do it here, on the unit.

Clive won't hear it now, what I did, but I need to face it. I need to be at Mum's funeral.

By absconding, I'm sabotaging any chance of release, but I can't stay.

It takes just ten minutes to pack my old sports bag with the few clothes I own, my toothbrush and the Black Magic box. It's time for me to leave this place.

I know that Clive will do his best; his report will argue as strongly as he's able that I still deserve my freedom, but I doubt anyone will listen. Pearl's death will put his expertise, the very working of the unit, in question.

I wait until no one is around and make my way to the fence, since I know the gate will be locked. I'm wearing my warmest clothes – my swallow jumper and a padded jacket – but still the air nips, and my trainers are quickly sodden from the slushy grass. Climbing the fence isn't easy; my cold fingers lace through the wire and I wish I wore gloves, and my feet are too large to get a grip within the gaps. I pull myself over, catching my jumper on the top, and land in a heap on the other side.

I'm cold and crazy, but I need to return to the scene of my crime. My head is already there.

He didn't ask my name, and wouldn't tell me his, so the tattooed man was simply The Leopard to me. After meeting him that Saturday in Spoons he told me to arrive at midnight, when the car park was long-since closed.

A boy wearing a hoodie met me, brandishing a baseball bat.

Up close, I could see he wasn't a boy at all, but a slight man with smooth olive skin. I waited as he lifted the grille that barred the entrance, pulling it up to his thighs. He took a pen-sized torch from his back pocket and put it in my hand.

'Go,' he hissed. 'And be careful.'

I ducked under the grille and into the total darkness beyond, gazing into a black hole so dark I wasn't sure where ahead was, fumbling with the switch on the torch. Behind me the metal gate shuddered down. I was on my own.

The tiny disc of light from the torch was like a firefly darting around a cave. All I could make out was the space, the vastness of the place with no cars, no people. Not at this level anyway. I could hear my breathing, and I hummed to stop my teeth chattering.

Overhead, cars rumbled on the ring road, people going home from night shifts, men looking for company, police cars doing the circuit.

I shuffled deeper into the car park, gingerly finding a way into my underground nightmare, expecting something to pounce from the shadows at any second. The slope was steepening, my feet careening downhill, torchlight catching letters as I passed: B, C, onwards, deeper, D, E, F. Two-foot-high fluorescent letters were my only guide. The deeper I went, the lower the ceiling, darkness closing in around me.

How much farther? There was no one to ask. My palms were sweaty, and my heart moved inside my chest, trying to escape, but my feet continued, blindly, stupidly, in a downward fall.

Voices.

I stopped and listened. A man's voice, then a woman's voice, quick and lively, that I recognised as Monica's.

I reached The Spiral's seabed, the ceiling so low I could jump and touch it, the ground wet and puddling. The end was marked by a breeze-block wall, and parked next to it was a white van, TOP KLASS CAR CLEANING emblazoned on the side, along with a list of prices, too small to read. Through the dimness, I could make out the outline of a couple sat in the front; the windows were down, so I could hear them, their voices rapid and foreign but unmistakably arguing.

I hesitated, my torch careening light across the ground, the darkness cloaking me in chill. Shaking, I stopped when the voices in the van fell silent. The driver's door opened, and he stepped out, the sleepy leopard from Spoons. His silhouette was lit by the car's light, a clean outline in the semi-dark.

'Come here, where I can see you.'

I moved closer.

He looked younger than I'd taken him for in the café, barely in his twenties; smooth-headed, but with a moustache and a stubbly chin. Eyes glinting. He pulled me towards him, hands running down the sides of my T-shirt and around my waist. I struggled back, thinking of the woman who'd been raped here.

'I frisk you or you go home. Which?'

I submitted as he checked and found nothing on me but my house key and the torch. I gave him the roll of money, £300 saved from birthdays and Christmases, and never intended for purchases like this.

From the other side of the van came the sound of high heels on concrete, then Monica appeared, hugging me and pulling back to touch my cheek.

'I don't want to help with this, Sam. You should go home.'

The man was still scrutinising me, and I was glad she was there, even though she wouldn't stop preaching.

'This gun will not help, Sammy. You will see, but too late.'

'It's not what you think. I can't let . . . It's just so . . .' The sentence cracked into pieces as my brain stumbled with doubts that knocked and jarred against each other.

Monica's hand moved to my arm, where she stroked my raised flesh. 'Shaking like a kitten,' she assessed. 'Go home, little one. This mess up all your big plans to be a photographer. You promised to make me famous, yes?'

I wasn't certain I could make Sonia confess, but without a gun I had no chance.

'I can't go home, Monica. Not until I have what I came for.'

The man took a bundle from inside his jacket, wrapped in a baby blanket. He unfolded the blanket and there, shining in the light of my torch, was a gun. Beautiful and dangerous. He held it between his fingers, its black flanks glittering with his sweat, and lifted it close to my face.

The Leopard gave me the full benefit of a grin. 'You like?'

Its beauty shocked me. I was afraid to touch it.

'Was my daddy's gun. He was in secret police, and this pistol never let him down. Many, many times she save his life. My daddy, he give me this gun, and she has travelled a long way.'

I didn't know whether to believe him.

'Take it.'

I handed the torch to Monica so I was free to touch its cool flank. I took it in both hands, reassuringly solid, but I dared not touch the barrel.

'She is Tokarev nine millimetre. Semi-automatic. You know why we come here?'

I looked stupidly at Monica for reassurance, but she was shining the torch away from her face, so I couldn't see her expression. The man was still waiting for an answer.

'So you can lend me the gun?'

'We are here so you can learn!' The Leopard was impatient with me. 'This is not a toy, you understand? Now you see.'

Monica, as if waiting for his prompt, placed the torch on the floor and opened the rear door of the van. It was empty inside; the seats had been removed, but a grubby mattress was propped against the front seats. It had dark stains and holes where the springs coiled out. My heart lurched and my mouth felt dry. I wouldn't get into the van, not for anything. I started to back away, but Monica's arm around my waist stopped me. Her mouth was close to my ear.

'Is angled to be backstop for bullet, Sammy.'

I had no idea what that meant, but realised she was telling me not to be scared.

The Leopard beckoned me to his side as he took something from his jacket. 'This is clip. In here you have nine shots. You push it in like this.'

I took a step backwards, shocked. 'I don't need to know how it works.' I pulled Monica towards me, urgently reminding her, 'I told you, the gun's just a prop. I don't need to understand it.'

I felt her body caving slightly, her breathing slow and pained.

'Oh Sammy. A real gun can never just be for show.' She reached and stroked my jaw, soothing the spot where I'd been burned.

Leopard reacted to the last word like it stung him, and moved in, his face close to mine. 'A show? You think this is some kind of theatre maybe? Not real?'

He held the gun steady, my hands still holding it, and slid the clip into the handle.

'I don't want to shoot it,' I said, but my words sounded weak. 'I don't even want to load it.'

'You put no clip in, how you think it will work as a threat, hey? Has to look like business. Besides this, you want to borrow my gun, you better know how it work. Is not a toy! You understand?'

I nodded, but my insides protested with a twist in the gut. I could never shoot anyone, no matter what they'd done.

'Now this, you pull back' – he indicated the top of the gun – 'and she is ready.'

I just stared at it, his instructions drifting away. He took the gun from me and sighed dramatically.

'Is very difficult to be . . .' He paused, turned to Monica. '*Presne*?'

She looked at me sadly. 'Accurate. He say it is difficult to be accurate.'

'Yes.' He continued: 'So you practise. I show how.'

Pointing the Tokarev into the back of the van, he pulled the trigger and I jumped from my skin at the sharp crack in the air.

'Shit.' My ears rang.

He laughed. Monica did too. 'Yes, is very loud. Now you.'

I took the gun, thinking it was heavier than just a minute before, and tried to point it, but my arms wobbled, and the tip of the gun moved alarmingly. The Leopard came up behind me, shadowing me and steadying my hands. 'You pull back to get bullet from clip. Like so.'

I smelt his vinegary sweat, saw the sheen on his skin, and realised that he was nervous too. He was risking a lot, just for money. We shared the weight of the gun, and he said, 'Now squeeze.'

I pulled the trigger, shooting the bullet into the open mouth of the van. My wrist jerked up, shoulders jarring, ears on dialling tone. I had no idea what I'd hit.

'Is no good. You not hit anything this way. Again!'

I prepared the gun, talking through in my head what he had told me. Pulled back and steadied my stance, this time unaided. Again my wrist jerked and I jumped at the noise. The metal handle burned my hands.

'You bad aim, little one,' Monica said, the torchlight catching her concerned eyes.

I lifted the gun and fired again and again, hand burning and wrist aching all the way to my shoulder, my ears buzzing. I knew how to use the gun, but my aim was crap, and even though that shouldn't matter given I had no intention of firing it, I felt like I'd failed.

'She is no good,' The Leopard said sadly.

Monica shrugged and took my hand, tugging me away.

'You want to hurt someone, must do it up close and personal,' he said.

I almost laughed at the hackneyed movie line, but he growled at me, and I felt myself stand taller.

'I've told you, I've told you both, I don't want to hurt anyone,' I said, dropping Monica's grip and reaching again for the gun.

No one believed me, not even myself.

CHAPTER 36

1 February

The shivering has set into my bones, and I can't feel my feet they are so numb, but still they take me away from the hospital grounds, towards the sea path. I keep my head down in the drizzle. My sports bag over my shoulder already feels too heavy, but at least I think I've got away when I hear my name being called.

I turn to see Sian, running towards me in her white canvas nursing shoes.

'Don't try and stop me, Sian.'

She arrives next to me, panting. She hadn't even stopped for a coat, and her navy uniform of trousers and tunic is getting spotted with rain.

'Sam! Living at the unit is a condition of your hospital order. If you leave without permission, we'll have to report it. It would be classed as absconding.'

Still I keep walking.

'Sam, they meet in just a few hours! Where is it you think you're going, anyway?'

'Orwell Estate. The funeral is today.'

She looked disbelieving. 'Ipswich? You think you'll walk all that way without collapsing?'

I shrug. I just know that I need to be there.

'Oh fuck.' She looks over her shoulder, up towards the Bartlet, then back at me. Then she rummages in the pocket of her neat tunic and brings out a small coin purse, tipping a handful of pound coins into my palm.

'You can get the bus from Hamilton Road. They're every half hour.'

'Thanks.'

It's an inadequate word, given what she's risking. Just these few coins are aiding and abetting. She hesitates, and looks again towards the unit, as if she too would like to escape.

'You sure about this, Sam? You want to go to the funeral?'

'Yes.'

Which isn't true. Since Pearl died, I'm not sure of anything.

'We could do this properly if you come back now. I'll apply for day release through the correct channels.'

But even as she says it, her voice wavers. We both know it's too late for that, that it would never be approved at such short notice.

I hitch my bag higher on to my shoulder, and turn left up Brook Lane, my back to the sea, heading towards town. Sian walks beside me, though she must be frozen.

In the bus shelter on Hamilton Road the rain starts to fall more heavily on the corrugated roof, and a slab of snow slides off, landing in a slushy heap on the pavement. Sian shivers, rubs her arms, and I wonder why she doesn't just leave.

The metal seat is thin and hard against my body. I listen to the rain, watching the grey mess of old snow and rain mingle on the pavement.

'You're not going to change my mind, Sian. Not after what happened to Pearl.'

'I understand why you're leaving, how much you need to be at the funeral. I just hope the board do too. I'll say I gave you permission. I'll tell them you'll be back this evening. You will, won't you?'

The pain in her voice makes me look up, and I see tears are falling down her cheeks. She could lose her job for this. She looks cold and wet and sad, and for the first time I realise that Sian is angry and hurt, just like me.

'You know what I did, don't you, Sian? You know I'm to blame?'

Sian shakes her head, defeated. 'I don't know who is to blame for anything anymore. I'm so mad, Sam. With myself, with all the staff. With Pearl too. But I won't let you down, I'll make sure Clive explains everything. The board can decide to discharge you if we say you are well. I'm going to fight for you, Sam.'

She reaches for me, and what may have been intended as a hug becomes all business, assessing me as her hand circles my wrist. Without moving her hand, her fingers search for my pulse, which will be slow as usual, just as I know my blood pressure will be low without needing a machine to tell me so.

'Be careful, Sam. Please look after yourself.'

Sian removes her hand as the bus approaches, sending icy water splashing up her pristine uniform. And then we hug, just once.

'Please come back this evening. I give you permission to go home; I'll take responsibility, but just for today.'

I get on the bus and pay for my ticket with Sian's money, taking a seat near the back, lowering my head lest any of the other passengers recognise me. Sian stands in the rain, watching. As the bus pulls away she lifts a hand and waves goodbye.

I haven't been on a bus in years, and the motion makes me feel sick; the air in the bus is musty and people are coughing, speaking into phones within the privacy of upturned collars, rummaging through purses with gloved hands. My bag is on my lap and I unzip it to check the Black Magic box is safe. It's really me I want to check on; I'm not sure how safe I feel, but the unit wasn't keeping me safe either. They failed Pearl, maybe failed me too. My recovery is now down to me.

I need to finally face what I did.

On Monday 27 June, the day of the press conference, I woke to find Mum standing over me. She placed her palm over my forehead.

'You cried out in your sleep. And you feel hot.'

I pushed her away, struggling to sit up, rubbing my eyes and looking to the window where sunlight streamed in; another scorching day ahead.

She had a tray – on it, a bowl of cornflakes and juice – and placed it across my legs, disabling any bid for escape.

'I brought you breakfast in bed.'

I considered the orange offering, but couldn't eat it; my stomach was tight as a ball. I checked my neck, but my glands were fine; it wasn't infection that was making me sick.

'Me and your dad have been talking. We want you to stay home today; Penny will understand. You're not well.'

'I'm fine.' Which wasn't true, but there was no way I was missing the conference.

She paused, and I could see she was considering whatever she was about to suggest. 'Why don't you do something relaxing instead? Go for a walk or something?'

There was genuine effort behind Mum's smile, as if she'd told herself she must appear calm for my sake, but the rift between us was wide and we both knew it.

'Can't. I've got something to do.'

'Oh well.' Her mouth turned downward, but then her shoulders lowered, and I saw she was relieved. 'I need to go to the hospital. Make sure Jena is prepared for what's about to happen. What is it you're doing?'

A few feet away was my rucksack, and inside it was the gun, my best and only prop.

'There are a few shots I need to take.'

I stirred the cornflakes, sodden with milk, but when I tried a small bite the cereal was claggy in my mouth. Irritated, Mum took my bowl from me, and dabbed my milky lips with her sleeve, then started to feed me, holding the spoon to my lips like she must have done when I was a toddler. Seduced by mothering, I ate more than I wanted, then pushed the tray from my lap, ready to get out of bed.

Her hand stopped me. Her fingers pressed into my upper arm, firmly but gently.

'Sam, I want to say sorry. I know things have been hard for you, these past weeks.'

It was nine weeks, exactly, since the attack. How I'd changed since then.

I made a sound of agreement, but couldn't meet her eyes.

'It'll be better between us, Sam. Once this is all over. Our family will be strong again.'

Because everything she did was driven by that wish, to keep her family together; I understand that now.

I peer out of the steamy bus window, my coat huddled around me. Familiar sights come into view: the Shepherd and Dog roadside pub that Dad took us to one Sunday for a carvery; the church with its fluorescent cross on St Augustus roundabout.

I leave the bus at Ipswich train station, and use the last of Sian's money on a single ticket to Westerfield. Where you are.

It was still early when I rapped on the front door of 5 The Terraces, but the sun was already warm. It was going to be the hottest day of the year.

The front door opened, and Keri the puppy pushed her way out, sniffing up at me and nuzzling into my thigh with her bony head. Sonia grabbed her collar and pulled her off. Her lime-green petrol station uniform swamped her, and she wore only one shoe, an ugly orange-plastic, Croc-style sandal. Her face was mottled red, and she swayed slightly as if she'd already had a drink.

'Where's Rob?' she asked, squinting a look behind me as if he might suddenly appear.

'He's not with me.'

She folded her arms and fixed me with an angry glare. 'He won't tell me what's going on, but he was all hyper last time he was here. You better not be messing him around.'

'I'm not, I promise.' It would have been the news of his dad's innocence that was affecting his mood, the possibility that the besmirched Campbell name was about to be polished to a shine. Not that I could tell Sonia this. Yet. 'I need to talk to you. Alone.'

She kept one hand on Keri's collar and reached behind her for the second shoe, whacking the puppy on the bum with it. The dog yelped, and cowered into the house. 'Serves you right.' She put the shoe on, leaning against the door frame for support.

'What's this about, Sam? My shift starts in five minutes.'

I'd pictured us in her front room, me in the armchair and her on the sofa. I'd imagined it all: pulling the Tokarev from my rucksack, the sight of the gun working like a charm, Sonia reluctantly but tearfully admitting she'd attacked Jena. I pictured forcing her to repeat her confession down the phone to Penny, the elation I'd feel. But Sonia made no move to let me into the house.

Just then the neighbour with the ginger cat came into sight, shuffling towards home, pulling her shopping trolley slowly down the pathway.

'Morning, Frieda,' Sonia called.

Frieda stopped, put a hand on the small of her back and said, 'Hello, love. Too hot for June, isn't it?'

Sonia looked up to the sky and blinked, as if she'd just noticed the white ball of sun directly overhead, bearing down on us.

'Can we go inside?' I said, jiggling from foot to foot.

'I need to get to work.'

Her work, at the petrol station – that was just yards from where the alleyway came out, where Jena was attacked. Since 25 April she'd got away with it; she hadn't aroused any suspicion. But Douglas had found a bloody raincoat behind the chip shop that they used to run together. The business she had lost when Douglas went to prison; to her twisted brain, it must have seemed that because of Jena she had lost everything. Douglas must have recognised the raincoat as hers, and got rid of it for her.

And here I was, Jena's sister, turning up like a bad penny.

Sonia stepped outside, pulling the door closed behind her, only just missing Keri's nose as she slammed it shut. Then she re-arranged her snot-coloured shirt, and slung her cracked patent bag over her thin wrist.

'I need to go to work, or my pay'll be docked. What is it, Sam?'

'I want to bury the hatchet,' I said. 'I know that you were right. Jena lied about Douglas raping her.'

Sonia breathed, shallow and quick.

'Really? She's finally admitted it?'

'Yes, she has. She's going to say it publicly, at a press conference, later today.'

Sonia looked into the distance, blinking from the sunlight or at a painful memory.

'After all these years . . . That little slut waited until I'd lost everything to say the truth.'

'My sister's not a slut!' I snapped, even though the image of her on the bed in Andy's studio popped into my mind.

Sonia sneered. 'Why else would she set up Douglas? She'd been fucking someone, and got caught. So rather than rat on her lover, she said my man raped her.'

I shook my head. 'She was only thirteen.'

'Old enough to have sex. Old enough to get pregnant.'

That idea, again. Mrs Read asking, *What happened to the baby?*

'There was no baby. I don't know why she lied about Douglas, but today she's going to vindicate him. And he's going to be there when she does.'

Sonia's jaw dropped. 'Eh? But he's in Scotland.'

'Not anymore. Nine weeks ago, Jena messaged him on Facebook, saying she wanted to meet, so he came back. He thought she was going to help him appeal his conviction, so he was hanging around the estate the night she was attacked. That's why he was interviewed by the police, why he was remanded.'

'Those bastards,' Sonia said bitterly. 'They're not trying to blame that on him too?'

'They were. But today, at the press conference, Jena is going clear his name. There will be reporters there, TV cameras too, and she's going to say that he didn't rape her when she was thirteen, and he didn't attack her nine weeks ago. Everyone will know the truth.'

I saw a range of emotions cross her face.

'After all these years . . . your sister is finally saying Douglas is innocent?'

'Yes.'

I could see how very much she wanted to trust me, but just couldn't allow herself. 'You're lying, just like your sister. You can't help yourself.'

'Then come to Westerfield Hospital if you don't believe me, this afternoon at two. That's where the conference is being held, on Minsmere Unit. Then you can see for yourself.'

She looked at her watch, swore, and started to walk away. 'I'll have to knock off early. Andy could give me a lift. I'd like him to hear it; he always blamed me for falling for Douglas, said I'd been an idiot not to see what a bastard he was. I'd like to be proved right for a change.' Then she turned and added, 'You better be telling the truth, Sam. I'm warning you.'

CHAPTER 37

1 February

From Westerfield station it's a short walk to the hospital, but the rain slows me, running in tears down my face. As I walk I catch my breath, gather my thoughts, telling myself that the people passing don't know who I am. Still, the closeness of others, the freedom, I can barely handle.

I think of my room on Ana Unit, and how being free would mean giving up that safety. But then I think of Sian waving goodbye, giving me her blessing. Even now, arguing for my freedom.

There is only one place to go. I have to finish this trip into the past.

On the hottest day of the year, Ipswich train station offered cool in the shade, a relief of iron-and-wood benches and steel girders supporting a roof that cloaked the whole platform. I bought a drink from the vending machine and sat on the nearest bench.

Out of the corner of my eye, I saw Rob walking towards me with speedy steps, his face already split into a smile. For a stupid second I wanted to run into his arms and tell him what had changed, that I had a gun in my bag, that I thought his mum attacked Jena. But good sense stopped me: he wouldn't take my side against his mum; blood was thicker than water. I was alone now.

'Where's Douglas?'

'Dad stopped at the shop for some gum; he said he'd catch us up.' Rob looked smarter than usual: his hair was gelled into neatness, and he had on a short-sleeved shirt; his usual jeans had been replaced with chinos. It made me sick, to see how much this meant to him, knowing it wasn't going to work out in his favour.

The tannoy crackled to life, announcing our train would be arriving shortly.

'We can't go without him, Rob. We'll have to catch the next train.'

'Don't worry, he won't be late. This is important to him, as much as to you. He's about to get his life back, and so am I. I won't be known as the rapist's son anymore.'

I could feel the slick worry in the palm of his hand, and thought of the pain that was coming his way. Because it was going to be worse, so much worse, than he imagined.

'Yeah, it's a special day.'

We found a seat with a table, manoeuvring ourselves around upturned coffee cups and discarded newspapers. I rolled my shoulders, feeling the pull across my chest and in my back.

I planned to confront Sonia in full view of everyone: the press, the police. I wanted a public confession. Sonia needed to believe I was willing to fire the gun, she needed to think her very life depended on telling the truth.

The guard put his whistle to his mouth and held up his hand just as Douglas came into view, sauntering down the platform like the world would wait. He jumped on just as the doors closed with their insistent beeps. The whistle sounded and the train pulled away.

Douglas slid into the seat opposite me, sweat on his forehead. 'Phew,' he grinned. 'That was close.'

We watched Ipswich station fall away as the train rattled past the boarded-up pig factory, travelling alongside the brown-banked River Orwell. Rob's mobile beeped, and he read the text.

'Shit,' he said, turning to me. 'Why did you invite my mum?'

Douglas raised his eyebrows in a questioning way at me. Both of them waited on my answer.

'I thought she deserved to come. Jena's going to say that Douglas didn't rape her, and Sonia needs to hear that.'

Rob accepted this, but Douglas started tapping the table with his hands, as if agitated. Rob leaned forward and touched his knuckles to his dad's to still his nervous tic.

'Don't worry, Dad. It's going to be all right for once.'

I could see how Rob's feelings for Douglas had turned around, now he thought he was innocent. I'd softened towards him too, but only a bit. He was still a shit; Rob had the scar to prove it, but he'd forgotten that. He closed his eyes, arms crossed, perfectly at peace, and I put my hand in his, and leaned my head on his shoulder, for the last time.

We let the sound of the train lull us, watching the scenery roll by like a film about a town in decline. Some of the flats in the suburbs were half-built, abandoned when the money dried up. Double-dip recession, right outside our window.

I was unable to sit still any longer, the adrenalin spiking in my body. 'Won't be a mo.'

The toilet was small and the floor was covered in piss, the space so enclosed I couldn't turn easily. The mirror, as opaque as tinfoil, showed me a blurry picture of myself. As I watched, I saw something shift, as if I was becoming someone else. I didn't blink; maybe it was that or lack of food, but my face morphed into a monster. Who the fuck was I? How had it come to me carrying a gun? I splashed water on myself, and when I looked again the monster was gone.

I opened the door to leave, but someone pushed me back inside, forcing me backwards and pressing me against the sink. Through the tiny window the world sped past, train wheels cracking on the track, and over me loomed Douglas.

'Cut the crap. Why did you really ask Sonia?'

He had me locked in, the small space, the rocking beneath my feet. 'Douglas, Rob will know we're here.'

'I told him I was going to the buffet car. So tell me quick. How did you work out it was Sonia? I never told the police the raincoat was a woman's. How did you find out?'

My breath caught, then released in a gush. 'I didn't know. Not until you just told me. But it proves my hunch was right. Doesn't it?'

He looked at me, and in that moment we both acknowledged something that I hadn't realised before: he too believed Sonia was guilty. And he had covered for her.

Finally, in a weary voice, he asked, 'So, what are you going to do, Sam? You'll have Sonia and Jena together, with half the world watching. What the fuck are you planning?'

I didn't answer him, couldn't. Because I didn't know the answer myself.

CHAPTER 38

We arrived at the hospital at a quarter to two. The patio doors had been flung wide, and on the courtyard were a gaggle of reporters, testing microphones and looking through notes. They didn't notice me, barely looked up as we arrived.

The few people gathered inside Jena's bedroom made it look hive-like, and I could see Penny talking to Mum. Dad was slouched on the bed, at the back of the room.

Just in front of the patio doors, on the yellow grass, four chairs had been placed in a line. To the side was a podium, the kind lecturers at college might use, and I guessed this would be where Penny would stand to guide the questioning. Two cameramen were setting up tripods, and I saw their T-shirts had logos: *Look East*, *BBC*.

Rob and Douglas hung back, but I needed to find Jena.

Inside the bedroom it was stifling and stank of hairspray and sweat. Mum was bent over, pouring herself a glass of water from a jug. Looking exhausted, she took a seat next to Dad on the bed, arms folded across her Pepto-Bismol-coloured cardigan from Primark. Her dress was fancy but faded, and gaped at the bust.

She took the cardigan off, folded it neatly, and patted Dad's leg, though he seemed to be lost in thought.

Then Jena was next to me, fizzing with energy, hair frozen into curls that made her look much younger than twenty-nine. She hugged me distractedly, and I sensed that she was alert to everything happening around her. Including the two newcomers in the courtyard.

'Sam, who is that you've brought with you?'

She was straining her eyes to see, but looking directly at Rob and Douglas, who were awkwardly watching the cameramen. Jena began to walk to them, and I followed, alarmed at what might happen, though I needn't have worried.

'You came!' Jena said, sounding genuinely delighted. 'Did you bring my usual: chips and mushy peas?'

Douglas managed to offer her a tight smile, now he thought she was about to clear his name, and then reached for Rob, a hand on his shoulder, his knuckles revealing his JENA tattoo.

'This is my boy.'

Jena blinked at Rob, curling her hand around her neck like a choke chain. Then she took his mottled cheeks in her hands, his face a mix of confusion and shame.

'You came to my house one Halloween.'

'I did,' Rob said. 'We were daring each other to knock on the mad woman's house, next door but one to yours, but I was too scared so I knocked on yours instead.'

'Ah,' Jena said. 'That's Mrs Read. But she's not mad.'

Flora floated up to us, wearing a tie-dye rainbow caftan and wafting her hand in front of her face like it was a fan.

'We're at thirty degrees. I said we should move the conference indoors in case someone gets heatstroke, but apparently we don't have time to move everything. You may want this, Sam.'

She placed a plastic cup of yellow-coloured squash into my hand.

'Places please. Just five minutes until we roll,' shouted the cameraman who worked for the BBC. Penny gave him a thumbs-up and came over to me.

'Sam, are you okay? Your mum says you're not well; I didn't think you were coming.'

'I'm fine.' I lowered my rucksack from my shoulder, so it was in close reach. 'Let's just get it over with.'

'Then it's time you took your seat.'

As I sat down, I saw a couple walking across the courtyard, towards the front line of reporters. Andy and – *my god, she had actually come* – Sonia.

Andy was dressed in an open-necked shirt and wearing Ray-Bans, confident as ever. His arm was held lightly around Sonia, who was pale and skinny, blinking up at the sky. I saw that the plastic strap had snapped on her orange shoes and she was struggling to walk, or maybe she'd had some drink or something stronger before setting off. Finally giving in, Sonia took off her shoes and walked barefoot towards Jena's room and towards her fate.

CHAPTER 39

1 February

I'm inside the hospital grounds; I just need to find your flat. The address was on all the letters you sent me, letters I never replied to, but always read.

My body is weak, and it's hard to think straight. Pearl's death is heavy on my mind, and so is Mum's funeral. Death, close around me. Oblivion, which is what I thought I wanted.

I wish I could feel something, just one scrap of emotion, for what is happening to me, but all I know is that this is the one place I need to be; you are the one person to see. I must finish my story, and be done with the past.

I'll try and be as clear as I can with this, but you'll have to understand that it just tumbles out from here, like falling dominoes, unstoppable pieces of action. Sometimes, I wish it was me who'd been attacked, so my memory was wiped clean. But then I remember that the whole point was that I didn't want to be one of life's victims anymore. I had a loaded gun placed in my rucksack, the handle easily reachable, and I was finally taking control.

'Okay, everyone,' announced Penny. 'We'll be live in three minutes.'

I checked the Tokarev's position in my rucksack: near to the top, handle toward me. I sucked in air, my asthmatic chest tight with anxiety at what I was about to do.

'Right,' said Penny, loudly enough so everyone stopped talking to look at her. 'Jena, if you'd like to take the seat in the middle, with your parents either side. Sam?' She looked over to me, then came closer and said quietly, 'Are you sure you're okay?'

I was so tired. My chest felt like a giant hand was grasping it. 'Get me water. Please.'

She looked around, but there was none to be found. I pointed to a bottle that one of the journalists was holding, and Penny asked her for it. I tried to drink, but my breathing was too laboured as I watched Jena sit down, flanked by Mum and Dad, then me, at the end of the line.

A crowd of reporters and cameras in front of us, all waiting to record every word.

The sun had reached its pinnacle, burning white. I noticed Douglas was speaking with Rob, then they approached Sonia and Andy. It looked a tense meeting; Sonia responded to something Douglas said, but her laughter was too loud and manic, as if she'd taken something to get over the emotional bump of today. I hated her, wanted to get this over with, praying that the gun would work its magic and just the threat of it would be enough to make Sonia talk.

Penny placed her hand on my arm. 'Sam, I really think you should just sit and watch. You're wheezing.'

My chest was cramped with asthma, and my head was as light as a helium balloon. I tried to relax, closing my eyes and concentrating on breathing. I knew what I'd come for.

'I need to do this.'

'Okay then.'

She moved away, towards the podium from which she would speak to the journalists. The press conference could begin.

The cameras began to roll, zooming in on Penny. 'Nine weeks ago, on Orwell Estate, Jena Hoolihan was set upon and left for dead. This is still an unsolved crime, and we are appealing for any information that will help us to find Jena's attacker. She was in a coma for four days, and is still living in hospital accommodation. This is the first time she has talked publicly about what happened.'

Everyone looked at Jena. The weight of silence was crippling.

Jena breathed; she looked out on all the people gathered there, and then she faced the camera and spoke. 'My name is Jena Hoolihan.' So calmly, with such conviction, it was as if all of the damage and memory loss had been a pretence, and here was my sister Jena, just as she'd always been.

'When I was thirteen, I said something bad. I said I was raped, and I accused a local man, who'd been my friend.'

Penny tried to interject. 'Jena, we're here to talk about the attack on 25 April.'

The reporters looked at each other, confused, but we were recording live, and Jena had to continue. Penny coaxed her: 'Nine weeks ago, Jena. What happened?'

Jena cast a sideways look at Mum, then down at her hands. It looked like she had forgotten what to say; the illusion of any normalcy was destroyed.

But then she spoke again.

'I can't take back the lie I said when I was thirteen. But I can tell the truth now. Douglas Campbell didn't rape me. He didn't attack me nine weeks ago either. He's innocent.' She turned, looked directly at Dad and said, 'I can't remember to forget anymore.'

From behind the line of reporters, Sonia stepped forward, and shouted, 'You should have said that sixteen years ago, you bitch! Do you have any idea how you've wrecked our lives?'

She pushed further forward, so she was wedged between the two cameramen, and directly in front of Jena. 'Do you know how much pain you've caused?'

I reached into my rucksack and pulled out the gun, standing to face Sonia.

'It's you who caused pain, you bitch.'

Like an actress in an action movie, I pointed the gun directly at her face.

CHAPTER 40

Sonia froze. Penny realised what was happening and left the podium, moving to stop me, but I resisted, wobbling the gun so it was aimed at the crowd. There was a single scream and several wails.

'Sam, please. Put the gun down.'

Everyone waited, frozen, to see what I'd do. The cameras were still rolling and no one appeared to breathe.

I re-aimed at Sonia, who was supporting herself on the BBC camera, gasping and afraid. I slid back the top of the gun like I was taught in The Spiral, felt the shot move into place.

Hearing the click, she began to beg.

'Oh nooo. Please, God . . .'

I experienced a rush of relief that this was actually going to work. 'Come on, Sonia!' I demanded. 'Confess!'

Sonia was hyperventilating, eyes wide and mouth slack, her face a picture of horror. I had a room full of witnesses; it would even be on camera. I could almost taste her confession.

Next to me, Dad was still and dumb. Mum gingerly leaned forward, red-faced and heaving, her voice no more than a wheeze.

'Oh sweetheart, what are you doing?'

Everyone was watching me, but I kept focused on Sonia. Her eyes were full of panic, beads of sweat on her brow.

'I'm waiting, Sonia. We all are.'

Douglas moved to stand behind his ex, he put his hand on her shoulder very slowly, because she was afraid and drunk and skittish. Jesus watched my every move from the cross hanging round his neck.

Douglas looked over Sonia's head to address me. 'Sam, please put the gun down. Let the police arrest her. She had good reason for what she did, given what Jena just admitted. A jury needs to hear that.'

Sonia flinched, her voice a high-pitched warble of uncontrolled terror. 'What the fuck are you talking about, Douglas? Arrest me for what?'

Her tears fascinated me, the way they dripped to her narrow chin, to the end of her nose, and she made no move to wipe them away. Rob was now next to his mum, wanting to protect her, but not able to reach her, flanked as she was by two cameras and Douglas.

'What the fuck have I done?' shrieked Sonia, losing control.

'I need you to tell everyone what you did to my sister, or I'll pull the trigger.'

From beside me, Dad, who had been silent until then, said my name. 'Sam. Please put the gun down.'

'Sonia deserves this!'

'Sam, no.' Dad's voice was cracking, barely audible to anyone but me.

'Admit what you did, Sonia. I'll count to three. One . . .'

Douglas barked, 'Just admit it, Sonia. We know you had your reasons. Jena ruined our lives!'

'Two . . .'

Sonia's breathing was irregular, and her eyes had popped; she was close to collapse.

'Three! Now, Sonia. Say it!'

Sonia whimpered, beginning to cry, mascara running down her inflamed cheeks. 'I don't know what the fuck is happening.'

'Don't lie!' My sharp voice made her flinch. 'Douglas found your raincoat. A woman's raincoat covered in Jena's blood!'

She began to sink to the ground, tears and snot and wailing.

'What raincoat? I don't know what you mean.'

A movement, unexpected. Dad stood up. He moved forward until he was directly in front of me, standing over me with both hands on my shoulders so the gun was aimed at his heart. 'Stop this, Sam. Please. That raincoat wasn't Sonia's.'

But I was so pumped with adrenalin I couldn't calm down. Something lurched in the pit of my stomach, an abrupt re-direction of thought. I jerked away from Dad, so I stood free of him, and found Andy in the crowd. I re-directed my aim at his smug face, now altered by fear and confusion.

'Was it you, Andy? Because of the porn films? I saw *Wedding Night*. How old was Jena then? Was she underage? Was she going to reveal your sleazy exploitation racket?'

Andy's designer glasses hid his eyes, but his jaw loosened, as if he was grasping for an explanation. Penny, still behind me, would be listening carefully to every word, I hoped, as were the journalists. He blushed, red from his neck to his cheeks. 'I didn't attack Jena. But I may have helped point the finger at Douglas for the rape.'

He looked to Sonia, who was knelt on the grass weeping. Andy looked apologetic, but also defiant. 'He was bad news, sis. I was just looking out for you. You and Rob were better off without him.'

Confirmation that Andy had been involved in setting Douglas up.

My thoughts were so muddled, my hands shaky, that I almost forgot Jena, seated two chairs away.

Finally, she spoke. Again, her voice was as normal as I could have wished for, clear and loud. 'You know it wasn't Andy, Sam, who hurt me. You *know*.'

I turned to her; she was still poised in her seat, her hands clasped in her lap. Our eyes met in a moment of total clarity.

My brain flashed back to that terrible day, 25 April, nine weeks before. The blinding rain.

I had just opened the camera, from Dad, and Jena had got so upset. I had yelled at her, because she was ruining my birthday, and she had tried to explain, but I hadn't wanted to know.

Finally, she ran out into the rain. To meet Douglas, I now knew. But she never arrived.

She ran into the rain, and then there was silence in the house. Mum and Dad had followed her.

Something shifted in everyone listening, or in me. There was a pause, and in the heartbeat of the moment it was as if the truth was so clear, so very obvious, that it dazzled.

I let my hand drop, and my arm went limp so the gun rested on my thigh. I sat back down heavily; I didn't know I was crying until tears blurred my vision, and when I blinked them away, there was Jena, knelt on the floor in front of my chair. She took my face in her hands and wiped my tears away. 'You must remember to forget, Sammy.'

'But we were both there, Jena. We can't forget.'

'Yes,' she said, pleading with me, her eyes full of wisdom and pain. 'We have to.'

Jena knew who had attacked her; she always had. And I knew too, though my traumatised heart had obscured the truth.

The face in Jena's painting was indeed female, but it wasn't Sonia's face. The face that Jena had painted was one I saw every day.

It was Kath's. Our mother's.

Mum tried to stand, but her legs gave way. Dad supported her, propping her up like he was all that was keeping her upright. She was swaying, ready to collapse, trying to escape. Her face was ashen, her lips pale, her eyes dark with fear.

Just as they had been when she pushed Jena to the ground, smashing her head against the pavement.

I could see she was in the grip of a panic attack, and Dad was telling her to be calm. This time, I couldn't help her. Police and journalists were hanging on every word.

'Mum?' Speaking as gently as I could. 'No more lies. Please?'

'I couldn't let her reveal the truth,' she said, but not to me, or to Penny. She was speaking to Dad, so softly that only Jena and I could hear. 'I had to protect you; I had no choice. She would have split us apart, and you promised me it only happened once. I couldn't let you be punished for something that happened sixteen years ago.'

Dad held her close. He kissed her. Even as I lifted the gun and pointed it at Mum's heart, he wouldn't step aside. It was useless as a prop; it had only one power.

'What are you talking about, Mum?' I wheezed.

Jena was the one who answered, still close enough to whisper. 'I was going to save you, Sam. When he gave you that camera, I knew what it meant. The dark room, the filming. I wasn't going to let that happen.'

Dad, still holding Mum. Silent, but in control. The four of us, finally talking. Everyone else too far away, distanced by the fear of my gun, to hear.

'I contacted Douglas because he was the only other person who knew the rape conviction was a lie. Together, we could clear his name, and make sure Dad was finally arrested. So you'd be safe.'

'But you didn't turn up to meet Douglas.'

Jena shook her head, staring back at Mum.

'She stopped me. She protected Dad, like always. Before her own daughter. Before her own granddaughter.'

Now my head was spinning. 'Granddaughter?'

'I kept the pregnancy secret until I was almost due,' Jena said. 'I was only thirteen; I hardly knew what was going on. They made me say it was Douglas's, then when his solicitor asked for a DNA test, I had to say I'd had a miscarriage. We hid the pregnancy.'

Realisation set in. Mrs Read had been right all along.

'Me?'

Jena nodded.

'Mum pretended she'd given birth to you, and I had to say you were my sister, but I promised myself I'd look after you. Always.'

The woman I'd thought of as my mother, who was actually my grandmother, placed her fist into her mouth. She looked to Dad for guidance, as she always had. And he turned to the cameras and said, loudly enough for them and for Penny to hear every word:

'I attacked Jena on 25 April. Arrest me, do what you want, but Kath wasn't involved. She had no idea.'

I could hear Penny radioing for back-up.

Abuse and secrets.

Jena had been forced to give me up; she'd kept the lie going that we were sisters, and created an alternative fantasy world to cope with her dismal reality. But when Dad gave me the camera on my sixteenth birthday, she decided to reveal the truth, because she wanted to protect me. She'd been silenced with violence.

For sixteen years, Mum had covered up the abuse. What kind of woman protects her husband over her own child?

Despite my intentions, despite all I'd said, I re-aimed the gun and pulled the trigger.

A single shot at the man who had been at the centre of this web of lies, straight at his heart.

CHAPTER 41

A memory:

I'm in our kitchen. There is the table, set for my birthday tea with a cake shaped like a heart. Just one present is unwrapped. A camera, a special vintage one, gifted to me by my dad.

I hold it tightly, even as the argument unfolds.

Jena tries to snatch it, and I know she would smash it to the ground if she could.

I think she's jealous; that's why she's so angry and upset. I don't understand what she means, when she shrieks at Dad that she won't let him, that she will stop him. That she will reveal the truth.

She leaves, running fast, and in the kitchen Mum and Dad turn to each other, both with terror on their faces. 'We have to stop her,' Mum says, determined. She grabs her raincoat and leaves the house.

Dad hesitates, looks at me for a long second, but eventually he leaves too.

I am afraid of being alone. There is a yellow flash in the kitchen: the fluorescent light blinks once then dies; creepy shadows are cast on the wall. I decide to follow.

I step out into the storm, and see Mrs Read watching from her bedroom window. She places a palm on the glass, where the rain looks like tears, and I see her mouth something, but I cannot make out what.

I sting myself on nettles, brambles scratch my arms, branches tug the hem of my dress and pull strands from my hair; rain in my eyes, in my ears even, feet sinking in the mud, shoes slipping, but I don't stop, can't stop.

I follow my sister, my mother and my father because I don't know what else to do.

Then I see, far ahead of me, that my sister is coming out of the pathway into the light. She pauses to catch her breath, and I want to shout at her to be careful, because someone is close behind her.

I am just fifty yards behind Dad, who moves slower. I call to him, but he is running now.

And far ahead, I see Jena turn around, but it isn't Dad who reaches her first, it is our mother. She lunges at Jena; I can feel her fury even through the storm, her determination to stop Jena at all costs.

I hear an almighty crack as Jena's head hits concrete. I stop, afraid. I have seen what my mother is capable of.

Dad reaches them. But he doesn't go to Jena, his daughter who lies broken on the floor. Instead, he opens his arms to his wife, who stands in the rain with blood on her hands and on her coat, which she discards in disgust, dropping it to the ground. They hold each other, desperate and shocked, and they begin to turn, to turn their backs on their damaged child.

When I reach Jena, she is alone.

It is just the two of us, in the rain.

And then, a second memory, from nine weeks later:

I have shot him. He is on the floor, and Mum is curled around him, clutching at the place where his heart lives and bleeds. Dad makes no sound, as always, but lets Mum comfort him.

Penny must have radioed for help, because soon paramedics arrive, and he is taken on a stretcher to the main part of the hospital, so they can save his life.

There was confusion; more police arrived, medical staff too. The gun was taken from me, handcuffs applied, but it all seemed far away. All I could see was how the setting sun cast an orange glow over the room, the last ray of light throwing a single path to my mother's face.

My real mother, Jena.

She knelt so her face was level with mine, and held my cuffed hands. Looking at Jena was like looking in a mirror. She'd always been an older version of me; now I understood why that was.

I believed, never questioned, that my mother had me when she was thirty, that my sister was thirteen when I was born.

Jena rubbed her eyes and sniffled.

'Jena?' I couldn't call her 'Mum'. Not yet.

Her mouth twitched into a sad smile. 'It's okay, baby.'

Tears were warm behind my eyes.

'Sammy.' She touched my face, stroked my cheek. She comforted me, and kissed my forehead. 'It's okay, Sam. It's going to be okay.'

And I wanted to believe her, really wanted to believe that, but I knew it never could be okay again. They'd taken Dad away, but his blood was still stained into the grass.

'We're free. Hush, now. My little girl.'

Jena held me, sick and bad though I was, crying softly as the day died and the sound of a police siren could be heard in the distance, coming closer.

CHAPTER 42

1 February

And now, there is no camera to hide behind, no place of safety.

This time, it's just me, a skinny teenager, who wants to come in from the cold. Turning up at your door, hoping you will let her in.

Because this story was never for Clive. It was never even for me. It was always for you, Jena.

I remember your first letter, after Dad was locked up, saying that Dr Gregg had pronounced your recovery a miracle. You were well enough to move into a flat within the grounds of Minsmere, with Lance. Broken people, caring for each other.

I look into the window of the flat and see you, lying on the sofa with Lance, and think of another time, on my sixteenth birthday, when it was you outside in the storm, in danger.

How different everything seems. The room looks warm and cosy; you're chatting, smiling too, and I see the last eighteen months have been kind to you. Or love has, the best medicine of all.

Dad's injury was superficial; he was quickly out of hospital, and arrested. He pleaded guilty to historical child abuse. My DNA proved it: I was the result of his rape of Jena. Mrs Read brought her notebooks to court; she'd known for sixteen years. But no one had listened. He also pleaded guilty to attacking Jena on 25 April. He took the blame for Mum's crime, and Jena and I let him. I said nothing of the bin bag of discarded clothes in our attic, which is where I suspected the raincoat was. In the end, she lost her husband and both her daughters, which seemed punishment enough.

He's in prison now, and will be for a long time. One day he'll be free, and we'll have to face him. Maybe even today, if he's been granted day release to attend Mum's funeral.

Your letters told me everything I needed to know:

Douglas was cleared of the historical rape charge, and compensated for the years in prison. He's living in Ipswich, trying to build a relationship with Sonia and Rob.

Poor Sonia: she was caught up in something that wasn't her fault.

So was Rob, who still writes every week, even though I never reply. I don't deserve his love, though it's been constant.

The films in Andy's flat were seized by police. Guilty of sexual abuse of minors and producing child pornography, he'll be in prison for a few years yet, and he'll never make films again. It wasn't just him; other men working at Pleasurepark had used it as a place to groom potential victims, filming the abuse in Andy's studio. My dad was one of them; he was identified in the background of some of the abuse tapes. The *Wedding Day* tape was one of his own creations; he was the cameraman.

What Mum said was true: he hadn't touched Jena since she was thirteen. But he had let others abuse her, and he had directed.

I like to think about all the victims who've been saved, as a result of the arrests. The girls and young women, who'll never even know the fate I saved them from.

Maybe my own fate too. I had no idea how close I'd been: the trips to Pleasurepark, being introduced to Andy, the gift of the camera. But somewhere inside, I must have sensed what was happening; I think it was one reason I started to starve. As Mrs Read wisely said, even if the victim is silent, the body shouts.

Mrs Read knew everything. It was her who called the ambulance on 25 April but, typically, she didn't give her name. I hope one day I'll get the chance to thank her.

I pleaded guilty to a lesser charge of Grievous Bodily Harm, aggravated by the use of a firearm. Three psychiatrists testified to my mental instability, on account of the anorexia, and I received a hospital order.

These are the facts, but there are still questions.

I still don't really understand why a woman would protect her husband before her own child. Kath always loved Dad best; perhaps it really came down to that.

Snow begins to fall lightly on my shoulders. I tap on the window and you look up, your dark hair falling on your cheek, which flushes with pleasure. You recognise me at a glance. I see your mouth speak my name.

I press the wet glass with my hand, wanting to touch you, and you must feel the same because you run then, to the front door. I hear it open and turn, and you are there, too close to see, your arms around me and your lips on my cheek and your skin against mine.

'Sam! Oh my beautiful girl.'

I let you hold me, and I think that I should have known, should have always known, that this was what I needed to make me better.

Later today, we'll go to the funeral together; we both need to mourn the woman we called 'Mum', despite what she did.

I'm not a child, not anymore, but as we pull apart and you look at me, I see that however long I live, however old I become, I will always be your child.

Because I always was. And I need to come home.

ACKNOWLEDGMENTS

This is the nicest part of the process, as I get to thank all of the people who made the book you now hold in your hands (or have downloaded onto your device!) possible.

My Sister has been through many changes, and different people have helped it along at various points.

For technical advice in relation to the muddy landscape of law and mentally disordered offenders, I'd like to thank academic and parole board member Nigel Stone, ex-probation officer and crime novelist Mike Craven and senior probation officer Robin Dawson. A big cheer to the members of Felixstowe Rifle Club, for candid advice on all things gun-related and for a fun evening of KitKats and cordite!

My writing group, Jane Bailey, Morag Liffen, Sophie Green and Elizabeth Ferretti, are a fixed point of support. We continued our monthly meetings (via Skype!) even when I lived in another country for over two years. These meetings are as necessary to me as air.

Maureen Blundell is someone whose editing advice is worth its weight in gold, and who has advised me on many occasions.

In 2010 I was accepted on the Apprenticeships in Fiction scheme and worked on an early version of this novel with crime writer Laura

Wilson; Laura, I enjoyed our meetings at the British Museum, and am grateful for your advice.

Maggie Traugott was fiercely supportive of 'Team Sam' and made me smile at times when I wanted to cry. Maggie, your emails cheered me no end. Thanks to Clare Conville for seeing the potential in the plot and making this happen.

The people at Thomas & Mercer have been simply wonderful, and I am eternally grateful to Jane Snelgrove for taking a chance on this book, and to Sophie Wilson, who made the editing process both challenging and inspiring.

I have a fantastic agent, Lorella Belli, who is as supportive, helpful and passionate as any author could wish. Thank you, Lorella, for all your hard work.

Finally, I am fortunate enough to have been born into a family who value storytelling, and no one has ever suggested I should return to the day job. As always, my husband, Andrew, is my chief cheerleader, which makes me one lucky woman.

ABOUT THE AUTHOR

Photo: © Chio Photography 2015

Ruth Dugdall was born in Hull and studied English literature at Warwick University before training as a probation officer. She decided to concentrate on her writing career when her novel *The Woman Before Me* won the 2005 Crime Writers' Association Debut Dagger Award. Her novels are informed by her direct experiences working within the criminal justice system and are published internationally. *My Sister and Other Liars* is her sixth novel.

Ruth lives in Suffolk with her husband and two children.